THE PRICE OF PERFECT

A NOVEL

WILLIAM ANDERSON

Publish Authority

ISBN 978-1-954000-24-7 (paperback)
ISBN 978-1-954000-25-4 (eBook)

Editor: Nancy Laning
Cover Design Lead: Raeghan Rebstock

Published by Publish Authority
Offices in Newport Beach, CA and Roswell, GA USA
PublishAuthority.com

Printed in the United States of America

INTRODUCTION

America is a divided nation today over culture and race. When millions of citizens differ in their opinions on this or other major matters, how they communicate their ideas between one another is critical—the words used, their nuances, metaphors, what they emphasize, and how well they understand the effect their words will have on those who differ. The most critical ingredients if we are to come together through language are first to listen, then have the freedom to speak our own truths. Today that freedom of language has been stifled in some instances where a host of words are considered taboo and offensive.

The Price of Perfect addresses this challenge to free expression through the frank, often very personal, conversations of the novel's characters. Some readers may think one side of the novel's racial discussions are offensive, or the opinions favor one side of the debate over another. This is not a story seeking comfort in its reading, but as an example of learning by listening. The goal of our nation to address today's racial issues should be to bring understanding and find commonality with each other while holding on to one's basic beliefs.

This novel invites readers to find common ground where all opinions are allowed and respected.

PROLOGUE

SEVERAL HEARTS with initials had been carved into the tree. The two workers gazing at them stood insignificantly against the tree's spreading base.

"I always hate to cut 'em down when they have a lover's mark," the tree man said from the shade of his yellow hard hat.

"And I don't like cutting down the really old ones. Too many stories it knows. All gone with my saw."

"Yeah, I played here as a kid when this was all woods." The other man held a large chain saw, which silently pulled against the thickness of his right arm. "This is the last one left and the one with the most rumors."

"What rumors?"

"Supposed to have been a hanging here in the forties. Black man pulled out of jail and hanged here. Now that architect is going to build where we're standing. Won't be no more stories about lovers or hangings then."

"Well, it ain't coming down today. This saw has a busted chain, and we got other work tomorrow." Looking up with some admiration as he patted the trunk, "You better find a friend fast, old fella."

CHAPTER 1

"HOW'S MY FAVORITE MOTHER?" Jack Collier held the phone close to his ear. He knew well that his mother Betty's voice carried little further than would a moth's fluttering wing.

Their talk was brief. Jack was driving to Athens from Buckhead for their planned lunch. He had called, just checking in, but also to ask if his mother had any memorabilia from his father that he could share with his nineteen-year-old son.

In the flight of days since her husband's death, Betty Collier had forgotten about the cedar box in the one-room shed behind their house. Perhaps it held some memorabilia? She saw the little room Wade used as an office and its contents as raw reminders of his passing. But with her son's request, she went to the backyard and the little wooden structure. There was a smell of absence to the room as she stepped inside.

She assumed the contents would be memories from high school, army medals, and financial records from his custom cabinetry company—the usual signature moments now boxed as though they never happened or mattered. Wade had antique carpenter's tools. She thought some of those might be nice to give.

Going through the various papers, she opened an envelope with no marking and saw a newspaper article with a grainy photograph under the headline "Hanging By Mob." With a casual look that became a stare, Betty saw that it was a picture of a very public hanging. Of a Black man. After the initial horror of seeing this limp figure in overalls, Betty couldn't understand why the article would be in a box with her late husband's private papers.

The photo was so emotionally unsettling that she wanted to fling its disgust from her fingers—to sink it deep in the trash pile of unnecessary papers that is the ritual chore for those serving the dead. Her hand seemed to shake more noticeably.

She found she couldn't let go of the picture. Her fingers lingered on its crinkling paper. But she held it tentatively, gingerly, like merely touching it diminished her. Perhaps there was a perverse beauty or starkness so real about the photograph's brutality that the ugliness was a lure. She felt a surge of revulsion in herself that she could be attracted to something so opposite of her morals that it held her eyes against their will. She studied the men in the circle around the oak and the man hanging from it in an ironic, casual slouch.

"My Lord," she whispered.

Written on the back of the photograph in the barely legible handwriting of her husband was the date October 10, 1940, and the words *Vinings Hill.* The man being hanged was black, and his cheekbones shone with sweat. He had on overalls with no shirt underneath and wore only one shoe. *Why,* Betty thought, *did that one shoe make the scene even more pitiful?*

She saw how the faces of the white men standing all around his body were a composite of expressions—from angry, to celebratory, to sullen. The details of the picture were glaring statements of a time and place scarred with mindless anger. Several of the men were holding cups upward in mock toasts to the camera. Their dress was workingman—stained khaki pants, rumpled white shirts, a few in overalls. Everyone wore a hat. She suddenly noticed just behind the hanging man, almost touching him, stood a boy. He looked familiar, too familiar. His resemblance to Wade's childhood pictures was too obvious. But that couldn't be. Betty cringed. He seemed to have a strange grin, with his face all twisted up and his eyes squinted. Or was he crying?

A large man stood behind the boy with his hands on the child's shoulders. What a cruel father, she thought, to take a son to witness this unspeakable act. The man's face had been scratched out—just the face. But why was such a photograph in her husband's papers? Surely, if that was him as a child, he wouldn't have kept it.

Wade had called Betty "The Family Compass." She stressed that the Colliers were people of values and certainty in their morals in a world she was convinced had turned upside down. Much of her concern now with Wade gone was her son, Jack. She worried that his creative drive had formed a man with visions too bold, even outlandish, in his architectural designs and his life. Betty felt a deep kinship with Jack's wife, Mary, and she worried over their marriage. Betty often asked herself how a wife could live with such a hopelessly romantic man who craved love and gave it copiously. Betty had seen the ease with which women approached her son. She prayed that it was all innocent.

But the speed of Jack's life concerned her the most. "Son, you run on full all the time. Slow down and let life catch up," Betty had urged him on many occasions. And now, a new project in Atlanta had become his life's masterwork, his obsession, his defining achievement. So, she had invited him on a picnic later that day where they could talk about creating balance in a life she saw as running without constraints.

If that young man at the hanging was, in fact, Wade and that scratched-out face was Wade's father—it would raise questions that could have shattering implications for their family's reputation. She knew the past, if let out, had a way of getting its own revenge. She jammed the article and its photo far into the mess of old check stubs filling the trash container. Any questions to be asked would go unknown in the dark of aged papers. It never happened now. It would never be resurrected.

At the bottom of the box, she found medals Wade had received for bravery in the Korean War. These would make a great statement about honor to her grandson.

Looking at her watch, she saw there was only an hour before her son came from Atlanta to pick her up for their picnic. She had eggs to boil and mustard to mix into the potato salad. Her buttermilk chicken was already fried and crusty, just the way Jack liked it.

CHAPTER 2

"YOU KNOW the only way you can get me here is to make your deviled eggs," Jack Collier said as he helped his mother out of the sunlit shine of his burgundy Mercedes. She stood next to him, and he could smell the lilac perfume that always walked with her. They waited as she gathered her strength in front of the unadorned granite tombstone that read "Wade Collier." Jack knew her fragility and knew her walk up the slight incline would be slow and careful.

"I brought some old photographs of me and your dad." She looked at her son with a faint smile. "We were pretty people back then."

Jack touched her shoulder. "Mother, you are pretty people now."

He saw sadness in her answer. "I'm now a were, not an am."

Betty placed her hand on the car door's edge to walk. She sought support to steady her movements. She could see her eighty years reflected in the car window. *My lips are now more lipstick than lip,* she thought; she had thinned all over. "I'm so skinny I'm like a kite ready to fly away," she complained as she wavered in her walk. "Better watch the wind. I might be gone."

Oconee Hill Cemetery's land rolls away in a quiet, slow wave from the tumult of the adjacent University of Georgia. The large water oaks cloud the sun with their long branches into calming islands of reflection.

Betty had prepared a picnic for herself and her son near Wade's gravesite. With a faint movement of her arm, Jack was directed to place her grandmother's handmade quilt under a large oak. And as Jack did, he watched his mother standing and imagining, as he knew she always had since Wade's death, that the tree was God's arm, all sinewy and twisting, as though it had just been mightily pushed out of the earth. She felt the tree and her husband were somehow nourishing one another. On this day, the June sun had abdicated its heat for a slight cooling. Still, the shade would be comforting.

For their picnic, Betty had worn what she called her "I don't care" clothes: a broad-brimmed straw hat, beribboned in red; a bright yellow, flower-punctuated dress, and red canvas basketball shoes. Her thinned ankles wore dark blue socks with orange dots. Jack gazed at his mother as he spread the frayed old quilt and unfolded their chairs. Betty was little more now than a gentle presence. A failing heart over the last year had reduced her already wiry body to more of a thought than a substance.

"Our friends here remind us of who we are and how short our stay is. You think it's forever because you aren't even forty," she said as Jack patted her chair. "If nothing else, we are southern and all the good things that means."

"The old South has gotten so old it's dead, Mother. In fact, I'm giving a lot of money to African American charities to erase it." Jack opened the large picnic basket.

"I'm proud of you for trying to help colored people. But they're stuck in yesterday. What we did to them was horrible and can't be erased, but they don't want it to be."

"The word *colored* is a part of that past that you like, and they hate."

Betty's eyes flared. "Don't lecture me on them. Your father and I have been nothing but fair to Black people all our lives. And don't tell me history and tradition don't matter. You can't change what is true."

"That's what artists do, Mother. We redefine what is real. Hemingway said, 'We make truth truer.'"

"That old drunk. What did he know? I heard he used to wear double shirts to make himself look bigger. No, there are absolutes, and we must hold to them."

"Great art is the only truth."

"No, son, being honest, caring, being fair—these are qualities of life that will never get old."

Jack gazed out over the marble and granite stones. "Maybe life is just a stage for lies. Maybe what is said to be real is just a sandcastle waiting on the next wave to say it isn't. I will say this, Miss Betty, I know I have designed the perfect building that will outlive time."

She gave a muffled laugh, "Perfect is a chase, Jack, not a find. It's a rainbow."

He pulled several plastic containers out of the basket, then took their tops off to display pieces of fried chicken, potato salad, and deviled eggs with bits of olive and bacon nestled on their whipped yolk tops.

Betty watched her only son and thought that nothing could be more beautiful than his face was to her right then. It was full in its features and glowed with the urgency and excitement she always remembered in him as a child.

Reminiscing, she said, "I used to say your blond hair looked like frozen sunshine. Everybody loved your curls when you were little. And you wanted it to stay long because of your ears."

"Ouch," he grimaced. "Only a mother would remember that pain. Yeah, I got bullied pretty good because they stuck out too much. I was called Rabbit Head and Elephant Ears."

He smiled wanly, remembering the taunts. "Then Daddy told me that I had the perfect ears, and everyone else's were too little. But when you're eight years old, there's no pain like being told you're different—that you're not perfect. I now know that different is its own perfect."

"So, is that why you still wear your hair so long?" She gave a muffled laugh. "Come to think of it; I haven't seen either of your ears in years."

Their relationship was one of sharp points soothed by loving admiration.

"What else do you know about me?" he teased in their casual interlude.

Her eyes crinkled into a sly look. "I think you want to be like one of those old Greek gods, not the main one, of course, but a god nevertheless, so your works will be emulated as the best designs anyone could ever make. You're Plato seeking the perfect. You want to be a marker, the golden ring that all others try and reach for. Maybe you're the Lord of creativity, so...," she touched his forehead with a chicken leg, "I grant you the power to do works so great that they are considered the ideal of design. But," she withdrew the chicken leg, "first, you'll have to tell me who you love the most."

"The most?" He screwed his face up as though this was a tough decision. "Well, that would be a tie between you and your deviled eggs."

Betty drew back in mock dissent. "You would disrespect the one who grants your wishes?" Her tone became more serious. "Tell me, son, what's so important about this particular building?"

"It's my most imaginative work. It's my life's creation."

Betty saw that his face was set with pride and conviction. "Your life's creation is your sweet wife and your son. The buildings come in second." She was scolding with a bit of hardness to her voice. "I worry that you might be giving the wrong answer to one of life's great questions: how much of our soul we will sell and how much won't we? We Colliers have a 'not for sale' sign on our souls and certainly not for a building design, for goodness' sake."

His response had a sharpness to it. "Mother, I'm not some delusional fool trying to stroke his own ego. I'm an artist that happens to design work environments that others call buildings. If you are driven by a need to create great works, you can't be stopped by some critic. Staying true to who you are isn't selling your soul. My creations are who I am. My work defines me." His face reflected the seriousness of his tone, the conviction, the attempts to placate and convince his mother.

"You're still trying to find the Easter egg the others can't find," she nodded at him knowingly. "I'll never forget when you were little, and you had to find the egg no other child could find. Just what will make you happy? Do you want to be a monument?"

"What's happy?" he asked rhetorically. "I may never find it, but I think I'm as close to it with this project as I'll ever be. And no, I don't want to be a monument. I want to do something monumental. Is there something inherently wrong about the pursuit of perfect?"

"The problem with chasing perfect is you don't know

when to let go. And knowing when to let go can be the most perfect part of perfect."

She thrilled about her son's extraordinary design talents but worried over his mood swings and almost blind pursuit of an idea. She worried over him being unable to achieve a level of excellence that only he could define. It made him complex and hard to fathom at times when at other times, he was all laughter, and his love was of a rare depth.

Betty let the heat in the conversation calm down. She finished her piece of fried chicken breast by savoring every bit of it, the skin and the meat hugging the tiny bone. She learned the completeness of eating from her mother, whose family was very poor during the Depression.

A crow glided out of the shading oak and landed in its black-robed body on Wade Collier's granite marker. It seemed unconcerned that Jack and his mother were only a few feet from the marble gravestone. Jack cut his eyes at the bird. He hated crows—their scraping cry, the dull dark of their wings. They seemed harbingers of something bleak to him. Watching it warily, Jack suddenly yelled, "I don't believe that!"

Startled, Betty rasped out, "What on earth?"

"That damn crow just crapped—went to the bathroom—on Daddy's tombstone." His voice was filled with indignation.

Betty's lips thinned out in mirthful acknowledgment of one thing life had taught her. "Now that was just an absolute truth; you never know what part of life is going to land on you and change everything."

Jack shook his head, answering confidently, "Nothing's landing on me, Mother. Just watch me grab my dream." He thrust his arm upward, and his fingers closed into a tight fist.

Betty saw the gesture and how his fingers had wrapped around thin air. She worried it was a prophecy.

Jack stood up and said, "Got to get back to Atlanta. Mary and some friends are at the club and looking for me to drop by the pool."

Betty looked up at his tall figure. "I know you'll tell sweet Mary I love her. She's the best decision you ever made."

Jack smiled. "Till death do us part, Moms. We're the Colliers, and we play for keeps."

CHAPTER 3

IT WAS ONCE a Fairfield joke said with a degree of civic pride. White people would never have crossed the street when Bradley and Connie Stevens came toward them. Townspeople would have come to greet them and ask them to be on their boards and charities. The Stevens, it was said, were the right kind of people, Bradley a surgeon, his wife a professor. Today, there was no more laughing about race. They were The Stevens—on every board, at all the charity fundraisers, at the The Right lawn parties. They were always greeted with broad grins and eager handshakes. The handsome and effervescent Stephens were a great relief to many.

The Stevens had secluded the possibility that they were the poster Blacks in their Connecticut neighborhood. They saw no prejudice toward them in any aspect of their life in Fairfield. They wanted to be the beacons of achievement to counter their race's deafening crime rate. When asked by friends in New York what they were doing for their race, the answer was, "We are showing how two people, raised in poverty in Harlem, can realize the American dream."

Their New York friends, all immersed in the BLM, said, "You mean you have turned white."

The Stevens had taken this as a shallow argument against achievement, and it moved them further into their cloistered world of Fairfield.

Their only child, John, at age eighteen, had shocked them when he said they were a family of privilege when millions in their race were struggling for equal justice. He felt guilty, he said, in a confessional of regret. Their response was to let him discover the Black experience in a place where achievement was not a sentence of being white but a token of pride. He had been accepted at Atlanta's Morehouse College.

Upon arriving, he had been invited to join a fraternity but was now so imbued with feelings of advantage he declined. He wanted to know the story of his whole race, especially the young men he could see on the street framing the college. To him, they were souls adrift carried by violent currents toward dark places.

John didn't realize how unmoored he was until his psychology class traveled to Montgomery to see Alabama's Legacy Museum and its shocking revelation of brutality. Thousands of names carved into metal slabs solemnly hanging like upside-down tombstones from the ceiling exposed a clarity to the true awfulness that had visited his race for centuries. It was wrenching to the young man. He now felt a connection with the street drifters, a brotherhood that made him want to march to their angry drummer.

In early June, at the end of his first year, when the weather had been of an undetermined mind, John Stevens, at age twenty, began the rest of his life with a series of lies. This was unusual for him as he considered himself a soldier for honesty in a corrupt world and a passionate idealist. He told his college friends and his parents that he was spending the summer in California studying the troubled inner-city African American male. He wanted to pursue counseling with those who found their family in a gang. But he realized he knew little about them or their world. He wondered if he could rise to their levels of distrust and anger.

Instead of California, John left Morehouse with some clothing in his backpack and a hundred dollars in his pocket and headed a mile south to an area of neighborhoods that were rare with hope. Here, the passionate young man felt he would study the anger, the destructive behavior, of men his race and age so he could better serve them when he began his career. And that meant living their lives.

But as evening cast hard shadows against the downtown buildings, John Stevens had to admit he didn't know how to be homeless. The first night he guessed he would try sleeping against some building to get the grit of life on the streets, or under a bridge or find a shelter. And now he wondered, having brought little money, how would he eat?

He had walked away from his life as a student with prescribed curriculums of study to be a student of chaos, where failure to learn didn't result in a bad grade but death. As John walked, he looked to his left at the salute to unbridled capitalism, the massive new Mercedes-Benz Stadium. So close, he thought, so glaring in its statement of inequality was this temple to extravagance. It took only minutes for him to enter the world he wanted to serve.

The evening quickly announced its readiness to cool. His sight and sense of smell seemed more acute. He realized how lazed the senses of people of means, like himself, could get. But this life was a Serengeti of dangers, where listening and sight and smell were essential for living in what he assumed was a predatory world. He almost smiled that hygiene was his first thought. He walked the streets in a garden of smells, from a bakery waft of freshness to urine on a wall. And the shadowy figures, moving as in an aimless slumber, caused John to wonder if he could ever relate to these people.

He was aware of how his senses seemed to intensify. John felt like an archeologist digging into another world, and for a moment, enjoyed being a student of the streets.

Three young men of his age and race approached him. These would be his future patients, he thought, and he was prepared to stop them and talk. But that thought was fleeting. One gave him a hard shoulder bump as they passed, spinning him back.

"Yo ass own the sidewalk?" came the sharp tone.

John notched his backpack up, and all thoughts of being on a crusade to help and understand this culture were losing out to a primal fear of being physically hurt. These feelings made him momentarily ashamed that he was stereotyping these men like the rest of society. He felt suddenly unprepared. How stupid of him, he thought, that he didn't have his act together about how he would even open a conversation. He stumbled. "Got a couple of questions for you."

"Questions? You sellin' stuff?" Appraising John, the larger of the three said with some annoyance, "Hey, bro. Ya'll don't look like no street man. Les' see what ya'll got in that backpack."

All three started moving toward him. Knowing this could go badly, he started to run as two police cars rushed from the evening, sweeping past him and sliding against the curb. Several officers jumped from their cars, yelling at the three. Two sprinted away, one fell, and as he was getting up, he was smashed back into the pavement by a thickly built officer.

Another officer suddenly appeared as if out of thin air. He held a pistol and a taser. "Which one you want?" yelled the uniformed man. Stunned and terrified, John raised both hands and meekly said, "I'm a college student here to study."

"Well, you're a stupid one. Get your ass on the ground. Now!" The words seemed to fill the air until there were no sounds left to make. John immediately started for the ground, but the young officer raised his leg, planted his foot on John's chest, and kicked him backward against a wall where he sank to the pavement gasping for air.

It was all coming to John in small, punctuated bits of time, like the frames of a movie now slowed so each word, each move by the police, was its own contained scene. The officer flipped John on his stomach, and as he turned, he saw two of the blue uniforms pounding on the man they had thrown to the pavement. He was yelling that he wasn't resisting. The blows had a thick, muffled sound.

The officer almost laughed as he talked. "Let's see how much dope our college boys got in this bag." He began jerking on the backpack straps, causing John's arm to be painfully twisted backward. A second officer had his knee pressing John's face into the abrasive grains of the sidewalk.

After rifling through the backpack and finding only clothing and several psychology books, the officer stood up, appraised John lying stiffly below him, and said, "OK, Einstein, you outsmarted us this time. Card here says 'Morehouse.' Didn't know you could get in there and be as stupid as you are. The streets are out of your league." He stepped on John's back as he walked away.

With a screeching of tires, the police cars drove away with the one bloodied young man. John was seized with an outrage and anger he had never known. It was all-consuming; his whole body was flooded with the injustice he had witnessed for the first time in his life.

John's only exposure to Atlanta's poor Black communities before this was the endless parade of young men committing crimes on the evening news. But that was another culture, as removed as if it was in another country. His was a world of promise and achievement with connections that mixed comfortably with whites of equal wealth.

No longer.

He felt he had just been initiated into the violence of inner streets, of a world of mayhem and randomness at every turn. And of judge, jury, and sentencing performed by both police and men on the street. There was no predictability here, no discussion or thoughtful pauses. It was all immediate and without reason. John now, more than ever, wanted to know more and to live in what seemed the eternalness of Black poverty and feelings of rejection and failure. It was an epiphany, surprising to him in its transforming suddenness.

The only certainty he felt about his life was his blackness, and now he wanted the world to know it. But his black eyes would rage when he was angered, as quickly as they softened with laughter. His thin lips had a pinkish tone. His nose was commanding on his square face. To assume the fullness of this new life, he would change his name. As he walked, John thought of several, but nothing came that would describe his new persona. It would come, he thought.

It was June, and John Stevens hungered for something he was once accustomed to at college cookouts. The steak felt wet and cold against his crotch and thigh when John slid the packaged meat into his pants as he stood next to the Walmart meat display. Pastor Randolph Struby saw the act, walked over, reached down, pulled the steak out, and asked the young man his name. John grabbed the meat back, pushed the pastor away, stuck the steak once again down his pants, and without thinking, answered, "A Man."

With an awkward laugh, the pastor responded. "I know you're that. I asked your name, not your sex."

"That is my name," was the defiant answer. And he felt good about it.

"Your parents gave you that name?" Pastor Struby was confused.

"No. It makes me realize who I am."

"So, do I call you A or what?" Struby thought this some silliness.

There was no answer as John Stevens was unfolding into a personality he had sought out but never was. A Man was a statement, he thought, for his whole race. It demanded respect. It was an assertion of worth, John thought.

The pastor looked long at the tall figure with the prominent face and didn't know what to make of him. His look, his stance, his words were all defiance. But the way he enunciated words without southern heaviness caused Struby to ask," You're not from here, are you?"

With a bored noncommittal, he answered, "From the streets."

Struby offered him supper, a bed for the night, and a little work for pay the next day if he would pull the steak out of his pants and put it back.

"No way," was the answer.

The pastor felt God had placed this man in his care, for what reason it was not his to ask. He had seen crime many times in his community but had never sought to bring a criminal into his church.

Believing he was being guided by the Lord, Struby said, "Come with me anyway. I'll give you a clean bed for the night."

John had no place to sleep that night or even to cook the steak he was stealing. He had been forced to develop the art of negotiation for the past four months on the streets. He felt the pastor must be getting something out of the invitation, so he would play along. He seemed a harmless little man, certainly no bodily threat.

"Does your church have an oven? I'll spend the night if it does."

Randolph Struby had been called to his Baptist church forty years earlier when it served a stable, middle-income Black neighborhood. The closing of the Ford Motor plant had started a domino effect that had caused an erosion of families to other counties seeking jobs. The selling of a house here, then one there, started a virus of sales that discounted the asking prices, which brought absentee landlords, followed by unkempt yards and homes. Most of the pastor's tenure had been like a man at the dike, saving a soul here and there. Then serving an aging population and watching families get destroyed in a tide of despondency and vanished hope for a better life. It was the system, many said, but few seemed to know how to describe what the system was. It was just "Them" and "They." There was no humanity, there were no names, and it was mostly whites to blame.

To be a part of the theft of a steak was a line the pastor couldn't cross. "I can't let down the God that has placed you before me by stealing with you. Let's go. I'll pay for it, and we can cook and enjoy it, but you do have to stay the night."

The young man had to think about what loss this negoti-ating might cost him in self-respect. He weighed whether a clean bed in a safe place was worth being controlled by this squatty little man versus not being allowed to steal the steak. He hadn't felt guilt at getting caught stealing, but he did feel disrespected in the way of the street, where no one would tolerate correction. To show some measure of control, he walked to the cash register with the steak sticking out of his pants at the waist, looked the cashier in the eye, slapped the steak on the counter, and announced with a surliness, "The little guy here is paying," which the pastor dutifully did.

That night in a back room of the small south Atlanta church turned into more nights. "A Mann" (the pastor added an extra 'n') was taken in as janitor and driver for the pastor who was aging and needed an assistant. It was a grace extended that A Mann, who preferred the whole name, knew was a rare offering. But still, he would continue to slip out into the night after he could hear the pastor snoring.

In the days ahead, he would break into a white or Asian business at least once a week, stealing chewing gum or cigars, small items for his own enjoyment, and no longer for selling on the street. He would trip the burglar alarm of a store, wait until he heard the sirens, then run joyously into the formless dark just ahead of the police. It was an act of freedom brought about by escaping through flight. With the wind rushing over his cheeks, he always laughed as he ran with his arms raised as though he were crossing some finish line as a winner. He loved to run away into the obscuring safety of the night to nowhere, to anywhere, away into his new life.

On the second night of his stay, Pastor Struby tapped on the door to the church storeroom, which now doubled as a place for A Mann to sleep. He wanted to discover more about his sudden guest whose anger reflected that of so many young men in the area.

The pastor was surprised to see him sitting on the edge of his cot, watching a small television. "We don't have that kind of television in the church. Where did that come from?"

"A buddy gave it to me," was the answer with a quickness that carried perceptible anger at being questioned. He hated being doubted or questioned about anything. He was so transformed in his new persona that he was comfortable in believing he had grown up in a world where escaping was the path to survival—escaping the truth, staying out of sight of the police, never acknowledging how anything was obtained. To be caught in a lie was to be defeated. Lying allowed one to maintain some degree of dignity and self-respect.

Sensing this could fast turn into a confrontation, the pastor calmly responded, "Well, that was generous. Not many people give away televisions."

"Yeah," was the only answer the pastor was given, and it had a finality that told him there was no profit in pursuing the issue. He assumed it had been stolen, and it took him a moment to reconcile that he was probably giving shelter to a thief and saying nothing about it. He whispered a quick request to the Lord for grace.

"OK if I join you for a minute?" The pastor sat uninvited on one end of the cot with the television blaring in front of them. "A good way to know something about a man is to find out about their people."

Looking at the television, the relaxed figure said, "I have no people."

"We all have people or had them. What about your mama and daddy?"

The answer was long in coming. He was really trying to

make up a plausible explanation. Being from an affluent family and leaving a prestigious college to become a common thief didn't add up, even to his transformed mind. So, he lied, "My mother was heartbroken and got so sad she stayed in bed all the time. Don't know where she is now." He was mentally sculpting a new self.

"Heartbroken? What happened?" The pastor felt he was getting a small bit of traction.

"Life broke her. No husband. Five kids. No job. She got so far down she couldn't get up. I used to steal to help her out; put food on the table."

"And your daddy?" the pastor asked.

"He would drift in and out. Wasn't a bad man, just couldn't make the system work for him." John realized that he had immersed himself in a make-believe world but let it develop.

His next statement was the first truth, a truth that had haunted him for years.

"Life has been hard on my race from way back." There was a pause; then, reflectively, he asked the pastor, "Have you ever been to the museum in Montgomery that lists our people that were hanged?"

"No, but I'm very familiar with it," Struby said.

You can't be familiar with the pain if you don't see it hanging in slabs from the ceiling."

It was his visitor's deep, resonating voice that had caught the pastor's attention.

Commanding and clear, it carried easily all over the small sanctuary. The next morning, he asked A Mann if he would say the opening prayer that Sunday. The pastor knew it was a sudden request, but he was trying to get some give from this scarred figure that, the minister thought, only knew taking, hurt, and hurting.

"Pray?" he asked in angry disbelief. "Pray to who, for what?"

"Pray for what's on your heart, and pray for the poor, troubled folk that live in this neighborhood." The pastor watched the young man's face as it seemed lost in the depths of its darkness. "For the young men who struggle like you."

"There is no God, preacher. If there is, he's a mean one to let all this hurt go on."

Then A Mann walked out of the room, cursing his new life in this tiny, confining place.

The next morning at the ten o'clock service, in the sanctuary that would hold no more than 200, the preacher saw the usual few dozen people sitting in the pews. A Mann sat off to one side. Struby insisted he attend service if he was to keep sleeping at the church.

The pastor nodded at A Mann and said softly, "Just a few words. Forget yourself. The Lord is the only hope some of these people have."

In resignation, A Mann muttered, "What the hell," and sullenly walked to the front of the sanctuary. Angry at himself for acting against his better judgment, he threw his head back and yelled, "Let the sun shine on the people in this room! They don't need no more pain. These folks are sick of being held back, looked down on, and beat on. They need a protector. That's your job, Lord, so I ask you to stand up for these little folks and make right the system that's hurtin' 'em. Let us run like the horses, freed of this being poor, freed of injustice! Show us how to run, Lord."

And caught up in his own words, A Mann started a slow trot around the church sanctuary. The congregation stared in amazement for a moment, then started peeling off out of the pews and joining in a line behind him until the entire congregation was moving in odd gaits, half-gallops, shuffles, whatever their age and infirmities allowed, throwing their arms up and yelling, "Run free! Run free!"

Feeling like a fool, as though his sense of who he was and what he was doing with dozens of near-hysterical people following him, A Mann quickly turned to leave the church but was startled when the small crowd started yelling a chorus of "Praise the Lord and bless that preacher!" And "He set us free, Lord." The reaction was authentic and unadorned.

A Mann felt a sense of confusion at the emotional, almost hysterical response by himself and the congregation. Then, it turned into a rush of excitement he had only experienced when almost getting caught in the middle of a robbery. It was like the exhilaration of escaping, expecting nothing from his short prayer. He felt that he had won, he had escaped being beaten by life again, and it was with some gift that was unknown to him. He sat in his tiny room afterward, filled with the strange rush of acceptance and accomplishment.

His world would start to change following that prayer. Word would spread throughout the area that a messenger had come to the small church, a charismatic young man, a true Negro, not a tan, yellow, or brown-skinned grandson of a plantation owner's rape, but a true Black man whose name, in fact, was a proud, maybe defiant, A Mann. The hoots, the hollers, the "I know that's right," which came from his name, had given him a mystique—all on the wings of his jog around the sanctuary. He was lost in this strange, made-up world he now embraced. Oddly enough, it was a skin more comfortable and real than the life of affluence and achievement he had left behind.

CHAPTER 4

AT MIDNIGHT ON THE TUESDAY, after he had arrived, A Mann awoke from his cot in the church, shaking in fear from a dream. It was as though the dream had broken out of some untouchable depths of his mind, immersing the tiny room in its own dark reality. He stood for a moment, awake in the dream. It was of being lost in a large building and being gripped in a sense of hopelessness at being unable to find his way out. His heart was pushing against his chest so hard that it scared him, and he put his hand over its thump as though his hand would calm it down.

Pastor Struby had told A Mann that the Lord had bestowed special powers on him.

The pastor said that he had the gift of a voice that roared like a lion. He had words that were like a mighty river, carrying the people along with it. He wanted A Mann to speak the following evening at the weekly singing and supper. The pastor said there would be no more than 20 people there. He said just to give a short little sermon on whatever came to his mind. Not to worry, the Lord would put the words on his tongue.

He felt, in a sense, he had experienced a rebirth. He was no longer John Stevens heading for medical school and psychiatry. He was the emboldened, angry man of the streets. It was becoming easy to be both a liar about his identity and to live in the lie, unabashed and unashamed. But it was creating anxiety. He felt the preacher was putting him in a corner. He had never been a public speaker, didn't attend church, had never been in prison as he thought the pastor assumed, but his fakery did haunt him. He had to escape. He had to outrun the fear.

The June night outside the church held an empty kind of darkness. No wind, no sounds of the solitary barking dog, not even a streetlight (they had all been shot out each time the city replaced them). A Mann walked several blocks to a series of small stores. Hair Talk was the local barber and a place of bonding and brotherhood. Pawn It was windowed in steel mesh. Soles for the Soul was a shoe store and cobbler, and further on down, squatting in its cinder block exterior, was Good Times, the liquor store reviled by mothers and wives who saw the damage its liquids had done to their men. Half of the shops were empty in the twelve-store neighborhood. Walmart's opening several miles away had rendered profits impossible for the small merchants. It was a walk through a culture abandoned on many fronts.

The crunch of A Mann's shoes against the grit of the sidewalk seemed accentuated against the night's still. He came to a small grocery store, which he and others had periodically robbed. It had a warning sign in the window announcing a new burglar alarm system. Before, he would kick out the glass in a door, reach in, and open it. Tonight he paused, not knowing why he walked to the back of the brick, one-story building and pried open the back door with a metal pipe he found in a refuse pile. The alarm immediately blared into the night. He hurried inside, past rows of canned goods and the meat display, passing various items he would typically take. Coming to the cash register, he paused. In his recent thefts, he no longer took cash or even steaks, which were easy to sell the next morning on the street. He had begun simply getting chewing gum and candies. Gazing over the impulse items, he reached out, and for a reason he couldn't explain, picked up a single peppermint in a basket the store offered for free. Pulsing blue police lights, accentuating the darkness of the streets, blared in their urgency through the little store's windows. He couldn't hear their sirens over the harshness of the alarm. With the mint in his mouth, A Mann walked slowly out the back door, giving the police time to get out of their cars and rush the front of the store.

Looking back through the store, A Mann saw their shapes rushing at the front door. Stepping out the back door he had jimmied loose, he started running. Shouts to stop, to halt, followed the fleeing figure as the police came around to the back in time to see him dash into the night. They watched his arms waving high and heard a joyfulness in his yelling and laughter as he vanquished the fears that had awakened him. No longer trapped, he was once again free.

The next night, the regular Singing and Supper event drew a rare, large, and boisterous crowd an hour before the six o'clock start. Pastor Struby cracked the church's front door and peeped out to see a mass of people on the small lawn, so large a crowd that it elicited a "Lawdamercy" and a whistle. He rushed back to the small kitchen where two women were fixing chicken salad sandwiches, then cutting them in small triangles without any crust.

"Better make some extras," he said. "We got a crowd like I've never seen."

He was afraid to tell A Mann about the crowd, afraid he would back out in fear of having nothing to say. But sensing that some divine hand was touching his little church and had picked the most unlikely of saviors to revive it, Pastor Struby walked around the corner to the young man's room.

He tapped on the door as a perfunctory courtesy, then opened it to see A Mann standing facing the window. The pastor had noticed how the young man would straighten up when he was angry or stressed, stretching his thin body upward in what the pastor felt was a subconscious attempt to be bigger, at least figuratively, than the problem. And at this moment, he looked tall.

A Mann turned to the pastor, who was taken by a new look on his face of barely contained energy and determination. The pastor put his hand on the young man's shoulder and said solemnly, "This is your time, son. You are the vessel. Now go empty the words the Lord is filling you with."

A news team from WMBB-TV, covering an afternoon shooting down the street, saw the crowd filling the church front yard and spilling into the street. A professor of journalism at local Morehouse College had said the MBB stood for More Black Blood because of its constant coverage of the tragedies of young Black men. Shandra Berry, the station's investigative reporter, had the station's camera van pull over.

It had been a slow news day, and she was mildly curious as to why so many were around this failing church in the middle of the week. It was known as a house of worship with few remaining worshipers and no chance of a resurrection. Shandra knew this neighborhood was ignored, especially by its various landlords, unless the rent was past due. Her crew had done an expose on the untraceable landlords who allowed the area to be known as 'The Target Range." She emerged slowly from the van in her camera-friendly blue dress and asked a woman, whose body formed an almost perfect circle, what was going on.

"I thought this little church had about closed," Shandra commented to the circular woman.

The woman let out a scream of joy and then answered, "The Lord sent a messenger who says it ain't gon' rain no more."

"How could you afford a new minister? I heard the place couldn't even pay its electricity bill."

"Well, we got plenty 'lectricity now," the woman exclaimed with certainty.

"Must be a famous visiting preacher," Shandra reasoned. "What's his name?"

"A Mann. He is such a man," the woman said joyously.

"But what's his name?"

The woman was lost in a hymn in her mind, in the milling, in the crowds moving in sway in the yard, which she joined. It was a yard of bees.

The reporter motioned for her cameraman to follow, and they pushed their way through the crowd and into the church. They were quickly enveloped by the impact of near hysteria in the sweltering room, generated by the power from the preacher's voice.

Shandra stood jammed at the back of the small room. Her cameraman couldn't get in, so she held her smartphone up and recorded. The tall, T-shaped young man behind a small speaker's stand wore blue jeans and a white shirt so wet with sweat it seemed a part of his skin. His face glistened with his exertion and from the effort of his fist smashing at the air. It was as though he was fighting against an unseen force.

"Out, you devils!" his baritone voice demanded. "In, you angels! Uplift us from this mud we have allowed ourselves to live in and clean our souls of hate, resentment, and despair. We're not mules. We're no longer born to the plow, but we act like we are. We're racehorses! Thoroughbreds! Give us the legs to run fast, to escape the devils of our own making. Run fast!" he yelled. "Run like the wind!" he demanded, then started jogging in place.

Already on its feet, the whole room began jogging in place in a crush of emotion and release. A window shattered in its frame from the pounding of the feet. Shandra found herself crying without shame or restraint, or explanation.

Squeezing herself out the front door, she saw her cameraman leaning against the station's van in the street. He held his hands up in confusion, like asking her what was going on. Working her way over to him through the crowded yard and wiping her eyes as she came up to him, he could only ask, "What is going on here? And why are you crying?"

"What's going on?" she asked rhetorically. "We have found our story, and I've found something I had lost in myself."

At that moment, the heavy, red church doors flew open and outward like they had no weight, like curtains in the wind. People came pouring out chanting, singing, and talking with an animation filled with joy. The service was over, and they mixed in general chaos on the small front lawn before moving off into the street for home or to their cars.

"Phil, bring your camera. We've got to get an interview with this...," she seemed uncertain of how to describe the man she had just heard.

"Oh, please. Don't tell me we've run out of robbery stories, and we're covering Holy Rollers." Reuben Gaines was a thickly built young man who could easily throw a camera to his shoulder and cover a fast-moving action scene.

Shandra ignored him, or didn't hear him, or didn't want to, and left him scrambling for his camera as she walked through the remaining churchgoers lingering on the lawn. She entered the church and saw the tall figure down front signing autographs and having his picture snapped with small children and women in large, flowery hats. Reuben caught up and stood next to her as she watched the scene.

"Shandra, what are we doing here? Where's the story?"

"It's called balance in the news, Reuben. It's called inspiring and elevating and hopeful in a forgotten part of Atlanta."

Shandra, a graduate of local Spelman College, had come under criticism from many in her race in Atlanta as the "cringe reporter," nicknamed "Bloody Shandra." Whenever they watched the Atlanta nightly news, here was another crime, and there was the picture of the criminal, a young Black man. They said her stories were too focused on the downtrodden, the constant gang activities, the druggies, the homeless, and they always, always had the same color of face. She was asked by friends at parties, even by her mother, where are the white criminals? When she stumbled into this story of hope at this tiny church, she saw it is as a way of addressing her critics and getting her surgeon father's circle of friends off her back. They felt she sought out and favored making young men of her race seem like predators. Shandra defended herself, touting all of her Black Lives Matter work, and besides, her station assigned what stories she covered. The messenger had become the hateful message, Shandra felt. She feared her reporting could hurt her civil rights work and her goal of advancing to a larger television market.

Shandra walked up to the young preacher. "Hello, I'm Shandra Berry with WMBB-TV. Can we have a few words with you? There may be a story here for tonight's news."

A Mann looked up from having written his name inside an elderly lady's Bible. The lady's enormous hat was white with a bouquet of plastic flowers on top that dominated the little scene. She smiled knowingly, "This man needs to be on the news. He is a heart-changer, a hope-giver. He brings light to a world that is stuck on stuck."

Shandra looked to her side at Reuben. "You get that?" He nodded.

"I'm sorry, but I don't know your name," she said to the tall figure. His face glistened. She thought of a prizefighter or race-horse now cooling down after the fight or the race but still swelled and glowing with the energy it took to finish the fight and run the race.

He stared at her fine features. Her nose was narrow. Her eyes, an intense blue, brought a flash of anger for the time-distant man that had probably raped a slave girl, and here, today, that lustful, humiliating moment still manifested itself. But her blue eyes, as reminding as they were, captured him, and he felt uncertain about how to handle this sudden atten-tion and thinking perhaps he should turn and walk away. And to be on the news—his face would easily be recognized by his college classmates. He would be exposed as John Stevens, a fraud, a rich boy living in a make-believe world of cruelties.

He said with educated clarity, "News? There is no news here, just people feeling better."

"No, to someone who knows bad news like I have been

accused of putting on every night, I would say this is very good news for The Target Range. But first, tell me your name."

The woman with the large hat, still in close attendance, said proudly, "A Mann."

Shandra's smooth forehead wrinkled in confusion. "Your name is...."

His dark features told no tales but seemed caught in a solitude suggesting stories that remained untold. His voice sounded prideful, almost boastful. "A Mann is my name."

This made her more inquisitive and a little annoyed that such a pretentious, and obviously phony name, would be claimed. Was this a sham going on here, perpetrated by yet another, though younger, money-grabbing minister?

"So, that's your preacher name? Surely you have a legal one, a name given when you were born, and it's certainly not that name." There was a cut to her voice, a noticeable doubt. She felt in that moment that she and everyone in the room had been played for fools.

"Are we to be known only by what we used to be, or by what we are now? Is forgiveness only with The Lord?"

"Well, that sure raises some interesting questions, like forgiveness for what? May I ask your background? You are not an ordained minister at your age—I wouldn't think. Where did you get your education?"

She saw his face become even more impenetrable as she tried to read beyond his words, but his voice was tinged with anger. It was the anger in realizing he was about to be caught in a lie, that he was no bedraggled man of the streets but a college man from a well-off family.

"So, you were brought up on the streets, you've been in prison, and now you're a preacher?"

The confusion of her question was reflected in the

curiosity of her look. There was something so primal about this man, who seemed her age but also far older. He was very African to her, from a distant time and place, yet broken in some way by the world of today, or maybe defiant against his own brokenness.

"Why would you call yourself by that name?"

"It is who I am," he answered.

There was an obvious intelligence in his enunciations. It made him even more of a contradiction to Shandra. She expected his background to have clothed him in street-culture language. But his enunciations were of higher education and demanding parents.

"It is all of me, my family and their families, my race."

Shandra was attracted to the physical beauty she saw in his spiral of a body, capped with impossibly broad shoulders. She thought of Maasai warriors and their exquisite thinness but fearless in their stance. She saw the way he held his head up as a symbol of pride. There was no slouching indifference to his presentation. He was either pure of soul and purpose or purely a false god to people so in need of someone to lift them out of their mire.

Pressing against Shandra were children and noticeably a boy, holding a little Bible, obviously wanting an autograph.

Shandra interrupted the rush, asking, "One last question, please? Will you be the new minister, uh, preacher here?

He was surprised at his answer. "I don't preach. I don't know how. I've never read the Bible. The preacher says the Lord does the speaking."

Seeing the effect he had on the congregation and knowing no scriptures, nor ever having spoken to an audience, he had started to believe the pastor was right. Someone, something, maybe God, was placing words in his mouth. It was a growing revelation, and it gave him a confidence he had rarely known. Hearing his words had her instincts telling her this was an upbeat story that would give her a little redemption and might find an interested, even intrigued, viewer while improving her resume. He was an unlikely star, she thought, but of definite star quality.

Shandra was finally squeezed aside as several teenagers pushed in to talk to and touch him. He turned away from her to answer their questions. She took a last long look at a man defying reality or chance. To her, he was raw talent, so basic in message and delivery, yet presented with a power that was entertaining, uplifting, and liberating.

At the back of the church, at the door, she couldn't resist, so she turned and looked back again as he looked up from the small crowd around him, and they realized they had made a connection. They had an attraction even in that brief moment of exchange. But connection beyond a short stare was too improbable, and Shandra quickly turned as though she had been caught peeping and walked out the front door. A Mann returned to the small group of admirers and to the unknown direction toward which he was now set.

The next morning, in the reporters' staff meeting, Tiny Smithers, Shandra's story assignment editor, made the morning inquiry about which of the reporters had anything new, what potential stories the police scanner was crackling in its static voice, and what stories the other stations were promoting for broadcast. This was before he would assign reporters and video crews to the usual crime and crash stories that were first up in every big city's leads.

Shandra was first to respond. "I've got something I found yesterday at The Target Range. We had finished covering our story on a shooting and saw a crowd in front of that little white

Baptist church. I went in and saw a remarkable young man, living on the street, that I think had the congregation on fire. And to put a real stinger on the story, he calls himself 'A Mann.' I mean, that's his name."

Tiny was so-called because he was anything but small—not morbidly obese, but full at the waist and thighs. His medium height accentuated the pooch and push of added body.

"This is a joke, right? A Mann? Where's the story?"

His laugh came in wheezing bursts; each laugh its only individual sound. It was accompanied by smirks and sarcastic looks by the other reporters.

Shandra knew she would get this reaction. "Tiny, I'd like to hit the restart with your coming in on what subjects we emphasize. We are very good at running young Black men down with our wall-to-wall coverage of shootings and robberies. This little church scene was a news story to me because it was filled with hope. You know the networks all end their evening news with a feel-good story. The whole country is sick of negative all the time."

"I'm okay with that hope angle, but this A Mann character, give me a break. That's so obvious he's a fake, a huckster. We're not giving airtime to another slick talker trying to make the poor people poorer."

"No, there's something very pure about this man," Shandra said. "Go with me on this one, Tiny. White people think all Black folks are mired in a hopeless world of their own making. Many do live in a world of no dreams. This is not just feel-good stuff, but a solution, a way out of sorts."

Tiny thought over her words. He admired Shandra. She was an aggressive street reporter with great insight, almost a psychiatrist, in her interviews. But he also felt she was colored by color. Her constant coverage of crime had made her achingly resentful of Black poverty and how she felt it had been a predator on her race caused by white prejudice. Tiny knew she wanted off the sad streets and on to stories of other significance, so he relented a little.

"From prison to the pulpit. Now that's a lead." He pushed his bottom lip out like he had just had a tasty morsel.

"Could be worth 30 seconds." His job as the editor would be to parcel out seconds like a card dealer.

"Actually, I think he's just getting out of prison, never having read the Bible, and now touching hearts—all news. If that's still what we do here. It's all so primitive—human nature at its most basic. I think our viewers will relate to this story of a fallen man and his redemption in a very improbable way."

CHAPTER 5

MEREDITH WALKED EAGERLY and with confidence, as though each step held a new promise. She was tall and trim, with a small face of pronounced features. Heads turned as she passed. Her hair brushed her shoulders in buttery curls. So rich in their blondness were the strands that they looked as though they were radiating their own light. She seemed to have been unpunished by life and felt no boundaries to her possibilities.

The newspaper staff had heard that Meredith O'Connor had been offered a job as a reporter before graduating from the University of Georgia in journalism. She didn't know that her so-called big mule of a father had leaned hard on the publisher of *The Atlanta News* to hire his daughter before she graduated and 'get her the hell out of the university before she writes another football exposé.' Her first-day walk through the expansive newsroom's clutter of cubicles was filled with the joy of accomplishment, a job before her senior year. She gave a slight pump of her arm, whispering an affirmative, "Yes!"

The receptionist had pointed across the broad room at the only enclosed office and said, "He's expecting you."

SAMUEL PRESTON EDITOR, the small sign read. The door was open, so Meredith stepped carefully into his office to meet with her first boss. She remembered his nickname was Press, which she heard captured his old-school, aggressive approach to reporting. Looking up from a paper-stricken desk, the editor barely remembered her from a very brief first introduction with the publisher. He did recall her as a pretty young thing who was going over his head—or her daddy was—to get a job. His publisher made no apologies. Inviting no comment, after she left the first meeting, Press was told to make it work.

At least she had already proven herself as a talented reporter in college, but Press knew she was hired to protect revenues, causing him to grumble that the paper's motto was, "All the news that's fit to be bought." It isn't a perfect world, the publisher had said. Press resented being accused of being too old school, and besides, the girl was talented, which meant hiring her wasn't a complete abridgment of the paper's morals.

When she entered, the striking blue of her eyes, which he could see were roaming over his office, momentarily captured him. She was thinking that the small room was a study in defiance of his newspaper's new commitment to all things online. Papers, newspapers, magazines lay where they landed as though blown in through an open window. As the editor, he still printed out his reporters' first-draft story proposals before marking them up with a pen. Or he gouged the paper with his impatient edits when he thought the writing was poorly rendered.

"Good morning, Mr. Preston, I'm...."

Ignoring her salutation, thinking it too cheery, too eager for seven-thirty in the morning, he simply said, "Meredith O'Connor."

He paused as though he was pondering some profundity or perhaps found musicality or poetry in her name. He held up a page from the newspaper. "Do you get a thrill out of getting ink on your hands? Do you love the feel of newsprint?"

She paused, now intimidated at where she was, looking at the obvious pleasure he took in holding his black-smudged fingers out at her. But it was a rhetorical question, with no answer expected as he pushed the newspaper toward her.

"This is sacred ground. This paper and this ink are the protectors of our nation more than all the guns in the military. I want you to feel that the ink on your hands will give you the same joy as does the ocean spray in a ship captain's face.

She thought it ironic he was alluding to ink when more news was now digitized than printed. He motioned for her to sit down, nodding his head as he waved his hand toward a green leather chair tightly placed against the front of his desk.

Meredith thought his voice had a rasp as though it had been washed with too many bourbons and clouded in too many cigars, the smell of which sauntered around the room.

"This isn't a poetry class. This is plain-Jane writing that reads clearer than a bell rings. Pithy, not poetry, rules here."

Press sensed there was a feistiness about her, maybe too much confidence, but he liked that. The scowl was curtained, and she could tell he savored what he was about to say like it was a tasty morsel,

"I see us as treasure hunters, the truth being the treasure we seek." He ended with a pleased grin that pushed his carelessly-shaved cheeks up into his eyes until his whole face squinted in mirth.

To the young woman, Press was like an actor on a stage

where she wanted to perform. Her whole being shuddered as though cold air had suddenly entered the room, but it was the chill of excitement and promise.

His countenance changed again as he hunched lower in his chair, both forearms flat against his desk. He loved assessing people, whether a politician or an employee, trying to see if they were wounded or lying or worthy of the paper's employ. In his heart, he wanted her to get the hell out of his office and go back to Daddy and say, "I'd make a better weather girl, not a journalist."

He wondered if she wasn't too damn pretty. It might be a distraction in interviews. Looking at her resume, he said in a gravelly purr, "We hired you before you even graduated."

He had pulled it up on his computer just before she came in. "You were making Phi Beta Kappa grades, Associate Editor of the college newspaper. And, of course, you broke that football cheating story about our university."

"Yes, sir. It was a big decision when your publisher called me at school and offered me a job. I was surprised that my dad was more excited than I was about the offer. He said I could always get a degree, but this offer was what I was in college for anyway."

Press smiled smugly. He knew the football cheating story had embarrassed her Bulldog-loyal father, even though it was an excellent example of investigative reporting.

Meredith was briefly bothered over the proprietary nature, the loyalty she heard when Press said 'our' university. Her face flushed. She couldn't tell whether in anger or embarrassment until she said firmly, "I found a professor giving math grades to athletes. I love our football team, but I hate cheating worse."

He liked her sense of moral indignation, but she had an overconfidence that could be worrisome. Maybe she liked the headlines about herself. He didn't need a college hotshot who would be byline hunting. But perhaps she was possessed with the essence of journalistic integrity, the irrepressible search for the truth.

"I like aggressive reporting, but 'controlled' aggressive."

Looking again at her resume, Press said, "I see that you studied architecture."

"Yes, sir," she answered quickly. "I like sketching buildings."

"Hey, none of that respect-the-old-guy crap," he gruffly ordered. "I'm not a 'sir,' I'm 'Press' even to the least of ye." He enjoyed his biblical paraphrasing.

Meredith found herself perplexed, liking him and then almost fearing him in rapid succession.

His dark eyes, secluded beneath heavy, disheveled graying brows, held her. They danced from threatening to inviting in a confluence of emotions that emphasized each word as he talked. "So, I'll start you out on a story that meets both of your talents," he said. "You'll shadow Trace Morgan, our business editor, listening and watching carefully to see how he handles an interview. Don't know if you've heard of the architect Jack Collier?"

Meredith was both listening and staring at her new boss. His billowing white shirt was obviously starved of starch, but more intriguing was his loud red tie emblazoned with a large, single black exclamation mark.

She noted how heavy his squared head looked. His face was governed by a wide mouth, which twitched along its length like thoughts were forever trying to express themselves on their own. She concluded Preston was a multi-tasker, and his mind flitted over assignments and deadlines with some thoughts forcing their way out in whispers.

"Yes, our professor brought him up several times. He said Mr. Collier was an example of a major talent who tries to out-design everyone but that he was too daring. Designs for the sake of daring and that architecture is supposed to be about function first, then how you shape a building around its use."

Meredith was a little put off at Press's sudden informality, even disrespect, when he rocked back in his tattered leather chair and slung a foot up on the right corner of his desk. She had never seen the bottom of anybody's shoe. But she was transfixed by his performance and uncertain of how to react to someone apparently so unimpressed with her presence. It was humbling, an emotion she had rarely known.

"He loves the camera, and it loves him, but that's my personal bias. He's a media manipulator. He plays us, and we have no choice but to let him—he's such good copy. Actually, he's a very good architect that has never hit it with 'The Big Design," but now brags about becoming world-renowned if he can pull off this mini-city he's proposing. Damn thing's costing half a billion dollars."

"Is the project all that different?" Meredith queried.

"You'd think he had reinvented buildings. I've seen the first draft he drew on a paper napkin. I was at a Rotary Club luncheon seated with Jack and the mayor. He had the mayor wrapped around his finger with words like *a revolution that starts in Atlanta—a world-class masterpiece.* All I saw was some childish scribble. The downtown power crowd is lit up about the buzz he claims it will bring to the city."

She could feel her shoulders lifting, almost like she was standing at attention and trying to contain her enthusiasm. She said graciously, but then she thought with much childish gratitude—maybe even being obsequious, "Thank you for giving me such an important story. I'll search the files for background information first, so I'll have a feel for who Mr. Collier is."

Press chuckled more to himself than to her. "Who he is? That's a good one. I'll just say, don't let him sweep you up in his charm. He thinks he's Atlanta's Picasso of the architectural world. You know, one of those really-out-there creative guys living in their own universe."

Press stared at her with a twinge of contempt as he remembered why she was standing in his office. Her father had pockets that were too deep for the publisher to ignore. More so, her father paid for his ads to be in print only, not the online version, and that kept the paper on paper on the street.

The editor didn't enjoy feeling like a whore. The publisher had made it clear. Meredith's father let it be known that he didn't want his daughter writing obits. He expected her to be put on real stories. The shredding finances of the newspaper demanded a certain willingness for subservience, for loosening ideals. But to this self-appointed gatekeeper of journalistic ethics, hiring this kid was butt-kissing of the first order.

So now, the editor thought, she can tell Daddy she got a nice first assignment, though it was as a shadow to a real reporter. Press smiled knowingly, feeling Jack would charm, hopefully not the pants off her, which rumor said he was good at doing, then everybody would be happy.

"Read some of our articles about this architect. Get to know what drives him to come up with these, I think, outlandish building designs."

He scratched his cheek, "I would go out to see the property. It's in the Vinings community, which is a high-end neighborhood but with a lot of history."

"Being from Atlanta, I know what happens to history here

—it turns into condos, townhouses, and restaurants. It's a town that lives in the moment," Meredith said.

Press stared past her. "Ironic, isn't it, that a town built on its history seems hell-bent on destroying it. That hill Jack is building on is a prime example. Sherman's troops had a big camp there before destroying Atlanta. A lot of old stuff from the Union Army has been dug out of the hill. Old rifle trenches still remain."

Press sat back in his chair and looked at her with a sober face. "Some of that history out there may not be so glamorous. Years ago, there were rumors about a certain tree in that area where a Black man was hanged by a group of rednecks that stormed the local jail. But then, Jack wouldn't want that story getting out, and neither would a lot of investors. Neither would this paper. His project has its arms—or hands—in many pockets, including those of the city fathers."

He could see how her eyes widened at the revelation of a hanging. Knowing how aggressive she seemed, he worried that he was setting her up to chase a rumor. "I think the tree is long gone. 'All gone' is the operative phrase. Ancient history. This is about the future. That's the storyline. Take a quick look and come on back. Probably just skinned ground now. Remember, at the interview, no questions from you. You're there to shadow Trace and to learn from his techniques."

To Meredith, that statement about rumors filled the room with its suggestiveness. Sherman was there? A hanging? She was already romanticizing all sorts of Civil War leads, putting this futuristic project in context with the past and giving the project even more interest. Perhaps Mr. Collier was even planning on bringing Sherman into the project's story.

Waving his hand toward the door, indicating it was time

for her to leave, he said, "Be patient. You'll get a byline soon enough."

The meeting was over. She walked out elated but a little angry. That last remark about her asking no questions in the interview was a put-down. She was a writer that had made the University of Georgia shudder at her reporting. To think she couldn't handle an interview about a building was indeed a put-down. But leaving the offices, she found herself more interested, intrigued about Jack Collier. And now to hear about a civil rights tragedy on his multimillion-dollar property that had the seeds of a powder keg of a story, she thought. And it was her first big story.

CHAPTER 6

MEREDITH HAD FAILED to dress for this kind of thorn-dodging walk. It was a modest hill but captured in a mess of affliction of stiff-limbed shrubs and briars spearing outward from tangles of brush. The property for the building was almost hidden in plain view. She had thought that because of its location in the middle of Vinings, one of Atlanta's most developed and chic neighborhoods, it would have already been cleared and ready for construction.

Rising from the small hill and towering in front of her was an enormous oak tree. Maybe this was the tree with a hanging that Press had hinted about. She wondered if it marked where a house was, so she used the tree's looming presence as her guide. She started through leafy, clinging underbrush.

"Oh, great!" A thorn pierced and held and stretched, then tore her skirt as she pulled away. She could feel the stiff resistance of shrub limbs against her bare arms and loops of vine snaring her shoes, but with a final determined push, she found herself standing in front of a small house shadowed by the enormous tree. Meredith thought its trunk looked like weary elephant skin.

As she stood in the small clearing in front of the single-story house, there was a decidedly unassuming, even tired look to it. The vestiges of a white paint job were now evidenced by flakes against the gray planking. A crumbling stone chimney poked weakly above the rusted tin roof. The windows, with no glass remaining, were partially boarded up. The house sat with a slight tilt on fieldstone pillars.

She was startled when the front door scraped against the porch planking as it opened. Stepping out of the vague interior was a man wearing a broad-brimmed hat. She was caught by his appearance, almost like a fashion model on an Indiana Jones set. He had an economical body with outsized shoulders. His starched blue jeans with a khaki shirt fit him with tailored familiarity. His thick hair was a rich chestnut.

He, too, was startled, but more by how pretty she was as he wondered what she was doing there. He took his hat off, seeing how edgy she looked.

"Harrison Stanton, here." He stopped outside the door on the small porch and smiled broadly. His face was unlined and tanned.

"Is this your house?" she stammered, not knowing whether to turn and head for the car or act nonplussed, even demanding.

"Hah. No, I think I can do better than this. And just who are you?" Harrison found himself staring at the perfect simplicity and symmetry of her face. It was without blemish or wrinkle. Her whole visage was a declaration of youth.

She answered officially, "I'm a reporter with *The Atlanta News*. I'm doing a story on the developer, Mr. Collier. He's going to build here."

"You mean the scalper." He pressed his back against the house and its little shade.

"What do you mean?"

The sun was breaking through the big tree and causing her to squint up at him as she remained in the yard.

"Jack will buy a beautiful piece of forested land and scalp it. I say his motto is 'If it grows, it's gone.'"

"I've not met him. Maybe tomorrow. I'm doing background on the building he's putting here. I just came out to see what the property looked like."

"Looks like," he scoffed. "See that magnificent tree? It's 165 years old, and Jack will make splinters out of it. That tree was a sapling when Sherman camped here. The condo frenzy in this area has so vanished history that it's now just legend. Except the tree."

Meredith took out a small recorder and repeated into it what he had just said. "May I ask how you know the tree is that old?"

"I'm an archeologist by profession, and I oversee the restoration of old buildings. I did a core sample on the tree out of curiosity. I'm a Civil War nut. I like the character of old stuff."

"My editor hinted that there were rumors about the tree. You know about that?"

"All kinds of legends surround this tree, but I'm not into rumors. I'm into facts."

Meredith thought that comment had a little edge on it, but he said it in such a pleasant way she let it pass. She gazed up at the stone chimney, which looked ready to crumble off the roof with any breath of wind.

"Hey, come up on the porch. That sun's too hot to stand in." He motioned with his hand in a gesture of invitation.

She had found his voice comforting in its softness and had lost her concern, or fear, of just who this sudden man was. She liked his casual nature, thinking there was a touch of romanticism about his restoring old treasures.

Meredith stepped up on the porch and into a patch of shade afforded by the tree. Subtly, her hand pushed against the tear in her skirt.

"I also wanted to record those trenches that Sherman's men dug over there before they are gone with the wind, you might say, or in Atlanta, gone with the bulldozer."

She was surprised. "The trenches are still here after all these years? That's special."

"After all the construction around here, this is like a little lost island of history."

She brought the recorder to her mouth. "I like that. A lost island of history."

She took her smartphone and snapped several shots of the grassed-over mounds.

"This is really cool stuff."

Peering through the door into the softly lit interior, she asked, "Wonder how old this house is?"

Harrison stepped beside her and walked through the door. "Come here. I'll show you something I found."

Light pierced numerous wall chinks beaming like burning darts. It then flattened against the flooring, creating a warm ambience. A fireplace of brick and stone yawned with the blackness of soot that coated its walls. To the left had been a second room, but its boarding had been torn off, and only wooden studs testified to its former presence. The floors of yellow heart pine had a clear, sharp response to their shoes as they walked. Meredith crinkled her nose in recognition of the room's musty smell. The air was so still she noticed its heaviness.

"Look over here in the corner." Harrison had pried planking from the wall.

"Look at these cut marks where an ax was used to plane it down. Definitely old craftsmanship."

"How old is old?" she asked. "Certainly not Civil War old?"

"No way this shack could be that old. But maybe over a hundred years. Still, don't know how it has survived surrounded by all this development."

Harrison's foot was on the stone flooring of the fireplace. He idly brushed his shoe against the flat stone hearth, scraping off a layer of soot.

"Hello, what's this?" He leaned down to look closely where his foot had been.

Meredith looked down at him. "What are you looking at?"

"There's writing scratched in this rock. I think it says, 'whupin hous.'"

Meredith almost pushed him aside as she leaned down for a look. "Is that English? No telling how many families lived here over the years. Maybe a kid scratched it; they sure weren't good at spelling."

Harrison instinctively took the end of the board he had pried loose and began scraping away an array of ashes, leaves, and pine needles that had come down through the chimney and amassed on the fireplace flooring.

"Ah, the plot thickens," he said in a false baritone solemnity. "Got some names scratched here where the logs would have hidden them."

Both of them leaned into the yawning fireplace to see

names crudely cut into various bricks. She read some of them off: "Ellie, Rufus, Joe John, Lizzie."

For a moment, they said nothing. Meredith started walking pensively in a slow circle around the room, listening to the sharp sound of her heels on the boards. They felt firm for a house in such a poor condition.

"What about this idea?" She surprised Harrison with the suddenness and conviction of her words. "What if those writings meant 'whipping house,' and this is a house as old as those trenches outside. Wouldn't that be an incredible story?"

Pulling out her smartphone, she held it close to the scratched words. A tiny flash captured their reading.

She looked intensely at Harrison. "I think we may have a story here. It doesn't take much imagination to see this house is from slave days, and slaves were beaten here."

He almost glared at her. "Wait a minute," he held up his hands. "Seems plausible, but you would have to research the records for this property. I don't use my imagination, as you say, to come to conclusions."

She resented that swipe at her integrity. "No conclusions, but I have some evidence worth pursuing. A story of slavery right here has the potential for important background and historical context for this development everybody seems to be talking about."

Harrison rebutted her with professional caution but with a decided bite.

"You haven't discovered anything. Don't let wanting to write your story get out in front of the facts. Yes, it's got some age on it, or it could be just a rundown shack no more than fifty years old, built with old wood. I know this area from a Civil War standpoint, and I see no way this house could go back that far. You might check the courthouse or archives building for property and genealogy records."

"I'll check records, but that bulldozer out there is about to flatten the whole place." She was oblivious to him in her nervous excitement, her words finding no space between each.

As she turned to leave the room, she said, "I'm going with a reporter to interview Mr. Collier tomorrow. I'd like to confirm what this house is all about before he tears it down."

Harrison followed her out on the porch. "Let me know what you find out about who owned this property in the 1860s. Here's my card."

She took a quick look and said what to him sounded like a flirt.

"OK, Mr. Archeologist, I'll let you know if I find anything. I think this could be a story the African American community would be interested in. A place of despair, now a place of hope. Old meets new. I like that. Maybe Mr. Collier could build around the trenches and save the tree." Her voice was filled with expectation.

Harrison warned Meredith as she stepped off the porch and down a path to her car to avoid the briars.

"I doubt that ego-maniac wants you to redesign his master-piece. Be cautious. He's a big dog, and big dogs can bite."

He worried that his name might get in a story by a naïve overachiever who was trying to make a name for herself.

Meredith stopped at the enormous tree, thoughtfully ran her hand over its trunk, and answered with an obvious conviction,

"Bite? So can this reporter."

There was a joy to her voice as she disappeared into the brush. She was on the hunt. Perhaps there was a story behind the story of another history-destroying Atlanta development.

She headed to the Atlanta History Center, where some of the area's oldest land transactions and wills were digitally defying age, or in a few cases, still available in their original paper form. It didn't take long for Meredith to run through the Vinings area records to one Ransom Steel's name in a heavy, yellowed ledger book of financial transactions going back before The War. In a florid script, it had a listing of his assets given to a bank for a loan application. At different periods during the Civil War, he had owned sixteen slaves.

Meredith drew in a sudden gasp when she saw one of the names listed as a slave was one Joe John. The other four names scratched in the fireplace either weren't there or couldn't be read in the swirling script of the banker.

She sat back in her chair, momentarily stunned and uncertain about how to handle this. Should she call Press and 'show him the money' as he had sarcastically requested? The records unequivocally proved slaves were on that property, but then there was no proof Ransom had beaten them. Should she jump in on the interview and confront Jack with the news of a potential historical building smack in the center of his grand plans?

Meredith was raised in Atlanta and knew it to be a city where new development trumped musty history. That meant a house, slave or not, would be flattened if it would jeopardize a signature building. She thought of Harrison's admonition that she be more circumspect in coming to conclusions. Well, she had her conclusions, and in her mind, she had found the gold ring on her first day at work. This arrogant architect who should know he was building on sacred ground, and the pain and suffering that went on there, could not be ignored by his ambitions.

The June sun created a palette of purples and oranges

across the afternoon clouds as Meredith walked out of the History Center to her car. The bite of the day had been momentarily softened. She stretched her tall frame, lifting herself up on her toes, and breathed deeply to calm herself, then called her editor.

"Mr...I mean, Press, this is Meredith."

There was silence. She feared he didn't remember her.

"Meredith, the new reporter," she said sheepishly.

Ignoring any pleasantries, the impatient voice of Press growled.

"What cha got? Pretty view of the city from that property on the hill, huh?"

She came back in a gush. "I have a whole new slant on the property. The lead is that this is an oasis of history that has been forgotten. There's an old...a slave house on the property, and they beat slaves there. Can you believe it?"

There was a pause, then a confused, "A what house? Slaves beaten in Vinings? What the hell is this about?"

"There was an archeologist there, and he found names under the soot in the fireplace, and it was written in the soot that people were beaten there." Her voice was breathless in its excitement.

His disbelief turned to a cynical pitch. "Let's see; you saw this house that has been sitting out in a ritzy area, that nobody has noticed or walked through, and you alone discovered that it was a slave's house. This better be good, young lady. What's your source of its age?"

He pounded on the last sentence.

She didn't like the 'young lady' comment but was so caught up in the excitement of her news, she responded with a joyous, "We found their names! In the fireplace, under soot and stuff. And I have just found their names on a will. So, there is a match."

There was a resounding impatience in her editor's quick response.

"Oh, and I guess beside their names it said, 'I am a slave, and I was beaten. Here's my email address; you can verify it by contacting me.'"

He gave Meredith his best Jerry McGuire intonation, "Show me the proof, Meredith!"

Meredith held the phone away from her head and looked at it like the entire instrument, and the voice coming out of it were crazy. She was hurt, angry, and suddenly wondering if this was the journalism she had dreamed of. She thought this was big news, and she resented his tone and mockery.

She answered firmly, "I'll bring you support for this tomorrow after I've interviewed the developer."

"Hold on. You are not interviewing anybody tomorrow. We've had this conversation, and you're shadowing Trace."

His voice rose again as he spelled, "S-h-a-d-o-w." Then realizing he was being hard on a young woman with no experience, his tone calmed.

"Look, I've pushed you into a story with a power player, and it could get tense very quickly if you try and bring long-ago abuses into it. This guy has been known to have the temper of a stick of dynamite. I want you to shadow Trace, listening and learning, no questions."

She felt she had blown it in her schoolgirl eagerness and had little choice but to buck up and answer with feigned enthusiasm.

"Yes, sir. I just saw a bigger story with important background context that could form a meaningful contrast between the old and the new Atlanta."

His response was measured and firm, like an exasperated father being patient with an errant child.

"If the background story relates to, changes, or adds new light on a story, then fine. That's good shoe-leather reporting. But I don't see any connection whatsoever. We can mine the past and say every event has some connection with what went before. But I see a slave story interfering here, not enlightening."

"Yes, sir. I see your point. I'll meet Trace at the interview."

His phone went dead. She didn't know if he even heard her last comment.

Tears came in a rush, riding out over her full cheeks and filling her nose with their sorrowful rain. Her body shook, and she found herself fumbling in her purse for a napkin.

CHAPTER 7

THE 8:00 morning air was so still in midtown Atlanta that it seemed to Meredith the whole street scene was a photograph. There was no humidity, and the buildings and trees had a dimensional quality as if every object competed to be seen with its own special clarity. She arrived early to the site of the interview with Jack Collier. She was dressed in brown pants and a tan blouse with a small string of pearls and sensible pumps. She had a small notebook and a recorder in her purse.

"Meredith." It was the small, somewhat starched figure of Trace Morgan, the reporter she was to shadow. He looked to be in his late thirties to her. His voice was deeper than his figure would have suggested. He was a fastidious business dresser, like a chairman going to a board meeting. He had a noncommittal look; his face was journeyman, of no special persuasion except he seemed to be blinking a bit much. She didn't see the passion she thought top reporters would show. She had romanced the image in her mind of a shoe-leather man, a little disheveled or inattentive at least in dress, to reflect his fervid commitment to reporting. That's what she wanted to be, impeccably honest and without favor for any side. A digger, unrelenting in a search for the truth.

She stuck out her hand, smiling. "Hello, Trace. Thank you for letting me follow you today. I read several of your columns last night. It is pretty exciting to be with an award-winning business journalist. Oh, and could I get a ride back to the office? I took MARTA down here."

His smile was a reluctant, one-sided shift of his lips, a faux smile for politeness' sake, on an otherwise unyielding demeanor. He stared at her in an appraisal she noticed, and she had seen all of her life, being heralded as a beauty since childhood. He imagined she was another of the blonde babes that seemed to be populating the media. His mind, in that instant of salutations, assumed she had enough talent to get the job but was hired to be the new Gen X face for the twenty-somethings who had abandoned print for catching news, meaning celebrity followings on the internet. She was window dressing—bait to be thrown to the selfie generation for which he had no use.

As they started to walk into the lobby, Meredith, in her eagerness to make an impression, joked, "Guess we don't need our scuba diving outfits today."

Trace stopped before the revolving doors, "Huh?"

Feeling overly eager and with a girlish excitement, she enthused, "I mean, the summer is so humid in Atlanta, it can be like swimming underwater. But not today."

She held a grin, waiting for his reaction.

"Yeah, not today," he said.

She thought it was a disrespectful tone and was given with a crooked smile that faked a compliment. Stepping in front of her, Trace pushed the revolving door for himself in what she felt was an Alpha move or just rude.

Jack's office was on the 20th floor of a building of his design. It looked from the street like crumpled aluminum foil unfolding skyward. The design had created controversy from nearby building owners, who said it defied the accepted look of Midtown Atlanta. Jack had won several architectural design awards from Europe, and a large spread had appeared in *Architectural Digest* for its "flamboyant freedom," one adoring critic wrote. Competing commercial realtors and architects of no-note derisively called it The Aluminum Foil Building. After work, Jack would often come out on the street and look up at the configuration, happy with his creation.

When Meredith and Trace were ushered into Jack's office, he was seated at a desk of richly polished wood from an old sailing ship. Mounted on a steel frame, it was a contrast in materials. In fact, Meredith noticed, the whole office was eclectic-- here, order there, but energy mingled with its feel.

Jack sat with his back to them, looking out at a sweeping view of downtown Atlanta. He was laughing loudly and exuberantly talking and gesturing. Meredith watched the theatricality of his mannerisms while she and Trace stood quietly waiting for him to turn around. She looked across the expansive room to see one wall covered in black-lined draw-ings on paper napkins, one on toilet tissue, and several encased as though they were special. All of the drawings looked as much like children's squiggles as they did building exteriors. To her right was a case arising from the yellow heart pine floors. Mounted on top of it was a paper and wood, architec-tural model.

But the singular object that caught Meredith's eye in the broad room was a life-sized drawing of a naked man standing with two sets of outstretched arms inside a circle, which was inside a box. Known as the Vitruvian Man, the line drawing was originally created in 1490 by Leonardo da Vinci as an example of the perfectly proportioned man. Da Vinci got the idea for the drawing from the notes of an ancient Roman architect named Vitruvius, who believed that man was the measure of all things so that even the design of buildings should reflect the human body. It became a study in proportionality and balance and a guide for Renaissance architecture. She would later learn that the five-foot-tall copy, looking ancient in its sepia tone, was Jack's inspiration and aspiration. The fierceness of the eyes, the prominent nose, and expanding cheekbones filled the room for Jack, like a talisman, a magical charm bestowing inspiration. Jack saw his own physical resemblance, especially when he let his thick hair grow almost to his shoulders or flair just beyond his ears. When he turned from his phone call to face his visitors, Meredith was immediately struck by how Jack's face had a definite resemblance to the drawing.

"Visitors from my favorite profession," he welcomed them as he stood. "I really appreciate you coming. I'm Jack." Walking around the desk with his hand out, he wore an obviously starched pale pink shirt with darker pink stripes and no tie. The shirt fit snugly. His over six-foot frame tapered up to his fulsome shoulders. He accentuated his height and his fit build by standing very straight. His expansive smile, his build, and purposeful movement around the desk toward them pulled her into an aura of energy. She consciously gave him a firm handshake with a quick look into his welcoming brown eyes. His grin was large and appeared to touch, push, and crinkle every feature of his face in one coordinated performance.

He looked intently at Meredith, almost stopped by her beauty, especially her bottom lip, so full it seemed to be pouting. "I've heard of you and your big story about cheating. That really rocked the university. I also heard you were hired by the newspaper before you even graduated. Well, no cheating to report here, but a design like the world has never seen."

Then looking at the small frame of Trace and placing his hand on the reporter's thin shoulder, Jack said, "And, I even get the award-winning reporter, Mr. Trace. I mean two heavy-weights to report on my little project." He seemed to find joy in speaking.

Meredith found herself trying to read between the lines of his words. Was he truly this humble after so much publicity and so many awards? Was this a setup, an overly obsequious act for favorable reporting? Or was he some Picasso-like creative genius you would never really fathom?

In these first moments, she did realize that he was a force of certitude and incredibly charming. And when Jack reached out and softly touched her arm to give emphasis to his words, she felt both uncomfortable with that immediate familiarity and drawn to it at the same time, which made her feel vulnerable in a way she was unfamiliar with. *Was he flirting?* she wondered.

"Your drawing indicates you are an admirer of Protagoras," Meredith said as she turned toward the Vitruvian Man poster.

Jack's face lit up in an expression of surprise. He held his hands out in astonishment. "I don't believe this." He delighted in philosophy, especially that of the founding fathers of western thought. But Jack knew no one with any interest in these original Grecian thinkers. It had long been a frustration of his, so to suddenly find someone with any knowledge of the subject almost made him giddy.

Her smile was a subconscious signal to Jack that she knew that he knew the history of his poster. "Protagoras was the

Greek philosopher who coined the statement, 'Man is the measure of all things,' which was the idea Vitruvian was trying to portray, and da Vinci was the only one who succeeded with that drawing."

His enthusiasm for further conversation was obvious. "This is too good," Jack exclaimed. He impulsively hugged her quickly, which astonished Meredith and shocked Trace. It was so quick that Meredith was still reacting when he was back to his normal stance.

"So, do you agree that man alone is the judge of and the measurer of all things?"

Feeling she had established an immediate connection with her first foray into interviewing, she seized the moment, although out of the corner of her eye, she could see the scowl on Trace's face.

"I pray that we individually don't determine what is right and wrong on all ethical questions, or there would be no commonly accepted code of ethics. It would be anarchy of sorts."

"A reporter I don't even know, who I am in agreement with." Jack's teeth were straight and white. She could see as his lips remained stretched back in a grin of appreciation. "I know that architecture, while subject to everyone's measure or opinion, still has levels of expertise that demand agreement."

Feeling he had been cut out of his own interview, Trace made a slight step forward toward Jack. "Are you saying that this creation we are here to discuss must be judged by everyone as excellence in design?"

Jack looked at Trace. "Not must, but certainly by those with the expertise to know great work when it is created."

Trace was having none of the charm. "Let's talk about this creation. Our paper wants to do a major story on the project now that you have the financing locked down. Although everyone has heard of it, you've built a real mystery around what the project is and what it will look like. In fact, I don't even know what you're calling it."

"Hey, ladies first," Jack pointed at Meredith playfully.

Trace interrupted, "No, as accomplished as Meredith was in college, she's just shadowing today. There'll be time for her questions as we do more stories on you."

There was a pause, which Jack irrepressibly entered with a breath of air that sounded like a beginning laugh. "From what I hear about that football story, I'd say somebody needs to be shadowing her. Take a shot, Miss Meredith."

Trace's placid face turned visibly red. Meredith looked uncertainly at both of them.

"Well, just one, if you insist," Meredith answered. "Creativity seems to be what you strive for, but will this design reflect something unique, something bigger than just you being creative?"

"Trace," Jack exclaimed. "Listen to that and just right out of college. Or still in college, sort of. She's going to be a good one. Like you." He closed with a placating compliment.

Trace was subtly but noticeably shaking his head in disapproval and glaring at Meredith. She was caught up in Jack's exuberance. It was like Trace had left the room.

Jack answered proudly. "I've created a structure of unique design, an environment, that inspires innovative thinkers to transition into higher levels of accomplishment. It's a work, play, and living community designed to stretch the imagination and the intellect of those living there." With emphasis, he said, "It's an environment for the mind."

Both reporters were recording and writing his comments. He motioned them toward the building's model. As they approached the large stand that held the model, Trace shook his head. "Never seen anything like this."

Jack responded without hesitation, "Never before. It's unique to the world of design because it isn't just about creativity, as Meredith just asked, but an instrument of collaboration." He put his hands on the table's edge in some affirmation of his authorship and his words.

"The town center is called The Agora, after the marketplace where Socrates taught. Here I plan on bringing innovative thinkers to speak on the commons. I want to invigorate the soul and the mind. The design reflects a cocoon from which achievement and excellence can emerge."

It was a large round metallic structure that partially opened like a flower, where a village with traditional little shops was abutting an urgent modernity of disparately-shaped offices and condos in twists and sweeps of odd materials, all working in a cacophonous arrangement, but an orchestration, nevertheless, that somehow worked.

"Are you ready?" Jack's voice was filled with a child-like expectancy. He then pressed a button. At the entrance to the town, wings suddenly unfolded and then rose in flight above the table before disappearing. Jack could hear their soft gasps.

"How on earth did you do that?" Meredith wondered aloud. The words had come without her intent. To question was instinctual for her.

Trace ever so slightly pushed his arm against hers and interjected, trying to stop her questioning. "This is some kind of hologram done large. I didn't know you could make them that realistic and that large."

"It's a technology I developed," Jack answered proudly. "It's like a dream unfolding into reality. It comes out just before dawn. Like announcing all of the possibilities of the new day."

The business section of *The News* was as much a promotional piece for the city's aggressive real estate community as it was a critical review of that world of ambition and buildings. Trace had never covered Jack's ventures. What he had heard from the other reporters was that Jack thought he was a creative genius—a master of self-promotion and a designer of outrageous-looking office towers. Trace had come to the interview in pursuit of the man as much as his building. "Let's be honest. Your work has been criticized with words like 'too expressive,' 'show-off designs,' 'narcissistic architecture.' Are you concerned that this will get the same kind of response with these flying wings? A building that opens like a flower?"

Meredith could see the slightest of change across Jack's broad face, a bare lowering of his eyelids. "If an artist is worried about being liked, he would never put down a stroke. Did da Vinci worry about people not liking the smile of the Mona Lisa?"

Trace's narrow mouth pursed up like he had just tasted something and was going to chew on it more. "So, you're comparing yourself to Leonardo?"

Meredith thought Trace was looking for a gotcha moment and feared Jack would abruptly and angrily end the interview. Ignoring the last question, which sounded more like an accusation, she said, "I don't mean to interrupt, but I have a question about the location."

Trace became obviously riled and said, "Excuse me, Meredith, let Jack respond to what he sees as true genius in his design."

Jack cocked an eyebrow up in a contemplative look. "I don't

have the range of talents da Vinci did. Maybe no human ever has. But I would like to think I could equal him in designing environments that fold around a unique concept. I like pushing the boundaries of creativity in architecture, not just to be creative, but to find the limits of functionality and purpose."

Trace was both taking notes and recording. To Meredith, he was obviously on a line of questioning which could embarrass Jack. "Would you say you're about to be known as Atlanta's Leonardo?"

Jack saw that as a pointless question. He answered with emphasis. "I don't design for Atlanta. I design for the ages, for centuries from now when critics look back at what set the standard for this era."

Trace was stunned at the audacity of the statement. Anger in his tone announced the next question. "That's a pretty boastful statement. Sounds like you believe you are the world's greatest living architect. That all the others should pay homage to your designs."

Jack felt his arms tense up. He knew he was being baited. He wanted to slap the glowering face of the reporter. But the slap came in the form of completely ignoring the question and pivoting to the dawn softness of Meredith's blue eyes. "How 'bout the location out at Vinings? Pretty great view back to Atlanta from that hill, isn't it? Oops, I forgot, I need to get permission so the shadow here can talk."

Trace felt the rejection, which drew more insistence from him to unveil this outsized, outrageous ego for which Atlanta leaders had fallen.

Meredith didn't hesitate this time. She thought the whole shadow idea from Press was demeaning and probably sexist. Her answer was without hesitation. "I understand a man was hanged on the property with the Union trenches, that beautiful old tree, and the shack or house."

Jack answered, "That shack was supposed to be knocked down yesterday, but the demolition man got delayed."

"Well, you may want to delay it some more. I've done a little research and am pretty sure the house has a story to tell."

"A story? What, that it's about to fall down?"

"Much more than that. I'm confident that it was lived in by slaves when Sherman camped there," she said.

Jack had a surprised look, putting his hands out in front of him. "Whoa, whoa, slaves? I don't think so. That house can't be more than eighty years at the most. And yes, Sherman overnighted in Vinings. In fact, I've got a boutique hotel I'm putting in called The Sherman Oaks. I always like saving old trees, but that one covers so much ground where the building is going, we can't keep it."

Trace started to speak, but Meredith's words rushed over his. "I found some convincing old records that show the house was built before the Civil War, and slaves not only lived there but may have been beaten there."

Jack's mouth opened; his face dropped in obvious disbelief. "What?! That beat-up old shack? Now we're entering the twilight zone. I might have to return you back to shadow status." There was a mark of fun in his voice because he thought the conversation so ludicrous.

"I think the evidence is compelling. When I was out at the house, I saw names scratched into the hearth along with the words, 'Whupin hous', which I take to mean whipping house. When I found the property records from that time, it had a listing of the slaves with the same names that were scratched in the hearth."

"Let's back up," Jack interjected, now showing some

concern. "I thought we were doing an interview on a real estate project. Where did this slave stuff come from? I think I need to give Press a call and ask him what this interview is about."

His normally jovial eyes had an uncharacteristic hardness. Looking at both reporters, then at the model before him, he was getting a hint that his lifetime's work could be threatened by a headline about Black people having been beaten on his property.

"Do you know Mr. Preston?" Meredith felt she was being warned.

"I know everybody, including Press," Jack answered with a sharp confidence.

Trace had a slight tick to his eyes that was now a more accentuated blinking and squinting around an interview spiraling out of control.

Meredith saw Jack's welcoming face compress into a tightened jaw and lips. He ran his hand through his hair several times. The three of them stood in awkward silence around the model.

Jack often knew people better than he knew himself. His wife had told him that once. He was a reader of nuances, facial expressions, and intent without revealing what he had discerned just through a conversation. He knew he had intimidated both of them with his threat to call their editor, so he continued to try and maneuver them away from all things southern.

"Well, all of that, if it can be proven, is tragic history. But you can pick out thousands of pieces of property in the south where horrible things happened. Do we want a world where the sins of the fathers, so to speak, determine and hang over every move we make today? There are old tragedies on most of the grounds around Atlanta. I don't see my property much different from them, sadly." He emphasized "sadly" for effect. "Any other property around here might share a similar story."

"Of course, "Meredith sounded apologetic. She was relieved to see Jack's softening response. "I don't see this as a negative. I guess I'm taking my reporter's hat off when I say this could be a positive opportunity for the project."

Trace's thin face seemed to draw together into a bitter taste look, as his eyes blinked like he was trying to rid them of an intrusive gnat.

"Meredith," he called out her name with a quickness that almost blurred the word. "We weren't sent here to help design the project or to give the history of the land. Jack's right. If slaves' sweat and blood prevented a building from going up, Georgia would be barren of any structures. Let's get back to the building and what it's about."

But she wouldn't be haltered. "Of course, but just this one more idea. Do we walk away from our history, or do we honor it? If the property is a little island or oasis of history still standing and hidden in plain sight in this rich neighborhood, you could use that to your advantage. You know, incorporate the past with this futuristic project."

Jack didn't know what influence this woman half his age had at the paper, but he couldn't let her wanderings stir up a civil rights issue where none existed. He admired her feistiness but saw the point of a spear emerging in her proposal that could destroy his design and how it was placed on the property. Jack tried to logically but politely stop her direction.

"The problem with slave time is that, yes, it was brutal and demeaning, but it was 150 years ago." He paused in his words then pointed toward the model. "Metamorphosis is all about a flowering of the mind and conscience and how in the right environment, it can be excited and stimulated to produce world-changing ideas and products. The last thing it is about is slavery. My concept is a million miles away from that shack and any cruelties that may have occurred there."

Trace interjected. "Let me remind our new employee," looking at Meredith, "this is a feature story about architecture. There is international interest in its design, and the paper is giving the story a lot of space. So, let's move on to the building."

Meredith could see the anger in Trace's face and heard the word employee to describe her. She meekly said, "Of course," and turned toward the model.

The reporters couldn't see how white Jack's knuckles had turned as he was gripping both hands behind his back.

"Well, I admire your digging into the history of the property. It might give some context I wasn't aware of. No wonder the newspaper wanted to hire you. But I can't believe a 150-year-old house in that high-end neighborhood with all the development around it would still be standing. If the house does have historical significance, we can take it apart and give it to a park."

Trace said, "Hmmm, *Gone with the Wind* has gone with the wind."

To make sure they knew he was kidding, he said, "Couldn't resist." Then he thought that actually might make a clever headline or perhaps, and he said, "' DaVinci Comes to Vinings.'"

"Well, that's actually true about this project. It has zero to do with that damn Civil War time."

Concerned that Trace could make him look like an egomaniac and Meredith could have the civil rights crowd storming the hill, Jack said, "Hey, why don't we wait on this Old South stuff until I can get a historian or architect who specializes in old structures to go out and determine the true age of the house. About a hanging, with so many trees that covered that hill, it could have been any of them. So, that can't be confirmed and is just speculation. Your paper, I don't think, prints rumors."

Meredith knew Jack was trying to stop the story by putting the paper in a box about writing without proof. She liked the subtlety of his maneuvering; there was a mastery in it, as facile as his drawings. She also noticed how easily he could move from firmness to graciousness in thanking the two reporters for coming as the interview ended. Meredith wasn't prepared for the emotion she felt when Jack again placed his fingers in a more prolonged touch on her arm at the door. Her mind was stopped at the moment, and she again looked away, afraid her expression, whatever her face was saying, might give away this momentary eddy of feelings. Jack then gave her his card and said he was available for follow-up questions. He didn't give one to Trace, who saw at once that Jack was playing this overzealous girl because he saw her as potential trouble and probably because her looks were so compelling.

"My last card," he apologized to Trace, who felt even more slighted since he was the lead reporter.

Meredith had never been in love. She had come to scorn her own face because that was all family and friends and schoolmates commented on for her whole life. She assumed that was the only reason so many men flirted with her. But now, this suppressed openness to love, like something primal, was giving her a strange lightness of being. She worried that once started—it couldn't be stopped, only fulfilled.

Jack watched Meredith walk away. She had broad, athletic shoulders like his wife. Her calves were full and rounded, like his wife. As she walked to the door to leave, she purposefully didn't turn and look at him, but she could see him in the distance in the reflection of the glass door, and seeing him standing and looking at her made her nervous at what had just happened to her. Jack shook his head and thought of the trouble he could get into with this woman hardly out of school. He felt a brief sense of guilt as thoughts of his wife intruded. But it was a very brief sense of guilt.

Trace said nothing as they rode the elevator down. Meredith saw he was containing his anger and tried to make small talk about the project. Trace said nothing until they were back in his car.

"I'm going to recommend, no, insist, that Press fire you before the sun sets. You broke two basic rules of journalism. You ignored your editor's specific instructions, which were to observe and not ask questions. And you tried to become a part of the story with that crap about slaves." He was glaring at the windshield, both hands firmly on the wheel. His head turned slowly toward Meredith. "You need to go back to college and find another major. You're no journalist."

Tears welled up in her eyes. Her mouth opened, asking for air, and the air seemed dry. A rising heat blushed her face. She had never in her life been called out like that, been called a failure, and to be fired from her first job! Her family would be humiliated. It would be shocking to her friends still at UGA and still admiring her getting such a prestigious job. But it would be joyous news to all of those Georgia fans who hated her for her exposé about cheating football players.

As they pulled into the newspaper's parking lot, Meredith was suddenly seized with anger over Trace's threat that revealed her independence. She said forcefully, almost in scorn at him, "I found the story behind the story. Who cares about another building in a town overrun with buildings built by another big ego developer?"

She turned toward Trace with a determination that had him move ever so slightly away from her. "I may have discovered a story of historical significance for Atlanta's Black community. It's a story of savagery and murder. They might even call it sacred ground. That means Metamorphosis could generate even more significance if it were used as a dramatic example of how the south has changed."

Trace cut sharply into his parking place. "You're clueless. A selfish member of the selfie generation. Everything is about 'look at me.'"

She turned toward him, holding the opened door, and said, "My approach to this story is called journalism—a search for the truth. You apparently want to do PR work for a developer." She closed the car door, surprising herself at the explosiveness of her temper toward an older man she was supposed to be working under.

Meredith had come to define herself by the lengths she would go to in order to find the whole truth. Journalism had become her love, her walk, and her contribution to society.

She walked briskly toward the employee door, her heels clicking against the parking deck's concrete floor. Trace cut the engine off and bolted from his car, thinking she was trying to get to Press before he could.

CHAPTER 8

MEREDITH REACHED her editor's office first. Trace had barely missed the elevator she took and stood in frustration for a moment, then went bounding up the three sets of stairs to the reporter's floor.

Meredith tapped on the editor's glass wall, but it was only a quick pause as she walked into the disheveled office. Press's head turned from his computer screen with a questioning look as Meredith seemed red in the face and exerted in her breathing.

"Yes?" His voice rolled out the word like it was a complete sentence.

"I've got proof that the Collier project is a bigger story than it seems. Slaves were kept in the house on the property and probably beaten."

She handed him copies of the records she had researched as Trace came in, also short of breath after sprinting up the stairs.

"What in the hell is going on here?" The words punched at both of them. "Are you two in some kind of footrace?"

Trace stepped up to the cluttered desk. "She's broken every rule of journalism, Press. She inserted herself in the story. She disobeyed your orders to shadow me and upset Jack Collier big time."

Determination flashed over Meredith's face. She, too, stood next to the desk, almost leaning into it.

"Trace was doing a public relations interview in the face of major news that could make this project even more meaningful in a historical way. I had no choice as a reporter but to pursue my lead, and I think you will be proud of what I have uncovered."

"She's trying to turn this into a make-believe civil rights story about something that may have happened a hundred and fifty years ago." Trace's voice was insistent, his eyes ticked as though providing a nervous support for the urgency to tell his side.

Press stood up with the papers Meredith had handed him. To her, everyone's movements seemed to be moving in a slower motion. She saw Press's short, thick fingers on the paper and how they were smudged dark gray from the print off the stacks of newspapers on his desk. She saw his paunch and the crumpled, careless folds in his shirt and his blazing red tie with the exclamation mark on it. She saw his jaw set, slightly jutting forward.

"I told you to ask no questions."

There was a pause as she waited for Press to say more, then realized he was waiting for a response.

Her fortitude began to weaken. It was in the diminished tone of her voice.

"I was hired to find the real truth, and there's more story here than just another building."

"And the real," Press dragged the word real out. "The real

story is not about a spectacular building that's going to get the attention of the world. The real story is," he glanced down at her notes, and having no patience to read them, held them out to her and demanded, "about what?"

Meredith was resolute since she had no other choice.

"In visiting the property, I found the house that sits in the center of it. The house turned out to be 165 years old. Slaves lived there, according to the records you are holding. And I found names scratched in the fireplace that match those listed as slaves. Also scratched were words that can only be interpreted as 'whipping house.'"

"So damn what?" Press stepped around to the side of his desk with Meredith close enough that she could easily see the veins running down his neck and the red mist of excited vessels covering his face. His eyes glared from their thick-browed setting, peered over his fleshy cheeks, and from under the weary lids gained after years of editing stories on the souls and the soullessness of men.

"If we followed your logic, almost every house and building in Atlanta should have never been built. This whole area," Press waved his hand at the window and the downtown buildings stacked outside, "would be empty ground, a memorial to the inhumanities that happened here. We're talking about over a century ago, and I doubt you can factually say a slave was beaten in that or any other house."

Trace followed quickly. "That's what Jack told her. You could argue that most southern land is a memorial to the evil of slavery. Does that mean we build nothing because we might build on the site of a cruel act?"

Meredith stood straight, feeling like the target of a firing squad and knowing she had to maintain her presence, uncertain of where this was heading.

Press emphatically put his hands on his hips. He had a sturdy build with a stomach that stretched his belt. His head seemed to sit on his shoulders with little evidence of a neck. Meredith's heart pushed against her blouse. She had to react and show a measure of control. Her charmed life had never included a confrontation like this.

"And regardless of the value of the story, I told you several times to ask no questions. Do we have a prima donna on our hands?"

Meredith pulled in a long but subtle breath. "You're right. I shouldn't have done that and wouldn't have, except Mr. Collier insisted I speak up. It was awkward. I couldn't say, 'My editor won't let me talk.'"

"Is that right, Trace?" Press asked.

There was a pause, and Trace answered, "He did, but then she took off with this slave house nonsense, and I can tell you, Jack Collier didn't like where she was going at all."

"So, a major story about a major development for the city gets sidetracked by something totally unrelated to it," Press summarized.

The reflection from his overhead lights on Meredith's watering eyes told Press she was tearing up. "OK, enough for now. Trace, write up the story you went for. Meredith, we'll talk more later." He motioned for them to leave.

When they were out of hearing range, Press called his publisher, Terry Stone's private line. "Terry, we've got a problem. I'm coming up there. I don't care if you're in a meeting. I'm on the way."

Press climbed the metal stairs to the newspaper's executive offices, walked past a surprised secretary, and strode in the spacious office of the publisher. Terry quickly rose from his chair and excused himself from a conference table where several suited men turned to see who had interrupted their meeting.

Stepping outside his door and closing it, Terry asked. "What the hell is going on? These are some of our top advertisers."

Ignoring any courtesies, Press said firmly, "I've got to let that college girl go, Terry. She's a prima donna because of that football scandal thing. Really hacked off Jack Collier, and looks like she's about to submarine his whole project with some nonsense about slaves beaten on the property. Which, she can't, of course, prove ever happened."

In the pause left by Terry trying to absorb what his angry editor had told him, Press said, "So I'm firing her, and you can deal with her old man."

"Whoa, slow down," Terry put his hands on Press' shoulders. "Cal O'Connor, her old man, as you call him, is sitting at my conference table right now. And he's proposing a multi-million-dollar advertising deal along with purchasing some of our stock."

"Damn it to hell, Terry, are we whores? The girl won't take orders, injects herself in the story, and, I believe, makes up stories."

Terry was a tall, patrician-looking man, close to elegant in his bearing, who looked down at the fuming, solid figure of a thirty-year employee. Terry knew Press was called the last traditional editor by his admirers and obsessive by many staffers, and that he was also considered the soul of the newspaper. Press had a national reputation, having been honored with a Peabody Award for editing excellence, and he was a popular speaker at journalism schools. Terry felt the pressure from both sides.

"OK, let's sit on this story for a minute. Let me get all the facts; then we'll talk." Terry thought he would speak the words he had heard Press say many times to overly excited reporters and get him to calm down. "Now, let me see if I can close this deal in here, and we'll all be getting bonuses, and more importantly, we can keep printing this newspaper on paper." He turned and disappeared behind his office door.

Press walked slowly back down the stairs to the newsroom, wondering if he was about to be overruled by a publisher who reacted to a Board that did the bidding of a media holding company concerned about falling stock value. Press felt the alters of truth and professionalism at which he worshipped were being defiled and by a good man—a man like Terry Stone for whom he had great respect. Would everybody sell out?

As Press passed Meredith's cubicle, he saw it was empty, and he asked the reporter in the next cubicle if she knew where Meredith was. The woman said that Meredith had gotten an email from somebody, seemed excited about it, and left, saying she needed to look for some clothes for an early meeting. Press stepped back to Meredith's computer, which was on. He tapped the mouse, the screen lit up, and leaning down, he read an email still visible.

Looking at the note, Press growled, "Jack, you bastard." Touching, then pushing hard against the screen on Meredith's computer, he said unequivocally, "You're fired, college girl."

CHAPTER 9

AN ARTERY RUNS through Atlanta's Buckhead, as essential and defining as any vein to the heart. It is a carriage route for the affluent, an asphalt symbol of old money, private clubs, and earned power. Some avenues, fountains, cathedrals, or statuaries become monuments to a place. West Paces Ferry Road is that symbol to Buckhead. It is art done in a residential format, but here, homes are the signature. Its mansions create the slack-jawed looks of envy from the tour bus crowd and small towners who come to gape and wonder about the rich folks who live in these broad-yarded homes. Oaks guard its length, supporting the oft-told story that Atlanta is a city of trees. It is also a place of dream chasers and those who have already grabbed their brass ring.

In other parts of the city, Buckhead is the synonym for wealth, privilege, power, inheritance, and consequently, it is both admired and resented. It is all-of- these things, but not in an exclusionary sense. There are cliques here, but for the most part, access is available if one is on the right boards, with the right firms, or is flush with money and proudly donates portions of it. The easiest way to a passport is owning a home, and there are no bad addresses.

Networking is the essential tool for further entry. The Creek Town Club on West Paces Ferry Road is one of those points of entry. Formally a mansion built in the 1920s, its broad lawn and massive oaks give it the feel of graceful, cared-for southern living. Entry is $100,000, and there is a waiting list of young lions filled with the rewards of their law firms, investment houses, and real estate developments. It is a place of anticipation, where one's children can meet the right children, business deals might be birthed, and invitations extended for lunch, or better, for dinner.

A large, broad-decked, saltwater swimming pool sits like a gin-filled sea at the back of the club. But on most afternoons, the only splashing heard is that of drinks being poured over ice. To get the new socially conscious to join and pay the $100,000 fee, applicants are told that The Creek is where you are when you have "arrived."

Jack's friends sat along the pool at the back of the club. They all watched, except for Jack's wife Mary, who was texting a charity that was asking for funds.

"Now, that's got to be an illusion," Frazier Hardy whispered. "Nothing is that perfect."

The young woman's breasts floated like porcelain suns on an afternoon ocean. They swayed in a ripened sultriness as the June air moved through The Creek Club's pool, furling its waters. She wore a one-piece, white bathing suit that clung in its wetness with near transparency against the caramel tan of her skin. The heat had driven her off her towel-draped chair to sit in the water at the shallow end of the pool. She leaned back against the pool's edge. Her elbows rested on the tile decking, which forced her breasts out onto the water's surface.

The three husbands peered across the water through their sunglasses. It was a gauzy apparition seen through the sweat and smear of fingerprints on their lenses.

They half-jokingly, but knowingly, called themselves "The Rich Young Rulers." They felt to their cores that they were kings of their worlds, cocky, ambitious, and handsome, all in their late thirties. They felt comfortable in defining themselves as the best of men, each a hustling entrepreneur with a solid bank account gained quickly and smartly and through connections—always connections. They worked names like plowing a field, cajoling the prospects into fecundity. All were sought by the most prestigious charities to sit on their boards and open their wallets.

One other thing they shared was that each of their fortunes was tied into Jack Collier, the fourth member of their group, who was yet to arrive.

Jack s wife, Mary, had wheat-colored hair that covered much of her broad face as she looked down at the blue glow of her iPad. Jack said Mary was lightning on a blue-sky day. Her studied approach to issues, her calming voice, often heralded by an easy laugh, were coverings for a fierce determination for community service and a quick intolerance for those who lived their lives without purpose. Her mother had worried about Mary before her marriage to Jack, that his purpose in life would always be about his designs. Mary's focus would always be others. But Mary saw a man whose talents were approaching genius. She was drawn into the rush of promise surrounding his persona and his designs. Jack was also a romantic with all the right, tender words, the attention to her needs, and an eagerness to listen to her.

They all watched the young woman sitting across the salt-infused pool waters, an icon forever taunting the sun's angry glare, flippantly defiant of its abrasive, aging rays. The men didn't miss a motion, sitting transfixed in a frozen leer. Like bird dogs on point, no muscles moved. Their heads craned ever so slightly and instinctively outward. As they gazed transfixed, they were each well aware that they were only an arm's length away from their wives' table.

The wives were of one basic body shape—lean and fit and crowned in varying shades of blond hair. Exercise under the direction of personal trainers was essential to their identity. They were as forward-leaning into life as were their husbands: aggressive, opinionated about politics, loudly into charity work, and especially focused on their children.

Conversations were normally filled with talk of remodeling one's kitchen or their second home at Lake Burton or the next Viking Cruise through France. But now, they were calling those who tended to the courts of their lives: interior decorators, gardeners, carpenters, cooks, maids, attorneys, travel planners, and cleaning services. The women were the actors seen on life's stage, supported by a small legion of handlers out of sight.

Virgin Marys and Arnold Palmers ran with crushed-ice coldness over their lips. They were resting up at the poolside before a tennis coach could work on their backhand strokes, then they would return to the pool for a cool down. When they looked up from their iPhones, their eyes bore in on the reclining figure of youth across the pool while simultaneously eyeing their husbands. It was a unique talent the women had, a kind of comprehensive fly-like eyesight that was forever aware of the direction of their husband's eyes, even when they couldn't see their eyes.

"Don't look now, but you're being watched," Frazier warned with a whispered earnestness to his friends about their observing wives. They were stalkers easily spotted. His petite wife Judy, nicknamed "Butter Bean" because of her small size as a child and from the baby talk of her doting father, heard the comment. In her brazen, raspy croak of a voice and loud enough for the men to hear, "I know a bird dog on point when I see one, and I see three. They're looking at her butt." She wanted to put the men on notice that the wives knew. It was a warning shot, said in a caustic, but kidding voice, but all knew she wasn't joking.

The husbands silently drank from their warming cups of beer, trying to look busy. Knowing they were caught in the act of lustfully gawking, they ignored the comment.

Butter Bean knew they were looking, knew they would look until they died. She croaked again, "A real man would only look at his wife."

They were boys of the south. Not men in their minds. To them, that heavy category described the gray, the wizened and stooped—their fathers. They were boys so defined by the ruling role of their mothers because the fortress of their homes had been commanded by their mothers and because their mothers' love was without bottom and with great favoring. A mothered, southern son could never allow himself to leave that nurturing harbor.

Marcus Sutton, the newest member of the group, was one of twelve African Americans out of the club's 1,800 members. Jack had sponsored him, knowing how well connected and respected Marcus was in Atlanta power circles. His laugh was quick, not overwhelming or too noticeable, but seemed appropriate for his confident demeanor. His eyes were green. His friends kidded him about his eyes being the color of money. He knew the color was from a plantation owner's son. He had tracked down the young man's name, and the slave woman he assumed was raped and whose particular traits were passed down to produce his captivating look. The thought of this rape was kept in a deep place. Much of his prideful bearing was done to show respect for that distant mother and to show he was getting his revenge by moving above her legacy of abuse and humiliation.

Marcus laughed softly, then said loudly for the wives to hear, "OK, we've voted. We're all southern boys, and we plan on staying true to who we are."

"Don't give me that southern junk, and don't call yourself 'boy,'" Marcus's wife Chancy said.

"Middle-aged boys? Is that an oxymoron?" asked Susan McLean. Her voice had a high pitch, as though she had pinched her nostrils together.

"I don't know about the oxy, but it is moronic, not to mention pathetic." Butter Bean's small mouth soured up in disdain as she spoke of the irredeemable immaturity of her husband and his friends. "Walk away from it, men. Your days in the sun are no longer about getting a suntan but about not getting melanoma."

Frazier looked at Marcus and kidded, "Blacks don't get melanoma, do they? You probably don't need to borrow my suntan lotion."

A soft but certain voice came from the women's table. It was Chancy. "Marcus, can't you find a smarter bunch of white guys to hang out with?"

"No, honey, these are the smartest white guys."

"Well, that doesn't say much for the rest of the race, does it?" Chancy answered, and the whole group smiled and snickered in the freedom they felt through friendship.

Cody McLean, the third member of the Young Rulers, said, "Who needs to be smart when you're on the Jack Collier ride to riches? At least we had enough sense to live in Buckhead where all things are promised, and all dreams come true."

Frazier responded with some caution. "We've all sunk our money on this horse named Jack. He's like all thoroughbreds— they can outrun the world until they don't."

Cody tapped his friend on the arm. "None of that. Jack is a sure bet. Our sure bet."

Frazier couldn't hide his concern over the monies each had risked in order to help Jack start the mammoth project. "I hate that word *sure*. I've lost a lot of money on that word."

CHAPTER 10

THE NEXT DAY, before going in the door of *The Atlanta News* building, Meredith thought she would get something at Starbucks to take to Press. He was hooked on it. No reporter or assistant was immune from his gruff order to run downstairs and bring him a large bold, no room, no cream. Any offer to gain redemption with her editor would help, she thought.

"Here, let me hold the door," Meredith said to a striking woman as she came to the entrance at the same time. Their eyes seem to sense a recognition of one another.

"Aren't you a local news reporter?" Meredith asked as they walked into the coffee shop. "Shandra Berry here. I cover the sweet streets for WBBM." She extended her hand. "And I believe I just saw you featured on *The News'* website as their newest reporter." Meredith felt a rush of heat on her face as her cheeks reddened with embarrassment. "Meredith O'Connor. I'm not sure what streets I'll be covering." She had an energy that Shandra found fetching but was blonde and a little overeager.

"Do you have a minute to talk? I may someday try my hand

at broadcasting after I've established my credentials as a reporter at the paper," Meredith asked as they stood in a short line to place their order. "Hopefully, covering Jack Collier will get me started on their using my byline."

Shandra had no real interest in talking to yet another hired-because-she-was-a-blond-bombshell. But with the mention of Jack's name, her interest was raised enough to agree. "Ten minutes. I've got an interview with the police chief on a story."

They found a small table, and Shandra asked, "So what part of the Jack Collier story are you covering?"

Meredith said, "His new project. Seems like it's got the whole town talking."

"Atlanta's swashbuckling architect sucks up all the oxygen wherever the monied and the powerful gather. That building is all anyone wants to cover. I heard it was just plain weird looking. And the name of it is strange too."

Meredith leaned forward on the table with a curious look on her face. "Let me ask your advice. You probably get all kinds of leaks and reports of a story in the making. How do you know when it's real or just a false alarm?"

Shandra, ever suspicious of why a question was posed, responded, "You must have a potential lead that's got you curious. Tell me more, and I'll give you my opinion."

Seeing no threat in Shandra and feeling in need of some mentoring, Meredith said, "I went out to Mr. Collier's property and found an old house still standing, which I am convinced was a slave house, possibly where they were beaten."

Shandra tensed all over, leaning into the table. Only her carefully measured voice hid the sudden interest, the possibilities of what she just heard. "Slaves? Where did this information come from?"

"There were visible names scratched in a fireplace, and what looked like "whipping house" was also scratched in the hearth. I know all that was forever ago and has nothing to do with the new building."

"Oh, no, I see it as an important part of the history of the property. I'll bet Jack would want to honor those poor people somehow."

"He not only doesn't want to have it publicized, but neither does my editor. They say it was all from another time and has nothing to do with the project. I guess that's what I'm looking for some advice on."

"Tell you what, I've got some interviews out that way later. I'll drop by and check out the house and the names. I'll give you my honest opinion." Shandra had no business in Vinings but sensed this might be the opening she had been looking for under Jack's immense light.

"Oh, I didn't mean to impose on you. I'm still learning this business, and I'm open to advice.

"Glad to help a rising star at the paper. I'll text you after I've seen the house. Got to run. It was a real pleasure." Shandra was on her feet and turning so quickly for the door that Meredith's hand was left untouched as she had reached for a goodbye handshake.

Shandra smiled and shook her head as she left Starbucks. Another white cutie. She was sick of them getting the choice assignments on the networks and in all media where one's face is seen. Shandra believed she was a token hire. She felt in her heart that the world loved white and especially blond. In the drive of her personality, she was going to turn her professional focus away from Atlanta's bloody streets. That out might be through some expose of Jack. But getting him on a racial charge could be difficult, especially with the Black churches and all the monies he had given them. Then again, the hypocrisy of his checkbook could be the angle.

On the elevator up to her office, Meredith's phone pinged that a text was waiting. It was from the reporters' pool secretary.

"Man called with interesting info on Jack's past in the Klan and looking for a reporter to prove what a phony Jack is. You want to take it?"

Meredith's natural curiosity became more puzzled than eager to pursue the call. What on earth could there be about this famous architect and the Ku Klux Klan? Did she really want to hear some gossip? Her initial feeling of protectiveness bothered her. Jack was getting in the way of her natural inclination to relish the invitation to pursue a lead. She thrilled to the chase, but suddenly, there stood this larger-than-life figure igniting emotions she wasn't used to feeling. She felt it threatened her professionalism.

The morning story assignment meeting was awkward for both Meredith and Press. She came uncertain of what she would be asked to cover. Press didn't want to think about her, but here she sat in a gray, pinstriped suit with a white shirt, looking like the cover for a magazine. *Damnit*, he thought as he sauntered in and sat at the long twelve-person table. *Got a prima donna on my hands.*

To the group, he said, "Let's go around and see what stories you've got."

Each reporter gave a status report of what they were working on or submitted in hard copy a completed story they hoped would make the next morning's paper with their byline. Meredith said to Press with some false bravado, "I wrote up the Collier interview. I know Trace is the lead but thought I would turn in my takeaways."

Meredith handed him her writing. The reporters sat quietly while Press scanned in his hurried fashion each reporter's various story lines. He quickly recognized in Meredith's writing that she was a first-class writer, more complete than Trace. But he didn't show it. There was a pause as he thought how it would become more difficult for him to fire her if her byline made the paper. The writing was too good, and insolence could be dismissed as what one would expect from a talented twenty-year-old. Insolence, he felt, was often the realm of the gifted, and that could be tamed with proper management, his boss would say.

Press looked at Trace; he would think Press had caved if he didn't fire Meredith. Worse, Trace was an office gossip that could, if he already hadn't, start bad-mouthing Meredith's behavior at Jack's interview.

Press went over the other stories, writing a large 'P' with a red felt tip pen. That was his go-ahead for the story to run as it was. The writers had coined it "The P OK." He looked up from Meredith's writing and said, "Meredith, obviously Trace gets the byline on Jack. I'll show him your take on the interview and let him decide if he wants to pull a line or two from yours."

Meredith felt she was getting shut out, so she spoke over his closing words. "I have a new lead on Jack Collier's background that may be far more interesting than any of these stories."

Without looking at Meredith, Press closed the meeting with, "No, we've been through slamming Jack. Let's not bring that back up."

He assumed she was back on the slave house idea. Press

scanned the table of reporters, "OK, let's get out there and dig today. Got to beat those television reporters to the punch, to the real story. They are shallow swimmers. Remember that. They get 30 seconds, maybe a minute, just time enough for sirens and blood on the streets. We dive deep."

Feeling good with his closing encouragement, Press was out the door to his office.

Trace glared at Meredith as he stood. "That slave stuff is a dead horse. Part of big boy journalism is knowing when to give up a bad story. Or maybe you should go back to college and look for some more cheating football players."

She was crestfallen and felt far removed from the table and its team of reporters. Press had given her no assignment, no new stories to pursue, and avoided even hearing about this new angle.

The Georgia fight song blared from her phone. It was her father. "Hello, my sweet reporter. How is the writer doing?"

He was always her cheerleader, though she had embarrassed him with her football story. She was his only child, and he adored her.

Meredith tried to buck up with some measure of enthusiasm.

"Hi, Daddy. Well, this isn't the school paper. This is, as they say, the Bigs, or big boy journalism, someone just said."

He knew her in some ways better than she knew herself. He could pick up the slightest change in her lips, her eyes, a drop or a lift in her voice. And he thought he heard a little less enthusiasm than he would have thought and liked.

"What about big girl journalism? Say, when do you think you'll get your first story?"

There was a pause that told him more than he wanted to know.

"I'm not sure. I'm still learning the ropes, and Daddy, I do have a lot to learn. I came here with my feet a little too far off the ground. The Georgia story put me too high too fast, I think. But it's all going to work out. Don't worry."

He knew she was faking any attempt at enthusiasm.

"I know you, and I know it will. Oh, listen, I want you to go with me tonight to the High Museum. They've got an annual fancy, smantsy fundraiser, and there will be a room full of Atlanta's movers there I want you to meet. Everybody enters the room by walking down a staircase, getting gazes and appraisals as you walk down. Kind of silly and pretentious, but all done for fun or funds, I should say. There'll be some important sources for you."

She didn't feel like going anywhere but to her apartment and drawing the blinds. She felt rejection, and it was a rare and harsh visitor for her. But she was her Daddy's little girl, and she couldn't resist his invitation.

Her father said, "Your mother and I will pick you up at six. There'll be heavy hors d'oeuvres, so plenty to munch on. Wear something swishy. See you at six."

And he was off.

The conference table loomed long and made her feel a solitariness that her life had never known. As she started to stand and leave the empty room slowly, the full figure of Janice Wood stuck her head in the door. She was the pool secretary and gatekeeper for calls to the reporters.

"Did you call the man back that was looking for a reporter?"

Meredith stretched her mouth in a regretful grimace.

"I forgot all about it. Let me have his number, and I'll follow up."

She took the info to her cubicle, dialed the number, noticing an Athens' area code.

A man answered, his voice clipped and rude. "I don't recognize your number; who is this?"

"This is Meredith O'Connor. I'm a reporter at *The Atlanta News*. You called with some information?"

"Yeah, well, I didn't hear from y'all, so I called some of the television stations and got a reporter that's real interested."

"Sorry, but I didn't want to disturb you over the weekend and was going to call this morning, so, if it's an important story, you'll want it covered in the state's major newspaper."

"I don't know, this Shandra woman, kind of a goofy last name, said don't tell any other reporters until she could verify what I told her. She'll have a tough time finding any of Jack's friends that remember or even know about it. But I do. I was there. I've even got an old photograph of Jack with the Klan hood on. And a copy of the hanging article."

What on earth? A hood? Did he mean hoodie? Meredith thought. But the real surprise was that her sudden friend Shandra would even consider a story about Jack without calling her, especially since Shandra had asked to hear about Meredith's story and share in it.

Meredith was back on her game. "Well, this may be good timing for me. I'm working on several stories about the Collier project, and I am the only reporter in Atlanta with some developing inside information about it. If you have something of news value, I'm your reporter if your story is verifiable."

"Doesn't really matter to me who writes it, but I absolutely don't want my name involved. You do have that Deep Throat thing going with your paper, don't you? You know, where everything's on the QT."

Meredith was shaking her head at what she was hearing in the man's voice, almost a suspicious, deviousness to it.

"Did you mean Jack was wearing a hoodie?"

There was a pause in his response, then an angry, "Are you trying to be funny? No, a hood. A pointed hood with holes for eyes. How old are you anyway?"

"Oh, that kind of hood. That was before my time, but I know who they were, of course."

She felt she had lost some control over the interview with her own naïveté.

"Back to your question of confidentiality. We do not disclose our sources, so you can trust us not to use your name. But I've got to hear what you have that we should write about."

"Jack walked with the Klan."

He let the words lay out in a kind of nakedness with no follow-up, letting the sentence make its own shock effect.

Meredith thought she might have misunderstood what he said.

"I don't know what that means, 'he walked with the Klan.'"

He gave a laugh that sounded like he was clearing his throat.

"You said you have heard of the Ku Klux Klan. Jack Collier walked down Broad Street in Athens when we were in high school. He was a Klansman. Now how does that sit with you?"

It was a confusing call. Who was this, and what was his purpose? Jack in the Klan? That defied logic. Meredith was only vaguely aware of the old racist organization, though it was embedded in the history of southern culture. Jack was a visionary. Those robed fools were so yesterday to her. She gathered her composure.

"And what proof do you have of this? When was this?"

His voice was so surly, almost like he was trying to disguise it, that she became more curious about what had drawn the man even to bring it up.

"You sound like that Shandra woman. Ya'll don't trust anybody. I'll tell you what I told her. We were in high school in Athens. The Klan was protesting some Black students at the university, and they publicized that they were going to march. Jack was crazy as a loon back then, and he got a sheet and a hood and joined the march. The newspaper took a picture of the march. They didn't know Jack was one of the marchers, but I was standing off to the side with some friends, and we were all hooting at the line. I've got the old newspaper, and I have Jack circled in the line."

"Did he attend any Klan meetings before or after the march? Was he involved with them?"

"Probably."

"But you don't know that for a fact. Was this a high school prank? And what's your purpose?"

Meredith was pressing on a story she felt was filled with doubt.

"Let's just say I don't like phonies. He always thought he was a big shot, dressing like some actor, and I think he should be shown for what he is, a damn phony architect doing show-off buildings."

"And what's this about a hanging?" She persisted, remembering well Shandra's phone message alluding to that.

"Yeah, his daddy Wade was at the hanging of a Black man in the 40s, and I have a picture of him grinning like a jackass eatin' briars right behind this poor Black fella swinging from that tree—that's now on Jack's property."

Meredith's mouth opened as though there were a weight

on her bottom lip, her jaw tightening at the momentary shock of hearing these accusations.

"Those are strong statements. I do need to see any photos you have. Can you scan or fax them over?"

He was quick in his suspicious answer. "No damn way am I sending materials. You want 'em, you come over here and get 'em from me personally. We can meet in a dark garage—you know, like it's done with reporters."

This guy has seen too many movies, Meredith thought. "Let me check into this more. Can you give me an exact date on the hanging?"

She could hear what sounded like paper being handled, and he gave her a date in August of 1940.

He warned, "Don't wait too long to call me back. That TV girl sounded real interested." And he ended the call.

Meredith felt like a fool, a naïve fool out of her league. How could she have been so trusting to share a lead with another reporter? Shandra was a competitor and obviously not to be trusted. She had her own agenda, commendable in some ways, self-serving in others. Should she call Jack and ask him upfront what this was about? It seemed impossible that he and his family had committed such reprehensible acts.

The urgency of the moment returned as she tried to determine what she was supposed to do the rest of the day with no assignments from Press. He would probably never give her permission to drive over to Athens and meet this man. But if she had nothing else to do, why not? She could at least call Jack and tell him what she had heard. She asked herself if this man was just another showboat and a racist.

CAL KNEW few restraints when he felt Meredith was in need. He wasted no time in calling the publisher, Terry Stone. Her dad knew all was not right with his daughter and wanted, in his subtle way, to make sure her work life was a priority with the paper's publisher.

Terry's secretary interrupted him to say that Cal O'Connor was on the phone. The signing of the major advertising contract between Cal's many real estate holdings and the newspaper was set for Wednesday—two days away.

"Hey, my friend, I think we have all of our contracts in order. Looking forward to Wednesday," Terry was pushing, corralling, controlling with his words of good news. The board of directors saw Cal's several millions of advertising dollars and healthy stock purchase as critical to allowing *The News* to build a robust online presence and redesign the printed version.

Cal's voice was cautionary. "It does look good right now, but I am under heavy pressure from my biggest investor, a hedge fund, to take a final look-see at broadcast. They think a printed newspaper is a dinosaur. Now, I obviously believe everybody over forty likes to touch what they're reading, but these guys are backing my real estate holdings with some serious money, and I do have to listen to them."

Terry stood up, clamped his teeth together in frustration, ran his fingers through his hair, and breathed deeply to control his anger.

He had been brought from New York to stop the newspaper from hemorrhaging readers and ad dollars. The deal would put his career as a turnaround artist in full sail. His credibility was dependent on this happening.

Cal's reassuring voice seemed to try and mollify the tension. But his money was too badly needed by the paper, and the slightest hint of retreating was met with dread. "But I do feel we can make this happen in time. I want you to know I'm on your side. You and I have been through a lot together on this deal, and you know that loyalty is very important to how I do business."

Terry felt a sense of relief. They had built a friendship, with many lunches, golf at three at the country clubs Cal belonged to, and several dinners with their wives, who had become fast friends.

"I know you're fighting for our deal, Cal, and I appreciate your loyalty to us here at the paper."

"Thank you. Oh, by the way, how is my favorite reporter doing? I'll bet old Press is really watching over her."

It was the shoe that Terry hadn't seen coming down. Could that be what this phone call was really about? His daughter? Surely, a deal of this magnitude couldn't depend on whether or not his daughter was happy with her story writing. Terry almost dismissed that as a possibility, but he could take no chances with so much hanging in the balance.

"Funny you would mention that. I've got a meeting in a few minutes. I'll confirm all is well there."

"My Meredith is a top-flight reporter, Terry. I'm sure your man has her on some major stories."

Terry had been on too many negotiations now to see the real purpose of this phone call. And it was all about "my Meredith." He courteously bid Cal a goodbye and dialed up Press as fast as his fingers could hit the numbers.

"Morning, Press. I need for you to come up. Just need a minute."

Press was in the middle of marking up a story on missing city government money and had no desire to break up his thoughts, but when the publisher called, it was not to talk about football scores.

Press could feel his sixty-two years, his failed attempts to stop smoking, his nightly love of Jack Daniels, and his expanded waist as he walked up the echoing metal stairs to the executive floor. Widowed, his lover was his work, except for an occasional fling with an old high school girlfriend, also divorced. When asked by family—worrying over the singularity of his life—if he would marry again, Press always answered that he was already happily married to *The News*.

To his surprise, Terry came walking down through the stairwell as Press came to his landing. "Hey, I thought I would just come down. We can talk while we're here. I wanted to ask how Cal O'Connor's daughter is coming along? Cal was curious about that."

Press's countenance fell visibly as he stepped down on the landing of the 10th floor beside Terry. He looked up at the patrician figure before him. Press stared at the very white shirt and the very pressed suit and the Brooks Brothers tie his boss wore. Terry made Press feel rumpled, which he was.

"We're meeting in a stairwell to discuss a college kid, oh, excuse me, the daughter of a very deep pocket."

Terry placed his hand on Press's shoulder in a gesture of gentility because he knew when he mentioned Meredith's name, Press would get hot. Terry didn't want him walking out of his office with his profanity-filled mumbles, turning the heads of the executive administrative people, so he came to meet him in the seclusion of the stairs. Terry was about smooth sailings, and his editor was a tempestuous storm when the integrity of the paper was questioned.

"I assume that no answer means you haven't gotten things

right with her, and I can't tell her father that. He signs the biggest advertising contract in the history of the paper in two days, which means you get to keep working here till we carry you out."

"Terry, the girl is her own newspaper. She's too damn good, and she knows it. She doesn't need an editor. Let's just let her roam the streets, creating her own stories."

"So, you recognize that she is a talent, just a little untamed?" Terry was trying to find some grounds for agreement. "Seems like a management issue. You can handle that. The potheads and drunks who have come through the press room, and you handled them all. This is just a headstrong kid. Big deal."

They both unconsciously shifted their feet on the landing. Its concrete seemed to be a sound amplifier to any scrap or step. Press put two fingers up in front of Terry. "Two issues here—one is her defiance of the soul of our newspaper, which is the unvarnished, unbiased truth. She's gone and dug up a story totally unrelated to Jack's project about some crap that happened in the Civil War. So, she's trying to tell her own version of the truth that has nothing to do with the project."

"Ok, I can see your side on that. But she may be looking for a bigger picture about the property. Still, I see your point. This is about the future and building Atlanta's brand."

"Number two problem with her is a management issue. We cannot have our reporters decide what story leads they will chase without it being cleared by me. She ignored my instructions; just flat defied my telling her not to conduct an interview yet. That makes me look weak, and the newspaper look weak to our staff."

Terry removed his hand from Press's shoulder and folded his arms. His negotiating included many moves. He had a facial expression, a hand motion, hands in pocket, arms crossed, a raised eyebrow, a lowered chin forcing him to look up. He knew all the body moves in negotiations, having hired a professional speech coach some years ago. It was an orchestral performance of all of his moving parts, designed to have the viewer succumb to Terry's managerial performance.

Press was having none of it. He was unrelenting. "It's the gorilla in the room, but we're talking soul-selling here. This kid is here because of her old man and his money. And I accept that we've all got to get in the door someway. But when she ignored my orders and betrayed what I think is good journalism by creating her own news where there is no news, then she crossed my line."

Terry leaned back just enough to feel the cold of the concrete block wall in the stairwell. It was a relaxed pose. He pressed his lips together in a smile of acknowledgment of Press's concerns, although at this moment, he didn't give a damn about Press's class on ethics in journalism. His posture, however, was nonthreatening.

"I hear you, my friend. A newspaper is nothing if it has no integrity, and you have been the faithful gatekeeper of our honesty and our commitment to the highest standards for years." He then slowly stood straight and put his right hand under his chin in a thoughtful pose. "Here is the other gorilla in the room. Newspaper readership is down everywhere. We're not a charity unless you and the rest of our employees want to work for free. We need cash to flow in as freely as our ink flows out on paper. That doesn't mean we sell our souls. It means we honor what we stand for by keeping the paper in business."

"I guess we need to agree on what selling one's soul means." Press noticed the slightest of echoes down the stairwell as they talked.

"Socrates on the stairs," Terry perked up with amusement over debating the meaning of a word.

"Listen, nobody is playing at being a whore here. But you've erected this fortress around your interpretation of the character of a newspaper. And you see a threat at every turn. This young woman is a threat you see that I believe can be managed. Of course, she should listen to you as her boss, and she should never create news. We agree. I say, let's all win here. You turn her great potential into a great reporter. Her daddy sees her byline. She tells him she's happy. And he writes a big check, and we all keep our jobs." Terry punctuated his ending with a large smile showing he was pleased with his portrayal of the issue. His implied instruction to his editor was to shut the hell up, get off this integrity wagon about the girl, and go fix the situation.

Press knew he was against forces much larger than himself. *The News* was a historic and respected Atlanta institution—a part of Atlanta's fabric. He may be an important weave in that tapestry, but a replaceable part with news going online from traditional sources. He nodded at Terry like a little boy, acknowledging that he had done wrong and his father was right. He turned and walked quietly down the stairs and back to his office. He paused as he walked into the sprawling room of reporters and immediately saw Meredith bent over her small desk. She looked up and saw him looking her way. He held his hand up with the five fingers in evidence, pointed toward his hand, indicating five minutes, then motioned toward his office. He needed a minute to gather his thoughts, to think through Terry's words. Had the newspaper become his only family and his only identity? Had his commitment to the best in journalism, as he saw the best, become an albatross, a light so bright that it became a darkness he could not see beyond or into?

His answer was no; he would not, could not give up his principles. To compromise over this young woman would be a betrayal to himself. But this job was his world. If he quit, with his wife dead several years, his two children, distant on the West Coast, and old drinking buddies starting to pass, who would he be then? He would whore because he had to.

Meredith pulled out a small brush which she used to tousle her hair up, then pressed her lips, seeing them as red as when she put the lipstick on, breathed in slowly, and felt good about herself despite the firing she thought was about to happen. She stood straight and proud. Press's door was open, but she tapped on it anyway.

Press wore the first smile Meredith had seen on his face, though it was not so much joyful as it was like a handshake, a perfunctory greeting. "Have a seat. I want us to understand one another. First me. I am a guardian at the gate. To paraphrase a man that I don't follow as closely as I should, 'Whoever follows me must take up the cross.' Too few in our business today are willing to give up their own agenda, their race for fame, their biases, and commit to carrying the cross that is great journalism. We have become a cause-pushing, sound-bite run for the ratings industry."

She thought Press was almost heretical, outrageous really, in his analogy to Christ and the cross, but it touched the passion she felt for the business. His belief in the sanctity of journalism was hers. She had risked her reputation, possibly even being physically harmed, certainly socially shunned, in order to bring honor back to a football program and a school she loved. She was a true believer, a zealot about writing truth.

Afraid her voice would break and seeing him as a blur

through the water welling up in fat drops along the edges of her eyes, Meredith nodded in agreement and answered with a wavering firmness, "We're after the same thing."

Press saw the impact of his words on the young woman, and her reaction lifted him to the point that his plans to fire her faded in the emotion of the moment. Press felt he was a forgiving soul, though it could be a high fence to jump to get back in his graces. His world moved too fast to coddle, to "understand," to sympathize. The god of his day was the deadline. The printing of the paper would not wait. A reporter had to hit the mark or come close on every story. There was not time for a lot of editing and rewrites. On one wall of his paper-immersed office was a target and its center held a single dart. That served as his only artwork, and all of his staff knew that it meant both threat and symbol of his insistence on hitting the mark the first time.

"I've thought about your talents, and I believe you can be one of our outstanding journalists. But no more working on your own. Make your choice. My way or your way."

"Your way," she said. It was not said in submission but with determination—like answering the clarion call. Press had given affirmation to who she was, what she could be, and what she saw as right. In doing so, Press felt he had paid homage to his company's management without selling out. He had laid down a gauntlet and forewarned her. He did see enormous talent in her, but he knew this talent had to be bound and bordered, or her father and all of his money be damned.

Now that they understood one another, Press had to deal with the slave house and get that out of the way. "Let's clear the air before I give you some new assignments. I want our disagreements laid out and eliminated. About this slave house —if true, it was a horrible place, but I see no connection at all with Jack's project. In fact, a story like that could harm what's going to be a big plus for our city."

She was delighted that he would bring it up. Was he reconsidering it as a valuable part of the story? Nevertheless, she approached the wound with caution.

"I believe Mr. Collier's project is, as he says, a revolutionary breakthrough in architecture. I minored in the subject, and I've never seen anything like what he has created. It is futuristic, for sure. At the same time, my research indicated that some terrible things happened on that land. Call it my idealism, my empathy, my guilt for what my race did to African Americans, that it seems not right to applaud the project and ignore the sorrowful story that it is covering up with its splash, flash, and sensationalism."

Press was listening carefully. "You said, 'it seems not right.' Your generation, thank God, has shucked off a lot of the racial bias of my generation and certainly earlier ones. But that means you can bring a new bias into your reporting, and that is the 'it seems not right.' You can want to interject race from the other side—the guilt trip/make retribution side. By making up for the sins of the father, we have created another danger, and that is bias in reporting. Everything through a racial lens."

Meredith shifted on the hard leather of the only visitor's chair in his office. She thought of what he had said. "I went after the football cheating story because I am idealistic. I love my school, and I couldn't stand a few cheaters bringing dishonor to its team. Aren't most journalists idealists? We want to right wrongs by reporting them." She smiled, "You could call us the ethics police, I guess."

Press stood up and made himself stand straight. His was a sitting job that had fattened his waist and weakened his limbs. He hated exercise but had started walking more throughout the office after his doctor warned him that death was an eager visitor to a sixty-year-old man with Press's intensity, who spent most of the day sitting.

"You're right. Journalists can be crusaders or, as you say, the keepers of society's ethics. But that is a two-edged sword because this can lead to blatant bias in story selection or which parts of a story they emphasize and which parts they exclude. That can make your reporting an opinion, not news. And that is going on at the networks and the major newspapers. They're run by cause-driven writers and be damned with a differing opinion."

Meredith felt she was in an experience-based journalism class, learned by long hours of doggedness, doubt, and anguish, then clarity, and then the joy of breaking a story of great enlightenment. She saw his slightly rumpled look as a sign of his dedication to his craft, of his long hours in that chair editing. His conversation was like a sacred ritual. She now felt that she had stumbled in her first assignment, too consumed in her own eagerness, her sense of fairness, and her natural love of the chase.

"My final word on the subject is this: don't look on a story as feeding a personal cause you have, but as a search for a revelation that is important for people to know. Let the story reveal itself in its totality. Stand back a little when it starts to play into your worldview. Again, let it tell you the way it is. You don't tell the story the way you want it to be."

"So," Meredith asked, trying to find some closure here. "My wanting some recognition for those poor people is creating a story where there is no story."

Press eased himself back into his large chair. His body seemed more comfortable when slightly hunched and always disheveled behind his desk. He was not a natural at standing. Meredith amused herself thinking.

"OK, I'll be generous. Yes, beating slaves, what, a hundred sixty-something years ago, was its own story. A horrible, unforgivable crime. As I think I said the other day with Trace, Metamorphosis is a story about a revolutionary way to design a community. It is its own story. If we go back over all of the bad things that happened to Black people in the Atlanta area and said we can't build there, or it insults what happened before, then this whole area would be a park to the deprived, the beaten. There were tragedies everywhere back then. And back then are the operative words."

"May I ask what you are being generous about?"

He leaned back, "I'll have to admit there is an interesting twist to it, but only if Jack could weave it into his plan. Otherwise, it would just be opening a can of worms that doesn't need to be opened. It is a story, just not this story."

Meredith felt she had permission, an opening to talk to Jack about. Would he agree to bring the old into the new? This sudden openness between her and her boss caused her to say without thinking, "I had a strange phone call that, in a weird way, ties into this conversation about race, or maybe it doesn't."

"What do you mean?"

"A man who wouldn't identify himself called here and said that Mr. Collier had been a member of the Klan in high school, and he had a photograph of him marching in a Klan parade in Athens."

Press shouted, "What?!" Then he burst into the first true laugh Meredith had ever heard from him. It was hearty and filled with the humor which an accusation so off the wall can generate.

"I had the same reaction. But what if it were true? Does

that have anything to do with Metamorphosis? The man sounded sneaky or vindictive and said he had given the story to a television station. But it gets worse. The man said Mr. Collier's father was photographed at a hanging from the tree that sits next to the house, and his dad was smiling."

"Wait a minute." Press placed his hand flat over his forehead and eyes and slowly slid it downward like he was trying to erase the words from his mind. He breathed deeply and rested back in his chair.

Two writers seated behind Meredith were pointing at their watches through his open door. He held a single finger up, telling them he was finishing.

"Have we entered fantasy land? Is this the twilight zone? What damn nonsense, but okay, this project has gotten too big to ignore any aspect. Why don't you check it out with Jack, and you might stop calling him 'Mr. Collier.' Makes you sound too young to be asking him anything. Obviously, I'm removing my no-interview order. You don't obey them anyway. Lastly, I'll email you several leads on some teachers reportedly changing student grades at a couple of Atlanta public schools. Probably nothing, but you might check it out. OK, out of here."

CHAPTER 11

AS MEREDITH LEFT Press's office, she felt a rush of enthusiasm. He had awarded her with a real assignment on investigating the school system, though she felt there was little to a tip that had been called in about grades being erased and changed by teachers.

She felt Press had just absolved her of her sins and blessed her to continue on under his guidance. She now had an excuse to call Jack.

"Hi, Meredith. Long time no see. What's it been, 24 hours?"

She could hear the mirth in his voice. It was a fun, teasing, maybe even flirting tone that drew her back into feelings she was trying to resist. She held the phone away from her ear, shook her head, and brought a more professional air to her words. She ignored his playfulness.

"I have had an anonymous call here at the paper from someone making some accusations about you and your past that I feel I must check out since they have also called a TV station."

His phone was silent for a moment. Then he scoffed at it being anything serious.

"It must have been that time in high school we threw toilet paper on the trees in our coach's yard."

"More serious than that, I'm afraid."

"Yeah, what's worse?"

"Whoever the man was, he said that you were a young member of the Ku Klux Klan, and he has a picture of you marching with them in Athens. We have no intention of pursuing this, but the broadcast people might."

"That son-of-a-bitch! I can't believe he still carries the grudge."

"So, did you? Were you in a march?"

His voice was matter of fact, not anxious or apologetic.

"I was a sixteen-year-old rebel, not a confederate, Black-hating rebel, but an artistic, angry young man filled with the need to express myself. My group of buddies and I heard the Klan was coming to Athens to march against Black students at the university. We thought it would be fun to screw around with them. We flipped a coin to see who would put on a hood, march with them a little, then start acting crazy and run around flailing their arms. The others would sneak over to the Klansmen's cars and let the air out of their tires. I lost the coin toss and got a sheet from my bed; we made a pillowcase into a hood."

Meredith was holding back a laugh, partially because it was so typical of what she would expect from this renegade called Jack acting like a boy, and also out of relief that it was all a big joke.

"I assumed it was something like that. But why would this person call the media about something so long ago and just a prank?"

"It had to be Melvin 'Skinny' Scarbrough. You know, I have found that the high point of some people's lives was when they went to high school. They talk about it every time you run into them, and they never forget the slights or perceived slights. These old hurts are like an open wound that never heals. I found this out at our twentieth reunion. The classmates who had stayed in our hometown lived in a high school time warp. Skinny is one of those. They live every day like it was twenty years ago. He's an architect in Athens, so maybe he hates my work. Who knows?"

Meredith felt great relief. She wanted this story to have a happy ending. She told herself she did not have a growing attraction to this taken man. She attributed her desire not to hurt Jack to her wanting her dad's investment to be protected. She also knew she was lying to herself, so she kept probing for an answer as to how anyone could be so hateful to this charismatic man. "Do you mind telling me what slight would make him try and hurt your reputation at a time like this?"

"If it was Skinny, and he was very thin in those days, he was kind of a loner who looked on our group of five or six guys and a couple of girls as the 'in' group. I didn't know it then, but he wanted to hang out with us. And he wanted to be a part of the Klan escapade because he thought it was going to be this daring, crazy, really big adventure. We hardly knew Skinny. He was always hanging around. He was pleasant enough, and we didn't try to exclude him. Anyway, the Klan thing was a big deal at school, with everyone buzzing about it, though only our group knew who had done what. Skinny had overheard us one day and knew I was the Klan guy that went crazy in the march. But I guess he saw it as a missed chance in his life if that makes sense, so now that I'm getting all this publicity, it's a payback."

Meredith pressed her teeth into her bottom lip. She knew

she was crossing the line once again, infusing her personal feelings into an interview, but she saw trouble coming, and she felt, and hated, her need to protect this man.

"Well, you do need to know that I assume it is Shandra Berry that he has told this story to, and I don't know where she might take it, if anywhere."

With obvious appreciation, Jack said, "This is really kind of you. We are in such a touchy world about race that an innocent act like that could get blown out of proportion. I'm open season right now, and the publicity hasn't even begun."

Meredith wondered what Jack would do now. It sounded like he was dismissing an incident that could blow up in his face. She felt compelled to feel Shandra out for no other reason than preparing *The News* for a response if the Klan story suddenly appeared on television.

"Again, it's kind of you to check this out. Nothing here but teenagers having fun. In fact, I should tell some of my Black friends and demand I get an NAACP award for making the Klan look stupid."

She almost didn't want to ask the next question, but she had to stay ahead of Shandra.

"There is a last accusation."

"This must be the toilet paper in the tree story. These just get worse and worse."

This bravado may be legitimate, or was he trying to convince himself that some very bad news was lying out there?

Meredith assumed her professional demeanor, which usually meant her voice lowered slightly in a calm but slightly threatening way, as she was 'in the hunt,' as she liked to say.

"The caller got to Shandra first and told her that he had a newspaper article with a photograph of your father at a hanging in the early 1940s."

Jack was standing at his desk and looking at downtown Atlanta when he had taken the call. He could see his reflection in the large window. He could see his face flinch in fright and could feel his heart now pushing against his chest, the heat rising from his neck across his head and down his face. He wanted to be careful. He wanted to scream at this young woman who had started a cascade of worries since he met her. And now this obscenity. His father at a hanging? But he responded with measure.

"Do me a favor if you would. Get a copy of the newspaper, and then let's talk. That's such an absurd statement—I can't even respond. I would call my dad a true southern gentleman. Reputation and honor meant everything to him. "

Meredith hurt for Jack, almost apologizing. "I don't know where an assertion like that could go, if it were true, except to damage you. I know for a fact that Shandra is talking to this man, and frankly, as a reporter, I also wanted to know your answer."

"You know what I've liked about you since the first? You're a purist. You put truth before all, and that's a rarity in this world. Again, I can't respond to something I haven't seen. If you get the photograph, give me a call."

She didn't know how to respond to his complimenting her. She realized her warning came across as more personal than professional. She focused back in on the house. "Oh, before you go, any luck on finding an archeologist?"

Jack was caught off guard. He had forgotten the promise, thinking the newspaper had said no to her trying to include the slave house in the Metamorphosis story.

"Honestly, I'm in over my head in writing contracts with engineers, contractors, water and sewer people, you know, the glamorous part of building something. But my secretary is on it, and I'll make sure she finds a name. Although your editor doesn't see it as a story, you've got me curious, and we'll get somebody with some expertise on old houses out there." He said with finality, "Hey, got to go. See you as the project gets closer." And his phone went silent before she could say goodbye.

What the hell was this about his father? He wondered. In 1940, Wade would have been about eight years old, so how could his father be in Vinings? It made no sense.

CHAPTER 12

JACK'S SMARTPHONE had Italian operatic music for its ringtone.

"Hey, money man. I assume you and Miss Mary are coming tonight?" It was Cody. "I've got all the Young Rulers here at the same table. That'll total 40,000 big ones for the eight of us."

"Don't send me any bills," Jack said. "I'm underwater. Got all my pennies, my house, and my wife's closet full of shoes pledged against the loans. You'll find me in Mexico if this thing goes south."

Both men snickered at the impossibility of that happening.

"Never felt so sure about an investment. Watch as we descend into the little people."

He could hear Cody's laugh about the stairwell descent onto the party floor.

The summer charity ball for Atlanta's leading cultural institution, The High Museum, was a major affair for the deepest pockets. It wasn't the big, crowded annual gala, but this was for Atlanta's inner circle called "THE 100." That was because access was limited to one hundred couples. Its coveted tickets cost $5,000 a person and were bought a year in advance because this one gathering would have Atlanta's most powerful and most monied group for one night of mixing with those you knew, wanted to know, and those you wanted to know you. *Vanity Fair* and *Vogue* magazines—not to mention the local press and a few paparazzi—would be there to interview and eternalize Atlanta's growing crop of motion picture and music producers, downtown attorneys and developers— all the local glitterati.

Jack had always been a media favorite because of the edgy design of his buildings and his persona—the force of his personality, his full laugh, the theatrical use of his hands and arms, the carved cut of his features. Metamorphosis would now force a commitment to the celebrity that he enjoyed on one level, but which also became more of an intrusion to his first love—his work. His true joy had become increasingly one of studying new building materials and the designs of others. He loved calling architects worldwide to discuss the art, as he called it, and then in his office, releasing all restrictions on his staff's imagination surrounding the creation of a building. That was his joy.

Everyone who entered the ballroom came down a broad, slowly spiraling staircase. It made for a grand entrance of sorts and allowed all to show off their clothing purchased specially for the night. A man stood at the bottom of the stairs and announced over a mike the names of the arriving couples.

Jack and Mary stood on the landing at the top of the stairs watching several couples descend into the noise. A small dance band was playing at one end of the room.

Jack had dallied a little at home, warming to and wanting

to be among the last to make the entrance. That moment on the thirty stairs was pure celebrity, and that was now his world. He worried he was risking his fortune and reputation by allowing this growing and glowing adulation, but he knew at the heart of creativity was its daring demand for failure on a large scale. The thought of losing so much made him try much harder to come as close to the white-hot touch of perfection as he could.

"OK, pretty girl, let's show Atlanta what real beauty is," he said as they watched a couple walk down before them.

"I assume you're talking about yourself," she nudged him in the side as she stepped down the first step. It gave them both an almost buoyant smile. They looked "right" to those below them who looked for the right look. In the partygoer's minds, the two were, in that short moment of glory, where they should be, like two Greek gods come to earth to mingle and spread stardust before ascending back into their rarified world.

Meredith saw them descending. She had come as her father's date, her mother saying the whole staircase thing was too narcissistic, too brazenly self-important. She slightly lowered her body so Jack couldn't see her as he gazed across the crowd. She hadn't thought of his being here and now couldn't understand her reluctance for him or his wife to see her. But he had, like a light in a darkness, seen her blond hair against the tuxedos, but only at a glance. There could be no stare.

Mary said softly as they stepped. "I feel like I did at my debutant ball. Isn't this the silliest thing?"

Jack smiled and nodded at the approaching crowd, "Oh, it's fun, and, yeah, silly, but we all need an occasional bit of applause. We all need a hug."

"A bit of applause?" Mary asked emphatically. "You need more than a bit."

"Jack and Mary Collier," the tuxedoed announcer at the bottom of the stairs announced with clarity. This was met by a series of catcalls from Jack's friends at their table, a lot of general applause, and the now-familiar yell of "Leonardo" and "da Vinci." And then they were consumed by the crowd and its wash of laughter and talk.

It would be an evening of friendships renewed and attempted. Jack was immediately surrounded by so many that others, not wanting to form a line, talked intensely to a friend while watching for an opening in the crush around Jack. Cal O'Conner gripped his daughter's arm and said, "Come on, sweetie, I have someone I want you to meet." She didn't see over the cloud of people that her father was taking her to Jack.

Mary had her own courtiers who would seek her hand. Rumors floated through the charitable community that Jack was about to become quite wealthy and that Mary would manage a trust for some of the fortune. She was a popular and respected woman, "born to the boards," Jack would tease her. She finally made her way to their table.

Frazier was standing in his solid stance doing a slow movement of his feet, rhythmically getting his moves down for dancing when the band was ready. He held a martini in one hand and was dipping an enormous shrimp into a sauce on their table. Medallions of pork tenderloin weighed on his plate. It was a heavy appetizer evening that made mixing easier than seated dinners.

"Welcome to fantasy land, Miss Mary," he said. "Where's Super Jack?"

She placed her purse on the table and gave Frazier a peck on the cheek. "Oh, he's over there surrounded by his fan club."

Mary went around the table hugging and air-kissing Cutie, Cody, and Sue Sue, and Marcus Sutton and Chancy. They were all resplendent in their formal wear, crisp and polished; all heads so perfectly coifed it seemed each hair had its own hairdresser. Their faces were plucked and shaved, perfumed, painted, scrapped, and otherwise an embellishment of good taste and good money.

Sue Sue thought Chancy's light brown skin was as smooth as a river's stone as she reached out and touched her face. "What's your secret for avoiding the clock, Chancy?"

Chancy's face was small and sharp-featured, including her narrow lips. She pressed her mouth together in resignation to the fact that it was her mother's doing. "You've seen my mother. She's over seventy and looks like one of us. We are what we are given, it seems, and I was given my mother's skin."

"And her mother's impatience and temper and...," her husband kidded.

"I worry that Jack, who is so visual, catches the marks the crow leaves as it walks across my face." Mary's upper lip had a way of pouting slightly even when she wasn't pouting, but it was one of her marks that Jack loved.

Sue Sue answered quickly, "Don't we all think about it more and more. I refused to walk down those stairs tonight because I'm too vain to be seen under that kind of light."

Her husband scoffed, "Can you believe we came down on the damn elevator? I pay thousands of dollars to be seen, and Sue Sue hides out because of a few wrinkles." His voice hit a high pitch of disbelief as he finished.

Everyone at the table laughed, then all went in a group to give a love hug to the small-figured Sue Sue. "We love you, elevator girl." Frazier gave her a smacking kiss on her cheek.

"OK, enough of the old age talk. Wait a few more years

when we hit fifty, then we can look back on forty-eight as the golden years." Cody raised a large glass of red wine. "Here's to now. The best year of our lives."

There was suddenly a break in the clinch around Jack, and there stood Calvin Murphy O'Connor and his surprised daughter. She didn't know her father was leading her to Jack. Her hand automatically went over her heart like some kind of salute, but it was an expression of her surprise.

"Jack, I want you to meet my daughter, Meredith, she's...."

Jack's face swelled into a grin of acknowledgment. "You mean the award-winning reporter? She's already put me through my toughest interview." And he reached out to noticeably shake Meredith's hand, which hesitated, then with obvious energy stuck out for a firm handshake.

Cal's lean and creased face reflected the surprise he felt at Meredith not having told him the subject of her first interview. He had always been one of her closest confidants.

Jack saw his surprise and filled the silence. "You'd be proud, Cal. She is very thorough—uncovers stories others miss. Now we may not agree on all of her findings, but I am open to new discoveries, new angles on my project, and we're kind of working or studying one of her stories about the property right now."

Jack was trying to preempt her going off solo again. He had them working together. She was too headstrong to let her get too out front. He had said more than he wanted to, but he was counting on a growing friendship, maybe more, with Meredith, as a firewall to keep her away from the slave thing until all the loan documents were signed.

"Oh, really? Well, what story is that?" Cal perked up.

Meredith quickly interjected with humor. "Oh, I was

tracking down a rumor that Mr. Collier was putting up an interesting building in Vinings. Just a rumor, though."

"Well, how about all of that? My daughter has barely arrived on the job, and she's on the biggest story in town." Cal pulled her shoulder against his with obvious joy.

The band started up with a slow song to encourage dancing. Cal turned his head toward them and asked, "Now, where is Mary? I want to ask her about a charity board I'm working with. You don't mind if we dance while I talk to her?"

"She would be flattered, Cal. Of course."

Cal said, "Keep him honest, Meredith. Don't let him spin you. Say, Jack, we have some negotiating to do about the stores I want to put in your place. Maybe next week?"

"I'll get you on the calendar, Cal. You wouldn't believe some of the international brands I've got coming in, but I'm saving space for you."

Cal worked his way through the crowd toward Mary. The dance floor was quickly filled.

Jack and Meredith stood awkwardly, then with a guiding firmness, he took her hand and said with confidence and a finality she couldn't resist, "Why not?"

She came in a stuttering movement, frames of instants through little hurdles of resistance. He swept her onto the floor, and before she could agree or refuse, she was in his arms and moving in a slow rhythm. His body seemed so powerful to her, though they were apart at a respectful distance. But this was confusing. At once, it seemed so wrong in a professional sense, assumptive on his part that she would even want to dance with someone she was reporting on. Then there was a warmth surging over her that was so capturing that she was afraid he could sense her flowing into him as they became one.

Her whole body seemed to be going through her hands and the intertwining of his fingers through hers.

Cal saw them dancing and said to Mary, "OK, there's one beautiful girl on the dance floor. Let's make it two." He held his hand out, and they stepped into the soft beat of the music.

"Mary, this has got to be an exciting ride for you with all of the attention of Jack's project and all of the potential it opens for you in the life of Atlanta."

Mary was five foot eight and fit well into Cal's six feet. He was an excellent dancer, a touch stiff and formal, but that was appropriate. Mary had had a flash of anger when she saw her husband take the first dance with Cal's college daughter, but she was at least relieved that there was no clutching, no too-close going on. And they seemed to be seriously talking, almost businesslike in their faces.

She looked up at Cal and said, "I'll be starting a foundation, which the project will fund. That's my excitement, and, of course, I'm proud of the recognition that Jack is getting."

"I've heard of what you're doing. I can tell you that in the not-for-profit world, there is a lot of anticipation about this foundation because you have such a reputation for smart giving."

She smiled demurely, "Well, thank you, Cal."

"I know you'll be on everyone's list for funding and very busy, but I've been asked to propose that you join us on Emory University's foundation."

She stopped dancing for a second, stunned by such a prestigious offer.

"Oh, I know," Cal said before she could answer, "you'll be swamped starting your new foundation, but this comes with the promise that you have to attend only four meetings a year, and there will be very few duties. Your name on our stationary is a rainmaker by itself."

"Well, this has turned into a lovely dance." Her smile became a grin, almost a laugh. "Emory. Good Lord. But let me talk to Jack and get back to you once he's got all the 't's' crossed on Metamorphosis. It's become his obsession right now. He sees this as the opportunity of his life."

Cal smiled, "You mean this is his da Vinci moment. Well, we all need heroes, don't we?"

Meredith had danced at high school proms and on dates in college, but never with anyone of Jack's grace and subtlety of movement. They became the music, living notes gliding, turning, stepping back then forward. Both felt something neither felt comfortable with or right with, but there was a magic to the moment where there was no sound, no floor filled with dancers, only their oneness. And then it filtered through to Jack that this could look a little intimate, and he brought them back, still in a soft voice. "I like your dad a lot. I can see his determination and drive in you."

"I am my Daddy's girl, for sure," she said sweetly.

Then there was a silence again where Meredith feared Jack could feel her heart, which felt to her like it was creating a pulsating bump on her chest. It was beating so noticeably. She tried to calm herself down and assumed her reporter's poise. "So, how is the project coming along? Any troubles? Holdups? All smooth?"

Jack's dance seemed to pick up with that, and he answered, "Well, aren't you a sneaky little reporter. This is a time to throw all of our earthly worries away and melt into the fun of the night."

She couldn't resist, and it came with a teasing look in her eyes, "Any trouble, any worries?"

Jack threw his head back in laughter. "I love it! The intrepid reporter that hunts news even on the dance floor. No, seriously, I couldn't be more optimistic. You wouldn't believe the list of companies that are trying to pre-lease space. I've developed a lot of properties, but I've never seen this kind of anticipation."

Cal and Mary were suddenly beside them, and Jack seized the moment to cut this flirtation out. He put Meredith's hand in her dad's and took Mary's, saying, "Thank you, Miss Meredith. Now go easy on this old dancer when you write your stories."

Meredith's mind was still in his embrace but had managed to make her dancing seem innocent. "Ah, the honest pen knows no bribery. A nice dance doesn't necessarily equal a nice story." And she and her father walked away.

Jack knew what was coming next, and as the last words of the band resonated, he reasoned, "Before you say I should have had the first dance with you, I'll say you are right. And I apologize, but this kid represents a real danger to our project. I am doing all I can to stall her until I can secure all of the loans."

"What in the world are you talking about?" Mary stepped back from their dancing as the first song ended, and hip-hop stormed the hall with its rhyming and beat.

"This girl embarrassed the Georgia football program with a story on players that were being given grades."

"So, she's the one?"

"Yeah, which means she's damned fearless. She went out to my property, did a lot of research, and claims there's evidence that slaves were beaten in an old house that's still standing. Oh, and she said a Black man was hanged on the tree that's there."

Mary stopped their dance. "Good Lord," was all she could muster as the revelation tried to find a place in her mind.

"Good Lord is an understatement. That's why I'm trying to build some sort of relationship with her. I've given her a separate interview, invited her to the Commerce Club, and asked her to hold off until I can get an archeologist out there and see if any of what she says is true."

Mary said, "This doesn't make any sense. What does something from the Civil War have to do with your project? Why would she even see a connection?"

"I think it's called idealistic youth. They want to right all wrongs, and she sees Metamorphosis as a vehicle for honoring those slaves."

The song pounded on, but they stood still among the twirls and stumbles and flailing distortions of the human body.

"I suppose you could do something, maybe a separate ceremony after the ribbon cutting. Make it a civil rights story."

"Only if I find out the paper is going to pursue this, and right now, her editor has no interest. So, hopefully, this whole idea will fade away."

As they started to walk toward their table, Mary asked, "I'm not sure what you're so concerned about?"

"The rest of the story, as they say, is that a guy I went to high school with has called a television station and said he has a picture of me marching with a hood on with the Klan in Athens."

Mary stopped a few feet short of their friends talking around their white tableclothed table and laughed out loud in more disbelief than humor. "Now, you've got to be joking. Everything you've just said was a setup, right?"

The band started some beach music. The three couples at Jack's table all went back out to dance, while Jack and Mary went to the table so they could hear one another over the sound. A server came by with a tray with glasses of red wine, offered it to Mary, who took one glass and handed another to Jack, who took a third glass off the tray.

"Remember some of the dumb things you did in high school? Well, some of us wanted to embarrass the Klan that was going to march in Athens. Call it our contribution to the civil rights movement. Well, I won, or lost, the coin toss and put a pillowcase over my head and marched for a few minutes, then started acting crazy, running all around, until they chased all of us off."

"When do the surprises with you stop?" She took an obvious drink while staring hard at his eyes. "All you need is a picture of you in a hood with a story about slaves beaten on your property."

Jack didn't tell her about the hanging photograph. That one had no answer right now and hopefully was too brutal, even as a rumor. Jack also lifted his glass, took a drink of the red wine, and looked at their friends dancing. Then he saw Meredith being led out on the floor by Chuck Reynolds, a recently divorced founder of an IT start-up that quickly sold for millions. He was in his late thirties, over six feet tall, with the face of a model. Jack was surprised at the jealousy he felt. Chuck's obvious youth made Jack feel older and vulnerable but also very competitive. He looked at Mary and wondered what the hell he was thinking. She was his one great love, and yet he could look at another with some longing. He looked back at Meredith long enough to make sure she was keeping a respectable distance from her dancing partner.

"I agree. We have a college reporter who wants to right the world's wrongs and thinks my project can be used to redeem us today for the evils of another age. On the Klan story, we have a social loser who is seeking revenge on me because my high school buddies didn't know he wanted to be in our group. Logic would say both of these stories are of no consequence. But this is not a world that prizes logic."

Mary held her glass and swirled the wine as more an act of thinking than affecting the taste of the drink. "Jack, you and I have a lot of our dreams wrapped up in this project. Cal just asked me to join the board at Emory University. Plus, I've indicated to a dozen charities that I want to see their applications for funding, based on the foundation which is based on Metamorphosis being successful. All the work you and I have done —our credibility."

"Let's don't get carried away. I can easily explain the high school stunt. In fact, it could show how I was into civil rights as a teenager."

Mary was eager to get in front of this. "Just go ahead and announce you're moving the house to a place where the public can come and see a rare bit of history—the civil rights museum, the Atlanta History Center. And maybe build around that big tree. You want to honor the lives that were ruined there."

Jack wondered out loud, "We should just go ahead and demolish it, and that would end the story. And there's no way I'll keep that tree. It's in a critical spot."

"You wouldn't dare tear that house down, now that the story is out there," she said abruptly. "That seems sneaky or hiding something. That's not who we are."

"Who we are standing on this dance floor, treated like celebrities, isn't who we would be if these stories get out of hand," Jack said.

"I don't understand. How does this college girl suddenly have the power to hurt your reputation and affect half the people in this room?"

"Her power is in her newspaper, especially its online version, not her per se. Her editor has told her the slave business has no relationship to our project. And normally, that would be the end of it. But this girl has grit and a sense of mission to right wrongs. She's a typical media crusader."

Mary took another deep swallow of her wine and gave the semblance of a laugh. "I know crusaders. I married one."

Their friends, tired of the dancing, returned to the table. Frazier was perspiring. He had ordered several beers before he had danced. Grabbing the beer, he plopped in a chair and turned the drink up, emptying it as though he didn't have to swallow—it just went straight into his stomach. His wife Cutie, as straight as he was round, also wearily sat down and took her shoes off.

"I know I have no class. You don't go barefoot at The High, but my husband would rather dance than eat. Well, that was an exaggeration." She poked Frazier's damp cheek in all of its fullness.

Cody loosened his tie and looked at Jack and Mary. "What's all the conversation you two are having? Jack, you're the master dancer of all time. This is a time for getting down on the floor if there ever was one."

Several men had walked over and were slapping Jack on the shoulder while their wives air-kissed Mary and then went around puckering to the rest of the table. No one shook hands, all hugged and air-kissed, with an occasional cheek kiss, depending on how well they knew one another. Never a mouth kiss.

Charlie Brogan, a slight man who looked even smaller in his tuxedo, a former Coca-Cola executive that was on the board of Morehouse and a major contributor, gave Jack a generous smile. "Jack, I want to thank you for bringing the races together on this project.

You've reached out to minorities to invest, and you're signing them up as contractors."

Jack nodded in a shy thank you. "It's one of the reasons I gave it a name that meant transition. The whole property is designed to bring people together."

"Well, it is a unique concept for our city, and that design is going to make you a worldwide figure." With great sincerity, he ended the conversation, "So, again, thank you for being a bridge-builder."

Marcus was standing just behind Jack. When Charlie walked away, Marcus took a sip of scotch and said, "Charlie, there was right. You've worked Atlanta like it's got to be worked. There's black, and there's white, and sometimes they make gray, but underneath they always remain true to their color, and you know how to make the gray."

"Kind of like a painting, isn't it," Jack mused. "Mix the colors together, and you get an endless array of possibilities."

"In the abstract, theoretically, yes, but under all the mixing, I remain Black, and you remain White. It was ordained by God to test us."

They both smiled and held their glasses in a toast. "Here's to the test. At least you and I passed. I love ya, white man," Marcus said, smiling broadly while showing his perfect teeth. It wasn't a supplicating grin but an acknowledging and accepting smile. It was his trademark, like a universal embrace that a friend had said reflected Atlanta.

Frazier had cooled off enough after pouring a beer down his throat. It was the way he drank and the way he lived his life —in a hurry, a mad dash to some. He jumped out of his chair and grabbed Jack by his arm. "It's our time, brother. We gone ride your little drawings to the bank. Hell, I might even ask for your autograph."

A loud, open-mouthed laugh had become a part of Frazier's rotund persona. Always quick to joke and poke and kid, he was the life of wherever he was. "The young rulers are about to be the rich young rulers."

Jack ran his fingers through his thick hair and its flow of curls and straights. "The only autograph I want to sign is the starter loan with the pension fund. Then you can start counting our money, and I can start my work."

Frazier twisted his face in a look of conviction. In the softened light of the room, Jack could see that Frazier's face was still reddened from dancing. "You creative guys are always worried somebody's not going to buy your art. Well, this painting has been bought lock stock and barrel by my investors and everybody else's."

Jack looked across the dance floor at the table where Meredith sat with her father and a handsome man she had just danced with. He was laughing and gesturing, and so was she.

The crowd noise, the band, all quieted into an indistinguishable hum while he looked and wondered and felt.

The band brought him back with a thumping, driving song, and he pointed at Mary, who was in close conversation with a Delta Airlines executive. She motioned that she would pass on this dance. Jack yelled to his three partners and their wives, "Let's dance."

They all yelled in agreement and danced their way out onto the floor. To Jack, dancing was passion, always fun, suggestive, other times beauty expressed in a rhythmic celebration of the body and its fluidity. He had taken lessons. He practiced in his office by himself and with the women working there during breaks. It was a release. Mary said he was so good that she would only slow dance with him.

He went to the table of several friends and motioned for the wives to come on out, and he danced with two and then three at a time, and they all gave themselves to the joyous abandon with Jack as the centerpiece. He was a peacock in full feather.

Meredith saw Jack from her father's table even though the young man was very expressive in trying to hold her attention. He said to Meredith, "That guy's a professional. He ought to be on *Dancing with the Stars.*" Meredith responded only in the quiet of her heart as it fell for the mesmerizing man with the precise but sensuous steps and tight twirls, the out-swung arms, and the gaiety of his captivating face.

The song ended. The crowd dancing with Jack all hugged one another. Mary smiled at the scene, thinking it was the best of times. Jack's face glistened with the energy of the dance as he approached her.

"Sexiest man alive," she smiled, an eyebrow cocked up.

'Married to the sexiest woman." He leaned in to kiss her, then realized he was a little too sweaty for any amorous moves. "Let's go home and see who is the sexiest."

Mary closed her eyes and turned her face up to her husband's. "I want to capture this moment in my mind. This is the start of a great ride."

He affectionately touched the tip of her nose with his finger. "Better hold on tight, babe."

As Jack and Mary turned to walk up the broad stairs, following others out, he saw Meredith walking beside her father and the young man. He wondered if she was going home with her father, and in the guilt of that thought, he put his arm around Mary's waist and hugged her toward him. He knew it was in the shame of this small betrayal of watching another woman that he had hugged his wife. Guilt, and the echoes of the raging love he had once felt, gave what measure of pause he still observed. A quick kiss on her cheek provided all the redemption he required, and they mounted the stairs to leave—the perfect couple about to ascend to an even higher plane of fame and fortune.

CHAPTER 13

JACK HAD DECIDED to wait a little longer before getting back to Shandra. The Klan march was such a prank that he felt comfortable in being nonresponsive, so if he called her in a few days, she might also think there was nothing to Meredith's slave fantasy either. But the conversation with Meredith brought the risk back to his mind, and he called Frazier, Marcus, and Cody, saying he wanted them to meet him out at the property about six o'clock. He said something might have come up, and he wanted to make sure they were on the same page. They all agreed to be there.

A grading machine sat ponderously near a small construction trailer. The brick-colored soil rose in a mist of dust around Jack's Mercedes' clean, black tires. The property consisted of eight acres and mostly up a hill of no great elevation. The June sun was blaring in its afternoon light, giving the day an overly lit brightness that demanded sunglasses.

Jack parked, left the leathered serenity of his car, and looked down with a scowl at his discolored tires. He saw a man out on Paces Ferry Road, scratching his head as he looked under the hood of his stalled car. Jack felt thankful his life had not faltered and that he had never been stranded and without. But he had been hurt and bullied for his ears being outsized enough that, as a child of eight years old, the words cut like deep wounds and had given him a lifelong empathy for someone stranded. He walked up the rise to the old house as his three friends came driving on to the site. A yell came up from one of the Jaguars.

"Hey, Leonardo. When you going to clear this briar patch?" It was Frazier, quickly joined by Cody and Marcus, the two being taller and trimmer than their shorter companion Frazier. They walked carefully through the whirl of brush coming up the path from their cars into the clearing of the house. All wore dress shirts and ties, and Cody and Marcus had on designer jeans. They often called themselves "Men of the Tie," a nickname that reflected their pride of tradition indress. They also favored what they called "interesting" socks.

The three men stood at the steps with Jack on the porch. Marcus stepped up on the porch, noticing how the planking gave, and quipped, "So this is where my ancestors vacationed?"

"Speaking of Black people," added Jack, "ya'll come on inside. Got something to show you."

They stepped into the room, noticing the sharp light shafts cutting through the structure's separated siding. There was no smell. The wood had long ago yielded its life to the dryness of age. Marcus stood in front of one of the light beams and watched as dust bits swam through its brightness. He wanted to sense what it must have been like to have lived a life of fear and servitude in this small space. But he couldn't place himself there. His world and his life had moved on to another place of power and freedom, and acceptance.

The blackened fireplace punctuated the room with its old field stones fitted somewhat into an evenness, mixed with what looked like handmade bricks. It looked older than the house. "We've always been totally honest with one another, okay, too honest sometimes. So, I want to show ya'll what I told you about at the pool." Jack said.

The three looked at one another with the uncertainty that lowers eyebrows and mouths into an expectation of something unpleasant coming.

"The coed reporter I had a dance with the other night is this idealistic type that believes the sins of the Civil War survive today and need to be reckoned with."

Cody interrupted, "Ah, the bombshell. I'll bet Miss Mary didn't okay that one."

"No, she's good because she knows I was trying to keep this little crusader from throwing water on our party here."

Frazier was feeling weak from the walk up the rise to the house but was more intrigued by where Jack was going with this. "Okay, enough of the buildup. What's this about?"

"She's Cal O'Connor's daughter. He has major plans for opening shops here, so I've been careful in telling her to be very sure. She believes this house is pre-Civil War, had slaves living in it, and that they were beaten here. And she thinks the hanging I told you about happened on that tree right outside."

"Damn," echoed in the small space.

"Where did she get that crap from?" Cody asked.

Jack pointed down at the bricks. "On these bricks are some scratchings that look like names and words that read like 'whupin hous' to her. She says she's tracked the names at the History Center to their owner. And she thinks the words mean slaves were beaten here."

The three walked over, bent down, and squinted to see if

they could read the scratches. It was difficult because they were soot-filled. As each backed away, there was no confusion in how Frazier and Cody reacted. "This is nuts," Cody said. "Slaves lived all over the place, and there's no way she could prove they were beaten here if that's even what it says. I can't make sense out of the words."

Frazier followed in his disbelief that anything could or should come of this. "Even if it were true, that was a century ago. Are you supposed to turn this house into a museum and cancel the project?" He felt a slight tightness in his chest and tried to control his growing stress and indignation.

Jack looked at the only Black in the room. "What do you say, Marcus?"

Marcus thought, trying to gauge his feelings. "The savagery to the slaves is in my race's DNA. It is the proverbial and eternal thorn that can lie unnoticed, but the slightest touching of it, and we feel the pain. The other side of this is that all of us here have major money and our reputations on Jack and his project. One aggressive reporter could have activists swarming all over this hill. One man's voice can now be heard around the world. We're talking a hell of a long time ago about an abuse that can't be proven. Is it true? Is this house that old? Seems there's room for this just being a legend." Marcus pulled his tie up tighter around his neck. He prided himself in having a starched look.

"But my Blackness gets its hair up when I hear the word 'hanging.' If it was on that tree, we've got a symbol that just compounds the slave story. And we, all of us, and our investments in this could have a problem."

Jack motioned for them to head for the door. "It's stuffy in here. Let's step outside. The afternoon sun was resting on trees behind them but was still intense from the west.

"As I told you, Meredith said that in the 1940s, a Black man was strung up by a mob who broke him out of jail. She said the hanging was on that tree but then backed off because this hill used to be covered in big trees."

"Surely that was in the papers. We could check to see if that's true," Frazier said. "Or is she just grabbing at rumors to make a name for herself?"

"As I'm getting to know this girl, yes, she's out to make a name, but she's a stickler for being accurate. She's a purist, and that's our hope for her not pushing the paper on any story she can't absolutely prove."

"Maybe you should dance with her some more," Frazier said, trying to bring some levity into the conversation.

"No, I need to start dancing with the Black television reporter, Shandra Berry. She's had a guy from my high school days call her about me, and she is one hungry reporter."

Marcus moved closer to the slight shade the house offered against the sun. "What guy? What'd you do in high school?"

"What didn't I do? The angry young man. Rebel with absolutely no cause. Then the Ku Klux Klan came to Athens. Some friends and I wanted to make fools out of them, so I got in one of their marches and acted like an idiot until they chased me away."

"Now I like that," Marcus sounded relieved. "You were down for the cause." Marcus reached his fist out to Jack in a quick tap.

"I heard that Shandra claims she has a picture of the march."

Frazier wiped a sheen of sweat off his forehead. The late afternoon was reluctant in relinquishing the warmth it had generated. His mind was on his chest as he monitored the tightening, a shortness of breath. "You're throwing a lot at us here, my man. A member of the Klan, a relatively recent hanging on that tree and slaves beat in this house. We are sitting targets for all hell to break loose." His voice rose in worried agitation.

Cody said, "Yeah, this has the Black Lives Matter crowd written all over it."

Frazier appeared nervous, though he always had an urgent nature. "What's the plan? I've got my ass on the line here. The damn media is out to destroy anybody today with a hint of racism about them."

Marcus quickly spoke up, either trying to reassure himself or give a truth. "You can call our Jack a lot of things, but not racist."

Frazier shot back, "You can call anybody anything today. Doesn't matter how ridiculous. Once it's said, it's true. All the good works Jack has done can be called into question with one story."

Jack tried to bring some lightness to the situation. "I hope I'm more than one story."

Frazier interrupted him, "You may be no more than one letter. The always toxic 'N.' Surely, they can find somebody who heard you say the 'N' word, and this big, beautiful dream of a project will never get off the ground."

Cody wondered, "How can one word, one letter in one word, said who knows when or under what circumstances, destroy a lifetime of works and deeds that counter that word?"

"We're in the age of accusation as maker and breaker," Marcus said, "and my people flat own the pointed finger. Funny, not ironical, isn't it, that your people owned my people because they believed we were inferior. We weren't, but it was believed. Now we own you through accusation, whether our accusation is true or not. Say it, and it's true."

"Well, all I know is the world's gone stupid," Frazier added.

Jack said, "Yeah, we can get philosophical, we can call names, but we've got to play in this game, no matter how stupid or unfair or incorrect we think it is. I'm trying to get out in front of the college girl and the TV reporter."

He knew he was lying when he called Meredith "The college girl." He smiled and said to himself that he was pulling a Bill Clinton and his calling Monica "That woman." Jack felt guilty about it. He felt he was betraying a woman he admired, and he had dangerously strong feelings for her. But he was living a lie with Meredith in every longing looks and flirting conversation and touches on her skin. So, Jack allowed the description of "the college girl" to come out, demeaning Meredith knowingly to himself.

"I hired an archeologist that is giving me a report tomorrow on the age of the house and anything he can find on the slave names. I'm thinking he'll say the house is maybe a hundred years old at the most, making the whole slave idea impossible."

"Yeah, out in front is where you want to be," Marcus rubbed his chin in thought. "I'll see if I can find out about a hanging here. Surely the Marietta or Atlanta papers had a story on it. Let's pray this never happened, at least not on that tree."

"This is our dream come true, Jack. We've all put in money. We've got our friends in it. You've got your reputation on the line. This is too big now for us to let it fall just because of some damn reporters." Frazier wiped his forehead again and moved along the porch into the shade of the tree towering next to and over the house.

He then impatiently asserted, "We can end this right now. We'll pry the bricks up and have your contractor push this tree down. When those reporters ask what happened, just say the demolition company came out early. And we don't say anything about the bricks. I'll chuck 'em somewhere."

Marcus had a growing discomfort with the direction of the conversation. He had become a central figure in this project, bringing in the investment of a host of Black national celebrities and local politicians. His power was in the trust he had earned. He was a bridge builder, a conciliator, but he was a man keenly aware of his race and the humiliations and savagery it had suffered. He tested himself from an early age to keep his heart filled with forgiveness. Still, it had been a continual fight when in small incidents, he would see the look, hear the remark, understand the feeling emanating from "The white folk," as his grandmother called whites.

"I don't know, my friends. I have to say I'm a little bothered by destroying all of this before we can verify its truthfulness."

His words were said with a softness like he was thinking about the subject, and the words rode out on their own. But they had a shock value in that they expressed a sensitivity to the subject the four had always avoided. Never in their years of hanging out and doing business did they have a disagreement or much of a discussion about Marcus and his racial difference. The four had conquered the reference to Marcus and any awkwardness on the subject by destroying it with humor or just ignoring it. If African American, they called him "Double-A." He called them "WB's" for white boys. The humor dampened the fire the subject could ignite, and they had grown close in their small brotherhood of business and social life.

The other three didn't know how to react, fearing Marcus had just thrown up a line they didn't want to cross. But Frazier was having pinpricks in his chest and was filled with a concern that swept his face in heat and sweat. He unobtrusively stepped back inside the house.

Looking down the hill and to the cleared land where they had all parked, Jack asked, "Wonder who that is?"

They all looked down the incline and over the brush to see a burgundy Honda with several antennae protruding from the roof, pulling up in a thin vapor of rouge-colored dust. And then out came Shandra, a man with a shoulder camera and a tall, dark man.

"This may not be good," Jack said in a thought that had escaped without his trying to express it. "That's Shandra Berry, the reporter I was telling you about—who is the Black guy?"

"Call in the bulldozers," Cody mumbled. "Cut the tree down. Knock over the house."

Frazier had gone unnoticed. He pulled a small knife from his pocket and walked as quickly as he could on the echoing wooden floors to the fireplace.

Approaching the house, Shandra directed the cameraman to make sure the big tree and the cabin porch were in the background of an interview she was about to do. The tall Black man did not approach with them. Shandra looked into the camera and spoke in what her mother called her daughter's "tell it straight" voice.

"This is investigative reporter Shandra Berry, and we're here at the site of what is being billed as the most innovative building in Atlanta's history. Designed by controversial architect Jack Collier and named 'Metamorphosis,' we have sources who claim that there is much more than a new building going up—possibly a brutal racial secret about to be covered up. After several attempts by this reporter to find the truth in the accusations, Jack Collier has refused to come before our cameras and answer what could be career-threatening stories from his past. Let's see if he's on the property. You can run, but you can't hide from the truth when station WBBM is asking the questions." It was her trademark close.

From the porch, Jack responded with a cautiousness. "Miss Berry, I don't think we had an interview scheduled today."

Shandra aggressively stepped forward to get between her cameraman and Jack. Any shots would show her in the picture. She looked combative in her red dress. Jack noticed her demeanor, a fierceness, a combativeness about her face, and the stance of her legs grounded firmly. Her hand pushed out a piece of paper.

"Since you have avoided my phone calls, you leave me no choice. And I'm here because I have some serious allegations that have been made about a history of racism in your family, starting with brutalities committed on this property, possibly with that very tree you are about to destroy."

She seemed to flame in the sun. Her bright red dress intensified almost into its own light with the sun hitting the front yard where she stood. "I have been told by a reliable source that you marched with the Klan as a young man and that your father witnessed a hanging from this tree and laughed as one Black man swung from the limb. I have pictures of both events." She held two pieces of paper out in front of her toward Jack and his two friends.

Jack's temper was verging on flaring as he walked toward her, getting close to her face. He said with conviction, looking not at her but into the camera. "This is exactly why the media is ranked lower in respect than used car dealers. You should be ashamed as a reporter for making accusations that have no basis in fact."

There was a noticeable quiet from the men on the porch,

as though both statements had left no air available in which to speak. Their faces had gone from wondering why Shandra and her group were suddenly on the property to shock at what she had just said.

Cody and Marcus looked at both Shandra and Jack for further reaction. It was about to be visceral. But Jack stopped himself. His first thought was how his friends were taking this, and he didn't want them to be photographed or involved. "We're just finishing a business meeting. Men, why don't you all go, and I'll be glad to speak with the reporter."

There was a moment of awkwardness in which Jack hastened them along by placing his hand behind their backs and urging them off the porch. The camera being aimed at them by Shandra's associate made them do what they instinctively did not want to do—abandon their friend. These were men who tried to create a world of certainty, and this situation had no certain outcome. But the camera's lens was a portrait painter that could create a damaging illusion.

Frazier could hear them talking outside as he leaned down into the fireplace, found the scratching, and tried cutting into the old cementing between the blackened bricks of the fireplace's flooring. He wanted to dislodge the bricks, pull them out and somehow hide them before the group came in. But his pocket knife was too dull and too small to cut through, so he began anxiously chipping and scrapping a brick next to the names adding a smiley face and the war cry of the University of Georgia's football team "Go Dawgs."

It was a frantic effort of chiseling. He then rubbed soot off the surrounding bricks and pressed it into his scratching, so it was difficult to see the difference between the old names and his cutting. Jack had said that Meredith had seen the names and would know something was up if he scratched them away.

Putting the renowned Georgia athletic cry and the smiling face nearby should make the whole affair arguably the work of recent teenagers.

As Frazier brushed by Jack, he whispered, "Have them look at all the bricks. Go Dawgs." He then walked away with the others, displaying a very satisfied smile.

A Mann had walked over to the tree. He thought its trunk looked like elephant hide with its gray, wrinkled bark. He touched the tree softly, feeling the rough and tumble of ancient growth and thinking on the memories it held. He wondered if the man had imprinted his pleas for mercy. Was the sound of his neck snapping now embedded in the tree's soul? Looking up at the enormous limbs, he wondered from which of these the man had strangled.

The men skirted around Shandra's group and headed toward their cars. Jack looked back into the house with curiosity, but in its soft light, noticed nothing different.

As the three men approached their cars, Cody said, "I don't like this. I've got a fortune riding on the development. The damn press can destroy anything today."

Frazier agreed. "I can't have my face on the news within ten miles of a race story. Damn, if there isn't always a downside to a driven man, which Jack is."

"This is sensitive ground for me. The Klan thing was a joke, and in fact, could help him, but the hanging, if it's his dad smiling, for God's sake," Marcus said. "And the names in the hearth? This is the stuff of a deal killer, my friends."

"Is it time to be thinking about Plan B?" Cody asked. "What if this goes from a few questions by an ambitious reporter to a national story about a racist developer? You know how news spirals out of control and becomes its own life form."

Marcus looked at the dust on his $300 brown leather

shoes. "Plan B? We've made verbal commitments to Jack and other investors. A lot of them are in this because we are. If we pull out, there's a domino effect, and we destroy one of our best friend's dreams and probably his reputation and money."

Frazier almost interrupted. "Hey, let's don't get carried away. We stand together. Nothing has happened, just another reporter trying to bring down a man at his finest hour."

Cody answered, "Yeah, I don't even like us talking like this. Jack is bigger than life, the most talented human on the planet. If she comes up with something, he'll figure a way to dampen it. I'm up for a drink at the club. Any takers?"

Frazier and Marcus both declined the invitation. Marcus said, "I'll call him tomorrow and get his sense of how certain he is that his daddy wasn't at the hanging."

Cody pulled his dark glasses off and squinted toward the house they had left. "I don't think we should just wait and see if this blows up in our face. We're talking best friend here. Let's be careful of what we say to anyone about all this. Friendship can carry a heavy price."

"Yeah, but what if the price is bankruptcy?" Frazier asked.

Cody had a sudden look of panic. "Whoa, don't even get into that. Jack will ammo up. He's as tough and smart as they come. No worries."

Their cars separately clouded the air as they moved across the dirt of the construction site and out into a chilling uncertainty felt by them all.

CHAPTER 14

JACK HELD HIS COMPOSURE, inviting Shandra's group to gather in the shade of the big oak.

One of his tactics was close-in persuading. He would stand physically, pressing an adversary in a negotiation, staring them in the eye, not in an unyielding, threatening way, but with a disarming familiarity that gave his physical presence and striking face an advantage and made his persona an intimidating force. He called it "influencing by proximity."

A Mann kept his left hand spread on the tree's trunk. Jack wondered what this somewhat mysterious, somewhat intriguing figure was doing there and what his involvement was with Shandra Berry. When Jack extended his hand to him, A Mann didn't move—in obvious defiance. To Jack, this man seemed like a black apparition that had emerged from the tree, not of this world but from that past terror. The thought, a thought he had never had of that emerging past in all of its horrors, struck Jack, halting his momentum for an instant.

Shandra was quick to reassert herself, "So, first, you have been accused of marching with the Klan, and this article," she held it toward him in all of its grayed-ink age, "it reportedly shows you actually in the march. What's your response to that?"

The burly cameraman stepped closer. Jack knew his face was filling the screen.

Jack creased a smile as he held the old clipping and stared at the photograph of hooded men. "This is a story of defiance to the Klan. As a teenager, I hated them and all they stood for. Some friends of mine wanted to make fools of them, so we drew straws to see who would join their parade and act like a fool to embarrass them. We had brought a bed sheet and a pillowcase. I drew the shortest straw, so I put on my outfit, and when they showed up on a Saturday morning, I slipped into the line. Oh, and while I was doing this, my friends were letting the air out of the Klan's cars."

Jack's face showed he was now enjoying relaying this tale. His voice tumbled through a laugh. "The march was underway, and I slipped in and started acting crazy, jumping up and down, waving my arms, and yelling, 'I'm suffocating under this hood!'"

"So then, I acted like I was suffocating and went running off, yelling that I couldn't breathe. The Klan didn't know what to do. It broke up the march for a while, as several of the men went running after me, thinking one of their own was in trouble." Jack looked pleased as he handed the newspaper copy back to Shandra. "So, yeah, you might say I marched with the Klan, but I definitely rained on their parade."

The answer caught Shandra off guard. Her momentum, which usually rose to a crescendo in this kind of close-in investigative reporting, was momentarily windless. But she was not to be outwitted. Quickly regaining her composure, she said, "Well, so much for pranks. The most serious allegation I'm asking you about is the hanging, possibly on this very tree. A source with kinfolks who knew your daddy swears that this figure, this boy in the picture just behind the body of the hanged man, was your daddy. At a hanging. And if you look closely, you can tell he's smiling."

The word *smiling* was said with a hint of disgust. Shandra had the talent of an actor in how she could very subtly inject emotions into her questions. She had cried once on camera at a murdered child's funeral while the production crew at the station watched and hooted over how ratings would surge with the tears.

"Never happened. My grandparents were from South Carolina. And they didn't move to Athens until the end of World War II. So, Dad would have never set foot in Vinings at that time."

"Can you say with certainty that you know all of the places your parents went before you were born? And do you know all of the things they did?" Shandra was pressing for quick answers to confuse him with the speed of her questions. She was on the chase and looking for any weakness, any stumble.

"Let me see the article," Jack said.

She handed it to him, and he could feel the camera zooming in on a tight shot of him holding the copy. His heart thumped noticeably against his chest. She caught his eyebrows in a bare move upward that suggested surprise, and Shandra noted his lips part. She had developed a sixth sense about the human face in all of its permutations. She felt she had accurate reads on one's innermost but unconsciously revealed emotions. She awaited his answer.

As poor quality as the copy of the old newspaper was, there was a definite similarity to pictures Jack had seen of childhood pictures of his father. He knew he had to react quickly and either with aggression or detachment. He decided to call her bluff.

"This is not my daddy. The photograph is so faded; it might just as well be yours. Beyond that, this hill was once covered in large trees. If a man was hanged in this area, it could have been on any of fifty trees all now cut down, but there's no reason to think it's this one. So, you don't have a story, Shandra. Now, if you would like to discuss how my project will help Atlanta's Black workers, we can discuss that."

Shandra had seen what she thought was an instant of recognition on Jack's face. She knew how intimidating, how masterfully intimidating, he was—his masculinity, his stylish clothing, his confident voice, and striking face, and she was feeling its full brunt. But she thought he was lying.

She sounded suddenly conciliatory. "I appreciate your thoughts. I'll check my sources again, so a little follow-up, then we'll have the whole story. Of course, my station would never broadcast anything we couldn't substantiate. So, let's say the story waits for a final judgment."

"Speaking of judgments, Shandra, there are a lot of investors in this project. If you start pushing a lie that could damage it and their investments, you and your station will be out here looking for jobs to pay off the judgments against you."

Shandra recoiled, "That's the oldest threat in the business —tell the reporter they will be sued. Doesn't work with me, Mr. Collier." She said Jack's last name with obvious emphasis to him.

"No threat at all," Jack responded. "The citizens who are investing millions in this project just want the truth told, and you seem like someone with an agenda, and, in this case, finding the truth is not a part of it."

She looked at A Mann slowing running his hand over

the tree's massive trunk. As he turned toward Jack and started to walk away with Shandra, he asked, "On which limb do you think it was?" The disgust in his face and how he carried himself appeared as if an aura had pervaded his body. His whole being seemed coiled, and Jack wondered if this very dark man would attack him. But he walked off in silence, with each of his steps showing their own determination.

Meredith had called Jack's office and was told by his assistant that Jack was out at the property and was taking no calls. She had a premonition that Shandra was about to push hard to make this a civil rights abuse story regardless of the facts, so Meredith thought she would drive out and warn Jack and show him the names in the brick which she was convinced were slaves. Their beatings had become more than a story to her. They were a wrong that needed righting, an unforgettable wrong against humanity.

She found herself more and more troubled by the thought of a slave being beaten in such close proximity to where she was raised. To her, this proximity soiled the ground. She could literally go out there and touch the place. It wasn't some distant Virginia plantation. It was her home. Meredith saw no negative consequences of such a revelation to the project but a historical fact that would enrich it and honor those beaten souls at the same time.

Meredith had never been what she would call "in love," but now, as hard as she was fighting it, she was, and it was blinding in its embrace as she was driving to Vinings. She wanted desperately to be true to her profession and realized this thing called love could be a form of insanity. She felt she was losing her identity. It was threatening her sense of self and her mission to report unvarnished truth.

She didn't see Shandra as she started to pull onto the site, but Shandra saw her as she was leaving.

"Oh, the blonde cometh. All hail the bleached one," Shandra said to no one as she got in her car. "What's with these damn blondes anyway?"

Reuben, a station cameraman, who had squeezed into the back seat, said, "Bleach yours and find out. Better bleach your skin too."

A Mann stood outside the car, staring back up the hill at the tree. He seemed reluctant to leave, as though he had uncovered a horror that might explain so much about how and why his father's family had left and fled the South. He got in the passenger's side with a slump, a giving in, that Shandra had not seen in him before.

"He was lying," she said to no one as she turned the ignition and pulled out onto Paces Ferry Road. As she did, she caught a glimpse of Meredith's Porsche pulling off the road and into the construction site. Shandra was talking to herself as much as to her passengers. "If she thinks she's getting 'The Get' on this story, I'll give her the Klan march, but I've had a bite on the hanging, and I'm not letting go."

Rueben asked, "What are you mumbling about?"

Shandra raised her voice and addressed both men. "I believe this hanging story could make national news, Reuben, and I want us to drive up to the Marietta newspaper and ask to see their archives. Could be something on the jailbreak and the hanging."

A Mann seemed lost in his own thoughts, but Reuben said, "No, I've got too much work at the station. Better take me back, and you two can go on."

"How 'bout it, Mr. Mann?" She was troubled by his downcast demeanor.

Still looking straight ahead, A Mann answered, "No, I need to go back to the church."

Shandra turned around and headed back downtown to their station. She looked over at her passenger. She saw his troubled, nonresponsive demeanor. "Tell me, what were you feeling at the tree?"

He was looking straight ahead, but not looking to see, just somewhere to place his eyes.

"A member of my race was murdered there. I felt his soul as I touched it. I felt his fear as he was tied, the burn of the rope around his neck, and the snap. I wonder if he has stayed there waiting for me to come and tell his story."

His eyes easily revealed the emotional anguish he was feeling, and it struck a quick fear in Shandra. "Let's not get too far ahead. Let me do some investigating and see how true all of this is or isn't."

A Mann asked, "Can I see that picture of the hanging again?"

"Sure. It's there in my purse. See it sticking up?"

He pulled it out, studied the photograph, and slammed his fist into her dashboard.

"What in the world?!" Shandra exclaimed.

A Mann held the article and its photo up. "It's the limbs, the same shape of the limbs on that tree back there. See how they stick straight out? So did the two big limbs on the hanging tree."

"Holy crap," the cameraman said. "He's right! This is hot, Shandra. Real hot."

Shandra remembered Jack's veiled threat of suing her. "But maybe all the trees that stood here had that shape," she said to the men. If this story was not as close to confirmed as she could get it, Jack and his investors could destroy her financially and end any hopes of a career. "Let's slow down a little here. We can't prove for sure yet that this was Jack's daddy. There are some powerful players in this property. I've got to be very certain before I go on the air with this."

Reuben said from the backseat, "That architect is full of himself. He's like an actor, always in role, always performing. I can see why the media loves him."

"People like him are the media's Achilles heel. We play to the brightest lights, the loudest voices, whether they're real news or not," Shandra said.

Then with some interior humor, Reuben almost laughed, "Ah, we're no more than moths."

Shandra was into her thoughts about the discussion. "Oh, for sure, Jack's a bright light. I'd say right now—he's the brightest."

"He works us with stories about his outlandish buildings. He's always in a high society magazine at some ball, and the press is now saying he's Atlanta's Leonardo da Vinci." Shandra had both hands on the wheel with her thumbs tapping as she did when she was excited about a story she thought was filled with treasure. Shandra had always told her father that she was born for the hunt.

The cameraman said, "Yeah, he may be a bright light, but we can cut the power on and cut the power off."

MEREDITH REMEMBERED TEARING HER SKIRT, pushing through the bush and brush that had not been cleared, and surrounded the house. An obvious path now led through the grasping briars. She could see Jack talking to several men in bright orange vests on the porch.

Appearing out of the tangle, Meredith gave a shy wave to Jack. Seeing her, he shook his head at another worker coming his way, but he also noticed how pretty she was, pretty always, but sunlit now in a faded orange shirt and tan pants.

"Thanks, fellas. Looks like we've got all the surveying we need. Got to talk to this reporter now." The men nodded to Meredith as they walked away.

"Guess this is my day to meet the press." His smile and tone softened Meredith, who had arrived nervous but determined to convince him of the beatings she believed had taken place there.

"Your friend Shandra just left. She hit me with the Klan march thing and now is pushing the idea that my daddy was smiling at a hanging from that tree." His head motioned to the right. "She even brought a cameraman and a strange acting young man."

He looked exasperated to Meredith, who realized she had come at a bad time. "I didn't realize you would be here," she lied. "I just wanted to look at the bricks one more time to see if the writings said what I thought they did, or maybe I made a mistake. I can come back another time."

Jack could see her embarrassment at following Shandra, but he also remembered the strange heads-up Frazier had whispered. He thought he would take a chance. "Listen, I know you have strong feelings about the injustice of slaves being beaten, so let's see if we can agree on this once and for all." He motioned, "Come on in."

The late sun was beaming its last rays before disappearing behind the Vinings hill. They were sharp stabs through the cracks in the boards of the old house, giving it a sanctuary look of pinpricks of light in an otherwise darkening room. Jack walked over to the fireplace.

"You say you saw writing. Where?" He knew but acted like he didn't.

Meredith walked around him, and with her tennis shoe, scraped at the leaves and debris on the blackened stones. "There, there is the writing. Let me clear it off."

She started to lean down, and Jack said, "No, no, don't get that soot all over your hands.Let me do it."

He leaned down and started wiping the black film until the scratches revealed names and the words, "whupin' hous."

"Well, look at this," he said as though he were surprised. "There is writing here."

Meredith's voice was filled with relief, "So you see it too. I wasn't wrong. And what do you think?"

With a touch of false enthusiasm, Jack said, "Let's see if we can find more names." He thought surely, Frazier had some reason for encouraging that the bricks be shown. Meredith scraped the edge of her shoe over the bricks next to the names.

"Oh, look, there's something else here."

With a relief that Meredith couldn't know, Jack said, "Are those names? I can't read it in this light. What's it say?"

There was an obvious pause.

"Go Dawgs." Her voice sounded reluctant and soft to Jack. He could see the flow of emotions over Meredith's face. Removing the debris had revealed the words "Go Dawgs" and the smiley face on bricks adjacent to the slave names. *Thank you, Frazier,* Jack thought prayerfully.

Jack stood up from the fireplace and placed a hand on her forearm, slightly turning her toward him. "I know you have put a lot of work into what you thought was a story. But this looks like a prank. That UGA cheer was first said, maybe fifty years ago."

Her mind was running over the possibilities. She pulled

her arm away from his hand and leaned down again to examine the names and the football war cry. They looked to be the same age. Meredith wondered how could she have found the one name on the will of a slave owner? It seemed too coincidental.

Seeing she was uncertain, Jack didn't want to act celebratory but understanding instead. He wanted to guide her away by casting doubt, and with doubt, she didn't have a story. But he wanted it to be her expression, not his.

"You came here today to confirm your suspicion that these were slaves' names. What are your thoughts now?"

Meredith wanted to run from the room. In one way, she felt like a fool if this was the work of some jokester, but it just didn't feel right. Maybe, she thought, the face and the Georgia cheer were later added. She did know an uncertainty had been created that her newspaper would not allow. Press would laugh her out of his office with this revelation.

Jack knew that Frazier had created enough doubt with his cleverly disguised scratches that the slave story was probably now too weak for her to pursue. But he wanted to preserve their relationship, or whatever it was.

"Okay, maybe there were slaves here. You said you found it in an old loan document, but the beating part now, I would think, it's too uncertain to run with. Here's a thought for you. Think of some way I might honor those people that my investors would approve of, and we can add it to the project's story."

Jack knew he was taking a chance on her coming up with something that still associated his property with slavery, and his partners would never go for that. He could tell Meredith had tried. It was both control of the story and a feeling of romance that was fueling these thoughts, he knew, and he knew it was potentially a stupid move on many levels. But he said it, made the offer, created an opportunity to continue seeing her. A light shaft lit Meredith's hair, giving it a halo effect, and washed her face in the purity of youth.

Jack looked away, she was too attractive, and the temptation to touch, to say something in that place of solitude was too great, so he walked toward the door.

She followed, saying, "That's a thought. I don't know." Meredith hesitated because it would mean she was giving up on the story of brutality. Slavery, whether these particular slaves were ever beaten or not, was unimaginable to her and weighed on her conscience as though she had been a party to it. "It would have to be outside of work. My editor has already said the only story here is your project."

Jack didn't know if she was pursuing the hanging and the photograph. He knew a great uncle of his lived in the Vinings area years ago, and maybe the family did visit about that time. It could be devastating if Shandra could somehow link the photo to his father.

He had to know if Meredith was pursuing it as well. With a nonchalance bordering on disinterest, he asked, "Oh, that hanging rumor, I expect Press has no interest in that either."

It was an awkward moment for Meredith. She had gotten too close to Jack and was feeling she was betraying him if she pursued the story, but she was a reporter and knew Shandra was hot after its truthfulness.

"Let's face it," Meredith said, and for the first time, she felt she wasn't talking to this legend but conducting an interview. "Your building is going up over historic land, whether it was a camp for Sherman, for slaves, or a hanging. With the world focusing on it and America in a racial divide, reporters will be looking under every rock."

Jack looked into her eyes and said to her, in a fatherly way, "Then you should be looking under the rocks before the rest of the world does."

"I have to."

It was a statement of independence, and it made her feel like she had regained some control over her attraction.

CHAPTER 15

AFTER THE CONFRONTATION on Jack's property, Shandra stopped at the station to let Reuben out, saying, "Keep that footage safe. If I can confirm it was his father at the hanging, we'll play that against his denial we just heard. This will be explosive and a huge driver for viewers."

"Yeah, I'll download it and do a little editing. To be honest," he said as he swung his legs out of the backseat to exit the car, "this is one light I'd like to put a dimmer on. Good hunting."

Shandra then drove A Mann to the church, stopped in front, and turned toward him. Without him knowing it, she had turned her iPhone's video on and was holding it, so it was focusing on him. "Something happened to you at the tree. I believe in a spiritual world, and I believe what you sensed could well have been that man's soul reaching out to you. What you do with that pain could determine the rest of your life."

"Maybe it already did," he said with a quiet certitude.

Shandra put the car in park. She didn't turn it off because

the June sun was weighing over the city, and the car would have immediately become too hot for a conversation.

"What do you mean?" She had wanted him to open up, to reveal more about himself and how he thought. Her emotions over this mysterious figure had gone from thinking he was a phony to being curious and now to a primal attraction that fed her feelings of Blackness and pride in her race. He represented purity in some ancient way, an African warrior to her.

"If that was Jack Collier's father smiling, I want that building stopped. I want him used as an example of what our people have gone through. To put a building there would mock the family of the man lynched here," A Mann said.

Shandra was shocked by the level of anger she heard in his voice. Each word was its own sentence, all measuring out to a conclusion that could become dangerous. She felt she had led him down this path with her own comments, but cutting the tree down bothered her more. She could care less about Jack's project. She worried more about her losing that towering oak symbol of the brutalities her race had suffered. She needed the tree as a symbol, a point of focus, not as some abstract that used to be there. And she needed this young man as a victim and a champion, not a revenger.

"We agree. That tree is a statement, a symbol for all to see about the wrongs our people have gone through. I believe Collier should be forced to leave it up and a plaque put on it that says, 'In honor of all those lives that mattered.'"

They drove in silence to the church. Then A Mann looked at her. His eyes glistened with water. She was a blur to him through the growing tears. His instructions to Shandra sounded with that deep resonance she heard when he preached, simple but now chilling. "Find out if it was Collier's father. And if that was the tree." With that, he was out of the car and walking toward the back of the church.

Shandra let the car window down and yelled, "No violence!"

Then she sat asking herself if she had loosened a storm in this man. She hardly knew him or what he was capable of. But she also saw a story of national magnitude, of a white racist hidden by the glamour of his achievements. It would be another example of how systemic racism hid itself under the guise of good intentions and 'helping the poor.' She saw how this young Black man was struggling to overcome the injustices of this world. But that wasn't news—it was commonplace. The hanging was the difference maker from all the others, and she believed that seeking retribution made it a winner. But she needed the rich, arrogant Jack and the tree standing. But first, she had to prove it was his father at the hanging, and it was that tree standing in mute testimony to a horror.

Marietta is fifteen miles north of Atlanta, a city preserving much of its heritage while accepting the ambitions of the developers who bring their traffic-rich office towers and luxury apartment complexes. It was the town closest to Vinings at the cusp of World War II that had a jail and a newspaper.

Shandra entered the modern, one-story, gray stucco offices of the *Marietta Daily Journal*. She inquired about any old issues on microfilm or in the original paper copies and any photo files. She was sent to a large room with cabinets by year and filled with old editions flattened in various drawers. At one end of the room, behind a small desk, Shandra saw a man she thought too withered with age to be there but with a kindly greeting in his voice.

"Welcome to the archives. I'm the research director, and

I'm older than anything in this room." He had a slightly impish turn of his face as he looked up at Shandra.

Without acknowledging his greeting, she said, "Hi, I'm Shandra with station WMBB television in Atlanta."

"Of course. I've seen you on the news. No crimes in here to report." His easy smile revealed a full set of perfect teeth, an anomaly on a face so creased there seemed a march of wrinkles. The comment annoyed Shandra.

Feigning a smile back, she answered, "Actually, I'm here because of a terrible crime that may still live in your files."

"And what crime is that?"

She didn't want to single out the one hanging. It was her reporter's habit of holding a big story close to the vest, so she lied. "I'm doing a series on hangings in Georgia, and I've just heard there may have been a Black man taken from jail here and hanged down near Atlanta."

A bronze nameplate on the paper-laden desk read Charlie Bagwell. His voice had a whistle to it. "That would be a Black man taken by a bunch of white trash September 23, 1940."

Shandra, astonished at his memory, said, "Well, that has sure stuck in your mind."

"Never will forget it. My daddy went down to Vinings to see if he could talk some of the men out of it. I rode with him. We got there right after it happened. Daddy made me look at the man hanging there, so I'd know what Black men had to go through."

Shandra could feel her pulse quicken and a rush in her eyes, which meant the start of tears, but she brought herself back, saying, "That sounds like the kind of story I'm looking for. Would that year of your paper be digitized or in an actual hard copy?"

"Both. Just pull the drawers marked 1940. It's also on the computer there."

Shandra walked over and pulled the large narrow drawers containing original copies of the newspapers in that year. Like mining for gold, her excitement built, and then, like finding a nugget, she pulled the old edition out. The article and its photograph of the hanging were both aged but far clearer than the copy she had been carrying around.

Leaving the paper on the large flat cabinet top, she walked over to ask, "Do you have photo files that may have the original photograph of the hanging?"

"We kept that one. Down there on your left in the blue cabinet."

Shandra thumbed through dozens of black and white photographs of various sizes from the year 1940, and then there it was on paper faded with age, but with enough clarity that the horror of the event was unmistakable. It had far more drama and reality than the copy in the newspaper. It gave her a visceral surge of anger. To stare at the limp figure was to be a perpetrator in humiliating. Even touching it made her a party to the act.

She asked Charlie if the names of any of the people in the photograph could be determined. "Bring it over here if you don't mind. I doubt it. Haven't seen it in years."

Shandra held it in two fingers by a corner, not wanting to hold it in her hand. She dropped it in front of Charlie, who put on a pair of reading glasses.

"No, I was only a child, and those in the crowd were already old men to me." He paused, then shocked her by saying, "Course, I did know the kid there behind the killed man."

It was an electrifying statement to Shandra. "How...why did you know him? Who was he?"

"He came that summer to stay a week with his aunt and uncle. They lived next door to us. I played with Wade every day he was there."

"Wade? What was his last name?" She had said she was doing research on hangings, but her obvious thirst for an answer to this hanging made Charlie wonder what her real motive was.

"Collier. Wade Collier. Wouldn't remember it, but his uncle Eugene, I called him 'Mean Eugene,' sure gave Wade a hard spanking after that, and when Wade's daddy came to pick little Wade up and heard about Wade's beating, he broke Eugene's jaw."

"I've got to get a good copy of this picture and your statement that this boy is Wade Collier. You wouldn't have the negatives, would you?"

"Lord, no. Those are long gone."

"I'll take it with my phone camera." She leaned in close and snapped several shots as the photograph lay on Charlie's desk.

He thought she was acting disrespectful of his little work area, almost bumping his head with hers as she leaned over and snapped her phone.

"Now, Mr. Bagwell, I'll turn my recorder on and get a statement verifying that this boy is Wade Collier and how you know it is."

As Shandra reached into her shoulder bag, Charlie asked, "Tell me, why are you so interested in this particular hanging?"

Shandra wasn't about to reveal the story she was working on. "Oh, I'm getting a few names from all the photographs I'm finding across the state, just to give some humanity to the story beyond the man who was murdered. I'll track people's family's down to get their side of the story."

That answer didn't square with him. "Look, the days of hangings are over thank goodness. Blacks and whites like each other here in Marietta. I don't want to be a part of getting things riled up again."

Shandra's reaction was quick. He thought her response was almost a yell. "Over? Over! Do you not watch the news? What's the difference between a white cop gunning down a poor Black man today and fifty whites hanging one seventy years ago? One used a bullet; the others used a rope."

Charlie's face warmed with a surge of fear at the strength of Shandra's response. He looked down at his hands on the desk, and they were shaking. His voice sounded tremulous but certain. "You've got your picture. I suggest you leave, or I'm calling the director, and you can yell at her."

Shandra saw Charlie's response as a typical white denial that institutional racism existed, and it made her even angrier. "Shut down, justice. Keep the story hidden. Let the killing continue. Lynch them with bullets."

Charlie lifted a phone and said, "Could you have Mrs. Stuart come in here right now?"-

Shandra glared down at Charlie. He looked small and withered but typical to her in his thinking of the dangerous assumption that race was now an American backstory, all solved and not worth bringing up.

"I witnessed your identifying Wade Collier. That's good enough for airtime."

She was out the door and into the parking lot, where she screamed at the sky before getting into her car. It was a release at the fury she had over the easy grace the old man had bestowed on what she saw as ongoing and indifferent oppression of her race.

Shandra felt confident she had her story. Jack's father was at the hanging, and it looked enough like a smile, maybe even laughter. She could say a credible source had identified Wade Collier.

She easily passed the speed limit on the way back to Atlanta as she phoned her story editor. "I've got the Get, Tiny. We've landed the biggest story of the year."

He caught the thrill, the exhilaration in her voice. "I'm always ready for a rating jump. Lay it on me."

"Jack Collier's father was at the hanging of a Black man, and," she waited for an effect like it was the punch line in a joke. "And he was grinning, maybe even laughing, as he looked up at the body."

"Damn, Shandra, that's pretty ugly stuff. But I don't know how we tie that into Jack."

She almost yelled as she answered. "Tie into Jack, you ask? Tiny, it was his daddy laughing at a man being hanged. You know that Jack knows it. He's already lied to me, saying his father was never in Vinings, and I know that he was."

"So, you want to bring something that happened, what, seventy-five years ago into Atlanta's story of the year?"

Shandra's thumbs were tapping avidly on the steering wheel. "This may be my destiny story, Tiny. And an exclusive that sends your ad dollars through the roof. Here's the thing: we can use the world's attention to his project to show the horrors our race has endured, a past that lingers in our soul."

Tiny was new in his position as story editor and producer. This had the potential to destroy his career with station management. They already talked of doing station promotions with Metamorphosis, doing remotes as it was constructed, hoping that the advertising agency for The Collier Group would send major ad dollars their way. Tiny had seen the drool from these sales meetings, and he became cautious in running such a potentially explosive story and souring his career.

"I don't know, Shandra. I don't see the connection between father and son, and I can tell you our management sees advertising gold in Jack's project. You know the civil rights crowd and how they could feast off this and maybe even delay the opening. You gotta know, Shandra, Jack is our golden cow." His phone went silent.

Shandra held her head back and yelled a string of obscenities. Her mind churned with the thoughts that Tiny was a Black man who had found his place, his job, his paycheck, his house in North Atlanta, and the strugglers be damned.

"There is no past to you, Tiny!" she yelled at her windshield. "But that's where the whites still have us."

CHAPTER 16

THE NEXT DAY, Meredith arrived at the Marietta Public Library as it was opening. She found her way into the archives section as Shandra had done, introduced herself to Charlie Bagwell as a reporter, and asked about files from 1940.

Charlie looked at her from his desk, now piled with books he was deciding to keep or throw away. The young woman looked like a student for a school newspaper. "Well, that sure is a popular year. Wouldn't be looking for a hanging story, would you?"

Surprised, Meredith said, "Actually, I am. How did you know?"

"In the years I've been volunteering here, I've never had anybody ask about that hanging. And now, in two days, two different reporters show up looking for the original story. Hope you're not as angry as she was."

Meredith knew he was talking about Shandra. She studied the crumpled but alert figure of Charlie. She thought she might get more help from him if she were open. "Okay, an accusation has been made that the father of Atlanta developer Jack Collier was at the hanging, and he was pictured as smiling. The reporter you mentioned seems to feel it would make Jack come from a racist family, and somehow that would make him a racist."

Charlie shook his head. "Does nothing ever change?"

"Not about race, and not with some people."

"Let me save you some time, but what I tell you is in confidence, no quotes with my name." He waited for her to respond.

"You have my promise on that."

"The hanging split our community. It was made more horrible because many of those in the mob who took the man from jail were thought of as better citizens. I mean business-people, bankers, lawyers, not just rednecks."

"What did the man do that was so bad?" She straightened her back as her purse with a small camera, a recorder, and large notebook was starting to exert their weights.

"The Black man was called a troublemaker and disrespectful because he would show up at Klan rallies with a hood on, then in the middle of the rally, take it off, yell they were all cowards, then run away. One night he caught a bunch of them trying to set fire to his house, and he came out with an ax handle and threatened to hit several of them. That got him in jail for attempted murder." Charlie looked up at Meredith with an impish grin. "They arrested him for defending his home."

Meredith said, "I do need to see the original photo."

"It's in the blue cabinet," Charlie responded. Then he watched her walk toward the end of the room.

Finding the picture, she took a small camera out, and photographed it, then walked back to Charlie's desk. "This was eighty years ago. Would you know anyone that might iden-tify people in the picture, especially the child?"

Charlie didn't know this young woman's motives and was now reluctant to get involved in what looked like a smear of a childhood friend. He answered her question with his own. "Why is this particular hanging suddenly so important?"

"It's a story of unforgotten and unforgiven sins; bringing the big man down in Atlanta. You know, the usual conflict story."

"That's all journalism is now, isn't it? You don't sound happy with your profession. What's your interest in this old story?"

"A terrible thing happened on the land that Mr. Collier is building on, which was this hanging. I believe if he somehow honored that hanged man, it would make the building almost a sacred site."

"Aren't some things so horrible they should just be left alone?"

"Absolutely not. If the reason for bringing them up is to make a moral point and see that it never happens again, then the victim should be honored and never forgotten."

"Maybe it's because I was so close to that night. It's my own nightmare, and I don't like reliving it and being quoted about it." Charlie's fingers were intertwined and resting on his desk, almost in a prayerful pose.

Meredith could see he was troubled by the conversation. She felt she was intruding into the old man's personal demons, but she had to pursue this as a reporter.

"There could be a real storm raised over this photograph that could affect many people's lives. It centers around the developer and the question of whether his father enjoyed watching a man being murdered."

"I don't know if Wade was smiling. I do know his uncle was a mean drunk and whipped little Wade after they came home from the hanging. Why? I don't know."

Meredith thought this wild goose chase after a child had no connection to Jack's opinions about race. The story she was now after had taken on tragic significance about a man who was killed by the hatred of another era. She assumed Shandra was trying to attach a seventy-five-year-old murder to a high-profile architectural design and its controversial creator. Shandra was trying to reignite the story of the past in hopes of changing the future.

"Well, I guess there's no way to know if he's smiling or if he's crying. I'm sorry I stirred up this part of your life."

She turned to leave, and Charlie said. "There may be someone who would know."

Meredith turned. "Who could that be?"

"If she's still alive, the housekeeper for Wade's uncle. July was her name."

"She was only fifteen and working for the Colliers. A skinny little thing. Her parents refused to give her a white first name, she told me later, so they named her after the month she was born."

Meredith asked, "But what would she remember about this? Surely, she's not still alive."

"I ran into her maybe ten years ago at the grocery store. The cashier repeated her name from a check she was using, and I couldn't believe I remembered her name and the peculiar kind of sideways smile she had, or I wouldn't have recognized her. July Jones."

"She still had her maiden name, so I guess she never married. You could do some searching in the obituaries to make sure she's still alive."

"In that day, white and Black people lived close, with a street or some landmark separating their communities. July lived in a house painted blue and was a few streets behind ours named Pope Street. I think a lot of the Black neighborhoods were bought up in the sixties, so I doubt her place is still there."

Meredith couldn't believe she had connected with a time that to her seemed so distant and so ugly in its inhumanity.

"Tell me how you knew Wade Collier."

"I was in the yard playing when Mr. Eugene, Wade's uncle, drove up from the hanging with Wade. Mr. Eugene was yelling, drunk yelling, how they had got rid of that man who didn't know his place. Wade got out of the truck and ran toward the front porch of the house. July happened to be sweeping, and the boy ran to her skirt and buried his face in it. She started to put her arms around him, but Mr. Eugene came on the porch, grabbed Wade, slapped him on his bottom real hard, several times—so hard it sent Wade sprawling on the porch. Mr. Eugene then went inside."

"Good, Lord." Meredith was disgusted by what she was hearing. "That's terrible. No wonder you still remember it."

"July took the boy around to a toolshed on the side of the house. I walked over and peeped through the slats. She was comforting him like he was her own child."

"You have been so kind, Mr. Bagwell. I'll start searching for Miss Jones right now." She shook his hand, feeling its protruding veins on the top and the joints in his thinned fingers. It was a warm hand that Meredith felt reflected his nature.

Marietta was still a small community where streets were easily found. Before going through the obituaries, she thought she would see if the Jones house still existed. To her surprise, a small, blue-flecked wooden house stood surrounded by new three-story, French-styled townhomes. The little house had an air of loneliness, an oddity, an anachronism in what was now a high-end neighborhood. Meredith parked her car and walked with little expectation to the small porch and blue front door. There was no doorbell, so she knocked. Nothing. So she tapped several more times, then shrugging her shoulders, she turned and walked back along the brick walkway to the street. She turned to look at the house again and could see the fecundity of a summer flower garden to the right side, and it looked as though a hunched-over figure was in the middle of the color. Meredith walked back to the house and around to the small, planted side yard.

"Excuse me," Meredith politely said. The bent figure kept at her work, which appeared to be pulling weeds. Meredith said the words a little louder and edged closer, not wanting to startle whoever it was.

"Yes?"

A thin, ancient face peered up from the flowers—hollowed cheeks, a soft mixture of gray and brown skin with riveting brown eyes. She had a small straw hat that cast her forehead in the shadow. Her voice was thin, a little high-pitched, but strong in its carry.

"Excuse me. I didn't mean to interrupt your work."

Meredith felt embarrassed and reticent walking up to someone in their yard, especially someone so frail-looking, though her gloved hands were clasping weeds with roots the woman had just pulled from the ground.

The woman stood quickly, belying her apparent age. She wore a brown work shirt and blue jeans. Meredith thought what a wisp she seemed, but her posture was perfect, either as a note of pride or just physical health.

"No, I'm a weed warrior on patrol. This morning, I won. Tomorrow they'll be back."

Meredith liked her obvious sense of dry humor. "I'm looking for someone who used to live here, a July Jones."

The woman ran the back of her glove across her forehead. "Used to live here is a good way to describe that old woman. And why do you want her?

Meredith stepped closer to the garden and the woman, though slowly. "I am Meredith O'Connor. I'm a reporter for *The Atlanta News*.I'm doing a story on a hanging that..."

The woman cut her off, "And why would you bring that awful thing up?"

"I'm trying to find the truth about a boy who was photographed looking at the man being hanged."

The woman nodded toward the house. "I've got to go in. The sun is showing me no mercy today. Can't even get a cloud to be a friend."

Her walk to the front porch had a certain briskness to it, Meredith thought, for someone who looked so old.

Meredith followed and asked, "Do you know if Miss Jones is still alive?"

"That's a question worth asking. I do know she felt the past was a weight she didn't want to lift again, especially with that hanging."

Meredith noticed the only mark on the woman's otherwise taunt-skinned face was a scar on one cheek.

"If you know Miss Jones, would you tell her I am trying to honor the man who was hanged, and I can only do it if I know some things about the boy in the picture?"

She handed her a newly printed business card. The woman glanced sideways, abruptly taking the card as she walked up the three front porch steps.

"Honor him?" She stopped at the door and asked with her back to Meredith.

"This sounds, well, silly, but I need to know if the boy was smiling and if his name was Wade Collier. You see, Wade was the father of an architect who is building on the site of the hanging. If it's proven his father was enjoying seeing a man hanged, then it will cause a scandal that could stop the building."

Still facing the door, the woman asked, "What if this young man was crying?"

"That could save the project and might get the architect to honor the man somehow."

There was a pause, and as the woman opened the door, she said. "Nice to meet you, young lady."

And she disappeared behind the closed door.

Meredith's phone song came on as she stood confused and frustrated at the incompleteness of the conversation. "Yes?"

"Miss O'Connor?" It was the voice of the man in the archives she had met. "Yes, this is Meredith."

"You left one of the manila files you came in here with. It had your business card attached, so I'm glad I could reach you."

"I can get too focused on a story and forget everything else. Thank you so much. I'm nearby; I'll run by there in a few minutes."

She didn't know what else to do with this older woman who had become somewhat mysterious. It bothered her that there was no closure here. Was July Jones alive? If so, how did this woman know her? She wanted to go up and knock on the door but thought it best to leave it alone and maybe come back tomorrow.

She left and headed back to the library. Entering the

archive room again at the library, she saw Charlie at his desk, head down over papers he was sorting. He looked up, "That didn't take long."

"I'm glad I left the papers here and had to come back because I wanted to see you again at some point and tell you that the house Miss Jones lived in still stands."

He noted that Meredith's voice was rising with an energy that gave her words a joyful sound.

"That area has been taken over by developers. I hear the houses in there are up over a half-million each. I'm surprised that one is still standing."

"An interesting older woman lives there now. She was in her flower bed when I drove up. She knew Miss Jones but wouldn't say whether she was alive or not."

The archivist thought for a moment then asked, "You say she had a flower garden?"

"Oh, it was beautiful."

"Did you notice anything about her face?" Charlie asked.

Meredith looked away like her answer was floating in the room, waiting to be seen.

"It was thin. Her eyes were large and clear. Her skin was smooth, stretched, I would say, and, oh, yes, a scar—there was a scar on her cheek."

Meredith could barely hear Charlie's subdued laugh. He shook his head. "She lives. Amazing. Let's see, that makes July at least 91 years young."

"I was talking to Miss Jones?" He could hear the astonishment in her voice.

"I suspect you were. I remember that July kept a flower garden that the white folks and Blacks would drive or walk by to admire. And she got a bad cut on her face by Mean Eugene. I never heard the word *nigger* used so many times, so fast, after

July stumbled over one of his liquor bottles lying on the floor. She dropped a pie she was taking to him, and some got on his pants. The story was he got up and hit her with his ring finger, and it tore open her cheek. Made a scar she carried with shame for years and later with pride."

Meredith was uncertain about whether to go back out to the house or to, at least for now, tell Jack that it was his father at the hanging. She knew her editor would reject any of this, so it remained a private pursuit. Meredith also knew Shandra was after the story, so whatever she did, time was becoming critical.

CHAPTER 17

MARY'S PHONE rang as she was handing her car over to a valet. She was having brunch with two of the charities on whose board she sat. She was trying to see if the one, a downtown homeless children's shelter, could have closer connections with one for abused mothers. Their two directors were asking for her guidance as well as funding. Mary's phone rang a lot in recent days as the noise about her husband's project became louder. The endless thirst of the nonprofits had them heading for that oasis known locally as the Collier Fund. Mary managed it. Her husband's architectural profits funded it, giving away a quarter of a million a year. Jack had never been particularly driven by money. The size and grandeur of his overseas projects had spun off some millions. His mother Betty could allocate twenty-five thousand dollars each year to several charities in Athens, one being the Oconee Hill Cemetery, where she had paid for several major improvements. The donation had garnered a plaque in her husband's honor.

The phone call was from Meredith's father. "Hi, Mary, this is Cal O'Connor. I have some bad news and some good news. The bad news is that my three years on the board at Spelman College are up. The good news is you have been nominated to take my place. Congratulations, my dear."

Mary could feel the chill running up her back to her neck. She wanted to giggle like a schoolgirl, to yell out with no restraint, but this was a professional call, so she paused to gain her composure, saying with obvious satisfaction, "I would be honored, Cal."

Spelman College was one of the premier schools for Black women in the country. Mary had donated over $100,000 from the Collier Fund to the school over the past two years.

She had also been a part of their mentoring program. She knew the school's president and other officials, having planning and social lunches with them often.Mary was considered a player in Atlanta's leadership circles in many ways, far more than Jack. His image was more around his theatrical presence and the controversial artistic expressions of his buildings.

Cal said, "There are rumors the High Museum has some plans for you also around the time of the opening of Jack's project. You must know, Mary, you and Jack are very bright lights on the Atlanta scene, internationally, really."

Jack's mother had once told Mary she thought her son should have been born in Paris or London or Athens, Greece, not Athens, Georgia. Mary knew the feeling but also knew the headiness of being a part of the life of a man capable of artistic achievement at such a rare level. And his money fueled her passion for involvement with charities, especially minority ones. Atlantans who moved in their circles saw Mary as the calm in the storm of the marriage—a steady, focused woman who knew how to bridle her husband. At times.

Mary was raised to be a part of the North Atlanta giver class, a group whose world evolves around competitive money-raising parties, auctions, 5K runs, cookouts, and mail-outs. It could at times seem a Disneyland world of galas with crowd-drawing themes of costumes and tuxedos and menu master-pieces. Since many of the same people were invited to the same parties, the competition for their money was fierce, requiring ever-more, evolving, creative themes for the parties. Mary and Jack's names were on almost every list, in part because she found meaning in giving to others, and he found meaning in giving to her.

Jack's phone rang with its operatic song. "Hey, pretty girl," he answered.

Her voice had a teasing quality, "Well, your pretty girl is a blessed girl."

"Because you're married to me?"

"That and I've been invited to be a member of the Board at Spelman. And by Cal O'Connor." Mary felt a true sense of accomplishment, of triumph about even saying these words of acceptance.

"Now that's a real honor. You've hit the top with that one. I'm proud of you, babe."

"And that may not be all. Cal said The High Museum could have an announcement about me to coincide with your opening."

"Good Lord. I may have to get an appointment with you to see if we can meet for supper sometime."

There was a pause, as though they both had to rest from the news that heralded Mary had arrived among the pinnacles of the charity world. Not wanting the spotlight to only be on her, she asked, "So, how was my rising young artist's day?"

His tone changed. "Better than yesterday. I didn't tell you I was practically accused of being a racist out at the property by that reporter, Shandra Berry."

Mary felt she had been punched. Her whole body rocked back, and weakness surged up her legs. "My God, don't say that word, especially in association with us."

Before he could explain, she felt all she had worked toward might suddenly be threatened. She knew well the poison, the toxic effects of even a hint of that accusation, whether true or not. It was more than a word; it was a dagger and could be an assassin's dagger.

"Jack, how can you bring up something like that right now? I wish you would save all your bad news until tonight. Or next week." Mary pressed her finger hard against the off button on her iPhone, feeling hurt that Jack would bring up a word that had no place in her world, a word that was said to describe him. But it also struck a fear in her, which she pushed away. She would savor her good news. Her life was about more than this combustible man she was married to. He was forever in some situation. Mary had told him he led the life of an acrobat who so far had always landed on his feet. But so far, she had advised him, only goes so far.

CHAPTER 18

SUNDAY, June 17, A Mann was up before dawn. The church was so quiet that he thought the silence made its own noise. He opened the back door and moved across the small backyard, through a vacant lot knee-high in grass, then up the sidewalk to the several stores in the Sweet City community. He went to the back of the Sweet City Hardware, a small operation that survived in spite of the Home Depots and Lowes. He knew the owner from when he was a child and living in the area. Mr. Jerry was the only name he knew the owner by, and A Mann knew what Mr. Jerry kept and where he kept it. No alarm went off as he jimmied the back door open, walked to the owner's small office, reached behind his desk, and pulled out a .38 revolver. Checking for bullets, he found the gun loaded with the short, fat ammunition. He then walked through the store's darkness until he found the rope section. Pulling out from its circular storage the thickest he could find, he clipped off a fifteen-foot section and left.

He was back at the church before the soft light from the east started sifting its way through the night's curtain.

Approaching the back of the building, he could see several cars parked in the street in front of the church, with people standing in small groups around them. It sounded like bees were in the front yard. It was 7:30, and he wondered what people were doing in the front of the church at that hour. Going inside, he hid the gun underneath the room's only chest of drawers, just as Pastor Struby trundled by going to the bathroom.

"Mr. Mann, do I hear you in there?"

"Just getting up," was the answer.

"I hear we have folks coming from some of the bigger churches. You've got a real crowd coming today. What's your message gon' be?"

He had no idea what he would speak about. His mind was filled with the spirit he had felt from the tree. It was a longing to give solace to that man's soul that A Mann felt was still trapped in the tree, constantly reliving the ordeal. He thought as he sat on his bed, what it must have been like to be dragged screaming out of jail, the abrasive hemp of the rope blistering his neck, the taunts, the curses, the fists slamming into his face as he was led to the tree, "that tree."

How could he free himself and all of America's hanged Black men? He wondered with a despondency that was almost paralyzing. He thought he might shoot Jack as a sacrifice to redeem the evil done to his kin. That meant the tree would stand, and the insult of some rich man's building would be stopped. He also thought of trying to hang Jack, but that might prove difficult with construction workers starting to come around. Then he thought he might hang himself as symbolic of what white society continued to do to his people. What a statement that would be, he thought. His plans were uncertain, but he was confident that he was being pushed or guided toward some resolution or some redemptive act.

His thoughts were broken minutes later by a thumping sound. Then he heard the pastor's voice telling someone they could not see A Mann as he was preparing for his sermon. There was pleading from a woman that drew closer and then a knock on the door of his little room, partially still a mop and supplies storage area. A Mann opened it to see two women, one about his age and quite lean in her build. The other, a frayed, older woman whose stomach and breasts challenged the flower-print, cotton dress she wore.

With them was a speck of a boy who seemed to A Mann to be eight or nine. His face showed only pain.

Pastor Struby said, "These good people wanted you to lay hands on this child and ask the Lord to bring healing to his body and mind."

A Mann thought they must be crazy. He felt put-upon and asked with some annoyance, "Why would I do that? I'm no doctor."

"We can't afford a doctor. Don't need one when God is the doctor. He works for free. You are like Jesus; you heal with words."

The young mother had a pleading, helpless look as she spoke. The older woman, who he assumed was the younger woman's mother, said with conviction, "You have a line to the Lord. You have the power of his words. We hear Him speak when you open your mouth. This child is troubled of mind, wakes up screaming. Can't hold food down. Can't go to school. He needs to be calmed."

A Mann felt resentment at the request. He felt he was a fake who wanted to take a life, not save one. A college boy playacting. But the more he looked at the child, the more he thought of the many at that age with a mother lost in depression and a little boy adrift in an unstable sea of dysfunctional adults.

With trepidation and embarrassment, he told the women, "I promise you nothing in this life, but...," and he placed his hand on the boy's head, his voice taking on that rumbling, resonant tone when he spoke from the pulpit. He didn't try and do it; the voice just came. "I ask the great healer to calm the waters for this child even for a moment. He has walked mean grounds, not of his choosing. He didn't ask for this pain. Calm the waters, Lord. We ask that you calm the waters."

A Mann said *Lord* because he felt awkward saying the word *God*, in part because he had never thought much about God. To say the name would be to admit he even believed in the God of the Bible, a being of love and compassion. He believed this poverty-ridden part of his race had seen too little evidence of those expressions in their lives.

But he had that impulse again that had, without intending it, risen within him. It was fueled by a rage against the oppressive world he saw around him. When he addressed the church, the emotion became a scream, a demand to whatever power was out there for a break, some help, some freedom. Having his hands on this tiny boy broke some of that insistence, immediately righting wrongs. It gave him a sweep of love that was as strange as it was remote and foreign.

He gently pressed his hand against the boy's head. It felt warm and firm to the child. He then placed his hands on each cheek and pressed slightly. It was a touch of tenderness the boy had never felt from a man. Tears bubbled up and out over his cheek. He impulsively wrapped his arms around A Mann's legs, who felt awkward and confused, but then accepting and relieved that something was happening to both him and the boy. He was this child all over again in the yearning for love and acceptance. He put his arms on the boy's back and pressed him into his legs in an acknowledgment of the boy's need to be affirmed.

"The apostle has calmed the waters, praise the Lord," the older woman cried out and wept along with her daughter. They both moved closer, placing their hands on the tall man they now saw as a messenger of God, a miracle worker like Jesus.

Pastor Struby was both stunned and seized by the belief that something spiritual had happened in front of his eyes. He, too, thought this complex man was a messenger for God, an apostle and disciple with miraculous powers like the original Twelve.

"We have witnessed a healing, a miracle in our little church." His voice was reverential and then with an uncharacteristic exuberance, where he raised both arms and shouted behind and to the women, "We have witnessed a miracle. Thank you, Jesus!"

A Mann wanted to say no. He was none of that. He wanted to run from the church, but the boy squeezed his legs as though letting go would send him adrift again into his troubled home life.

"Little boy," A Mann awkwardly said, "I've got to get ready for my speaking. You're okay now. You can come back and hug my legs anytime you need to."

He gently tried to uncouple the boy's arms from around his legs and lead him toward his mother. The mother was in tears and kept thanking the Lord over and over.

Finally, with Pastor Struby's urging, she pulled her son away, and they walked toward the front of the church. The boy gave a skip and smiled up at his mother, which sent her rushing toward the church's front door and outside yelling, "It was a miracle! He drove the devil out of little Anthony. A Mann is God's man."

A voice came out of the gathering dozens, "Maybe he is God."

There was a gasp throughout the crowd. "Jesus is in the church!" Another spoke out in a quivering voice and then fainted backward.

Although it was only around 7:30 in the morning, and the church service didn't start for two hours, many had come early, driven by social media about the amazing new voice of the Lord coming to Atlanta. With the woman's fervent yell about a miracle, iPhones were pulled out, and friends and relatives were told that the new preacher was performing miracles— bring your pains and brokenness for a healing. Within minutes, cars were screeching to a stop as near to the church as they could park. Wheelchairs, canes, bald cancer patients, shaking people with various brain disorders, all were moving across the small lawn toward the front door, then knocking, then pounding and pleading for a miracle.

The pastor leaned down on one knee as he looked up and said to A Mann. "Father, you have blessed my church with your holy presence."

A Mann glared at the pastor as they heard the commotion outside the front door and now the back door. "Are you calling me Father?"

"You were sent to me in disguise, as a lowly prisoner, just as Jesus came as a carpenter who no one expected." The pastor was quivering in reverence.

A Mann was seized with anxiety. He had to escape. Calling him Jesus and Father was, he thought, madness— people caught in a hysteria of need. His day had started with angry thoughts of the hanged man's death, and now this was spiraling out of his control. It sounded and looked like a mob scene.

"Pastor, go to the front door and tell the people I will see them in thirty minutes. I've got to talk to the Lord. He'll tell me what to do."

"I should call the police and get some control over this. These people sound desperate."

"Do that. I've got to be by myself now."

He pushed the pastor away from his door, and as the stout little man scurried up the aisle, A Mann went to the pastor's office and grabbed the keys of the church's only car. He went to the bathroom at the very back of the church. There he opened the window and climbed out into a thick hedge pressing against the building. No one saw him, with a rope in his hand and the pistol in his pocket, as he got into the church's old Chevrolet and drove out between some cars just arriving and onto a side street.

Pastor Struby cracked open the thick wooden front door and spoke against the buzz of the crowd. "The miracle worker is seeking guidance from the Lord. I'm going to get him now. Just stay calm."

He moved his short legs quickly down the aisle and back to A Mann's room.

"The people are ready for your healing words," he said loudly as he walked.

When there was no response, he peered into A Mann's empty room. This started the pastor's search for the healer and a growing feeling of panic when he couldn't find him. Walking out the backdoor, he was confronted with a jam of people.

"Have you seen A Mann?" he asked above the praying and singing.

"Nobody's come out," someone answered. "But we're ready to come in."

Struby was worried and wondered. *Where in the world could the young man have gone?* He hurried around the small building, searching. A Mann had closed the bathroom window he had crawled out of, so it looked like he had just vanished into thin air.

Desperate for an answer, as the pounding on the doors resumed, Struby decided he would draw on scripture for what might have happened. He decided he would say, like Jesus at Nazareth, A Mann had simply disappeared through the crowds unseen. And then later, after his death, Jesus simply walked through the closed door of the room at the top, miraculously ignoring the laws of nature. Struby restrained his conscience as it reminded him this was not what happened here; there was a reasonable explanation. But it was an answer that would feed the needs of the gathering crowd and build on the reputation that was saving his failing church.

The pastor wanted a way out himself. He wanted to retire with a success that had escaped him after years of kindness and caring for his community, but he couldn't provide the explosive, electrifying effect of this young man. And he couldn't stop the slide toward financial ruin facing the church without him. The pastor would edge and hedge along the truth for the greater needs of himself and the flock now pounding on his door. No one had ever knocked insistently on his door, but now they were.

The pastor pushed the heavy blue door against the pressing bodies and stepped out to see a lawn and street filling with people. He told them the stories of Jesus mysteriously vanishing at Nazareth and miraculously walking through closed doors, and this is what A Mann had done. He had gone to another place, perhaps to be alone and pray for the stricken that had come. He had the power to disappear. Surely this was a man of God, a man of miraculous powers.

When the crowd buzzed with confusion, then with a few notes of anger, the pastor soothed them by saying God worked in his own time. This moment was not the time. The people there had not prepared themselves enough with prayer and asking for forgiveness. That was it. They weren't ready for the miracles that A Mann would perform. God would tell him when the people's hearts were ready.

Struby was amazed that he had mounted such an effective defense. He could see by the quelling of their disappointment and anger that they believed him. He then seized the power he felt he had over the crowd by saying, "A Mann needs your support in another way. He came from prison with few clothes and no money to even buy food. Our little church has gone into its meager funds to help this amazing man. Through your prayers and any other way the Lord moves you, your support will be appreciated by him. And, believe me, with his powers, he will know of your support and touch you personally."

The pastor had been caught in the moment and was using this adoration of an accidental preacher to fill the church coffers. He pushed aside a worrisome thought that he had succumbed to the church's financial needs and was stretching the truth, but then it was true. First Bethel was broke, and the pastor told himself that the Lord had made A Mann disappear for this very reason. If he was lying, the pastor was lying for the Lord.

He thrust out a small basket to a man in a wheelchair. It was a chance Struby took, but if a crippled man would make a donation, the others would be shamed into doing the same. The pastor thought that prayers would not keep the electricity running—it was cold cash, or he would close a bankrupt church and leave his profession in shame. Surely all the years of service he had provided warranted a kindlier end to his career.

The disabled person leaned back to the woman pushing him and ordered, "Let me be the first to give my support to the miracle worker. The poor who had less than we do gave to Christ. Surely we can give to this son of Christ."

The woman, with some reluctance, pulled out two dollars from a bag but then forced a broad grin, held some cash up high for all to see, and forcefully pushed it down into the basket.

Glances of guilt scattered across the crowd as a growing embarrassment seized them. Hands went into pockets for change and into purses for bills as they shuffled forward until the basket was overflowing and the pastor raised his hand.

"I know each of you, and I will give the miracle worker your name." Raising his left arm with hand open, he gave a benediction, "Now go to the quiet of your homes and get right with the Lord. He will bring A Mann back to the earth when you all, all of you, are right in your faith."

He turned and quickly went inside, closing the door as though he was afraid the moment would reveal what he had just done. He sat on the back pew and eagerly counted out $410. He asked forgiveness for the truth he had stretched, the tale he had told, and himself believed. He then hustled to the back of the church and placed the cash in the church's safe.

A Mann remembered the route to Vinings. He felt a sense of great peace as he drove onto the cleared parking area and looked up the hill at the tree. It was 8:30 in the morning, and cool air hung like a hush over the area where Metamorphosis was to be built. The sky was like clear water with a delicate blue, but none of the quietude would hold as the emerging sun, like a caldron tipping over, would singe Atlanta with more ninety-degree heat.

Parking Pastor Struby's Chevrolet, A Mann took the length of rope and the .38 revolver he had stolen and walked through the brush toward the old house and the tree. He would spend the day at the tree, losing himself in its majestic size and what he felt as the spirit of the man. He would fast of both food and water. He would spend the night there on the ground in a ritual that was unfolding to him, and the next morning, Monday, he would hang himself, feeling the terror, the choking gasping for air, then the release to join the murdered man. That world, whatever it held, had to be better than this one.

CHAPTER 19

SHANDRA WOKE up alone on Sunday morning. She had dated through a list of Atlanta's most desirable African American achievers. They were the music and film producers, attorneys, bankers, all living in rarefied atmospheres. Many of the men, attracted to her beauty and local celebrity, found Shandra too intense, too immersed in a Black movement of reprisal and anger that they wanted to take a step away from but still say they were "Down with the Cause." One record producer had told her, "I'm moving toward money, not another movement." They had made a necessary peace with white bias being an ocean of subtleties, but never overt enough to make them feel like victims and being held back. Her circle of Black professionals did give their time and money to minority children organizations. And they mentored through groups like The 100 Black Men. The forlorn and lost young men of the street were a distant shore they had sailed away from through hard work and good fortune.

Shandra was on a personal crusade brought about in part by her feelings of guilt at her news stories of too many young

Black men as criminal predators. But she also saw their plight in part the fault of enduring white oppression, now veiled in liberal homage paid by political correctness and bottomless government fundings. It especially angered her when North Atlantans would bring their children to help the poor by serving food or bringing clothing to homeless shelters for an hour then quickly make a break for Buckhead.

Shandra believed that Jack Collier offered her the chance of a lifetime to show the underlying racism she believed dwelled in the "cream at the top." Shandra was driven in part by the need for personal achievement while feeling she was betraying Atlanta's social injustice movement she quietly worked within. At one point, she had slept for a week in a women's homeless shelter, ostensibly to encourage and mentor the women. Afterward, she realized she was there for redemption from the stories of Black crime she reported. Now she sought peace in trying to know the feeling of being poor and hopeless and desperate. She had wanted to suffer, to flail herself and draw blood and feel the pain of oppression.

So damaged had her psyche become by this confluence of emotions that she needed to leave Atlanta to have her own exodus to a more promising land that didn't know her and would accept the renewed version of herself. The hanging would be her passport while bringing a national light on what she saw as the dark side of even the whites who had given their time and money to Black charities. It was all a sop, she felt—the flavor of the time—the trendy thing to do. And no more.

Looking at her clock, Shandra saw it was 9:00 and thought a visit to Pastor Struby's church might be interesting. She could see the new preacher that had grabbed her attention and possibly, she knew, a growing piece of her heart. When she arrived, the churchyard had several dozen people holding hands in a packed group. Some held their faces up toward the sky, while others bent their heads downward. All seemed to be praying. Shandra walked with some reverence up onto the lawn and asked a solemn man dressed in a dark suit, "Why aren't they in the church. Is it filled already?"

The man who was leaning on crutches just outside the group said, "They're getting right with the Lord so the Savior will come back."

Shandra was confused. "Yes, Jesus will be back some day, but why not go inside and hear the new preacher?"

"Oh, he is the Savior, and he's disappeared. Gone to the Lord to talk, we've been told."

"Wait a minute. A Mann is who you're calling the Savior?"

"Oh, he is that. He performed a miracle earlier and will be back to cure more folks, but we have to first get right with the Lord, one by one."

Shandra impatiently walked around the man and the group and pushed against the church door. It opened to an empty sanctuary. She walked to the front, past a small stage, and heard Pastor Struby talking in a beseeching voice to people at the church's back door.

"You might as well go on home. Maybe next Sunday, he'll be back. I know, I'm sorry too."

The pastor looked around and saw Shandra standing nearby.

"What's going on, Pastor? Shandra asked.

He shrugged, "Gone. Just disappeared into thin air. Nobody saw him go. But the church car is gone. Guess he hot-wired it."

"I'll have to tell you, Paster, I don't like some of the talk I heard outside. You're not pushing this guy as some savior, are you?

"Struby sensed a flash of heat run across his cheeks. He felt like a sudden fraud that had been caught. But he stammered a quick, "Oh no. The people themselves feel he is a man of special gifts."

Does he have a phone?"

They were standing next to the pastor's small office, and Struby glanced in. "He might have one now," he said, seeing an empty space on his desk where the church iPhone normally sat on a battery stand.

"Would you give me the number on that phone? I'll see if I can reach him."

She dialed the number. A Mann was walking up to the tree when the phone rang. He thought it must be from the pastor.

"I want to thank you for what you did for me, Pastor, but I've found my place in this life, and it isn't in this life."

Shandra almost stuttered as she spoke, "This is Shandra. I'm at the church with the pastor. What are you saying?"

He had reached the tree. He hesitated in speaking with her. There was such certitude about his mission; he wanted no discussion. But he had started to feel an attachment to the beautiful reporter. He was attracted to her intensity, her ferocity over "The Wrongs" as he now titled centuries of unrecorded incidents of Black oppression. He paused, not meaning to have her interfere with his emerging plan.

"I now see my purpose. You'll know when I know because I want you to carry my story." And the phone went silent.

Jack's phone vibrated as he sat with Mary at the church known for its "A-Listers," Buckhead Presbyterian Church. Gerald McCoy, the senior minister nicknamed "The Real McCoy," was closing his sermon with a self-deprecating joke about his golf game. His humor was a part of his widespread appeal and how he had made Buckhead Presbyterian the most successful church in Atlanta in fundraising. The Reverend McCoy was a minister to some of Atlanta's most powerful leaders. He had a southern way, people said, that just made him likeable, a quality almost separate from being a minister.

Jack looked down at the text unrolling on his iPhone. 'There's a Black man on the property sitting on a limb in that big oak. Should I call the police?' Jack could see it was from the security man who was now staying in the construction company's trailer at the site.

Jack thought nothing of it, then realized it might be the man who had come out with Shandra. The sullen, very dark-skinned man. Jack assumed he was just being nostalgic. He certainly didn't want any incidents, so texted back, "Leave alone if that's all he does."

Mary elbowed him lightly, whispering, "Is there no place sacred?"

Jack dutifully put the phone back in his coat pocket, but she could see by his face that the text had bothered him.

Shandra stood in the back of Pastor Struby's church, perplexed about where to go with the young man. She had undeniable feelings for him, though their encounters and time together could be counted in minutes. He was now making little sense to her. The church doors were being pushed open, and inquiries made as to when the miracle worker would be back.

Struby apologetically would say, "Hopefully next Sunday."

The pastor concluded that the miracle man was off praying, that he had asked the people to get right with God before he could come back and perform any more miracles.

The whole scene only made Shandra angry. She was sick

of pitiful, and that's what she saw here—people so desperate for hope they would grasp at any answer, regardless, in her opinion, of how false it was. Even Pastor Struby was in on the game. She now saw him as another of the so-called Black leaders making up their own reality.

And making money at it. In Struby's case, he was giving up his truthfulness by making Christ out of this possible criminal no one really knew.

Her drive back to the station was wetted by tears of frustration at the path of her own life and the plight of her race. She arrived at lunchtime, and the Sunday news readers were live on-air. She quietly walked behind the cameras and into a small editing suite. James, one of several editors, was mixing footage of another home invasion in Buckhead. The suspects' photos were already on the screen—three young men of color. The owner of the home that had been invaded stood on the steps of the elegant French chateau. He was being interviewed.

"I don't want to sound like a racist," the elderly homeowner apologized, "but somebody needs to talk about the African American culture. They seem to be committing all the crimes. Don't white people commit crimes anymore?"

The picture of opulence, split-screened with the faces of the suspects, hit Shandra like a bolt. Her body had a rush of anger-driven stiffness, making her face tighten into a glare, her fingers balled up into fists.

"Hey, we can play the blame game too, you damn racist. James, my friend, we have a story to leak that this station won't release."

"And why not," he asked.

"Because they've sold their souls. They are looking at the golden goose of ad dollars with the Collier project."

James had a square face with a close-cropped beard. He

rubbed it with his opened fingers. He spoke in a low tone, not wanting the conversation to leave the small room. "And I'm assuming you want to tell the world about the tree on Collier's property?"

Shandra felt her conscience, her professionalism, was trying to block what she wanted to say. She had no confirmation that Wade Collier was happy as a child to see a Black man murdered. But her life, she felt, was at a crossroads, and fate was not helping, so she concluded that she would either spend her career as the recorder of Atlanta's mean streets or make herself a national name.

"James, I want you to put together two minutes worth of my encounter with Jack Collier at that tree. And include the footage of a Mann standing close to it. I want to put it up on the internet."

"The station will fire you in a second and me too. I would love to knock that guy down, but I've got bills to pay."

Shandra was sick of money as a weapon against courage. It was the curtain behind which too many of her friends hid. But the potential for a national story was too great here. She thought, as they talked, there would never be a more powerful tool for her than Metamorphosis. James watched her facial expression relax away from its tightness into a hint of a smile. "It's destiny, my brother, that this building, or whatever it is, has such an ironical name. Its meaning of transition is exactly what the freedom from oppression movement is about."

"How's that?" he asked.

"After all these years, we're still trying to get the mind of the white to transition out of looking at us as inferior and unequal to them."

"I did finish editing the Jack interview. It was ninety seconds and needs to include the results of what you found about Wade's father. Right now, it's too inconclusive for management to put it out. Tell me, what do you want Jack to do?"

"Admit an insult to humanity occurred on his land. Admit his father was at a hanging. Admit he knows of the horror of that hanging and is trying to erase its memory rather than be known as a closet racist."

James shifted in his chair. The room was partially lit so the various screens and console boards with their lights could be seen more clearly. "You're in fantasyland. This man and all the money behind him aren't going to roll over and admit anything. And what if his father was a child racist? What's that got to do with him?"

"Okay, you could argue, 'nothing,' but it's the opportunity his property gives us. The movement needs the spotlight sometimes in whatever way it can get it. The publicity is going to be worldwide. His father's behavior and Jack's guilt by not admitting that brutality occurred on his land can be that door opener that lets us in."

"I've done the marching thing, Shandra. It was a rite of passage fifteen years ago. I yelled at whatever it was we were yelling at until I was hoarse, chained myself to a cop car, maybe threw a rock or two. We've stuffed overt racism under the covers, and I can live with it staying just out of sight. And that means just out of mind. I'm through enslaving myself in victimhood."

Shandra could see him slipping away from her need to use this moment of blinding attention to focus on the evil she saw barely hidden in the shadows of American life.

"James, we can't let go of the fight. You've got a job, a paycheck. Those men we photograph on the street—they have no future. We can't leave them behind, or we have no cause other than ourselves."

"A lot of those guys are just plain criminals. It's their culture. I can tell you this station wants no part of a civil rights story built around that project. You need to move on."

Shandra had heard this loss of passion at many of her friend's cocktail parties. Yes, they all agreed white feelings of superiority were alive and well, but "some of their best friends" were whites, and at work, many of their peers were lunch partners, baby shower invitees, and all of the other relationships of life. It was a vague world, undefined in many ways as to where exactly to stand. But Shandra was adamant in what she saw as unremitting, sometimes subtle, sometimes blatant, oppression.

She looked at the screen on which James had been editing.

"What do you have there?"

"I put together some footage of the interview you had with Jack. Once you're satisfied you've got Jack pinned as a racist, it will be easy to insert those few sentences together, and we're ready for a newscast."

A young woman stuck her head into the suite and told James he was needed in the main editing room.

"You need more than a grinning kid to get this on-air, babe."

Then he was out of the door, leaving Shandra looking at a freeze-frame on the screen with Jack's face large and in focus. In the background was the tree with A Mann leaning against it. She thought how easy it would be to take the footage and put it on the internet. It would cause the explosion she wanted, but it might end her career.

The reporter was stymied by her station and her sense of journalistic integrity or was it greed, not to mention having her career destroyed if Jack's investors came after her. But in a tease against herself, Shandra made preparations to put the footage up on social media. She ran her finger almost seductively across the button that would send it up, and her phone buzzed. To her surprise, a live video was streaming over FaceTime, and it was A Mann in a selfie that showed his face with what looked like a rope around his neck. He panned around, and she could see he was sitting on a tree limb. A sweep of his arm revealed the house on Jack's property.

"What on earth are you doing?!" she yelled into the phone.

He had a serene look on his face. The anger or sullenness she had only known from him was gone. She was touched by how relaxed he appeared.

"I'm joining the 4,000. I've found my purpose, and this will fulfill it."

"What 4,000? Don't do anything until I get out there. I want to hear what this purpose is. Now just relax. I'll be there in a few minutes."

She thought this event gave her permission of sorts to go ahead and release her interview to the world. She would deny she had done it; maybe James had hit it by mistake, who knows? But she needed cover, so she called in a station intern who was just a college girl and an assistant editor, both minority staffers. When they entered the small room, Shandra said, somewhat nonchalantly.

"Just want your thoughts on this footage we got. You think we need to add any more to it before airing?"

Both were somewhat intimidated by Shandra's reputation as one of Atlanta's top reporters and uncertain of what she might want them to say.

The intern saw the footage and seemed disturbed by it.

"I'm shocked by this. This man is trying to hide a murder. Yeah, it was years ago, but his father laughing at a hanging?"

The editor, a thick-shouldered young man with obvious energy about him, said with emphasis, "I would say the son is trying to cover up an obscene act by his father, and that's its own form of racism."

Shandra felt verification in how she viewed Jack. She wanted company in what had emerged for her as a cause against the modern subtleties of white oppression.

"I agree. Can you believe this guy is denying a photograph of his father and about to destroy the evidence of how he enjoyed watching a murder? At some point, I'm going to put it up on the web and show the world what kind of man they are about to give millions to."

"Well, why don't you upload it right now?" the young woman asked.

"I'm so close to confirming a last-minute fact that I could, and it would probably be within our factual guidelines, but you know me, I want to cross all the t's."

She was lying and pushing and opening the door for one of them to move the mouse and put the arrow in a place that would upload the ninety seconds into eternity.

With a sudden hurriedness, Shandra said, "Anyway, I've got to run to a big lead I've got on this story. Thanks so much for your opinions."

Shandra ran out of the room, across the studio floor, and into the main editing suite, where she grabbed Reuben, her cameraman, by the arm and pulled him out the door.

"Get your camera right now. All that we wanted is about to happen."

"What the hell are you talking about?" he asked.

"The young preacher is threatening to hang himself on

Jack's property. He just called me. We've got to stop him after we've got some footage."

Confused but moved by Shandra's insistence, Reuben went to get his shoulder camera and microphone.

The intern saw Shandra practically run toward the station's front door. He looked at the assistant, and they both put their hand on the mouse and, without a word, pressed it, and the interview was uploaded to the world in a decidedly raw form.

After the church service, Reverend Gerald McCoy invited Jack and Mary to a light lunch of shrimp salad in his expansive office. Anytime he issued a lunch invitation, parishioners with means knew it was not as much about taking his food as it was about the reverend taking your money. He was a man with a generous laugh, a thick-bodied former college wrestler from the University of North Carolina. Gerald had always said he could have been governor, but the Lord had other plans for his life.

"Jack, we've had several lunches in your office, and I'm always intrigued by your da Vinci drawing of the perfect man. That's what I'm selling, you know, the only perfect man who ever lived."

Jack nodded as he paused before his mouth with a large shrimp forked and red with sauce. " Perfect is an interesting word. My mother says it's a chase that has no end."

"Well, I know you're trying to achieve a memorable design with this building. Our church is so proud of what you're doing with a lot of support from Mary."

Jack knew what was coming next. Gerald put his fork

down, clasped his hands with a prayerful firmness, and leaned forward. "I'm trying to make this church a more perfect place myself. I'm hoping the two of you will bring your talents to help me in this effort. I want to get a contemporary church service built, and I can see the name on one of the doors." He gazed up as though he were looking at a sign.

"Jack And Mary Collier Youth Center. Wouldn't that be great?" His lips almost smacked as though he had just had a taste of something delicious. He often ended sentences where he was seeking agreement with "Wouldn't that be great?"

Jack had a love for the minister, but he knew staying too close to him could get your time and wallet burned. "Sounds interesting, Gerald. Let's get my project up and running; then, I'll have more time to hear about your dreams."

"The dream team. I love it. I'll put together a group. Maybe you or Mary can chair it."

Jack's phone played its operatic notification that someone was calling. "Oops, thought I had turned it off." He glanced down and quickly read a text. "The grand opening for your property is about to take place. See it on the evening news, Shandra."

Trying not to look as though the text had his heart racing, Jack told Gerald that he must be tired from preaching all three morning services, and they were honored he had invited them to his lunch.

"No, Jack, it sounds like you are the one that's about to be honored across the world. God has blessed you with special gifts. One is visionary. I'll be calling on you to head up an important committee on the church's future."

Jack knew every strategy this expert fundraiser used, and he knew Gerald had focused on him and the money and attention Jack was expected to receive. Jack drew a deep breath, a weary sigh, and said, "Better give me some time on that one. I've got a dream to get off the ground."

When they were in the hall, Mary said, "We've got to buckle up, love. We're at the top of everyone's call list now. Got to keep our heads in a calm place."

Jack had an annoyed, impatient look on his face. "I got a call from security about the property. I'll drop you at the house and run out there. Just some guy wandering around. No big deal."

Shandra's phone lit up as she drove toward Jack's property. It was the Associated Press asking what was this story on the internet about a hanging at the Metamorphosis site?

"What? What do you mean?" She knew, and she smiled and nodded her head in agreement. One of the young staffers had become so incensed they must have uploaded the footage.

The reporter continued, "It is you interviewing Jack Collier next to a tree where you seem to think his father watched a man being hanged and laughed about it."

"I didn't release that. I'm still working it; in fact, I'm on the way to put the final touches on it. Check our evening news. There will be more to this."

Reuben's phone rang at the same time. It was the station manager, Floyd Akers, yelling into the phone. "What the hell is the footage about Jack doing uploaded?! I told you this was a dead-ass story, and your ass is dead at this station!"

"Wait a minute, Floyd. I didn't upload anything. I don't know what you're talking about."

There was a pause, then, "The footage you shot at Jack's project. The stuff Shandra wants to put on the air, and we said no way. Now somebody put it out on social media, and all hell is breaking loose from the mayor's office to the Chamber and news organizations everywhere." The man's voice ended with a high-pitched, "Where the hell is Shandra, and where are you?!"

Reuben put the phone on speaker. "She's driving us out to Jack's property. She seems to think something is about to happen out there."

Floyd demanded. "Put her on the phone!"

Shandra shook her head. She knew it was pointless to debate the story. She had freed herself of the rule of her bosses. She was going for broke on the story. She whispered to Reuben that she didn't upload the story.

"She said she'd call you from the site, and she didn't upload the story."

Floyd's voice yelled into the car, "Tell her she is fired! She no longer works for the station and to bring our car back!"

Reuben cut the phone off. He knew his career might be shot along with hers.

"You heard that. Let's get back to the station and see if I can salvage my job. Who the hell put the story up if it wasn't you?"

Shandra had accelerated the car up Paces Ferry Road. It was Sunday, so quiet with little traffic. She now wanted to get to the site before James forcefully made her turn around.

"I showed it to the intern and Maggie Lacy. They must have done it after I left. The story wasn't ready, so you know I didn't do it."

Reuben turned toward her and said firmly, "I mean it, Shandra. This white injustice obsession you've got has now put my job on the line."

She cut sharply into the cleared area at the base of the project. There was a man standing outside the construction trailer looking up the hill at a figure sitting high on a tree limb.

Shandra pointed to her right and said, "Forget our station. You're about to shoot gold for the networks."

Looking out his window, he could see the figure in the tree. "Is that what's his name?" Shandra was out of the car, motioning for him to follow. She walked some feet away from the man on the steps, who asked her who they were and told her this was private property.

"We're here to talk that man out of the tree. I know him." And they were off through the bramble that remained at the base of the hill.

The security man redialed Jack's phone. Getting no answer, he left a voicemail.

"Mr. Collier looks like some reporters are here. Say they know the man in the tree." Then the man shouted not so much on the phone but as if himself. "My God, he's got a rope around his neck, and he's tied the other end to a limb above him. I'm calling 911. We need some cops out here fast."

Jack had dropped Mary off at their house. His phone was constantly vibrating, which she could hear.

"What is all of that about on a Sunday?" she asked.

And then, as Jack pulled up into their driveway, her phone lit up. "And now mine. Don't know if I can handle being married to such a famous man," she kidded and kissed him on the cheek before getting out of the car.

Jack sat for a second as she walked into the house. The messages were from his three best friends, and it looked like his biggest lender. Then there was the security guard's terrifying yell from the site, yelling about a man with a rope. *So that was the grand opening that Shandra had texted him about,* he thought, as his car screeched out on Tuxedo Drive and raced for Vinings. He thought he would at least call Frazier to see why all three of them were calling.

"Hey, buddy, what's up? Got a call from...."

Frazier cut him off. "Our butts are in a bind, my friend. I can't believe that reporter put your interview on the internet. My phone won't stop ringing from clients who've put up money."

Jack was shocked. "What do you mean on the internet?"

"You haven't seen it? Yeah, that attack dog Shandra put her interview about the hanging online, and I've got major clients in a panic that you are being called a racist could somehow tank the project."

Jack's car slid to a dust-clouded stop in the cleared space of the site. The guard walked swiftly over. "Sorry, Mr. Collier, but I had to call the police. My boss said I should."

"Of course," was all Jack could say as he jogged toward the tree. He could see A Mann clearly had a rope around his neck. Jack emerged from the brush to find Shandra and Reuben— recording the scene. Reuben then suddenly turned the camera on Jack, who forcefully pushed the camera away and stood underneath the tree. A Mann was high up, and if he stepped off the limb, his body would not stop low enough to be held up by a rescuer.

Jack ignored Shandra's burst of questions. He spoke loudly but with some compassion to A Mann, "I'm going to come up and let's talk about this. I want to hear how I can help you."

He started to find a foothold in the rough bark and a shot rang out from above, hitting the ground next to Jack. He was shocked that A Mann had a gun, and he ducked around the tree out of sight.

Shandra yelled up. "A Mann, don't make this worse than it is. Why did you shoot at Mr. Collier?"

"Nobody comes up this tree. It is a sacred place that no

white man is going to desecrate. Now have him come out and stand so I can see him."

Shandra looked at Jack, whose back was pressed against the trunk. Feeling emboldened for a reason he couldn't explain, Jack stepped out into the patch of ground between the house and the tree, clearly visible to A Mann.

"Tell me how I can help you." Jack didn't know what the purpose of this man was, but he didn't think it was to kill him.

Shandra swallowed and tried to appear controlled. She nodded at her cameraman and stepped out so he could get a video of her with A Mann in view above her. "I've got you on camera. You can relax and tell us what point you are making."

He looked down at them. "This rope is the flag of my race. I've come here to honor the 4,000 who were hanged. I'm here to raise the flag and show the world how my people are being hanged every day, not by ropes, but by control, by hatred, by robbing us of our dignity."

And suddenly, three police cars and a fire truck moved quickly onto the site, with the police rushing out of their cars, their hands on their guns. They could easily see the man sitting in the tree, but they saw no weapon—he had it in his lap. Jack had moved up on the porch and could also be seen staring up at the tree. One of the officers yelled, "What's going on? Is anybody in danger?"

Jack shouted back down the hill to them. "Nobody is hurt. We're just listening to this man. We're hoping then he'll come down."

"Oh, I'm coming down alright, and it will be a statement about how whites continue to kill my race just as they murdered the 4,000. The slights we always see, the rejection for a job, the cop quick to kill—these are the new ropes. But I want the world to know what it's like to see a real hanging like your father watched, Mr. Collier. Maybe you'll smile as my neck is broken."

Shandra yelled up, "It's a waste. There is a better way to tell the world your story. Use this as a loud trumpet to send the message of oppression. Don't give them another victory. You've got Jack's attention! Tell him how his project could be dedicated to those 4,000, how he can save this tree as a symbol of white hatred and Black hope. Tell him now."

Jack's phone was now in an endless ring. He saw Mary's name, his partners, investors, all were clamoring for attention. He felt naked in front of the stare of the camera. He saw disaster in what was unfolding here. He could see crowds from the neighborhood gathering and two television trucks rolling onto what had become the parking area below. He recognized several local media personalities running toward the tree, though police tried to hold them back. Only Shandra and the cameraman stood at the base of the tree, with Jack just feet away.

A policeman walked slowly toward the tree and, looking up at the figure on the limb, calmly said, "My name is Mike Terry. Could you tell me yours?"

A Mann pointed the gun down at him and said, "Get the hell away from the tree. I'm not playing mind games with cops."

The policeman was a negotiator and calmly backed away a few steps. "Of course, I just wanted to see how we can talk through this."

"Talk? You want to shoot me, don't you? Another sass-mouth Black boy you want to take a pop at. Well, this field nigger has had it with cops, had it with white hate."

Looking down at Shandra, he said, "I'll give you a picture,

Miss Shandra, that you can show to the world that tells the story of my race."

He slid closer to the edge of the limb, and they all put up their hands as though the opened palms and outstretched fingers would stop him. Almost in unison, they all yelled, "No!"

A fireman, a muscular man, had sneaked behind the tree and was slowly climbing up the opposite side. His foot slipped on bark, and A Mann turned to see what the noise was, and as he turned, he fell off the limb. Jack could hear his neck pop. He seemed dead in an instant as his body was calm at the end of the rope.

There were screams from the crowd in the parking lot. The television reporters pressed through the police, who were running toward the tree. Shandra cried out, "He's hanged himself."

Jack moved instinctively and began frantically reaching for limbs and outgrowth on the tree that he could grasp, pulling his body upward. The fireman worked his way around the trunk, and with a large knife he had in his hands, he started cutting the taut rope.

Jack had climbed alongside the slumped body and grabbed A Mann around the waist, holding him as best he could until another fireman climbed up and took over the figure's body. Medics and police all hurried to the tree, and A Mann was soon on the ground.

One of the blue-coated medics put his fingers on the reddened throat and announced, "He's got a pulse" He then looked at Jack's disheveled figure and said quietly, "You've pulled him back from eternity."

A Mann's open mouth pushed out a loud breath as an unmistakable flutter moved his eyelid.

Jack's white shirt was twisted and wet with smudges of bark streaked over the fine threading. Several buttons had been sheared off. He stood stunned for a moment, then walked with uncertainty toward the house where he sat dazed on the steps.

Shandra wasted no time walking to him with a microphone in her hand. This was her moment, the culmination of her career, the bridge to a new universe of fame and respect.

Reuben had the heavy camera saddled over his shoulder and captured the scene of Jack with his head down as he sat. Then Shandra walked into the frame with a serious look. She stood almost next to him. "Mr. Collier, what have we witnessed here?"

Jack barely heard her voice, and then it came to him that she was there and with a camera. Without a word to her, he walked over to the fire truck and watched as A Mann was placed on a gurney. Jack asked one of the firemen if the still figure was still breathing. "Wheezing, but because you moved so quickly, he may be okay. Gotta have a broken neck after that fall."

Shandra had followed him. "A Mann said there was a Black man hanged in this tree, and he felt it is sacred ground that you're desecrating by cutting it down for a building. What's your reaction to that?"

Jack knew he could avoid her no longer. Other reporters had now rushed around him, flaring lights from their cameras. Their microphones jutted out like plump knives at his face, with their questions now unfurling in a cacophonous blare of words overlaying and obscuring meaning.

"First of all, this isn't about my reaction, but a man's life. I think we have avoided a tragedy here. I'm praying he will survive."

Shandra was momentarily stopped by the tenderness of his

response. She wanted the civil rights angle. A story of compassion undercut her agenda of oppression.

"But he was in that tree because your father laughed at a man being hanged here. He called this sacred ground that you want to destroy for a building." Shandra could feel the surge of power this moment gave her. Her opinions, her hatred, and her belief in the continuing subjugation of her race were a singular driving focus that left the other reporters suddenly mute.

The ambulance with A Mann inside ran through and over the bushes and undergrowth surrounding the house in a scraping noise. Its siren shrilled in the languid air, causing all of those to momentarily jerk their head away as though an inch or two would diminish the sound. Then it was gone out onto the highway.

Two policemen and a tall, plain-clothed man with an angular face approached the reporters. "I'm Detective Price. We need to talk to Mr. Collier. You'll have to hold your questions." It was said with authority as he brushed through the cameras and up to Jack.

But the reporters kept shouting, and Shandra stood her ground.

"Let's step inside this house," the man said with clarity and put his hand on Jack's soaked shirt, directing him toward the porch and the dark interior that seemed as though it would provide some privacy.

"Wait a minute. I've got to answer these accusations," Jack protested.

But the man was adamant. "Sir, we've had a man hang himself on your property as he was accusing you of something. We need to get this cleared up. Then you can talk to the press."

Jack was stunned and furious over Shandra's assertions

about his father but was moved away before he could say any more. Through the lens of the cameras, Jack was seen being escorted by the police up the three steps of the old house and inside.

"Shandra, you seemed to know this guy. Who is he?" a narrow woman in a light cotton pantsuit asked.

"What's this about Jack Collier's father at a hanging? You're on the internet today, questioning Jack about hiding a murder." A man in a cotton Polo shirt with Associated Press stitched on it had elbowed his way close to her.

Shandra was exhilarated but holding on to some control. She was determined to look professional and hide the thrill of this unexpected dream-making moment and not sound as giddy as she felt. She knew her side of this story would be the authoritative one picked and quoted by the national press. This was, in effect, her interview for a major market job, but it was also her expression of a set hatred for the lingering injustices she saw from all whites.

Obfuscating ruled the landscape to Shandra, especially by the likes of the Colliers. They were known for giving substantial money and time to minority charities, but she felt they were masking their feelings of guilt by their patronizing, feel-good check writing.

"I've been working this story for some time after receiving a tip from a reliable source that Jack's father was part of a mob that broke a Black man out from the Marietta jail. Now his father was very young at the time but still seemed to be laughing as he watched the man being murdered."

"And how do you tie Mr. Collier into, what, a sixty, seventy-year-old story?" a reporter asked.

"My research shows the hanging was probably in this tree, and when I told Jack, he said he was going to cut it down. It was in the way of his great building. He also said his father never was in Marietta as a boy. I have proven that to be a lie."

The AP man asked, "And who was this man that tried to hang himself?".

"I understand he must have led a tragic life but has recently turned it around and become an electrifying preacher. It seems he saw hanging himself as a symbol of all that Blacks continue to suffer through. They are hanged every day, he is saying, in a thousand different ways."

"Why did you release the story on social media before you confirmed your accusation about Jack's father?"

It was Meredith's voice, and it caught Shandra by surprise. She acted like she didn't know the blond in a tan dress. "I'm glad you asked that. I didn't release it. That was a working draft that someone at the station must have accidentally uploaded."

"Then are you admitting now that you don't know what state of mind Jack's father may have been in, and you don't know for certain if a man was hanged in this tree on Jack's property?"

The scrum of reporters went suddenly silent as though asking themselves if all of this was a fabricated story by a reporter with an agenda?

Shandra was seized with the fear that she had been caught because there was not yet full confirmation. In a pause, she considered that her cause of exposing white suppression had perhaps pushed her too far. But she couldn't relent. It would ruin all she had within her grasp. She tried to change the subject by showing bravado in her response and turning Meredith's questions into a racial attack.

"Oh, so you're saying this unbelievable act of courage, this sacrifice of a life to save the future of others, is meaningless because a 'T' wasn't crossed somewhere. I'll stake my reputation on the painstaking research I did in digging into this story." She looked at the surrounding reporters and said with authority drawing the attention away from Meredith.

"Now, let's talk about the man we have just witnessed, who would give his life to save his people." She then spun an off-the-cuff story of A Mann, which held him up as a mysterious figure who appeared out of nowhere. Stating that he had recently broken free from his life to electrify hundreds with his powerful words, perhaps even miracles—what a magnificent martyr he was willing to be for his race.

The reporters became rapt in their attention to her story and saw headlines and ratings and readers, in this man of mystery, maybe even a romantic tale, and the potential ruin of Jack. It was taking on the guise of a Greek tragedy, a Shakespearian account of power humbled. It was news at its most delicious. And it had legs.

Inside the house, the detective stood in the dull light with Jack. A police officer stood with him, turning his eyes around the room as though there was danger in the softness. The detective said, "I'm Jared Holley with the Cobb County police. Could you tell me what just happened here?"

Jack was still trying to calm himself. His mind was playing over his climb up the tree and the incessant attacks by Shandra. His phone had not stopped vibrating since he arrived. He knew his world of friends was shocked and curious, but he was trying to assess in his mind what had just happened before calling anyone back.

He answered the detective, "The man came out the other day with this so-called reporter named Berry. She is a community activist with a television camera who is trying to create a story where there is none. She got the idea that my father witnessed a hanging at the tree when he was a little boy. She's trying to tie my father, when he was eight years old, into this project, now seventy years later. It's crazy."

The detective seemed as puzzled as Jack. "So, you have no connection with the man other than he came out once with the reporter?"

Jack nodded in agreement. "That's right. I have no idea who he is."

The police officer said, "Sounds like we need to talk to the reporter before we go to the hospital and talk to that guy."

"OK, Mr. Collier. We'll be back in touch if need be. Looks like you and that fireman saved the man's life."

The officer paused then said, "By the way, Mr. Collier, mind if I call about any extra security work you'll need on the project? All the officers are talking about it."

Jack couldn't believe the officer would ask for a job after what had just happened, but he had always stayed supportive, maybe cozy, with police.

He responded with some marshaled cheer, "We'll need a lot of security. I always enjoy working with our police."

They walked out on the porch to see Shandra getting into her car, still trailed by camera crews from other stations. The officer said, "Well, we know how Shandra loves the camera. I wouldn't be surprised if she didn't cook this whole thing up. Let's go to the hospital and see if the man is conscious."

"Bet he's got a sore neck," the policeman said with a noticeable smirk as they stepped off the porch. Jack stood speechless, still bruised from the hurricane that had just blown through his life.

CHAPTER 20

MEREDITH HAD WAITED beside the tree, hoping to see Jack when he came out of the house. Her mind was wracked with anger toward Shandra's unfounded accusations, her impulse to get the complete story to her editor, and this maddening feeling for Jack, who had saved the life of a man who was damning him.

The whole affair was schooling to Meredith. She couldn't believe a reporter of Shandra's stature was designing a story to fit a narrative. Truthfulness appeared to have no gravity. She knew Shandra had no idea that July, a witness at the time of the hanging, even existed. Even more disappointing to Meredith was how the press had accepted Shandra's story and were rushing to get it out on their evening news and online versions of their newspapers. She saw a dejected-looking Jack walk out on the porch. He was on the phone, and she felt like a schoolgirl stepping back to one side of the tree, contemplating if she should hide behind it. She impulsively put a hand on her chest, as it felt like it was skipping beats, and she drew in a deep breath.

Jack saw her and motioned for her to come up to the porch. The area had cleared. The reporters and Shandra had gone to file and edit their stories and then go to the hospital to check on A Mann. It was like they had forgotten that Jack had gone inside the house to be interviewed. Shandra had the official story of injustice by a racist, hiding behind his philanthropy. They had their footage, and the police and fireman had gone to the next 911 call. A big man was about to fall, and the blood of the press ran fast.

There was a quietness in the yard, like the aftermath of a battle, where the field had been cleared of the dead and wounded, and only souls now hung reminiscing in the air. She walked over to the steps looking shyly up at Jack, his bark-scraped, rumpled, sweaty shirt, his dark cotton pants torn at one knee and his hair tousled, some strands stuck to his forehead. But then he stood, legs slightly apart, hands on his hips in defiance and a strength of manhood that left her drawn irresistibly toward him.

"Have you come to praise Caesar or to bury him also?" He was trying to bring some levity to the moment, uncertain of why she had lingered while everyone had gone. She stood in all of her youthful radiance, sun-glistened—a picture of perfection, a fantasy he would bring into the darkened room behind him in a breath. But for all of her sexual and romantic appeal, he had to be wary of any member of the press fraternity, even her. She had, after all, been the first to bring up race with her pronouncement that slaves had been beaten in this house.

What had happened here this afternoon was too serious to be ignored by some play-like romance. Jack sat wearily on the steps, stretching his legs in front, and leaning back with his elbows on the porch.

"I was surprised, no, disappointed, at our profession in the way Shandra has created a false story, and the press bought into it," Meredith said.

"What do you mean?" Jack sat up straight.

"Shandra did confirm at the Marietta archives that your father was the child in the photograph at the hanging. But she got angry with the archivist, who was actually there when your father returned from the hanging. Because Shandra got mad, she left without finding out the real truth."

Jack's lips had parted in wonderment at how she appeared like a vision of purity against the brutality of the day. "And what was the real truth?"

"Your dad was visiting his uncle who took him to the hanging. The uncle had a maid named July, who saw what happened after the hanging and said your father was hysterical with fear."

"Surely she's not still alive. Do you think?"

Meredith said, "Oh, I'm pretty sure she's alive, and I've found her. I'll know for certain tomorrow."

"Well, that could show Shandra's accusation to be based on a lie. I feel like I'm in the theatre of the absurd. What my father was doing at eight years old has nothing to do with me and this project. But all of a sudden, it does, and whether or not a child was smiling could bring this whole world down." He shook his head, then smiled with a corner of his mouth at the flimsiness of life's dreams.

Jack stood and came close to Meredith. She looked away for a second to gain composure, and then he put his hand on her arm, and the waves quickened. Her heart became a movement of waves cresting, then cresting higher again, which caught her breath as she tried not to show in her face how his mere presence quickened the forces of her body.

"What I've come to admire so much about you is that

you're true to yourself and your profession. You're after the ideal just like I am. We chase after the perfect."

She thought his words poetic, rubbing her gently, not seductively, but repairing and comforting in their own way. She wanted to cry out that he was breaking her will to stay true to being the unfettered explorer, the unbiased, incorruptible seeker of the actual. She wanted now to protect him from hurt as much as she wanted to protect her profession from the swiftness of judgment that she witnessed with Shandra and how lies took wing like a kite losing its string, flying on its own whims, but tied to nothing else.

"I'm learning that speed is the enemy of seeking the ideal. Getting the jump on the other station, the other online news is imperative now. But Shandra is after more. She's got a civil rights agenda, and I think she sees the glare from this project as a platform from which to shout it."

Jack was impressed with her analysis, but he knew he was being outraced in getting his story out, and he had to have a plan quickly. He still had not seen the online release of Shandra's first interview with him, but with one glance at his iPhone, he could see the chorus of concerned friends and investors who bore witness.

"Meredith, if you would pursue this person, it might bring some truth to the slander from Shandra, not to mention that it would make a great story for you." He removed his hand from her arm. He hated his rashness in even toying with a romantic fling as he witnessed all hell breaking loose in his larger world.

Meredith also seemed to regain her composure and said briskly, "We'll see where my research takes the story. I know you have calls to make. I want to find where the facts are here."

She turned and walked back toward her car. Her face was damp, as were the palms of her hands. Witnessing a hanging, the confrontation with Shandra, and just the presence of Jack, had Meredith feeling dampened by perspiring and almost exhausted. This was turning into a story of many moving parts. Meredith wanted to concentrate on the hanging photo since it now was the centerpiece of Shandra's assertion that Jack was a hidden racist, symbolic of all whites. She cared little for getting into a civil rights war of words, but she had been intrigued about this ground from her first visit. Meredith realized that she was trying to come to grips with a story of Atlanta's past. Her conscience was driving her as much as the trail of a very hot story.

Jack followed her slowly back to the parking area. Then he called Mary. Her voice had a sick sound, full of hurt, confusion, and disbelief.

"My God, Jack, what is going on?"

He tried to be calm, but her voice almost pushed him to tears. He said, "I live in reason; I'm not very good at insanity, and that's what all of this is. This reporter is on a racial injustice tear. She's trying to use the attention Metamorphosis is getting to push her blame for her race's problems through me to all white people. I just happened to have created a big megaphone for her."

Mary's voice was filled with tears. "I just want you to come home. I need you home right now."

CHAPTER 21

MEREDITH LEFT the Vinings property anxious to confront the elderly woman in the blue house to determine the truth about Jack's father at the hanging. She parked on Marietta Street in front of the little house. She had never had qualms about approaching someone about an interview and was usually in an aggressive frame of mind. But as Meredith stepped up on the porch, she found herself timid and apologetic, feeling like she was intrusive. July had been so frail but still intimidating in the prideful, untouchable way she had carried herself. She was not of this time but a vestige of a distant era to a twenty-three-year-old.

After several knocks, the front door opened, and July stood with a blue striped apron over a cotton dress of blue background and spotted with tiny flower prints.

"Miss July, I'm sorry for disturbing you," Meredith said her name without thinking she was ignoring that the woman had not told her who she was.

July's face had a stern, appraising stare. "Why do you call me by that name?"

"The gentleman that works at the library lived next door to Wade's uncle and was there when Wade was brought back from the hanging. He saw the uncle hit little Wade, and he saw how Wade was clutching your apron for protection."

Meredith caught a brief look of pain that passed like a shadow over the woman's face then vanished. "The gentleman also told me that the uncle had hit you with his ring finger, and it had...."

"No more, no more." The woman interrupted Meredith as though the words were still too painful to hear. Her face had twisted to one side, and her thin hand went to the scar. She started to close the door, and Meredith's body leaned toward the woman in urgency.

"Miss July, a story is all over the media about that little boy Wade, who ran to you for safety. The story says he was a racist and was laughing at the hanging. You know the truth. Is that what happened?"

July stopped closing the door in a long pause, then asked, "Would you help me water my flowers?"

With a youthful eagerness, Meredith almost blurted out, "Oh, yes. I would be honored."

She stepped aside as July came out on the small porch and walked to the garden to the side of her house, now a palate of perennials and annuals. She stood in her smallness, very straight, which made her look taller, and had her head almost tilting backward in a prideful way. It was a smooth walk that belied her years. July picked up a metal watering can. "You can fill this over at the spigot."

Meredith dutifully filled the can and could feel its heaviness as she walked into the fecundity of the plants.

"These yellow ones are verbena. They last much of the

summer. These are phlox of different kinds, and my knock-out roses over here will keep blooming."

July thought for a moment as Meredith started watering through the many holes of the spout.

"I like plants that hold their purpose, not ones that show off for a few weeks then do little but take up space."

"Sounds like a philosophy for life," Meredith observed as she poured.

"Could be," July said. "But living this long, it's hard to hold your bloom and to find a purpose other than to take up space."

Meredith slipped out of her low-heeled yellow shoes and felt the dirt still holding onto its late morning coolness. "Miss July…"

"Child, you don't have to call me 'Miss.' I can see you are a child of the south whose mama and daddy were rooted in its customs."

Meredith shyly nodded. "I am that child, but I'm not sure what being called, or being a child of the south, means today. But I'll take it as a compliment. I would argue the saying that you can't go home again would be more accurate if it said you can't ever leave home."

July felt comfortable in their casual and natural conversation. She liked Meredith taking her shoes off. At her age and with only a niece who brought her groceries once a week, July had little interaction with others except the occasional social worker that dropped in and her minister. Meredith, in her yellow dress, seemed a flower herself.

"I am so enjoying your garden, but I have to ask you to help me find the truth in this story about race that is exploding all over Atlanta. And you may be the only person that can calm this down."

"I am a reader, not a watcher of the television very much.

But I did see last night where a man tried to hang himself, and the man that owned the tree helped save him, but it seems the reporter said he was a racist."

"The man that tried to save him, named Jack Collier, is a famous architect who is putting a new building on the property where the tree is. And it is claimed to be the very tree that that man's father, Wade, who ran to you seventy years ago, was seen smiling at as a man was hanged."

July moved her jaw back and forth in nervous energy, then said with some intensity,

"Oh, no, that's not what happened at all."

"I worked for little Wade's uncle. He was a mean drunk who hated 'The Negroes,' as he called us in a mocking way, over-pronouncing the word Negro. Called 'Mean Eugene,' he made Wade go with him to the hanging, and when they got back, that child was hysterical. He was scared to death and crying. He ran to me from the truck, grabbed hold of my apron, then his uncle grabbed him and popped him so hard it knocked the boy down, making his nose bleed. No, he wasn't laughing at all."

Meredith felt a chill shake her shoulders. This was the true story, she thought. This could undercut Shandra's accusation that Jack, by association, was as racist as was the photo showing his smiling father. It would be Jack's redemption, but Meredith realized this would also be her big story, her time in the light after the social rejections she received at Georgia for her cheating expose. She had become something of a pariah, where only several girlfriends showed their loyalty to her, but few of the men even glanced at her after the football story broke. She left the university nationally acclaimed as a rising star journalist of uncommon courage, but one scorned by those school chums whose love and friendship she needed most.

Meredith had wondered if this need for approval and affection had made her so attracted to Jack. He, too, had garnered scorn by many for his daring creativity. But he had parlayed the notoriety into power and celebrity. She had arrived in Atlanta wounded, and to her, this powerful, charismatic man accepted her, and in effect, validated her through his immediate acceptance and praise. At a place in her mind— she hated to admit—Meredith felt a satisfaction, a thankfulness, at being handed the ability to save Jack through July's revelation, possibly. But more importantly, this discovery of what really happened could be the jump-start of her journalistic career.

"You have the opportunity pretty much to save the reputation of Wade and his son Jack. The news media is saying Wade was a racist, and now his son is also because of the hanging in 1940."

"Do you know this man, this Mr. Collier?" July asked.

"I've interviewed him about his project on several occasions. He is a brilliant artist and seems very honorable."

Meredith was suddenly aware of not divulging any emotional connection, but July saw the barest of change in Meredith's face as she spoke about Jack and heard a joy that sneaked into her words. It suggested there may be more than a professional relationship behind her wanting this story.

"I'll video an interview with my phone, but I would love to take you to our newspaper to meet my editor."

Meredith could see the reluctance come over the creased face. "No, I don't like all of this. It was so long ago and a terrible day in ways I never got over. A hatred has lived in my heart, and I'm not a hating person."

Meredith turned her iPhone's video on with its voice recorder. She held the phone in her hand with the camera facing July. This casual conversation had become too much a part of the story not to have it, at least, recorded.

"This hanging in 1940 has become a sensation overnight in Atlanta. It's destroying Wade Collier's name, picturing him as a child racist laughing at the hanging of an African American."

July shook her head, "I only saw that little boy for the one week he was staying at Eugene's house, but I grew fond of him. I was practically a child myself doing housework. After Eugene hit him, I took him to the toolshed to try and stop his crying. He was scared to death and hysterical about the hanging."

"So, he hadn't been laughing at the hanging?"

"Laughing?" July scoffed. "He was terrified. He was crying, not laughing."

"You can save his reputation and maybe that of his son with those words. May I turn on my video?"

"That means I would be on television?"

There was a certain fear that could be heard in her voice.

"It's still a mean world, kind of like it was in lynching days. Folks would be throwing rocks, shooting at my little house. Sometimes it is better to be hidden from the world than be a part of it."

Meredith couldn't let this revelation go unreported. "I guess you have to ask if your heart would stand for letting Wade and his son be destroyed by lies. It was lies that murdered the poor fellow. He was an innocent man that no one stood up for. Only a child named Wade was crushed by what he saw. Now Wade, or his memory, needs somebody to stand up for him."

The strain of the conversation and the events of that day weakened July. She walked over to an old chair whose cane seat barely grasped the wood frame. She called it her "weed'n chair." Here, the persistent weeds would feel the still firm grasp of her hand as they reluctantly gave up their roots from the nourishing dark dirt that made her garden such a hurry of colors.

July reached into a growth of white, frothy phlox and held one bloom under her thin hand. "When you get to this age, you would hope all the old fears wouldn't matter anymore, only the good memories. But you can't escape where you're going if you can't escape from where you've been."

Meredith listened and watched July leaning into her flower bed from the small, rickety chair.

"So, you still feel the anger from being hit by this Eugene?"

July sat up straight and glared at Meredith standing just away from her. "There've been a lot of Eugenes in and about my life."

Meredith wanted to nail down this interview but found herself becoming more engrossed with this woman, so ancient in appearance, so wise in the measured way she talked.

"That man's name seems to have taken on a larger meaning for you."

"Seems, in the same way, the man that tried to hang himself said the whites had hanged him in many different ways. I could say I have thought of Mean Eugene so many times over the years in the slights I've received, or plain meanness from white folk."

July's face creased into a slight smile, " 'Course I don't mean all white folks. But slights do wear on you, and soon you group everybody in the same category."

Meredith knew how getting someone comfortable and trusting was a critical and time-consuming part of an interview. She also knew a reporter had to be careful in controlling the conversation. She could see July losing her train of thought about Wade and talking herself out of helping as she remembered how many times over her life she had been hurt by whites.

Trying to distract away from where the conversation was going, Meredith said, "I like this picture of you as a gardener, someone still bringing beauty to the world in this little flower garden. And tell me, is there a story about that chair?"

Meredith had learned while at Georgia that if a reporter was seeking confidential information, they didn't confront or demand answers; they sided up, came from an angle, kind of snuck in like asking about a chair that had nothing to do with anything but served to maneuver the interview into where the questions could be asked in some innocence.

"I've had this chair for over fifty years. It was my mother's. She always had a garden, so she could cut the blooms to put in the house. My father made it for her. Never was much, but now it's still upright and as creaky as me. We're friends falling apart together, but we're still together."

"Then I would appreciate videoing you in something that represents family and something that was important in your family, and it seems that was flowers. So here we go. I'll click this on and ask you just two questions, and that should do it."

With no hesitation, July held her hand up and said, "No pictures and no name, but I will speak into that thing if you want."

Meredith had no choice, so she asked, "You, as a witness that day, are convinced that nine-year-old Wade Collier was forced by his Uncle Eugene to go and watch the hanging of this Black man. Wade came back terrified and crying hysterically, not smiling at what he had just witnessed?"

"I felt his little hands gripping my apron, crying and terrified after he ran from his uncle's truck. I saw his uncle slap him so hard for crying that it bloodied the little boy's nose."

She then sat silent and seemed to retreat into her own thoughts, and Meredith knew not to press further, that she had enough solid evidence to write the story that would counter the hurricane that Berry had started. Meredith was holding herself back from running out of the yard and racing back to show this to Press. She had found what she thought to be the kernel of truth that was the essence of a story and often the most difficult to find.

"I want to thank you for telling the truth of what happened. You've saved the reputation of one and maybe two good men."

July looked firmly at Meredith. "I don't know his son, so I don't speak for him. I knew Wade Collier, and that is who I speak of on that day only. I can't speak to the rest of his life."

"I understand this is about a very specific event. And that's the way we will write it."

July reached out and gripped Meredith's wrist. Her face looked fearful. "I can't have my house being shown on the television or my name given. No pictures even of my garden. My last few days on this earth can't be lived in fear of mean folks burning my house down. Will you promise me I'll be a secret?"

Meredith feared this could weaken the interview but knew she had to honor July's request. She also feared the passion that was driving Shandra. She had created a whirlwind that was based on condemning Wade and Jack. She could arrive at this little house with a camera crew and intimidate July into who knows what story?

"I'll do better than that. Let me photograph you from the back. I won't show the flowers, and I'll put your words over the back of your head with that hat on. I'll do all I can to protect you. I promise."

July seemed satisfied with that and stood while Meredith videoed within a tight frame, the old hat and some of July's hair puffing out from it. The background was blurred.

Meredith walked around to face July. "This has been an honor for me to meet you. I hope I get to come and visit your garden again soon."

July stood with a firmness that pushed her shoulders back. She said, "Any time. These flowers are my gift to the eyes of whoever wants to look on them."

Meredith nodded, smiled broadly, and was quickly into her car. It was late enough in the morning that the usual congestion from Marietta to downtown Atlanta had loosened its grip. She was soon in *The News'* parking lot and pressing the elevator button as though her urgency was being communicated to the elevator.

Press was leaning back in his chair, feet on a corner of the desk, head back, and looking up as he talked on the phone. She stood at his opened door. He glanced at her, waved casually, almost lazily to her. She held up her iPhone and pointed at it dramatically until he ended his conversation with an annoyed concession.

"I hope this is good," he said. "That was another teacher saying she had been instructed to change student grades. This may develop into a major scandal. What's on the phone?"

Meredith consciously tried to hold her excitement back. She swallowed, dropped her chin, stepped into his office, and handed the phone to Press, hitting the video button. "This is what I've got."

Press held the phone up at an angle so the sun from his window didn't blind its video.

Meredith could hear the clear voice of July giving her testimony.

Press took his feet off his desk, wheeled his chair straight, and looked at her with a rare grin. "This is powerful. Can you verify what she says? Any other sources?"

Meredith knew if the paper was to print this as a rebuttal to Berry's accusation, it had to be better supported by multiple sources, which Berry's wasn't.

"Yes, there is a man who works in the Marietta library that witnessed the whole thing."

Press exclaimed, "Now, this is a story! You have made my blood run ink-black today, and that may be my highest compliment."

He referred to printer's ink, which dated him, but he was old school and proud of it. Press looked up at Meredith, who swelled with pride at being accepted into the journalism profession at its highest level by his congratulatory remark. She could feel tears of joy wanting to well up and sniffed as though that would stop them. He motioned generously in a silent invitation for her to take a seat next to his desk.

Press knew a game-changer when he saw one, a revelation so searing and irrefutable that it defined an issue. Normally, these revelations would be that. But then he suspected the story of a wealthy Atlanta architect being destroyed by itself may have already eclipsed his father eighty years ago. First, they had to break this evolving narrative out into its many parts. They went back over the story in its entirety with a detailed analysis of all the players. Press called this Grind Time, where fact-checking turned away fantasy for unerring truth. Shandra and her motivations, her ambush, and accusations of Jack at the house were reviewed and examined. A Mann and what they knew of him was insufficient and needed discovery. The 1940 hanging, Wade Collier's photograph, and the recent attempted hanging? What was that about? Jack and his place in all of this maelstrom of racism. Why was he, a major supporter of the Black community, being so vehemently accused? After an hour of roughly typing out the information they had—and didn't have—on her laptop, they concluded that this was a larger story about race in today's America. The Collier project was being used as a platform from which Shandra and apparently A Mann could garner worldwide attention for their agendas of racial injustice. The fact that they could destroy Jack and the project were irrelevant collateral damage.

Press called Terry Stone and told him that Meredith had shown this sudden media storm to be based on a false premise. Terry expressed great relief, hoping this revelation would stop what could be a major money loss for the paper if, caught in a firestorm of racial animosity, Metamorphosis was not built.

The publisher told Press that Jack's project was Priority One at the paper. If Meredith had proven Jack innocent, then put it out immediately. When Press said the school cheating scandal was white-hot and had Pulitzer Prize written all over it, Terry almost yelled at him that the schools could go to hell. His newspaper was facing losing the print part of the business if it lost the mammoth Collier project's advertising dollars. The century-old News would be just another online news presence. To Terry, the only glory was in print on paper.

Meredith could see the grim look cascading over Press' face as he pushed the "off" button on his phone. Press almost resented Meredith again, this time for having uncovered July. The discovery of teachers changing student grades to make the Atlanta Public School system gain more federal funding was far more dramatic in scope than a guy trying to hang himself and failing, which really made it no story of import. The cheating scandal would be the Press's signature story, the final curtain of this editor's illustrious career. And he was now ordered to slow it down, move it below the fold so that the newspaper could stand in line at the Metamorphosis trough.

Press knew he was in the twilight of his career. He had wearied of the American racial story that seemed to have no ending. His publisher had asked him to bend to the economic needs of the company on a number of occasions. Stories were to be hidden in the innards of the paper when it would hurt a major advertiser. Press couldn't let a story of widespread cheating be sublimated to another race story. These had become like a broken record to Press, the same cry of injustice in a different verse.

He would turn this one over to Meredith in a promotion that would infuriate Trace and other reporters who had worked the Atlanta vineyards for years. Now, "that college girl," as they called her, would be given the lead byline for this overnight earthquake of Atlanta's architectural genius being a hidden racist.

"Meredith, you're the lead reporter on this race story, and you've earned it." Let's get Collier cleared quickly because I have a much bigger story for you. He had a satisfied look that said he had faith in her. Excited, she almost ran out of his office.

CHAPTER 22

THE DRIVE HOME was slow and otherworldly. *Is this for real?* Jack kept asking himself. He saw that his closest friends Frazier, Marcus, and Cody had left quizzical messages centered around the theme of "What the Hell?" Now there was one from the mayor's office, several lenders, and Gerald, his minister. His whole world was reaching out, some grasping, all perplexed, confused, and very afraid of how the hanging and Shandra's online release might affect their own interests. They were all in that place of aloneness where no answers are available except those provided by the imagination and its garden of afflictions.

As he turned off West Paces Ferry Road and onto Tuxedo Road, where he lived, Jack saw several media trucks and vans in the distance in front of his house. "My, God!" he exclaimed and quickly turned around to go to an old driveway behind his house where he could park and walk unseen through a tall hedge and into his backyard.

The blinds were closed on the large windows across the back of the house. As he started to step onto the stone patio, he heard his son's familiar voice from above. "Social media has been very social, Dad. And you are the main star."

Jack looked up to see his son Paul, lying flat on the back-side of the roof and peeping over the top at the camera crews out in the street. The roof was their favorite father-son hang out, where they would share a cigar and attempt to think great thoughts. But usually, they discussed the chances of the Atlanta Falcons or the Georgia Bulldogs to conquer their respective football worlds.

Jack gave him a wry smile. "Don't worry, philosopher. My work will be for the ages."

He stepped through the back door that opened into an expansive kitchen. He had designed it after an Italian villa he had visited and had brought many of the pots now hanging from ceiling racks back with him. Jack loved all things Tuscany. Although his building designs were called radically modern, he always found a part of every building to include the soft earth tones, a stone arch, small elements that paid homage to the architects of ancient Rome.

Mary and Jack's mother were startled by his sudden entry. They were standing, almost huddling, around the sink as though the kitchen held some powers of resistance and defense. Their faces were torturous for him to look at, frightened, sad, like they were on watch for an impending tragedy. They saw his torn and smudged clothes, his hair still askew. He put on a brave face with a comforting smile and a bit of bravado to challenge the crush of news now streaming over the internet and being edited in local newsrooms for six o'clock.

"Well, what a day. The good news is I helped to save a man's life."

"And the bad news is you saved a man trying to hang himself in your tree." Betty quickly responded with a cynical scold. "Let's not paint this in any other way than as a bad picture."

Mary tilted her head forward as Jack saw a tear, shining like a small jewel escaping from her eye in a slow fall to the floor. And then tears were coming in easy streams, wetting her cheeks in a glistening shine. She rushed for her husband, grabbing him in childlike desperation that demanded solace and assurance. He held her tightly. His mother, standing behind her, turned to leave them alone for however long they would need to talk through this.

"No, Mother. I need both of you right now."

Betty said, "What's going on is you are being accused of trying to hide a murder scene where your father was photographed, supposedly smiling."

Her face was a picture of both hurt and anger, like saying the words created its own repugnant world. She remembered well the photograph found in the attic. It had terrified her, as she had considered that the blurry child behind the hanging man had a resemblance to her husband. She had felt that by pushing it deep into the trash, it would forever be hidden. And now, somehow, here it was being broadcast across the world.

Jack said nothing, just looked his wife in the eyes and guided her from the kitchen and into their living room, where they sat on the yellow sofa. Betty followed them with a box of tissues which Mary quickly took to dry the tears and clear her nose.

"Jack, no couple has done, is doing, more for the African American community than the two of us. And to be accused..." and her voice broke in a cry, "of being, I can't even say it, is....," she couldn't finish the sentence.

Jack said in a calming voice, "It shows you how dangerous a lie can become. Fiction is fact. She got this guy worked up who thinks he'll be a martyr, like one of those suicide bombers, I guess. It's all about facetime in the media. The more outrageous, the more media coverage you get."

Mary blew her nose, carefully folding the tissue and holding it in her palm.

"Everyone has to know the work we've done with minorities. This is so unfair to us."

Her shocked and helpless pleading moistened Betty's eyes as she stood near a side table at one end of the leather sofa.

Mary's voice hardened, "But what in the world was your daddy doing at a hanging?"

Jack sat up and put his elbows on his legs in a thoughtful pose. Shaking his head, he said, "It makes no sense. But this whole thing has come down to a photograph, and I'll have to admit, it does look like a picture of Daddy as a child."

Betty's heart raced in fear and embarrassment. The picture she had found in Wade's papers and then stuffed in the trash was now all over the internet. She had convinced herself that it wasn't really her precious husband, her rock of morals and honor. She felt weak, leaning with her legs against the sofa's edge. Jack could see the paleness, the unsteadiness, and quickly stood and walked to her side.

"Mom, I think you need to lie down. This is tough to take. We've got to be calm and work our way through this. I'm sure there's an explanation. Dad would have never voluntarily gone to something so terrible."

Betty felt off-center and weak. Her mind went to her partially working heart. She should go to her purse and take a nitroglycerine pill, lie down, and breathe slowly. Her heart failure condition was now in its sixth month. Her arteries had been severely compromised with plaque, but she wanted life. When she asked her doctor how bad her condition was, his answer was for her just to enjoy every day and not worry about "what-ifs." It was his way of prescribing the illusionary healing powers of denial.

Betty walked carefully toward the room where she slept, and Jack looked at Mary. "This could kill her," he said softly.

"Kill her and destroy us. What are you going to do to get a handle on this?"

"Right now, I don't know what the media is saying or how much of this guy hanging himself has even made the news."

Mary looked at her wristwatch. "It's almost six o'clock. The local news is coming on in a minute. Let's take a look."

Their son walked through the back door. He had climbed down from the roof. "Dad, there's a group of people with signs down on the street, and news people are interviewing them. This is getting real crazy."

"There's no real anymore," Jack said philosophically, "except real crazy."

Mary held the television remote out and punched the "On" button. "Let's see what the news stations are saying."

The hanging was the lead story on all four local Atlanta stations. Jack was shown dramatically climbing the tree then pushing the hanging man upward. After A Mann was taken down, Shandra was pictured, accusing Jack of trying to hide the fact that his father had been at the 1940 hanging and seemed to be laughing. It was a confusing message—a many-layered message, with accusations of racial injustice, of murder, of heroics in saving a life. The reputation of an Atlanta-born creative genius and his greatest creation suddenly was threatened. It was opera and tragedy on a large scale, and the press dove into its banquet of storylines.

"This is a nightmare," Mary said, shaking her head. "This can't be happening to us, Jack, not us. All the work, the fundraising, and mostly for minorities. How could they close the door on all we're doing for them?"

Jack stood and walked to the living room window. He placed his finger on a blind and barely moved it up, so he could peek out. There was a small group of both races with signs reading, "Hanging Lives. Every Day."

"My God, how can they have signs already made?" Jack asked no one. He turned and walked back to the sofa. "You asked how the door could shut on us. I think that we, any whites, never really have opened the door to the Black community. To many of them, their identity is defined by their history and everyday afflictions. Unless you're of their skin and one of them, you can't pretend to be accepted by them. How does this ever stop? I can never be Black. They can never be white."

Mary looked at him quizzically, then with a touch of anger, he could see. "Are you a social scientist now? That's nonsense talk. We both have many close minority friends. Look at Marcus. The two of you couldn't be closer."

"We're about to find out. I'm calling him, Frazier, and Cody. I need their advice. We'll hook up at the club."

"Where can this go, Jack? I've never had anything bad happen to me in my life."

Jack looked at her face. It was a look he had never seen, of defeat and confusion.

He sat close to her, pulled her head to his shoulder, and stroked errant hair away from her forehead. She felt like a child to him at that moment, and he had to be strong, though he had no idea to what shore this sudden hurricane would carry them.

"Oh, we'll come out on top, sweetheart. We always do. Stay close to Mother. This is her husband that's at the center of it, and she worshiped that man. I'm going upstairs to my studio, make some calls, then try and get together with some folks."

He kissed Mary on the cheek and held his lips there to emphasize his feelings for her.

Jack then climbed the carpeted stairs to what he called his "Icarus Room." He named it such because it was where his mind was free to push the limits of creativity that would bring him close to rejection or even the destruction of his reputation as being too outlandish and impractical.

Jack called Marcus. He was one of Atlanta's most popular and often powerful, behind-the-scenes African Americans. His advice and counsel were sought by many. Marcus had practiced diction as a child because he had an early penchant for precision in everything he did. His clothing always had a pressed, starched look. His hair was meticulously in place. Jack heard his perfect enunciation. "Hello, this is Marcus." But his voice had a certain distance, a leaden tone to Jack's.

"All hell seems to be breaking loose caused by one of your brothers attempting to hang himself in my tree," Jack said.

Marcus responded, "I've never seen something blow up so quickly. Everybody's confused about who this guy is, what's Shandra Berry so worked up about, and what was your daddy doing at a hanging? She's succeeded in planting the idea that you are trying to cover up the whole hanging thing."

"I've got to get my arms around this, Marcus. I'm asking you to give me some advice. I wanted the four of us to get together, and ya'll help me with a plan. I don't want the project to be impacted."

Marcus sighed. Jack could hear the soft passage of air pushed out of Marcus' mouth into the phone.

"It may be already affecting it. In the last hour, I've had some heavy hitters with money pledged to the project ask me if they should rethink committing money. We're talking race, which is more explosive in this town than gasoline."

Jack felt an urgent need to see his friends, to find comfort in the way they often showed their love for one another in their biting humor. They were his circle of wagons. For fifteen years, the group had sustained one another in tough times, talked through their trials, and extended grace when one stumbled. More important now was the fact they saw one another as very bright observers of the Atlanta world of commerce and politics. Their individual wealth and wide popularity had made the group an economic force to be reckoned with and a point of jealousy of many businessmen. Jack and his high-profile creations were the easiest target for derision and ridicule—a flamboyant artist the press adored and now seemingly ready to destroy.

Marcus seemed cautious. "Let's wait until tomorrow and see what the start of the week brings before we know what you're dealing with."

"What I'm dealing with is an ass-kicking," Jack corrected. "Your reputation is in this. Frazier and Cody have some millions of their clients' money ready to invest."

"True, but it's your tree that nutcase climbed on. Secondly, this Shandra Berry has it out for you, and she's carrying the lead horn in this parade."

He paused, then said, "And third, that old photo of your dad seems to be the real story. I'd find out what that's about."

Jack didn't get the warmth he wanted out of the conversation, just analysis.

Marcus then said, "I don't know if you've heard this, but a reporter snooping around in Athens just called me. He said he had heard your group of high school buddies used to go out at night looking for Blacks walking along the street. You'd throw water balloons at them, and this is the real toxic part, you called the rides 'Niggah Knock'n.' What the hell is that?!"

Jack was shocked that this long-forgotten, one-time episode had gotten out.

He answered with a measured, "That one is true. We were sixteen. One of the guys picked us up to show off how easy it was to steal his parents' keys. Another boy came up with the idea of throwing water balloons from his car at any Black man we saw walking. I think two were thrown. None by me. But I was there. But then, one of the balloons splashed on an old man that looked exactly like Uncle Remus, who we all loved from the movie. No one said a word in the car. We all felt ashamed. My friend let us out at our houses, and we never did that again."

"Oh, then it's okay, you had a conscience. The duality of the white liberal. That little water balloon story could well drown your project and you with it." Marcus had a sharpness, a cutting sarcasm that Jack had never heard.

"You'll no longer be known as the next Da Vinci, but as Da Nigga Knocker.'"

Jack was shaken and perplexed, "I think I know who put that out."

"I think you've got some fence-mending to do in Athens or butt kissing. Somebody there is feeding this stuff to the press."

Jack realized who it had to be. Skinny had carried all his life the rejection he felt in high school, and now his jealousy of Jack's success was driving him to exact his revenge.

"We were only high school kids," Jack mumbled into the phone. "Nobody hated Black people. We didn't even know any, except our maids."

Something about that statement, *we didn't know any*, didn't sit right with Marcus.

"My family is on the way to an evening church service. I think I'll save my prayers for you and maybe all of us. We'll talk."

The sudden silence of the phone was its own goodbye.

Jack's world was a world of the forever future. He rarely thought of the past, and certainly not that it could destroy him. And that it would be the south's eternal disgrace, the abused Black man that would emerge as the avenger.

The press left the street in front of Jack's home as the sun was setting, and the dozen or so activists went home for supper. They were moth-like in gathering around the eye of the cameras. None cared to be a sign holder in the dark, while few in that neighborhood wanted to hear their beseeching cries for justice.

Betty had extended her stay with them because some old Atlanta friends had invited her to play bridge. Jack was worried about his mother in this storm of criticism about him. She saw any disparaging comments as a slight on the family name. Betty felt her role was the protector after her husband's death. Wade was the family coat of arms—a statement of honor and honesty. Without his good name, there was no Collier family identity, no distinctiveness.

Jack walked with some jaunt into her bedroom, trying to show he was unscarred by the attacks against her husband. He worried her heart was too delicate to handle this sudden assault on their reputation. Jack felt his own ambitions had opened this ancient door to the long ago. Without the dream of his grand design, the futuristic Metamorphosis, his life and his father's would have remained bound in the cords of the past.

Jack walked to Betty's bedside. Four small pill bottles stood like sentinels against the stopping of her weakened heart. She was reading a book on the parables of Jesus and how they can guide one's life today.

"I've always gone to the Lord when my world seems to be falling apart. He's my safe ground when the waters get high."

She asked, "Where do you go, Jack when life gets hard?"

Jack didn't answer, then said, "I go to myself."

She ignored that response as to her. It had no value. "All the good works of a good man, a lifetime of honor all means nothing in a mean world. And that's what we have created, Jack, a very mean, finger-pointing world. There is no grace left."

Jack sat on the edge of the bed. "There has to be more to Daddy's being at that hanging than we know. There's one reporter who has found an old lady who may have the real truth. The reporter's calling the woman named July tomorrow. Her story will show how Daddy is completely innocent."

"Your dream has been caught up in the times. Black people are madder than I've ever seen them. These police shootings have been like matches to gasoline."

Jack stood up. Mary had called them from the kitchen. She was warming up some split pea soup she had made earlier, along with some egg salad sandwiches.

"Race is like an ember that never goes out. I'm starting to think some Blacks don't want it to go out. I'm not one, so I can't speak for how they feel. Mary and I have spent many hours trying to help them, and this is what we get."

"I'll pray on it, son. If you don't mind, bring me some of Mary's soup. I'll eat in here. You two have a lot to talk about. Maybe tomorrow will be better."

Betty touched his arm, her lips creased in a gentle smile as she looked into her son's eyes. And then she couldn't because they reminded her so much of her husband.

CHAPTER 23

JACK KNEW he had to make the one call he dreaded above all others, to Martin Savoy, the project's major lender. Martin had left several messages, each rising in obvious frustration. His pension fund's millions were the foundational money that would allow the project to start. All the other committed funders would dutifully follow suit. Such was Martin's hard-nosed reputation that his approval of a project told the world to come on in; this water is fine for investing.

Martin's phone identified that it was Jack calling. There were never greetings given or the perfunctory "hello." Martin would just start talking. "This whole project has been skating on thin ice with our fund. It's always been on thin ice with me because of the outlandish design, but now the ice may have broken. We can't get within a mile of anything racial. The R-word is doomsday."

Jack's body visibly moved back in his chair by this pronouncement. His mind was caught in a place where words retreat, in fear of showing how vulnerable he felt.

Martin heard a silent phone and barked, "Hey, you there?!"

Jack summoned up a response, delivered calmly. "Martin, this story was made up by a reporter with a civil rights agenda. I would urge you to hold everything until a news story comes out that will show it has all been a lie. You'll see, this has all been made up."

"You don't understand modern media? You haven't heard that race is the great American guilt, and it lies in wait to destroy anyone challenging its legitimacy?"

Martin's voice said these words with more accusation than a question.

"What has not been made up and is swamping the media is that an African American tried to hang himself on your property for what many see as a heroic sacrifice. That is red meat to the race crowd, true or not. In today's media, the first lie can be the last truth, no matter how big a lie it is."

Jack was surprised at Martin's analysis of the media. He had seemed so dry and intellectually empty, but then their relationship had been one of numbers, risks, and return on investments. They had never had a drink together. Martin wouldn't give him the edge that might come from some collegiality found in a glass.

Martin was filled with certitude in his tone. Race was something he had obviously thought a lot about.

"My concern is that the seed has been planted, and no amount of your trying to dig it out will change minds, especially African American's. The belief that you're rich and your kind are racists under all the glitter is set. See, you are a coin; when a newsy guy like you falls because of their accusations, it makes the activist crowd's validity rise. You're valuable by being made worthless, and my fund cannot fall with you. You're now toxic, Jack."

It was a crushing conversation, so sudden was Martin's conclusion that Jack felt he had been swept up in a wave of insanity, where rumor and innuendo and lies ruled. But he remained calm and determined.

"Martin, you and I have been through a lot in putting this deal together. Give me until tomorrow before you call it quits." Jack punched the off button before Martin could respond.

Martin smiled as he felt the rush of power, the satisfaction of bringing down a trophy like Jack, a hotshot, self-proclaimed genius. Damn architects, he thought. It's all about them and their next building so they can strut around. And Jack is the biggest peacock in the yard. Martin laughed to himself, thinking of Jack as a peacock with his feathers shorn. It was all risk and reward to him. He held the power of the pen, and his signature had made the small, big, and the big, small, depending on how he dispensed his fund's millions. The ultimate enjoyment was financing a successful project, but the fun was toying with these butt-kicking developers and bringing them down to butt-kissing for his coin.

Sleep for Mary had been roiling, turning, then waking with surges of anxiety. When her husband slipped out at six o'clock for his office, Mary had fallen into a deepness where the ears know no sounds and the mind is clearing and filing and erasing the outside furies.

Mary's phone played a brief operatic singer when she had received a call. It had rung continually last evening and started at 6:00 this morning. As she jogged to her car, she saw Cal Connor's number come up. Mary's mind was not on defending the morning news shows about her husband as a racist, but she thought Cal might have some words of support, so she took his call.

"Mary, this is Cal. I wanted you to know how shocked I am at all this news." He let it stop at that, making it obvious to her that he wanted a reaction.

"Oh, Cal, thank you for your call. It's like our world has been turned upside down by these terrible lies about Jack and his father. No two men have done more for the minority community."

"Well, I didn't know his dad, but I do know you have been a leader in Atlanta in your charity work."

She noticed he didn't mention Jack. His language seemed careful. Was he afraid he would be quoted and concerned that his words of praise of either Wade or Jack would be used against him?

"Few have been as generous of their time and money as Jack," Mary said.

"Yes," Cal's answer was noticeably brief. Then he continued with a somewhat distant tone, "Confidentially, Mary, my advice would be to email Spellman's president and Emory's board chair and tell both that until this event is settled, you ask they put in abeyance any consideration of your joining their boards."

My God, she thought. Cal has talked to them, and he's their messenger. Jack has had no chance to respond, and already these institutions are moving away from us.

The flame was burning quickly. Mary found it astonishing in its rapacious enveloping of the city's leadership. A reporter was practically accusing one of Atlanta's most controversial and admired architects of hiding an awful truth about his father. A Black man, so disgusted with what he saw as a cover-up and its example of America's racism, had attempted to hang himself on her husband's property. The reporter had said the hanging tree was the man's cross he was willing to die upon to expose the sins of the white man. And rich, arrogant, self-serving Jack Collier was symbolic of that sin. Mary's world had fallen in an eye blink.

In the early press reports, the story seemed to be one of good versus continuing, unabated evil. Whatever the truth, it was too hot for Atlanta, known as America's Black Mecca. Many of the minority community's most powerful had money committed to Jack's project, and many more saw it as a golden goose for their shops, offices, and condos. But the race drew blood, and no institution in Atlanta wanted its blood drawn or its sanctimonious commitment to equality besmirched. Jack was being swept away by the great tidal crusade of The Movement.

Mary was too professional, too astute in how institutions branded themselves and zealously protected their brand, to argue with Cal. "That's sound advice, Cal. I would never put these institutions in an awkward position. I'll just ask that any considerations concerning me be put on hold until we can get the truth out."

"Jack is a communication master. I'm sure he'll quickly have an answer for all of this. Again, be patient, Mary. My best for you."

She felt a weight pushing her down, a shroud of inexplicable sorrow, shock, and disbelief weighing and weakening. *How could this be happening to people like us?* she asked herself.

CHAPTER 24

AT 7:00, Meredith called Jack. "Hi, I wanted you to know we are about to release my interview with the lady who was there when your father came crying, not laughing, from the hanging."

Jack could feel the weight coming off his shoulders. "Good Lord. That could turn this whole mess around." Pausing to absorb the rush of emotions about Meredith personally and her discovery, Jack said, "You're the best. Let me start spreading the word. Talk soon."

Feeling confident for the first time, Jack called his three friends. It took several minutes, but he finally had them all on a conference call. Jack was at once tense and curious as to how loyal his friends would be after a night of reflection and feedback and watching, he assumed, in shock, as the Atlanta news stations were convicting him.

Each man said a stunted, "Morning," uncertain of what else to say. Jack was quick to assume control of the conversation. "Hey, guys, breaking news, as they say. We may have an answer to this bullshit. That girl reporter at *The News* just called. She found a witness to prove Daddy wasn't laughing at the hanging. He was terrified."

There was a short and obvious silence as each man absorbed and calculated what this news meant. Marcus was reluctant to see this as the answer to the storm. "Don't get too excited because your daddy is no longer the tail that's wagging this dog. It's that damn tree and the glow around the guy."

Jack felt a victory was being taken away from him. "I thought we had a winner with this. What would make a strong statement is your standing by me at a press conference I might call at noon tomorrow."

"Can't do it," Marcus answered quickly. "I'll be at a luncheon with the mayor and can probably do more good there. So, what would you say at a press conference?"

"My main defense, if I do it, is going after the reporter that lit this fire. Shandra has done more than any Atlanta reporter to create stereotypes of Blacks. Watching the evening news, you would think every Black is out tearing up the town. 'Bloody Berry' is what some leaders call her."

Frazier was his usual robust self in asserting to the group, "You need to kick somebody's ass for this slander. Good, you're on the offense."

Then, with a noticeable drop in his assertiveness, "You do have some kick-ass answers for this, don't you?"

"Like I said, we'll go after Shandra in particular as the face of the new journalism, which is sensation-driven at the expense of facts and context. This new information about my dad should be a powerful example of how she's writing her narrative," Jack said.

"Destroy her credibility up front. I like that." Jack could see Frazier hitching up his pants as he did whenever he made a pointed assertion. The hitching of his pants was like a period, a finality at the end of whatever he had said.

"I gotta tell you, Marcus, and don't get PO'd, but there are too many in your race that won't let go of the past."

Marcus could feel his demeanor change. He then smiled at himself, knowing the past still held to him in ways he could never escape. Frazier's statement put him in a defensive mode, a place their years of friendship had never called up.

"You can't erase our color, my friend. It's part of our culture. And for centuries, our color resulted in chains and whips and beating. Whether we bring color to the surface too easily or keep it suppressed is our choice, not yours."

Frazier felt uncomfortable responding because the four of them had kidded about race unmercifully, finding laughter as the valve that let the steam out. But in this situation with Jack, it seemed a side had to be taken. The four couldn't keep it in a gray area any longer.

"I hear what you say, and I can't relate to it, 'cause it never happened to me. But at what point does past become present and future, a prison really, with no escape?"

Jack interceded. "Let's say you're both right. Shandra Berry, to me, is fixated on believing her race is intentionally being held back and disrespected. And I'll say it. I respect her for her stand. To her, there is a clear villain, and it is white people. She truly believes this and is willing to wreck my name and this project to draw attention to her cause. Frazier believes this story of white oppression is nothing but a bargaining chip to keep whites on the defensive and fearful of speaking up." Jack was trying to keep his tight group tight. The last thing he needed was for his three closest friends to start fighting among themselves.

Cody had given no response. Jack knew that he had a lot of

his personal money committed. He was also the one of the four of them that had mortgages and investments beyond what a big loss could sustain. Jack said, "Cody, I may call a press conference. My PR people have several Black ministers and a bunch of charities I've helped that will be surrounding me. Each will give a short testimonial attesting to what my foundation did for them or what I personally have done in free architectural work. This will create a shield of sorts that challenges the credibility of the accusations before the press can start with them."

Cody finally responded, "I like that. We all know what you've done for Black charities and the money you gave Morehouse. But I think the horse is out of the barn. I agree that the tree and the Black guy hanging himself have swept your daddy's story below the fold in the newspaper. Afraid it's too little now and too late to turn the tide by itself."

Marcus was unimpressed with Jack's answer. "It's going to take more than charity work you did, Jack. That's weak against a determined reporter and a willing media, and you are the target of a rare opportunity."

"What do you mean? My history of aiding the Black community...."

Marcus interrupted, "That doesn't mean crap once the story is set. You wrote checks, did a few drawings. You never marched, never got clubbed for the cause. Just handing out money doesn't make you untouchable. Now it's made you a bigger target. To be effective, a cause needs an enemy. Sadly, my friend, that's you if you won't leave that tree alone."

Jack felt both angry and helpless. "Let's be honest here. Without my funding, a lot of these charities would be closed. What am I supposed to do, wear blackface to get the color experience?"

Frazier said, "Then you would be a true racist. You, we, are attacked because we don't understand the Black experience. If you try to act like you're Black, you're a phony. There's no out for white people here."

Cody wanted none of this back and forth and said, "Jack, we're all connected here as long-time friends and investors. You've got to stop this train, or all of us are going to be run over."

"I'm trying, but I need your backs. I need you...," and his voice almost broke. "I need to have you guys standing with me. You're big dogs in this town. People trust you with their money. If you're there, just standing there, it says you believe me. Ok, I gotta run." And Jack was off the call. He wanted to hear no more excuses. He was appealing to the sanctity of friendship in the face of fire.

Cody said to the remaining two, "All I know is that fiction can be fact in this upside-down world. We know this is crap, but my investors know what they hear. Yeah, Jack is an eccentric, creative genius, and genius is a lofty place that people love to tear down. But we all know that we should be there standing beside him."

There was a quiet from Marcus who, in a measured voice, said, "Jack is a brother to me. Just like you two. If we go and stand in support and these accusations hold, then we are tarred with him. We would have to be prepared to give it all up, literally give up all we've worked for, and be labeled as racist supporters."

Frazier then gave a whizzing laugh, more air-carrying words than expressing mirth. "Your reasoning sounds like grounds for divorce from that clothes-buying wife of mine. Seriously, we could all be broke and shunned—no more country club, gala invites, African safaris, or Viking river cruises. But we would be true to ourselves and our friendships if we stand with him."

Cody didn't want to say it, but he did. "You haven't seen my debt load. You guys have money squirreled away. I'm on the line big time for some investments. If I get branded as a supporter of a racist, I'm dead meat. And, yes, Jack is like a brother to me also."

Frazier's voice had settled out of its anger, "Brotherhood. Friendship. What price do we pay before the price is too much? God, I hate this conversation. Backing Jack should be a no-brainer. For all the years the four of us have spent together, I shouldn't ask, do we walk away from our friend and protect what we have?"

Cody answered. "Time for honesty, right? Jack wouldn't knowingly ask us to fall with him. I believe he feels really confident that this is a bullshit story and no one will be hurt." He paused and said quietly, "I just wish I felt more certain about the outcome."

Marcus' voice was brisk and confident. "If I can break away from this meeting with the mayor, and Jack holds a press conference, I'll stand with him. But I might be more effective being with the mayor in calming him down. Let's stay in touch." With that, his phone went silent.

"Did Marcus just find his excuse for not being there?" Frazier said more than asked. "Are we all running away now?"

"Sadly, we are," Cody said. "What's your excuse going to be, old buddy?

Within an hour, Jack had been advised by his PR agent Sampson to forget a news conference. He had called around to see which Black ministers and other downtown business leaders would come and form a phalanx of support behind Jack. No one would come. The story was now too hot regardless of how much Jack had given to their charities.

Jack called Marcus back, remembering Marcus was supposedly at the mayor's office. "Looks like you are off the hook. I changed my mind about having a press conference. I think I'll try and work something out with the mayor."

Marcus sounded a little cold in tone, "The mayor wants to use me as an intermediary between the two of you."

"So, by the mayor not being seen with me, he has deniability if it got out that he was negotiating with me." Jack knew Sam Hayworth well. He had contributed thousands of dollars to Sam's campaign for Mayor and, along with Mary, had introduced the candidate to many of their North Atlanta friends known as connectors and money raisers—the Queens and the Kings in the big houses of Buckhead. The Mayor thought Jack a flamboyant, egotistical artist, but brilliant in his designs, fun, and always ready to help with a minority cause. But now, the mayor's phone was swamped with wealthy Blacks who had money pledged to Metamorphosis. They were seeing their anticipated quick returns lost and their names caught up in a racist scandal.

They saw the hanging episode as a grandstand play that threatened their potential profits and all the Black businesses to whom Jack had promised space in the development. This small cadre of minority movers were no slouches when it came to demanding Blacks get their fair share of the Hartsfield-Jackson Airport array of food courts. And they would stand behind Congressman John Lewis when he called a press conference about the latest slight. But Metamorphosis was to be The Big Payoff like the airport was, and the man could find another tree to hang himself on. They quietly demanded that their friend, the mayor, get with Jack and that out-of-control reporter Shandra Berry and save the project.

"Tell him, 'Thank you, Mr. Mayor, for all the networking

parties I set up for you and the thousands I gave to your community,'" Jack said sarcastically to Marcus.

"Welcome to the world of black and white. Here's the deal, Jack. The mayor has backed you on your project, even has some side money in it. But this hanging tree is a bridge too far for a Black politician. He badly wants the project to go forward, but even though *The News* has found the story about your dad was crap, this A Mann character and the whole hanging thing has given that tree a symbolism that gives The Movement food. The mayor says the way out is for you to modify the building's design and save the tree. If I can get agreement, he then wants to announce that you are coming to City Hall where the two of you will try and come up with a solution."

"So, how much blood do I give?" Jack asked.

"You'll have to tell me now that you want to save the tree. Then a grand announcement is made. And the city too busy to hate will once again rise out of the ashes, so to speak." Marcus offered.

"Pictures with you two shaking hands with prominent Blacks, and you dodge the race bullet, and the mayor looks like a bridge builder."

Jack had to laugh. "This is pure politics, where the mayor gets the credit for saving the tree and the project. There's no way, Marcus. It would highlight the tree, make the hanging a part of the branding, and make the project a symbol of Black oppression. Let's find another way."

Marcus wasn't prepared for his friend taking a sudden and unyielding stand. "Jack, I don't believe you understand how this tree, as a symbol, has caught on with the Black population on a national basis. The tree is already a part of the branding. *The News* reporter saved you from some of the racist accusations. Getting the tree out of the picture will return you to the rich white friend of the downtrodden. I see real PR value in this for you. Atlanta is about compromise. Let's do it."

"We'll dig the damn thing up and move it, along with the so-called slave house, to a park or somewhere, but it doesn't remain on my property." The more Jack thought about it, the madder he got.

"I'll put that out to the mayor and leak it in confidence to Shandra Berry—get her take on it—and to the guy that tried to hang himself. I'll get back to you."

Jack saw the Dean of the University of Georgia's School of Architecture was calling. Jack answered with an ebullience that caught the droll administrator off guard. "Glad you called, Dean Lawson. Just want you to know the million-dollar scholarship check will be delivered Friday at the ceremony."

The Dean's voice was a monotone that suggested a distance, unlike his recent celebratory comments when Jack announced he was awarding the school some significant money.

"Mr. Collier" (it used to be Jack), "the university is calibrating the recent events and will have to see how your project reflects on our school. Thank you for the generous offer, but we'll have to press the delay button on accepting the funds as of today. I'm sure you understand how the university honors diversity and stands for inclusion. We can't have any association where race is involved that would threaten that image."

There was no point in blowing up, as he wanted to or getting into a debate, so Jack was gracious in his response.

"Of course, I understand. But know that all of this is about to come to a positive conclusion, and I look forward to rescheduling the scholarship. Talk to you soon, Dean."

The Dean gave no response and was off the phone.

That one hurt, Jack thought, as he shook his head. His alma mater could now be added to the list of those who would have taken his money. Race had become untouchable.

The solitude Jack felt was overwhelming. His three best friends had indicated that they would not stand with him at any news conference. Okay, maybe Marcus needed to be with the mayor, Jack thought. But Frazier and Cody? Frazier had answered with an apology in his rapid-fire, whiskey-hoarse voice way. "Hey, Jack, I know you canceled the press thing. I was coming, but I'm on a new blood pressure medicine and got so dizzy I could hardly stand. I started to poison that damn tree."

"Well, *The News* has a reporter who is a real reporter, and she found a witness that cleared my daddy.

Frazier said, "Well, Daddy isn't driving the story anymore."

Jack was reluctant to reveal the bad news but had no choice. "I've just talked to Martin Savoy with the pension fund. They could out unless something dramatic happens."

"Oh, my God. This could topple the whole thing." Jack knew Frazier well enough to hear the strain, the panic in his voice. "Well, do something dramatic. We can't let this go down over a guy who wanted to hang himself." His voice ended with a wheeze like he was out of breath.

"The mayor wants me to change the design and include the tree, says that will take the steam out of the tree."

"Can that be done? Hell, do it. Do whatever; we gotta save this!" Frazier's voice was now a shout, and Jack was worried Frazier's heart wouldn't stand this kind of strain.

"This is my life's dream come true, Frazier. Who am I if I agree to destroy it because of a lie?"

"Dream on another project where your best friends and half the city can't lose their asses."

"Okay, calm down. I'll meet with the mayor and see what we can work out. The whole town has its money and pride in the project. It's too big to fail."

Jack then tried to call Cody but got his voice mail. He knew Cody was on the brink of bankruptcy because of several failed investments, and he was counting on Metamorphosis to bail him out.

He called Marcus back and said he wanted to meet with the mayor as soon as possible. Jack got a quick call back saying the mayor would meet him at 4:00, but to tell no one of the meeting. What Marcus didn't say was that the mayor had already put out the word to certain ministers, civil rights activists, and major downtown business leaders that he would try and save the project and the tree. For the sake of the city, he was entering into negotiations with Jack Collier. He told each person he contacted not to mention the negotiations to anyone else. Sam used this whispered confidentiality as a tool to make people feel they were a part of his inner circle.

At 4:00, Jack walked into the sprawling office of the Mayor of Atlanta. Sam had an erect posture and wore a perfectly tailored grey pin-striped suit. His hair was cut short, looking almost like a tight-fitting cap over his cherubic face. His skin was quite black, accented by a barely seen sparkly cream he applied every day. His friends called him "The Star" because of the sparkle. His lips were broad and constantly moving, either in conversation or spread in an easy smile. He got up from behind an orderly, orga-nized-looking mahogany desk and reached out for Jack's hand. He was a booster for his city and gregarious with anyone he met.

"Jack, from the first time you drew Metamorphosis' rough

image on a lunch napkin, I have believed this would put Atlanta on the world map in architecture. It's just damn brilliant, you know. And I'll always be grateful for all the support you gave me when I was a candidate."

Jack said, "You're easy to support, Sam. And your backing of my project helped pave the way for all the initial financing. It's going to make a lot of people a lot of money."

After these effusive remarks, Sam sat on one corner of his spacious desk and looked hard at Jack.

"And it's going to make you world-famous. We need to work together, so we all win. It's the Atlanta way."

"Sam, this racial thing is nonsense, and you know it. Other than the Woodruff Foundation, not many have given more to the Black community than my wife and I have. An ambitious reporter has ginned this up, and I don't know who this guy is that tried to hang himself. Don't you see that they're using the publicity Metamorphosis generates to push their agenda, which is that all whites are racists? You know the systemic thing."

Sam let out a long sigh. "Race is the white man's Achilles heel. It may be a weakness you are never allowed to escape by my people wanting to play that card for whatever reason. It can be the kiss of death, and right now, you and maybe the project are being kissed."

"So, I have been chosen to play sacrificial lamb? Another white who gave, but giving wasn't enough when a lamb was needed?"

"If you want to get poetic. You know what the Good Book says, works alone are not enough. You gotta believe too, and in this case, believe in the pain of the past. I asked you here today for the two of us to work out a solution that keeps your reputation and keeps the project on track." The Mayor walked behind his desk and pointed his hand at a plush leather chair for Jack to sit in front of his desk.

"Jack, your creation is the talk of the architectural world and one of my proud achievements, to the degree I helped you get zoning and gave it my administration's approval." He let those words of his taking credit hang as though he were waiting for an agreement from Jack. He didn't get it.

"It's not just a masterpiece, Sam. It will put Atlanta on the map as far as building designs go. It will be a destination point like Arthur Blank's new stadium already is."

"We both agree on its significance, but this tree and that slave house are in the way, and you by association. I've got an idea that will clear your name and make sure this great project is built."

He was taking heat from Atlanta's substantial number of Big Mule white liberals that had voted for him, and from the powerful Blacks who expected big returns for having been promised store leases, insurance contracts, legal fees, banking money—a host of ways to make money off a major real estate project. This was a massive pie, a golden goose for so many, and a loudspeaker for activist groups across America. All were attracted to its mighty light.

Jack was intrigued and suspicious of what solution Sam was about to propose.

"This is insanity, Mr. Mayor. How does one deal with crazy?"

"Here's how—the tree has become the big focus. It has opened an overnight online explosion of vilifying you and all whites for being shadow racists." He shook his head. "One activist in California has changed the project's name from Metamorphosis to Mephistopheles."

"Ha. So now I have created the devil's workshop. That guy must have read Faust."

Sam agreed. "I know. It is an irrational world the internet has unleashed. But it just shows how hysteria can destroy the most innocent of us."

"And what's your solution, Sam?"

The mayor leaned forward, and with a voice Jack thought had been lowered for authority, for gravitas, for putting his full meaning behind his proposal. "You slightly modify the design to include the tree. On something that big, we're just talking a few feet. The tree can then become an honored symbol of white generosity—of asking for forgiveness."

Jack leaned back, feeling the leather in the heavy chair. He put both hands on his forehead and ran his fingers back through his thick hair. His mouth broke into a broad grin. "Is this a joke, Sam.? That would not only destroy the entire design; it would have a hanging tree as part of the brand. You can do better than that."

The mayor had been given the idea by Marcus, who was now pressing his ear hard against the nearby storeroom door, listening. Marcus had worked up the idea with several ministers and businessmen and had an envoy go to Shandra and get her take on it. She liked it. She told the envoy that she would expect a sign announcing the tree as a historical site, and she wanted a guarantee from Jack to list it in his marketing materials for the project.

Marcus told the mayor that he had a consensus and to lean on Jack to accept it. Otherwise, his architectural career in Atlanta was over, and the entire project may fall from lenders bailing out.

"Don't be too quick. I have confidentially run this idea up the flagpole and have gotten very favorable responses. This is a dramatic way that restores you and saves the masterpiece you created." Sam sat back as though he had just finished an enjoyable meal.

Jack put a hand on each of the chair's arms and stood, all six feet two inches that seemed to dominate even the spacious mayor's office. The mayor admired the manhood before him, then stood himself, trying to stretch as tall as his five feet ten-inch frame would allow.

"A masterpiece is called that for a reason. It is one because of the uniqueness of its design. No tinkering around the edges, no fudging here and there. Oh, it may be great art, but it's not perfect. I have tried to achieve perfect, and that is its true value to the city."

Sam said quickly, "Oh, perfect, my ass. There is no perfect about anything in this life. You're chasing a rainbow and working to destroy yourself and humiliate the city."

"A perfect creation is rare, eternal, and acknowledged by everyone. It's beyond the grasp or even the dreams of all the others who try for it."

The mayor was starting to sweat in his anxiety and impatience. "Don't give me that creative crap. I'll start pulling the plug on this thing, starting with reviewing the zoning. I'm sure we can discover some problems with your application."

"Okay, calm down. Here's my offer: I'll dig the tree up and ship it anywhere. The tree is situated in a critical part of the design. It has to go."

"Damnit, Jack, don't you know the hatred this has generated toward you and now toward our city? Think of Atlanta. You won't be able to design a doghouse after this, and all those Buckhead liberals you hang out with, well, those doors will be shut. At least talk to Mary. She's a level-headed woman. And call your buddy Marcus. See what he thinks. He knows the politics of both money and race as well as anybody."

Jack had a look of resignation and said as he started to leave, "I'll talk with Mary and some close advisors. I'll call you back in the morning, but as of now, the tree goes, and the project stays the same."

Jack left, walked out into City Halls' marble-floored hallways and a swarm of reporters. One of the Mayor's supposed confidants had tipped them off that a grand compromise was taking place. Their yells and poked microphones made the scene look like a medieval battle with mikes being thrust like soft-tipped swords into Jack's fleeing face.

"Did you strike a deal?"

"What about the tree?"

"Are you a racist?"

Jack walked with confidence between their cramped bodies, looking straight ahead with a smile that looked to them like a strange peacefulness. He hated the incessantness of the press, but his career was in part due to their fascination with him.

He said to them as he walked, "Would a racist give $250,000 to Morehouse? Would a racist bring Atlanta's churches of all colors together in a meeting of understanding with one another?"

There was a moment of stammering and thought gathering as they were without questions. But their fervor and incessant pursuit intensified like a predator chasing a running animal as they trailed him out of City Hall to his car, jamming against his windshield and windows.

Marcus pushed the door open from his hiding place and, stepping into the mayor's office, pronounced, "He's a stubborn damned mule. Call him obsessive, a crazy artist, ego-mad, dream chaser, whatever, but I don't think I saw any movement, Sam. He would rather lose it all than walk away from who he is."

"This can't be, Marcus. The publicity about the building has made it a gold mine. We've all got money in it. The city will look stupid."

The mayor's demeanor changed. He balled his fist up and struck the top of his desk. "I'll crush him, Marcus. I can't let some egomaniac embarrass me and the city. He can kiss Atlanta goodbye."

"Alright, alright, let me set something up with Shandra Berry and that loon she's protecting and see what they'll concede on. I'll tell her it's strictly confidential, and we'll meet late tonight at the guy's room at the hospital."

"How far do we take our past as our shield and sword?"

The mayor seemed suddenly philosophic to Marcus. "It's double-edged; the word racist can destroy a man, but like all weapons, it should be used carefully."

Marcus knew the mayor was struggling with this whole incident. He knew Jack's project would be an economic boon for Atlanta. But he couldn't resist the accusations now sweeping the country about the tree and the man who wouldn't budge to save it.

Sam then relinquished those thoughts to say, "I think the cause of this whole thing is the ambition of this one reporter and that nutcase. A Mann, my ass. Jack's no damn racist. Ask Shandra what she wants. See if she'll let the tree be moved. Tell her the Black community has jobs and investments to lose if she keeps pushing this. Find us a way out, Marcus."

∽

MARY WAS on the phone in their kitchen when Jack walked toward the house from the hidden backyard entrance. He looked up at his son sitting on the roof.

"Sing in me, Muse," his son said, "and through me tell the story of that man skilled in all ways of contending."

Jack had to smile at the opening line from Homer's Odyssey. "My son, Homer. I love you greatly, Muse."

"Love you too, Wanderer, but worry over how you will weather the seas you are on."

As her husband entered the kitchen, Mary asked, "So, how did the meeting with the mayor go?"

Jack reached into the refrigerator and pulled out a beer. Popping the top off, he took a slow swig relishing its sparkle and body. He looked at Mary and said with soberness and a tone of defeat she had never heard from him. "I feel like a small boat on one of those gigantic Hawaiian waves. The wave, I guess you would say, is race, and it snuck up on me and now has me in its grip. I don't know how to get out."

"That's a creative way to put it, but what exactly happened?"

Jack relayed the cancellation of funding by the pension fund, the failure of his three best friends, and all of the Black charity directors refusing to show up if he gave a press conference.

Jack saw Mary's face turn into a rare pleading, frightened look. "So, all of this could be ended by a slight change in the building? Jack, we're getting destroyed. Change it, for God's sake."

Jack stepped back from her and said nothing immediately, as he let her emotional appeal run through his mind. Nervously uncertain of how to express his feelings to her, Jack absentmindedly ran his fingers over the wet sides of the beer.

He saw Mary as his last line of defense, the ultimate supporter of his need to create, regardless of the winds against it. But this was not the world of Mary. Hers had been genteel, respectful, courteous. Hers had been a life of helping others, and now she was being swept up in these awful accusations where their good works were being painted as camouflage.

"Let's talk in a bit. I've got some calls I've got to make. Hold your thoughts." And he headed upstairs to his office.

CHAPTER 25

MARCUS CALLED Shandra at her television station. She had just finished being interviewed by MSNBC, CNN, and the Black Entertainment Network. The station receptionist said *The New York Times* had also been trying to reach her. Shandra was happy for the first time in years, truly happy. She was, at last, being recognized for getting The Big Get, a story so impactful that it threatened to derail a half-billion-dollar project and end the career of an architect about to be crowned one of the world's most uniquely talented men.

"I'm between interviews. What do you want?" Her voice was abrupt and condescending, Marcus thought.

"The mayor has asked me, off the record, to meet with you as soon as possible and discuss a solution that will address the issues A Mann has brought up that will allow this project to move forward."

Shandra responded, "I'm not negotiating this, but I will tell you what A Mann told me he wants: the tree stays, and a metal sign is placed in front of it honoring the historical persecution of Blacks. Also, the tree and its story become a part of promotional materials that advertise whatever this building is going to be."

Marcus figured she would use her sudden national visibility to drive a hard bargain. He knew Jack wouldn't go for these demands. It would turn the whole mammoth enterprise into a memorial to murdered Blacks. He was annoyed with her self-proclaimed champion status of Black oppression but avoided showing it.

"Actually, I should have first asked what is your goal here, Shandra? You started out covering a story; now, you are the story. Is this journalism or promoting a cause?"

"That's an accusation hidden in a game of definitions. According to the nation's press, this is a story far bigger than a damn egomaniac's design. That's why the nation's press is calling me for my opinion on this. It is my honor as a reporter to break this story of continuing injustices on our people. This is called news."

It was all he could do to restrain himself from calling her a phony for her sudden defense of Blacks after years of reporting on their murdering one another. But for the moment, he had to placate her. She was in the spotlight and could make this go away. "That's a very honorable pursuit. And there are several ways we can fulfill that without destroying a project that is going to provide hundreds of jobs to our race and make a lot of money for investors, many of whom are Black."

"And?" Shandra asked with a noticeable sarcasm.

"To keep the tree in that exact location would destroy the overall look of the building. That uniqueness is why all the money is flowing into it. And that money will mean jobs for Black people. Let's have Jack move the tree close by, but so that it doesn't force a redesign."

"I don't know. If it's moved, it is no longer in the light this project is creating. It is a second citizen just like Blacks are now, unfit for a place of honor." Shandra was offended by the suggestion of placing this sudden national symbol off to the side.

"Shandra, if you keep pushing this hard-line, the project could fail, and you will be accused of destroying the jobs and fortunes of people of your own race."

"You don't know hard I can push, Marcus. This has brought me off the police beat to a place of national prominence overnight. You're a slicked-up-behind-the-scenes country club boy. You don't have a voice beyond that Buckhead crowd. I've got the voice, Marcus; you weren't interviewed by *Time Magazine* today. I was."

His jaw tightened. He bit his bottom lip. She was playing hard ball. His hand gripped the small phone tightly. She had made a blatant assault on one of Atlanta's most powerful men.

"An hour ago, I took A Mann out to the property and interviewed him at the tree in his wheelchair with a neck brace on and burns from the rope. Go online and look, and then call me and tell me to forget the tree."

Marcus made the offer again to Shandra, and she shouted "No!" so loudly all could hear her defiance. Marcus then told her the city would turn on her and make her the real problem here, not a brilliant architect who had given much of his time and fortune to Black causes. Shandra seemed to pause, which indicated to Marcus that the threat of a popular Black mayor turning on her had some resonance.

Shandra said with an obvious bravado, "Well, I'll match your mayor for a call from the White House telling me how the President was following the situation and wanted to bring A Mann to the new Civil Rights Museum for an interview. Here's what I'll propose to A Mann: we drop the demand for the mention of the tree in the project's promotional materials, but the tree must stay where it is. That's like moving a battle-field somewhere else. It's where the event happened that gives it authenticity."

"See what he says," Marcus advised her. "But also tell him Jack can move the tree a few feet away, and all is well. To change the design would ruin what everyone is excited about."

"I've already told the President that Atlanta thinks the dollar bill is more important than honoring the thousands of African Americans who were hanged. You talk to Jack, Marcus. A Mann will talk to the President," she proudly repeated.

Marcus shook his head. "Your idea to save your people has become a cause to promote you. That's not how this city works. It's a place where we all pull together."

The phone was silent on her end.

Marcus called the mayor, who answered immediately, "What do you have?"

"What I have is a potential disaster. Shandra has gone from being a reporter seeking the truth to an activist creating her own truth."

"Tell me about it. Social media has exploded again with her and that guy out at the tree. She did a close-up on his neck, showing the rope burns. She's good, Marcus, and she's control-ling the story now. My phone is burning up from the NAACP and Black members of Congress demanding we save this tree. Oh, I'm looking at the news on my computer now, and some-body has designed a logo that says, 'Don't Hang the Tree' with a noose hanging from a tree limb."

"I've got to get Jack to make some compromise. She as sure as Hell isn't. As she told me, she has the nation's microphone, and everyone's listening."

The mayor sounded despondent. "You know, Atlanta dodged all the civil rights riots with the image of 'the city too busy to hate.' Atlanta is an economic engine where the only color is green. And I'll tell you, a lot of minorities are going to miss out on jobs and investments if this project collapses. Jack has got to get off his creative high horse and make some modifications."

Marcus said, "I'm on the way to his house to see if we can get some movement on his part."

"Well, make it fast. She's turned the tide against us, and we've got to save this project. Hell, we're only talking about a slight alteration in the design."

Marcus arrived in the driveway behind Jack's house along with Frazier and Cody.

Cody said what they didn't want to say or hear or admit. "What price is friendship? The three of us love our Jack. He's our brother. But if we back him on digging up this tree, our clients and we stand to be called racists. And nobody can be called the R-word and come out alive."

Their faces were somber as they came through the back door. There would be none of the usual jocular kidding or asking about one of their latest business deals. It was a light-hearted competition they had, but not on this evening.

Mary hugged each one as they came in. As she did, they could hear a muffled yell outside. A member of the press would periodically knock on the front door and yell out a question. For the most part, they had lights and cameras set up on the street next to their trucks, using Jack's house as a backdrop for periodic updates on the unfolding story.

"I can't tell you how happy I am to see you three." Jack had heard them as he entered the room.

"Jack, you're in a hell of a fix," Frazier said. "That damn

reporter Shandra has turned this into a national story on race that has every liberal and Black in the country demanding you keep the tree. That 'Arms up, don't shoot' slogan is now 'Don't hang me' and 'Save the Tree.'"

Cody seemed nervous. Jack could tell by a slight twitch in his mouth. "What can you do to make this go away, Jack"? Cody asked.

Implicit in that question to all three of his friends was the fact that Cody was hanging by a financial thread. He went all-in on a surefire technology start-up whose founder had a nervous breakdown and the enterprise folded. Cody lost four million dollars.

Investing the balance of his assets into Jack's project was to be his savior.

Cody said, "I saw some protestors on the news in New York wearing 'Keep the Tree' T-shirts with a picture of a tree limb and a noose hanging from it. These professional race hustlers feed off events like this. This is a feast for them, and you're the entree."

Jack said, "I met with the mayor today. He wants me to redesign the front of the project and keep the tree. It would destroy what is acknowledged by international architects as the perfect design. That's not just about me creating some-thing for me, but about the design being perfect. This is the value it holds for the three of you also."

Marcus was reluctant to bring up his meeting with Shandra but had no choice. "At the mayor's request, I've just come from trying to negotiate a way out of this with Shandra. She wants the tree, wants it featured in the project's literature, and...."

"Stop it, Marcus. Don't want to hear anymore. She wants

this entire project to be a monument to white oppression, and there's no damn way I'm letting that happen."

Marcus's worried look carried into his tone—a pleading kind of request. "I think we can get her to move off putting it in our literature. But the tree is her ace, and she is rallying millions of people in social media to save it."

Cody said to Jack, "Aw, just make a little tweak. Nobody will know the difference."

Jack stood, his legs apart in intentional defiance, and said, "I will."

Frazier was obviously annoyed by this answer. "Wait a minute. This is now about more than a drawing you did. This is about us losing our asses and having our reputations affected because we are known as your best friends. This is bigger than you and the perfect building."

"It's about who I am, what I stand for, my identity as an architect and a man."

Marcus said impatiently, "Don't play the misunderstood artist role. We all know the whole city says what you have designed is brilliant. But this is now about more than your design or who you are. It's about four centuries of racial injustice that you just happened to get caught up in."

Jack could see a film of sweat glistening across Cody's brow, though the house was cool. Cody looked at his hands as though he were off alone pondering something. "My family is counting on this, Jack. That's as plain as I can put it to you."

Jack was both disappointed and angry over the conversation. He felt hemmed in by his closest friends. He thought they were abandoning him, and he was learning there are limits to every friendship and what those limits are.

He sounded solemn to them. "Changing the design is bad enough. Having the tree featured as a part of it is a bridge too far. You want me to say we'll make the tree a national symbol of how horrible white people were and still are to Blacks—then I've created a monument to bigotry and hatred."

Marcus countered, "No, the mayor, me, all the big steeple ministers in Atlanta, will say this an example of how our city can solve any issue of race. This is your gift to honor those who suffered. You are showing how the races can come together with compromise on both sides."

"There's no damn compromise. Shandra gives nothing. I give up my gift to the world," Jack said.

"We'll shut her down as an angry person that would destroy the image of our city and hundreds of jobs for minorities. The city will back you. Make the change as small as you can." Marcus was intent on rebutting any of Jack's complaints.

Jack had been listening but was unmoved on redesigning and said, "Here's my last counter—I'll move the tree, still on the property, but away from the building. And it won't be featured in any property advertising. In fact, I'll give the plot of land the tree is moved to, to the city."

Frazier almost shouted, "I like it! See if the mayor will back this, then call her and say the city is satisfied. Everybody wins. Call the mayor, Marcus."

Marcus thought for a minute, then called Sam, who thought moving the tree showed little sacrifice and sought no redemption. He thought it would be seen as a way to dodge a white man sacrificing for a Black. He said he had become more enamored with taking a piece of the design off. There was a beauty in such a costly seeking of redemption, and he told Marcus. Otherwise, Jack would be viewed as selfish and not a team player—not on board with the city's "too busy to hate" theme. But he told Marcus to call Shandra and run Jack's idea by her. If she went for it, he would relent too.

Jack, Cody, and Frazier were waiting in anticipation of what the mayor said, but Marcus held his finger up to symbolize their patience. Actually, he didn't have the heart to tell Jack what Sam had said—how the mayor now supported Jack being humbled before a Black symbol, the tree, and its noose.

Mary was sitting silently in the adjoining dining room, listening. The lights were turned off, but the light from the kitchen and the afternoon sun cast a subtle, subdued light through the room. Feeling herself hunched over in the chair, Mary straightened her back in the act of pride and resoluteness, regardless of what was about to happen to her family. It was a scene she never thought she would see—four close friends now being split by their own needs away from the brotherhood of love and respect.

Mary had been half listening and half following social media as the story raged on about the Jesus-like, heroic act of a man willing to hang himself for a cause larger than himself. As Shandra had just said, it was reported that the first Black president had been briefed on the story and had called A Mann at his hospital bed. Shandra was being hailed as America's hot journalist, who happened to be in the hospital room when the call came in from Washington. She also got to say a few words to the President.

The four were only feet away in the kitchen, so it was easy for them to hear the shock in Mary's voice. "My, God, the White House is now supporting this insanity."

Frazier stood up from the kitchen table, his face florid with worry. "What do you mean the White House?"

Marcus interjected, "Yeah, Shandra just told me the President had actually called that guy's hospital room and thanked him for his courage. Shandra, of course, got on the phone and was also commended. It just got bigger than us, my friends."

Marcus looked at his phone. "It's the mayor. Better take it."

"You seen the latest, Marcus? The President is now backing that nutcase, and Shandra thinks she's America's Black Bob Woodward."

Marcus had punched the speaker on his phone and held it up for the others to hear.

"Yeah, I'm here with Jack, Frazier, and Cody. Tell them what you think."

Sam breathed out a laugh. "You men are about to get your butts kicked if Jack doesn't keep that tree. With the President in on the act, the momentum is too great even to move the damn tree. Jack, you got to suck it up and take a couple of feet off that front entrance. We got to keep this project on 'go.'"

Cody looked at Jack, whose eyebrows were deeply furrowed. His long hair had slipped slightly over his cheeks. His face was a study in dejection, but suddenly an electric energy seemed to lift his shoulders, and his face had a peace about it.

"The design is who I am and what I have worked toward all my life. I can't change anything, or it's no longer a master-piece. There are no shades in perfect."

"Oh, cry me a river," Frazier said. "The four of us and sweet Mary in there are going to be wiped out if this isn't built. The only perfect we will be is perfectly broke and with reputations as racists."

Mary walked into the room and up to her husband. "Jack, life isn't about getting all you want. It's about being happy with what you can achieve, and this building is so incredible that redesigning just a portion doesn't detract from its achievement. You can't take the people in this room down with you."

She had the rapt attention of the three friends. They waited for an answer as Jack looked at each—his best friends and the wife who had honored their wedding vows even when he hadn't. "I can't let you all be hurt, and I can't change a design that people might be talking about for centuries."

"What are you saying, Jack?" Mary asked for the group.

"The strength of all of our relationships has been that we stand beside each other. This design is the most important thing in my professional life. I have created something rare. I expect each of you to help me fight to preserve the project exactly as it is. And stand against these absurd racial accusations."

Silence held the room for a moment. They all felt a sense of guilt and uncertainty. They knew this was Jack's lifetime dream—more like an obsession. They had always stood together if one needed help, and by the sheer magnetism and intellect of their personalities, they always came out on top. But there was now this career-destroying charge of racism that they could be tainted with by association.

"Let's be brutally honest. In America today, race rules. It never went away as anger, a divider. It is a permanent ember waiting on a breath of air to flare up. Your project has reignited it. We can all be stained, lose business and reputations if we get on camera and start arguing with Shandra Berry, or now the President, for God's sake." Frazier's argument seemed to satisfy the other two.

Mary was angry with her husband. She saw his demand that his friends risk everything as an act of selfishness, of a narcissist's need always to be right and be alone at the top. But she couldn't show her feelings in front of the three men.

"Do I have a choice? I have no support, including the four people in this room." Jack's frankness made his friends and his wife uncomfortable, a little put out by its starkness. Their responses had a tone of anger.

Cody spoke first. "Hey, that's a little rough on the people that have stood by you when your work was laughed at, and you were on the edge of going under emotionally and financially."

"That is unfair, Jack," Mary's tone was more scolding. "We are your biggest supporters and want almost as badly as you to see your dream realized. But we could all be hurt badly by you getting on a creative high horse."

"Oh, I think it's more than me chasing something perfect. I would ask you four, what price would it take to change who you are into someone you don't value? Someone who throws away basic principles?"

Frazier was quick to respond. "Oh, I would say, I would hope, that protecting and honoring your best friends and your wife makes a bigger statement about who you are than cutting a few feet off a damn design."

Jack knew he was cornered by them putting their friendship over his dream. Before he could respond, Marcus went back to the mayor.

"Yes, Mr. Mayor?"

"Before this blows up in all of our faces, I may have a way out. I've talked to several big developers in this country and overseas. There is a strong interest in buying you out and building the project using all of your designs, so all would know you were the creative mind behind it."

"And what about the tree? Would they keep it and change my design?"

The mayor hesitated, then sounded like a doctor telling his patient that, yes, the tumor could be removed, and they would only have to take out a little bit of your brain. Jack knew the mayor had made the calls. What he didn't know was that the White House had called Sam and said they wanted this standoff ended. They gave the mayor several international builders that were looking for access to the American market. And what a jewel to open with, the president had said.

"I can promise you that the redesign will be so slight no one will know. It will still be seen as the crowning achievement in architecture. It will always be your baby." Sam was attempting to sound upbeat, even cheery.

"Can't do it, Sam. It would be destroying all I stand for as a man and an artist. If we don't hold on to who we are, then we're nothing." Jack's face was one of defeat to his friends.

"He's found a way out, hasn't he?" Marcus asked Jack. "Forget everything else, Jack—artistic pride, achieving your dream—you're out of money, friend. If Sam has found a buyer, he's found a way out. But I'd drive a hard bargain on keeping your name out front as the designer."

"How did this happen?" Jack asked with bewilderment.

Mary walked up to him, put her hand on his shoulder, and tried to offer some comfort. "Call it bad luck, fate, a world that often makes no sense, but you can't be faulted."

"For me to be taken down by being called a racist is...," he searched for the right word and couldn't find it. "It's just crazy. I feel like the sacrificial lamb for America's racial sins."

"It's the power of social media led by a reporter with a cause. And it feeds on the idea that Black people are conditioned to feel oppressed. Being a victim is part of their culture, their identity." Frazier gave his unbridled explanation.

It was the first time in their long friendship that Marcus felt a pull away from Frazier. It was visceral and primal, and it brought up a wave of anger and defensiveness toward his friend he could not contain.

"Leave it alone, Frazier. Not all of us walk around wearing chains from the old days. But the old days, in a more comfortable form, are here every day. The slights, the disrespect; you don't know."

But Frazier was moving beyond the bonds enforced by friendship. "Sorry, Marcus, but it's true. Your race has no sense of forgiveness. Whites can never apologize enough, give enough because the life of a victim is never having to take responsibility for your actions."

Marcus had a glare that Frazier had never seen in their years of friendship. He was suddenly a stranger. "Just when you think you've met a white man that respects Blacks, you find his white skin might as well be a sheet on a Klansman."

Frazier's easy temper rose. "Oh, that's cute. Every white man is a closet Klansman. Oh, it's systemic; we were born hating the color black. But that works into the narrative that justifies all Black people being the victim. And all the unwed mothers and missing fathers; why we can't mention that. The truth about all the good that whites do is not allowed in the conversation or is dismissed as patronizing."

Marcus felt sickened. This brother, this man like family, was suddenly a stranger.

Cody tried to change the subject back to Jack. He said, "I'll bet every masterpiece has a slight imperfection that only the artist knows about. If a buyer shaves off a small portion..."

Jack quickly rebuffed him, "Unfortunately, Cody, this is all about race and nothing else. And no, that front section where the tree is will be critical. And the damn tree will stick out like a sore thumb for everyone to see and be reminded of brutality toward Blacks, not the uniqueness of the project."

While his mind boiled with anger, Marcus also felt he had betrayed Jack; he feared being called an Uncle Tom for standing beside a man labeled as a closet oppressor of Blacks. He failed his friend, and he knew it. But he wanted to be acknowledged by Atlanta's power structure as the man who found a solution; that was his currency. He was the go-to, behind-the-scenes connector.

"Jack, let me get with the mayor, see what offers are available from these developers, then check in with Shandra and get back to you. Honestly, you're too hot right now to be negotiating with any of these parties."

Jack was also saddened at that moment that he had lost the years of trust he had built up in Marcus. He realized how times that were so predictable could fly fast away, as though they never were. He thought how life was so in the moment. He knew Marcus was looking to be the great compromiser who saved the project and the tree. None of this group around the kitchen table, including Mary, was standing with him. It was the first time in his life of indefatigable optimism that he felt truly alone and abandoned. He was losing the creation of his life, and he knew it.

Marcus stood then, in his lean look, his dark suit perfectly fitted, his small face and sharp features giving the picture of elegance. "Jack, you have no choice but to cut the best deal you can, turning over all of your drawings and selling the title to the land. We can say that all you ever wanted was to design the building, and now you want someone else to go through the rigors of building it. It will be known as your creation forever."

Jack felt alienated. He was suddenly with people who had no clue what achieving true art meant. His friends and his wife lived in a world of right now. Jack felt that he lived in a world that didn't yet exist, and he was giving it life.

"Isn't that the best we can hope for in life? That we're all given just enough happiness to make it work?" Mary asked.

"Your mother has told you that chasing the perfect is a chase with no end. Perfect exists somewhere else but not on this earth."

"So, our goal should be mediocrity?"

The comment made Frazier stand quickly and place his hands hard on the kitchen tabletop as though he were anchoring himself to emphasize his remarks. "Don't give us that philosophical crap. 'I'm the tortured artist that nobody understands.' All of our butts are on the line here for you—our businesses, our investors, our reputations. My clients are threatening to pull their commitments, and that's some millions. Any association with this race thing is toxic. I swear it's more deadly to a businessman than a bullet."

Cody stood in his lanky, almost disjointed way. It seemed suddenly imperative if one was going to state their opinion with any authority, they had to be on their feet in some affirmative stance. "I think you should ask yourself, is one masterpiece all you're good for? Surely, you have more in you. If you think this one won't be perfect with the tree included, do a new one somewhere else. And as far from Blacks as you can get."

Marcus said, "Yeah, but only if you can shake this godawful accusation. You can't leave Metamorphosis with the reputation you're a racist. It's got to be a graceful and forgiving, maybe a magnanimous exit."

"In other words, kiss asses and be a sellout." Jack was standing feet wide, hands on hips, in his best pose of strength, though he felt nothing but heartache and anger.

Frazier quickly responded. "I wouldn't call it kissing asses, but saving asses, including ours."

Jack's face lost its iron determination and fell with a melancholy, reflective downcast where he didn't look at them, but out the broad back windows of the kitchen onto the flower garden at the edge of his backyard. Not seeking an answer, but mostly speaking to himself, he said, "The big poster of the Vitruvian Man at my office has a plaque beneath it quoting da Vinci. 'He who is fixed to a star does not change his mind.'"

The exasperation in the kitchen was palatable. They were all now wearied of what they perceived as a dangerous avoidance of reality.

Mary responded quickly. "Oh, please! Spare us, da Vinci. You mess with race in America today it will destroy you in a flash, which is where we are all headed."

The three friends stood silently, embarrassed at hearing this woman they so respected turning on her husband, who was, or had been, their best friend. She said what they all thought—that they were all terrified of what Jack's chase for perfection was about to do to all of their lives.

Marcus said, "We've all said enough. So why don't we ease out? Call me in the morning, and let's see how we make the most of this."

The three men touched Jack's shoulder as they filed out the back door. They were touches of assurance, love, silent pleadings for him to walk away from the project. Their footsteps across the intense green color of his lawn and away from the house were like a funeral procession of solemnity. At the end of the large yard were tall shrubs, fat with their summer growth and a narrow path through them to the rarely used drive where their cars were parked. Once through the hedges, they stopped in the quiet.

Cody said, "What do you say when the world you've known no longer makes sense? I hate the hell out of this for Jack, but dammit, I've got almost a million in this project, and if he loses all his funding and can't start, then I'm busted."

Frazier hitched his pants over his protruding stomach. "We

all three put up a million. My clients have pledged about ten more. I want to stand by our man, but I've got to think of my family and my business. It's a tough spot he's put us in."

Marcus offered, "His art is his life, we can see that, but his art isn't our life, and this obsessiveness with being known as a genius is his issue that could destroy us. I'm going to push the mayor to help attract a buyer."

Cody asked, "Yeah, but will he sell? Or does Jack think he can find new money and work through the race stuff?"

Frazier answered, "Once you're tagged, it's all over. Slavery in the south branded all of us. We just lay low and keep quiet and hope the Shandras of the world don't look our way."

"No lender will let his brand be associated with Jack," Marcus said. "He's giving us no choice but to pull away. We've got to tell our clients we are trying to help him work through this and condemn any association with the old hanging. But our best friend is now our toxic friend."

Cody opened the door to his car. "At some point, a man's got to save himself and all he's worked for. I can't go down in flames because of Jack's ego. I think the fabulous four have just seen their friendship fold."

None of them felt honorable about the conversation. They almost wanted to hide their faces from him, not look directly in the eye out of shame for what they knew was making a choice that overrode friendship and loyalty. But their choice had become clear, and that was to distance themselves from Jack. The losses from publicly standing beside him would be too great for them. It was Jack's fault now.

Jack had walked through the dining room and tipped a blind open to see the spectacle on his front lawn. He closed it in disgust.

CHAPTER 26

THE PRESS TRUCKS squatted in their white, boxed shapes on Tuxedo Drive, their satellite dishes worn like round metal ears listening to voices bounced up to space then down. Their reporters stood speculating live before the intensity of their camera's small suns. The word that the president had now intervened for A Mann and what pressures that would bring for Jack to give in and save the tree, released a wave of conjecture by the reporters.

And then the one-time shrill of a police siren announced that Shandra Berry was being escorted onto the scene. Cameras swung toward a long, black SUV. Shandra stepped out with the look of royalty. She was a star arriving at some red-carpet gala, and the older reporters would recognize her dress color as Coca-Cola red. The car's driver, a burly man of no apparent humor, quickly came around to offer crowd control or camera assistance to a light man and a videographer. It gave Shandra the appearance of having an entourage. The press scrum yielded before her confidant walk up on Jack's lawn. The fading evening struggled to present its last urges of light, softly bathing the dozens of people with an orange tint.

Shandra's camera crew set up their equipment with Jack's house in view up the slight rise of the front yard. Her face swelled in the exultation of the moment. She nodded at the various press members like a queen to her subjects. And then lights from her crew went up, and she spoke with alternating gravity and energy.

"We are here before the estate of Jack Collier in tony Buckhead. The city is tense tonight after the firestorm of controversy raised about the attempted hanging at Mr. Collier's tree—the new symbol of Black oppression he refuses to honor. Cries and demands from across America focus on Atlanta, the so-called city too busy to hate, to see if it puts business and the dollar over this heart-wrenching cry for social justice. Known as A Mann, the inspiring new preacher willing to give his life for his race is now being hailed as the new hero of America's civil rights movement. He has been encouraged by none other than the President of the United States by phone today. By his stunning, selfless act, he has come to illustrate how racial hatred remains alive and well, even though some write fat checks to Black causes. A Mann has shown how his people won't sell out for a few pieces of silver and how they will never forget the past."

Shandra paused as though she were getting a second wind. All the other stations were focused on her. "But I'm just a reporter. Why don't we let the man who would free his people speak for himself?" As if on cue, the back door of the square-backed SUV swung up, and two large men dressed in black climbed out and pulled a wheelchair out of the back with the lean figure of A Mann sitting in it. A gasp was heard from the press corps, then a frenzy of questions. They were ignored as the wheelchair was rolled up on Jack's lawn next to Shandra. A white, thick brace still claimed his neck, which had a cracked vertebra, but surprisingly to all who saw him hanging, he was not severely injured. The hospital had allowed him this short escape from his bed with the promise he would return quickly.

His eyes were alert and had a hungry look to the peering, gawking, clamoring press tribe. The sudden adulation, the presidential call, and Shandra's incessant claims of a destiny for him had changed John Stevens from an idealistic college student into a man of purpose, now comfortable in the moniker of A Mann who represented all men of his race.

A reporter's voice from CNN carried above the cacophony. "What did the President say?"

His voice still had a whiskey roughness from the jerk of the rope but also retained that resonating quality that had made him an instant success at the small church. Shandra held her mike next to his mouth, making sure she was in any camera shot.

"The President said racism remains America's great burden. Hangings are alive and well, not by the rope, but by the insult under the breath, the denial of a job, the under-funded education, the oppressive police." A small smile seemed to work its way into the next remark. "He said I didn't have to kill myself to prove a truth everybody already knows."

A five-year-old Porsche drove up unnoticed. Meredith had a new sense of what this story was about and wanted to experience the show before Jack's lawn, then try and reach him for a final comment. She saw a situation spiraling out of control, where millions could be lost and lives destroyed, all based on a lie. She had never been so close to the fury that social media could cause—literally like a raging fire that created its own weather and its own reality.

Meredith felt deflated, even defeated. All of her hard work, her front-page story in *The News*, in peeling back the truth on Jack's father, and therefore Jack was now forgotten. She had driven to Jack's house, not to become involved in the scene on the lawn, but to report from the edge. She was proud of the investigative work she had done in finding July and the truth. Her editor had even praised her. But Shandra had outmaneuvered her own sloppy work to make saving the tree the "new news." She had shrewdly shifted the story from Wade Collier to his son and how Jack was, at the least, cruelly insensitive to the suffering of Blacks. The President of the United States had given the attempted hanging a national spotlight. It was now in the world of politics, forcing both Democrats and Republicans to take sides.

Meredith had watched as Shandra, and her entourage had driven into the mass of reporters. She felt alone and imagined what Jack was feeling. But Meredith prided herself on not letting go of a story. Even though a more seasoned reporter had seized the moment and turned it into a maelstrom of growing magnitude, Meredith was determined to remain a player. She wanted to know his response to this disruption of his life. She wanted the personal, the behind-the-scenes picture of a man being destroyed because of his dedication to his art. Her interests now focused on the man whom she saw as a victim of her profession and the power it had to birth and feed innuendo and suspicion and hatred.

Hearing a commotion from his front yard, Jack separated the blinds to see the spectacle on his lawn. His phone vibrated. Looking down, he saw Meredith's name.

"I need to take this one," he said to Mary, who was close by in the kitchen.

"Who is it?" she asked.

Jack started to lie. He rationalized the ease at which he could bend the truth on his being a natural teller of stories, all a part of the mind of the artist. But his sensitivity to Mary's hurting wouldn't allow him to lie. But then he told a lie of emphasis as he tried to diminish Meredith's impact on his heart.

"Oh, it's that college reporter. That girl has been the only honest one in this mess."

And he walked through the kitchen toward the back door.

He knew it would look too suspicious if he just walked out now that Mary knew who had called. So he started the conversation in the kitchen and started slowly making his way to the back door.

Jack didn't exactly know how to open the conversation and didn't know why she was calling.

But when he answered her call, she heard a different voice from his usual bravado and cheer as though she were the only person in the world he wanted to talk to. It was a subdued sound.

"Yes, Meredith."

She halted, analyzing his tone and feeling what she perceived as hurt, even despair.

"Thank you for taking my call. I have a storyline I want to submit to the paper, not on the tree and all that."

He interrupted, "You mean there's more to this story than me hating Blacks?"

She paused, then, "I'm after the truth here. There's a larger story here, and it's not just about race."

"My God, I've been called by America's only curious

reporter." It was a false cheeriness. "The racist accusations are bogus and a handy way for Shandra to promote herself."

Meredith responded, "She's using the voice of the press in a way that degrades our profession."

Jack was curious. "And what is the truth here?"

"It's about an artist who believes that he has created something truly unique, and he won't compromise even in the face of his personal ruin. It's also about a young Black man who is willing to die to shine a light on what he believes. You both actually have a lot in common."

Jack was almost brought to tears. Someone finally understood him. He was swept with feeling for this young woman but held himself back from expressing his feelings about her.

She continued, "But here's the other side, the dark side, of this chase for the perfect. It can hurt and destroy, and I imagine if you don't redesign around the tree, you'll lose the project, all the hopes of the investors, and maybe a lot of your friends. So maybe the universal question is, what's the price of perfect?"

She heard a half-laugh. "Where have you been all of my life?"

"Not born for most of it."

It was a pointed appraisal at the more than fifteen-year difference in their ages, an embarrassing reminder to both about what they knew—that they were all wrong for each other on many levels.

Jack didn't want her to point out the obvious. He wanted to see her. He was at the back door and quietly opened it and went out to the lawn. Mary had walked into the dining room.

Once outside, Jack said, "Now that you have the headline, when do we do the interview? Better be soon. I may pull out of the project in the morning."

Meredith held the phone away from her face, staring at it as though the phone itself had shocked her.

"Well, that's news."

"Actually, it's a scoop, a get. And you got it."

Meredith was flattered but more interested in the details.

"Can we talk in the morning?"

"No, all hell will break loose tomorrow. Where are you?"

"I'm by the NBC truck on your lawn, watching Shandra perform."

"You mean my worldwide lawn now known by millions? Maybe I should go out and cut the grass. That's too funny you're out there too. Listen, here's a quick way we can do this interview. There's a little alleyway behind my house that few know about. Drive around to it.

I'll come through my hedges and meet you there by my car."

Jack moved quickly toward the back of the lawn. Looking at the house through the kitchen windows, he couldn't see Mary. She had walked over to peep through the closed blinds that showed the mass of reporters on her lawn when opened. She immediately saw the pale orange dress of the young reporter who had danced with her husband, and she remembered the blond hair now glowing under the late rays of the June sun. She was on her phone. An instinct, a curiosity, made Mary turn and look through the kitchen windows to see Jack near the backyard hedges talking also. And then he disappeared into the thickness of the hedges. Turning back, she saw Meredith put down her phone and walk toward her car. The thought of what she thought was happening was crushing to Mary. Her husband and that girl were going to meet in the alley. *Maybe it is just a reporter doing her job;* she offered to herself—an explanation with which she could live.

The terrible accusations against her husband and the potential loss of all they had worked for caused Mary to wilt into a kitchen chair. She put her arms on the table and lowered her face onto them. She cried fully and without restraint. The hurt was now transformed to water, and it flowed in a torrent of pain.

On the weed-sprouting dead-end street, Jack leaned against the door of his Mercedes in a pose. Meredith drove up with some reluctance. She feared meeting with this magnetic figure alone, even though she could get the last scoop and find redemption as a journalist. Jack walked over to her silver Porsche. Meredith was determined to make this her final contact with Jack, and she steeled her emotions, so nothing showed but professionalism.

"Let me set my recorder on the hood. I can have the story online by twelve tonight. I'll have to run it by Press, of course."

She gave a weak laugh. "Which means I may have to wake him up."

Jack stepped out of the way. Meredith avoided his eyes. As she walked, Meredith felt she was stumbling. Her legs were so weak. She had a small digital camera, screwed it into a tripod, and put that on the top of the hood, pointing toward them. Taking a small mic and attaching it, she did a sound test, played it back, then held it to her mouth and started the interview. Her movements had been almost unwelcoming, detached, very controlled, Jack thought. He wanted nothing but to take her in his arms and cover her perfect face with kisses, but he took her direction.

"This is Meredith O'Connor, reporter for *The Atlanta News*, in an exclusive interview with our city's most talked-about architect, Jack Collier."

Then looking away from the camera and at Jack, Meredith

said, "Mr. Collier, your design has been heralded as one of the most important creations in modern architecture. But over the last several days, it appears the entire project is in jeopardy because of racial accusations, first against your father, now against you. Since your father has been proven innocent, the focus is now on a tree on your property where a man attempted to hang himself to honor 4,000 of his race and the racism he still sees today. You have been accused of all sorts of racial biases because you refuse to save the tree and respect the heritage of African Americans. What do you say to these charges?"

Jack was always aware when a camera was on him. He could strike a pose that was appropriate for the moment, and at this moment, he didn't want to appear either angry or pleading but sincere and sympathetic in his explanation.

"I believe in life that we should reach for a place of excellence that we thought we could never attain. I have tried to do that through my designs but never achieved it until now with Metamorphosis. To keep the tree that you speak of would mean destroying what is being called a masterpiece of design, not by me, but experts across the globe. I believe we should all applaud one another when we achieve our best."

"Critics say a small change is all that is required," she said.

"There are no shades of perfect. It is, or it isn't," Jack said. "This design's strength is in its integrity, and changing any of it is to change all of it. I can't do that to what I see as my gift to architecture and to my city of Atlanta."

"How do you weigh that against this tree now being viewed as almost sacred? A tree so special that a man tried to hang himself on it. Now even the President sees it as a national symbol of African Americans trying to honor those murdered by white racism."

Jack refused to bend. "There is no proof that this tree was the one a man was hanged on. This was a forest of those big trees back then. But since many want to believe it was, I've offered to move it to a location where a park I would pay for, could be built around it. I am very sensitive to the sudden importance of this tree. I respect the belief that our nation isn't equal when it comes to minorities. But to mix the horror of a long-ago hanging with the celebration of the future, well, they don't work together in this case."

Meredith felt that she had her story of two men, both seeking the perfect expression and how opposing dreams can destroy one another. She now wanted to interview A Mann for his side.

"What one thing would you take away from your experience?" she asked.

"What has happened to me should be a call to all Americans. In this media-charged world, how well one lives their life, how many people they help is not necessarily how they will be judged. It just takes one reporter intent on destroying you for their own cause. But I won't yield. It would be a betrayal of all artists and of Atlanta to change my design."

"You must be surprised that you have been accused of racism after the money and work you have donated to the Black community."

"You know my first hero as a boy was a Black man that worked for my dad. He was the proudest and the strongest man I ever saw. As a boy, Gordon was a lifelong influence with how passionate he was about his work as a cabinet maker. But I'll let others judge the degree to which I have supported the African American community. What I will say is that this project was going to be an economic engine for that community. We had arranged for a sizable minority percentage to get construction work and have their own shops. The reporter, Shandra Berry, has hurt the community she claims she wants to help."

Meredith turned toward the camera. "There you have it. A media story starting with what Mr. Collier says is a lie that took on a life of its own. This has become a conflict between two men, both seeking what each believes is right. But the collision has resulted in one man almost killing himself while the other stands to lose all he has worked for. This struggle for the true truth could be called a metaphor for America today. Is it the price we pay for having a nation built on diversity, where everyone's truth is asked to be respected? You decide. Meredith O'Connor in this exclusive interview for the online edition of *The Atlanta News.*"

She lowered the mic and looked relieved.

Jack smiled for the first time. "I owed you a story."

He stepped closer to Meredith, now bathed in the orange glow of daylight, reluctant to dampen the final embers of the June sun.

She rubbed her fingers against her palms and could feel them dampen—an odd thing that she noticed her hands did when she was around him. Not knowing how she could say no, Meredith reached for the camera on the car's hood in some attempt at professionalism.

"Meredith," he said in a way that made her name sound poetic or the beginning of a song to her. She was surrendering to whatever was happening or about to happen and fought against it with all she could as she put the camera in its case.

"Yes," her voice broke as she spoke, but if she didn't look at him, it was like he wasn't there. She couldn't fear or fall in love with what she couldn't see. She turned her face away to fumble around with the camera's tripod until she could feel

Jack's hand on her shoulder, pulling her softly around to face him.

Meredith rubbed one hand's fingers over the palm of the other. They were wet with the emotion that was gripping her body. With her last bit of resistance, she moved to one side with her equipment, walked to her car, and pushed the bag into the car. With determination and what she thought was some wisdom, Meredith said, "Sounds like what shouldn't be said, shouldn't be said."

And she opened the car door. "Got to get back and get this to Press before I release it."

Jack walked to the door, put his hand on it, and said, "There's a follow-up to this story. It may be in Italy with my new company and new work. You have a free ticket to fly when you want to come over for an interview on what happened to this scorned artist."

The invitation both angered and thrilled her. He was married with a child, he was twice her age, a giant in his industry, perhaps a genius, and she was months out of college with a college football scandal as her only byline. But reason—what was right and wrong—were escapees from their restraints when confronted by the power of love, attraction, and adventure.

She paused at the car door. "All of that's tomorrow. And tomorrow is always a place of dreams. Not always reality."

Before she could finish breathing out the sentence, Jack had stepped next to her and, almost in a whisper, said, "A hug for the future and to thank you for all you've meant to me during this ordeal."

Meredith, in her twenty-second year, had rarely been hugged by a man other than her father and a few flirts. But this hug, the capturing into this man's arms and against his chest, was to enter a new world of a heart pushing to fuel the intensity of her feelings, a mind in flight to a place she had never been, and her entire body was suddenly without form or strength. Her arms at first just splayed out in surprise, then moved on their own up and around Jack's neck as though clinging for life in roaring water.

The hug felt eternal. Then Jack took her chin, turned it up, and kissed her, barely touching her at first as though full contact would free him from the last few constraints he felt. Then, when she kept her chin up, he melted into the fullness of her lips as they both left this earth for another place where only they existed. Their breathing was exhausted and deep like a runner, almost dizzying or desperate as though this was their last gulp of air.

And then Jack caught himself. He knew Mary, and he knew she might curiously walk through the hedges to see what had taken him so long, and he knew that with this kiss, he had immortalized this intensity and captured it forever in both of their hearts. They would meet again, maybe not in a romantic Tuscany setting, maybe back here in a year after all had cooled down. But he hoped this wasn't the last time they would lose themselves in this abandon.

"You're very special to me, Meredith. And we both know this can't be, but for this one moment, I found perfection."

He then stepped back. She looked stunned, still lost somewhere in the kiss, thinking her heart was now on the outside of her chest. "Please wait thirty minutes so I can tell Mary before you release anything. I'll be in touch with you when things make sense again."

He calmed her hair, now a swirl on her forehead, in the heat of the evening and the passion of the kiss. He said with a smile, "You're a special creation, Meredith."

With that, Jack turned and disappeared into the tall shrubbery.

Meredith staggered back into her car, where she was caught between laughing over the admission that she had felt the sweeping power of true love, then shame that she had kissed a married man. And somewhere in the mix of emotions was an exhilaration that she had another first on this very hot story. She drove off slowly, checking her watch for thirty minutes when her fingers would rush over the buttons on her phone, anxious to reach Press and tell him of her coup. She had to give it to Jack—he was resolute in his beliefs.

Before stepping out of the shrubs, Jack peeped through them. Across the lawn, he could see Mary through the broad kitchen windows. She was in the kitchen looking back toward the hedge, and he felt a deep sense of guilt about how their marriage was now residual debris, a result of the explosive racial accusations. Meredith's lipstick had become a remnant, a red echo of their kiss moments earlier. Jack rubbed the back of his hand across his mouth and saw Meredith's red lipstick on it from his lips. He wiped the color off on a leaf.

He stepped out on the lawn and walked briskly toward the back patio. Afraid if he went into the house, any lingering perfume Meredith had on would be a fire alarm to his wife, Jack motioned for her to come out and tipped his hand up as if he were drinking. She turned and went to the refrigerator, got a white wine for him, and quickly poured a cabernet already opened for herself.

Jack sat at a round table on the back patio of their home. Mary sat down opposite him, placing the long-stemmed glass in front of him. She couldn't bring herself to drink; it would show too much cordiality and seem like this was everyday kitchen table talk. Wanting to avoid opening with an accusation, she asked if he had heard from his mother.

"Family is everything to Mother. She is old, old school. This hanging stuff is crushing."

Jack let the wine sit on his tongue. He knew his wife and how in her heart she had a lingering uncertainty about him and women, so he got in front of what he figured she was about to ask him.

"Oh, yeah, as I was leaving, that college kid reporter called me, saying she was in the front yard and the newspaper wanted a story about how this was all going to end. Well, I wasn't going out to the vultures on the lawn, so I told her to come around back, and I'd give her ten minutes."

It irritated Mary to no end that Jack insisted on calling the young woman "This college kid." No one in their full womanhood, as she was, could be relegated to a mere college girl. Mary knew the game and that he was trying to dismiss any threat this beautiful young woman might pose.

"So, what did you tell her?"

She wanted to say, "That little blonde," but that would have revealed too much of her feelings, shown her anger and disappointment and mistrust.

Jack knew she was suspicious, and he didn't want to hurt her, but the fire had been diminishing between him and his wife for several years. Their schedules had become their loves.

"I told her the reasons I can't change the project."

She said nothing for a moment. Mary stared at her husband as he held the wine glass. It was a look he had seen before when she was fed up or angry.

"That's no story. Do you realize how many lives will be hurt if you let this fail? Not to mention what will happen to our son and me?"

"I'll spend the rest of my life hurting because of the pain and embarrassment this is causing you. Believe me. I'm looking for a way out that I could live with."

Mary sat back in the wooden chair. "You don't have a solution, do you? Your life has been all triumphs and praise. You have no idea how to take on a rejection, an accusation of this magnitude. Compromise is not a part of your makeup. You don't know how to appreciate somebody else's point of view. So, my husband, Custer, is going to make a stand with the same results. Your legacy in Atlanta will be that Jack Collier really was a selfish man. He put his need to be a hero in the architectural world above a symbol of inequality. One thing that could happen is I'll lose my ability to do my life's work."

He laughed in a disbelieving way that was more statement than laugh, more telling than words.

"Oh, you'll stay as the queen of boards. You have our foundation and far too much respect and leadership, and charities have too much need. You stand apart from me to Atlanta in all of the service work you do."

Jack shifted forward in the chair, picked up the glass, and took a sip.

"I've realized that you and I have denied our differences for our whole marriage. And I also realize that no woman could be as consumed by their husband's work as he is. None of this is fair to you, but the obsession, the need, the perversion, whatever it's called to create something unique, is who I am. To bend and change what I believe to be my life's great achievement is to lose my life's purpose. How can I do that?"

She was obviously not accepting his explanation. Anger filled her voice. "You're running from something, Jack. You're terrified of failure. It makes me wonder what happened between you and your father or something in your childhood.

The way you've been acting is crazy, and it's driving your friends and me crazy because this obsession can destroy all of us."

Mary was probing into his most basic makeup, into the dark places only he knew about and had kept covered with his outward personality, his bravado, and unflinching certitude. He knew he had been humiliated as a child for his outsized ears. He knew his father lived in a world of praise for his exacting craftsmanship. Even deeper in his closet of hidden fears was that Jack couldn't accept the inevitability of his own death and leaving little that was unique behind. He knew he found control in achievement and the acceptance it brought. It was control that helped him overcome these fears. To let his project be altered in any way was to lose control.

Mary looked at him, lost in what thoughts she didn't know. She knew that far-away stare when her husband had moved into his own private world. And then the fullness of his attention was back.

"I'll make it work somehow," Jack said with a certain innocence. "I'll protect you and our son. Keep the faith."

"I feel like I'm competing with some god called 'Perfect' that you're controlled by. And don't dare say I've not stood by you in our marriage. The list of demands, God knows what indiscretions, and selfish acts. I could make a list as long as my arm. Damn right, I've made personal sacrifices to put up with you, but what you're doing here is an act of utter selfishness. The fact that you could financially destroy your closest friends, not to mention hundreds of other investors, says that you don't have character or a moral compass."

Jack saw his wife in sorrow and with an emptiness that said he was out of answers for her, their marriage, and the loss of his best friends. It was all now cascading down in sheets of regret.

"Of all the reasons for me to be brought down, I would have never thought it would be about race. The efforts made by both of us to the Black community have been substantial."

Mary breathed in deeply. "If you had been demoted all of your life in whatever you did and held back for centuries, it would affect the way you saw the world too. Unfortunately for us, the anger is being exploited by a very savvy reporter. She sees herself as the new champion of minority rights, and she, like you, is obsessive in her chase."

Jack's face reflected a touch of anger. "I know Black people have been through hell, but they won't let hell go."

"You and I, and all of our friends, have lived in a bubble most of our lives. We've never known hell, as you say." She lowered her eyes in despondency. "I can't get into anymore talk about race. I can't talk about any of this anymore. I'll stay in the guest room tonight." And Mary turned in an exhausted, slumping way toward the quiet of the house, seeking only refuge.

CHAPTER 27

"YOUR ASS IS FIRED!" Drake Tumlin, the owner of Shandra's television station, screamed through her phone.

"You were told to leave this story the hell alone. We'll lose millions in advertising dollars if Collier's project fails."

Shandra was at the hospital early that morning, waiting on the doctor's report on A Mann's condition. The hallway where she stood was crammed with local news people and the curious and sudden admirers of the hanged man. It was awash in the conjecture of who this unlikely hero for the cause was that would even give his life.

Shaken but firm, Shandra answered calmly. "You can't fire me. It's the story of the year, and I am the lead reporter. Your little station will be known nationwide, thanks to me."

The owner roared back. "Yeah, we'll be known alright, as the station that was played for a complete fool. The man is a liar and a phony. He's a Morehouse Man, for God's sake. He's no street guy. This is all bullshit. And you bought it."

She was stunned and confused. Walking out of the hall

and toward the broad emergency room doors, Shandra cautiously asked, "What do you mean, fake?"

His voice was heavy with sarcasm. "Ever heard of a little Atlanta college called Morehouse and maybe a wealthy town up north called Fairfield? Well, his mother, whose summer house is in The Hamptons, tracked this station down and wants to know what the hell is going on with her Morehouse college son? Who sure as hell isn't named A Mann."

Shandra held the phone away as though it was suddenly an instrument of exquisite pain. Her ears rang, and her neck stiffened. She wanted to ask more, but there were no words in her drying mouth.

Her boss roared, "We gotta get in front of this and fast. Once this news gets out, we're ruined."

His voice rose into a shout, "How could you be so sloppy in not investigating who this guy was? He played you for a fool, and now we look like fools. You've got to get out front! Then I'm still firing you."

Her voice almost sounded dazed to the owner. "I'll get back to you soon." And she pressed the "end" button.

Shandra's world as a crime reporter had prepared her to move quickly and with composure, as she chased police radio chatter to urgent gang scenes, many still in progress with bullets flying. Her friends called her a war correspondent. But this call left her shaking in fear of her career in ruins.

She held her head back and breathed deeply. She first had to accept this call as fact and suppress the shock and deep disappointment of being lied to by A Mann or whatever his name was. She was a storyteller, and her answer began developing itself as she walked down the hall and toward his room.

"Officer Marshall." She knew the young officer, and they all knew her from her crime reporting. "Could you allow me to give an urgent message to A Mann from his parents? I just heard from them in Connecticut."

"Hard to believe, but he's awake. Maybe a little groggy."

A nurse opened the door of his room and stepped between Shandra and the officer. "Nurse, is A Mann awake? I have a message from his parents. They're terrified."

"Shandra Berry," the nurse smiled with an eagerness. "I want to thank you for how you have told the story of a man who tried to give his life for us."

The nurse lightly put her hand on Shandra's shoulder in a semblance of a reverential hug.

The reporter's instinct for an opening was almost primal. Quickly looking at the nurse's embroidered name on her white jacket, Shandra said with an ingratiating softness, "Nurse Sara, I have a way you can help the movement our hero is fighting for."

The nurse looked puzzled, then exclaimed, "Me, what could I ever do?"

"I found his parents in another city. They saw the hanging and are panicked. They have asked me to give him a message personally and no one else because of the trust he has for me. But is he even awake?"

The nurse answered, "Oh, yes, he's awake." The nurse looked at the officer, then back at Shandra. "Since the parents asked you, but just for a second."

Shandra moved quickly to the figure wearing a large neck brace. His eyes fluttered open as Shandra leaned down to whisper in his ear. "If you want to honor the 4,000, cut the A Mann crap, or our fight for freedom will be laughed at and lost, 'John.' Your mother is horrified about all of this."

She emphasized the word John into his ear to let him know what she now knew. Shandra then rose and pressed her lips, showing the perplexed nurse and officer all was well.

Walking out into the hall, the reporters saw her emerge from the room. She walked toward them with a self-assured composure that they all sensed, and it made them hungry for her words, for what she had seen of A Mann.

Stopping in front of the gathering crowd, Shandra announced, "I have just spoken with the bravest man I have ever met. You know him as A Mann, the man who would give his life to free his people. But I know him as John Stevens, a man who was resurrected into a new life as A Mann."

Confusion reigned in the packed waiting room. Reporters and admirers started a quizzical buzz that elevated into shouts seeking an explanation.

Shandra thrilled at the moment. Her mind had found the answer, which created a broad smile on her face.

"John Stevens is a Morehouse College student from Connecticut. He had planned to give his life to helping young Black men of the inner city. But coming from privilege, he didn't fully understand that life. What did he do, this passionate young man who had a rich life ahead of him? He gave his life to the streets, to become A Mann."

A reporter near her was heard to say, "Sounds like Clark Kent and Superman." A giggle rustled across the crowd like leaves along the ground.

"It would have been wonderful," she continued, "if a young man of the streets had risen to be a spokesman for justice."

Pausing and gathering a deeper breath so she could deliver the next thought, almost like a preacher bringing home the message, "But a young man from a wealthy, loving home, a student at the nation's finest Black college, gave it all up,"

She paused as the crowd leaned forward for the payoff. "To learn of the systemic racism that is oppressing our young men and then offer his body up to express the anguish of his race—he climbed to his own cross. My God! That is heroic!"

The cameras clicked and flashed, voices started yelling and laughing, some wept and rushed around the preening figure of Shandra.

"Damn, if she didn't pull it off," the station owner shook his head and said, "I think she saved her ass and ours too."

CHAPTER 28

BETTY WAS WATCHING the 10:00 news at her home in Athens and saw Jack's interview with Meredith. Sleep, and its curtaining, did not come easily anymore. She called her son.

"Mother. Why are you calling this late? What's wrong?" He knew she usually went to bed early.

"There's a lot wrong, son. A lot you don't know. A lot I didn't know."

The statement was such a surprise with ominous implications all over it that he didn't want to ask her anything, so his response was silence.

"I've finally been going through Wade's old papers, including personal and business checks. One of the checks was written to Ramsey Defoe, a man suspected of being the local Ku Klux Klan leader. Attached to the canceled check is a note from this man."

Jack was stunned and could barely ask, "Do I want to hear what it says?"

"No, you don't, but here it is. Because it's driving home a point that I want to make to you."

Her voice cracked with the delicateness of age. Clearing her throat, Betty read with such determination that each word was almost its own statement.

"To my friend, Wade. I can't thank you enough for your contribution to The American Way. We need funds for the newspaper ads to further public support for the white man's culture. We both know that there are good colored people, like those working for you, and we're not about them. Then there are niggers, like the ones trying to destroy our way of life. As you requested, your support is confidential between the two of us. Maybe someday, you can come out in the open with your belief in preserving our great country.

Your friend,

Ramsey"

"My God, Mother," was all he could whisper. Jack didn't know how to respond. He had known his father as an outspoken friend of African Americans, doing repairs at their churches at no charge. His most talented carpenter was a Black man who made, to some consternation, the same salary as the white workers. He remembered one day his father berating a white carpenter for calling a fellow worker a *nigger.*

Betty said into the quiet of the phone. "I'm telling you this because I believe you are about to destroy yourself trying to create something no one else has. I suspect that may come from your father, who, Lord knows, I practically have worshipped as the best of men."

"I always wanted to be like Dad. He was the best man at everything he did."

"Well, now we know he wasn't the best for the Black race. I can't even say out loud the name of that terrible bunch he gave a check to."

Jack frowned as though he was in physical pain. "Yeah, this is crushing."

"Look on it as a realization that we're all human. Maybe good is a more worthy, less selfish goal than best. Sometimes being good is good enough. I do believe a part of you is trying to live up to the image you've had of your father as being perfect. Well, you now know your daddy wasn't perfect after all. Like all of us, he had dark places. I want you to find a way out of this mess. Your daddy has let you off the be-perfect hook."

And the phone went silent.

The house was quiet. The front yard media trucks had gone back to their stations to download, edit, and put on the late news what their respective reporters had unveiled. Much of their coverage would be the dramatic arrival of A Mann. Shandra had been the orchestra leader and was playing her colleagues with sensational comments and the surprise appearance of the man of the hour, rope marks and all.

Jack carefully opened the door to the bedroom they called "Betty's Suite." Mary was sleeping on her side. She had a soft night light on that erased all age lines on her face. Jack loved looking at her as she slept. It was an eternal look of peacefulness he saw, and it made him hurt for what he was putting her through. Whether their marriage survived or not, she would always be The One.

He walked back into the kitchen and was shocked to see Martin Savoy, the lender who had shut him down, of all people, looking in the kitchen window. Jack thought he was hallucinating. *What the hell,* he thought, as he walked to the back door.

"Martin?" It was all Jack could say or ask, as in what is the man who would destroy him doing at his house at this hour?

"Yeah, I know, this looks nuts. Well, it is nuts, but I had to wait until the press cleared out and the front of your house was dark, so I wandered around here. Come outside. I don't want to be seen, to say the least."

As though his senses had returned, Jack stepped out to the patio and the dark of the night. The day's heat had rapidly calmed its force, and the air was so still, it was like there was no air.

"Jack, the stars must be with you. The president of our pension fund admires your work. He has been telling his friends about how we were the primary funder of what was going to revolutionize the way work areas are designed. He agrees with you that to have a tree associated with a hanging at the entrance to your place would destroy your whole idea. He thinks you have been railroaded by the media and wants to work something out."

After the last few days, Jack could believe about anything. "What does he have in mind?"

"He wants you to declare within 24 hours that you are offering the property for sale. But here's the redemption part for you—you will give the area around the tree to the guy called 'A Mann' to do with as he wishes. Then announce you have become too much the focus. The project needs to be what everyone is talking about. Say you will insist that any buyer has to honor the needs of the Black community by having a percentage set aside for Black construction companies."

"So, you're keeping the tree?"

"That damn tree has become a national monument." Martin stared hard into Jack's eyes. Jack felt there was something implicit in the finality of Martin's words.

"The last stipulation is that you take a break from Atlanta, so you are no longer a target for the press, which means the property is a target. We would prefer you find a reason to go to Europe or somewhere for a while, maybe getting some work over there."

Jack knew they had him over a barrel. They were vultures, and the world of the developer knew the lender circled every project they financed.

Martin said, "We'll let you keep the shirt on your back. That's it."

"Assuming the tree is still standing, you're going to cut part of the building to keep it?"

"We will. It's the only way to quiet the anger. The herd wants you to lose something, and they know how you value the whole design. We will have a small museum in some area of the development, honoring the man hanged in 1940. The museum will also have ongoing workshops on how to improve race relations."

Jack saw his dream burning on the fires of Atlanta and its past. "Why not let me stay in Atlanta, at least."

This stubbornness angered Martin, who felt he had come with a solution for a man about to be ruined.

Martin said, "Damn it. The project can only be cleansed by getting you out.

Don't you know the perception the media has created about you? Plus, we have several million sunk into this property that we're willing to take a hit on. You're out, or we'll wipe out this company and sue you personally for non-performance of contract."

Jack knew he had no legs because of the pressures from his wife and friends and with the project's brand now ruined in Shandra's racial assault. Jack felt a strange sense of relief but didn't see Shandra softening.

"You're going to reap the same wind my accusations have

sown. Shandra and the president and the rest of the civil rights crowd will descend on you, and you will be the new racist. Never underestimate the power of generous giving. Individually, we have been major contributors to civil rights organizations and this president. The fact that a museum will be built assures we won't have problems. Oh, and your being gone helps."

The tall figure, still wearing a very cinched tie, gave a weak smile. "Do it for your wife. I know of Mary and her work in the charity community in Atlanta. Save her further embarrassment. Get out and give everyone a break from this. You've worn out your welcome in this town. People don't understand artists other than thinking they can be strange."

Jack realized redemption of a sort was being offered. Martin was right; Mary deserved better. Jack had a sense of guilt about the woman he had fallen deeply in love with and married.

"I'll think on it. But I'm not running from town like I'm guilty of something."

"You are guilty because of what you believe in and blindsided by an angry time in our history."

He reached out with an unenthusiastic hand. Martin equally offered a limp hand in reply. "I'll let you know, Martin."

CHAPTER 29

WHILE MARTIN and Jack were talking, Shandra had left their front yard and its gaggle of reporters and took A Mann back to the little church and his room. The day had wearied and relinquished its hold on the light so that it was dark. The hospital had wanted him to stay several more days, but he insisted on leaving. Randolph Struby greeted them at the back door of the building, and his cheer was obvious.

"Now, this is a story for the ages, my son. From riches to rags to friend of the President. I saw you on the news a few minutes ago, talking about your phone call." He smiled at Shandra, "And being interviewed by the beautiful Miss Berry."

Shandra was tired. It had been a long day of interviews and job offers from local stations across the country, but she was waiting for one of the three major networks or a cable to make the big call. Maybe even a Hollywood producer saw a movie in the emerging story of the man who would die for his race. She had little interest in what this stubby, always apologetic, pastor had to say.

"I have to get home and grab some sleep. Surely this will come to a head tomorrow. Collier can't keep holding out. The tide of public opinion is now a mighty wave, a mighty river, as Dr. King said."

She noticed A Mann's demeanor, and it made her pause. He walked away from them toward his room, not even commenting on the day's activities, not even a note of gratitude to her. He seemed removed from the moment and somewhere else. It was a look of despondency that bothered Shandra. She wanted to follow and come close to the man that had propelled her out of the insignificant television station and her Bloody Shandra moniker and onto the national stage. She hoped to guide the young man as a national figure for civil justice, maybe be his agent. But he was in his room, and the door was shut.

She awkwardly said, "Looks like A Mann also needs some rest—not even supposed to be out of the hospital yet." Speaking louder to his unrevealed figure, "Good night, sleep tight. The eyes of the world are on you." And me, she thought, as she smiled at the pastor and left.

An hour later, the pastor heard some steps from his study and got up to make sure the young man was alright. Walking down the hallway between the study and the small bedroom, he peered in and saw the thin figure had apparently gone to the bathroom. The pastor stepped into the room to wait, and as he did, he noticed the fibers of a thick rope barely protruding from a backpack on the floor. Easing the rope up, the pastor was shocked to see a noose formed and knotted, and it looked ready for use. Hearing A Mann coming back from the bathroom, Pastor Struby pushed the rope back and turned as A Mann walked in and went over to the backpack and hoisted it to his shoulder.

"Pastor, I need to borrow the church car." It seemed a strange request at nine o'clock at night.

Struby was seized with a fear of what might be about to happen again. He thought quickly. "Okay, but you have to wait a little bit. I was coming to tell you I have a church member who is near death, and the family begged me to come to give final prayers."

Without waiting for an answer, Struby turned and left quickly to find his car keys. "Won't take long," he yelled as he almost ran before the larger and younger man could argue that he was in pain or some reason to say he needed the car first. Struby was quickly out the back door and into the night to save his church.

The ride gave his heart a chance to calm and his mind to formulate a plan. A Mann was his church's meal ticket out of quietly closing into oblivion. His new national notoriety would draw crowds and contributions. Struby himself would be given credit as the man who saved John Stevens and saw the God-given talents no one else saw. It could be like the old glory days when Dr. King ranged the land like a budding colossus and Struby had him preach at his little church. There had been the echoing eyes of press cameras, which gave a reality and importance that Pastor Struby could never generate on his own. He simply could not allow the spotlight to be dimmed by A Mann going back to the tree and hanging himself. And that's what the rope and the request for the car meant. He pulled into a gas station, retrieved a small gas can from his trunk, filled it, and was gone again.

But A Mann wasn't all that was on the pastor's mind as he drove. That morning several of the big steeple Black ministers had called him. They saw these accusations of Jack being a racist as not only a lie, but the Black community could lose badly needed work if the project were closed. They also refused to refer to A Mann but called him John Stevens. They thought Shandra was actually hurting The Cause by her blistering attacks on a major white supporter of their community.

They suggested that the pastor call Jack as a representative of Stevens and tell him the pastors would move in behind him if he would donate the tree to Stevens and sell the property. They said the vitriol was too great for Jack to stay. They would assure the press that Jack was not a racist after he had left. He would be seen as redeemed, and his wife could continue all of her good works.

Struby felt a power he had not known since Doctor King preached at his church. He had been anointed as the one man who could save this coming financial loss for his race. One of the ministers gave him Jack's private number.

It was a special number and Jack took the ring. "This is Jack."

The voice had a resonance to it like someone comfortable in speaking, Jack thought. "Mr. Collier, this is Pastor Randolph Struby. I'm the minister of the First Bethel Church. I was given your number by several very prominent Black leaders who you know but wish this to remain confidential."

Jack didn't know what to say other than, "Okay."

"I am the minister who found John Stevens, now known as A Mann, and he stays at my church. I have heard the shrillness of the voices against you, and I can tell you after tonight they will become a roar. I would urge you to send a statement tonight to John, offering something that will end this for both of you. You are a creative man. You know how much this must be costing you. And it will cost more after tonight. I apologize for so much secrecy, but there are a lot of powerful Atlantans of both colors who want to be able to support you. Give them a reason. Good night, sir."

The phone was silent.

What the hell was that? Jack thought, but he was shaken by Struby's ominous tone. *What was going to happen that I would regret so much? Why tonight? Am I about to be shot?*

But the call was another compelling reason to stop his lone stand and let it go. His wife's pain made it more imperative. The fight was finished. He had to give.

He wrote an email to Meredith.

I have come to realize I need to protect my family, friends, and our city more than I need to fulfill a dream I had for all of us. To continue standing for the truth in this angry environment would be to continue hurting those I love. Sometimes the price of a dream is too costly, and that's what this dream is, too hurtful for too many. I am putting the property and my plans up for sale today. I am deeding the area around the tree to the man who tried to hang himself to do as he will to further the civil rights movement. I have job opportunities from around the world. I will be out of the country for a while doing work where the past doesn't rule the future, and all can agree on what is truth if that place still exists.

Regards,

Jack Collier

He hit 'send,' and within a minute, she was trying to reach him by phone. He couldn't answer. He was exhausted with the whole mess, and he wanted some time away from her, also to see if she could be cleared from his mind and affections.

Meredith immediately sent the message to Press, who said to hurry ahead and put it online as an exclusive.

∿

THE TRIP to Vinings was swiftly taken. Struby parked on a dark spot just above the project's site. He could see the construction trailer down below with a light on, and he could see a man standing on its stoop. The guard went back inside the trailer, and Struby rushed toward the silhouette of the tree.

The June evening was still removing the last of its light, so the pastor could see well enough to wind his way through shrubs above the old house and the tree. The lights of the Vinings community with their restaurants and condos gave a jeweled backdrop to the dark hill. The night, of itself, was quiet, but the cars coming and going out on Paces Ferry Road were hums of rubber against pavement, giving a background ambiance of soft sound.

Coming up to the massive shape of the oak, Struby uncapped the gas can. He began dousing the tree, splashing the toxic liquid as high up the trunk as he could. The fumes were noxious and burned his nose. Standing back, he lit a match and flicked it toward his work. There was an immediate whoosh of flame, a sound like it was sucking air, and then the flames climbed up to the highest gas splash. The fire roared angrily in its brilliance, causing Struby to back away and run as fast as his short, heavy steps could carry him back through the brush toward his car. As he drove away from the scene, the pastor could see the tree in his mirror, like a great torch. He felt good that this thing of evil was being destroyed and his church saved because its savior could no longer hang himself from one of its limbs.

The guard was now back outside the trailer. He had called 911.

"Damn tree's on fire. In Vinings, where that guy tried to hang himself. Better get a fire truck."

Knowing how suspicious and wary A Mann was of

anyone's motivations, Struby headed for the home of an elderly couple. The woman was dying, but death would not visit tonight. She would be his alibi if A Mann or anyone suspected him of the burning. His visit was brief, and he was back in the church before an hour had passed. With some pleasure, he handed the keys to A Mann and asked him not to be out late.

"Pastor, I believe for the first time there is another place where I'll see you and the man killed here." A Mann could smell the odor of gasoline on the pastor's hands. "Smells like you gassed the car up."

Struby gave a quick, energetic, "Yeah. The hose dripped on my shoes. Now hurry back."

A Mann noticed that the tips of the pastor's shoes seemed blackened, maybe burned, but he let it go. He took the keys, and with a kindly, lingering stare at the man who had taken him in, he was out with the backpack over his shoulder.

With a knowing smile, the pastor wondered what would happen when this man, intent on sacrificing himself, drove to the property and saw fire engines and police cars and a flaming tree. Struby prayed that A Mann would forget Morehouse and become the soul-saving, income-producing preacher he was capable of being.

The pastor went back to his study, where his imagination gave life to cameras and lines of people at his church. Maybe even a cable ministry could be started with the booming intonations of the charismatic A Mann. And always on camera, seated behind the speaker, would be the purple-robed pastor, possibly even made a bishop by then. He knew of Jack Collier and knew him to be a friend of the Black community. He had given Jack an escape by announcing an offer before the world learned of the tree burning and would verbally crucify the architect for burning it down.

He lowered his head at his desk and prayed for God's forgiveness that he, one of God's workers, had been thinking of himself so intensely and imagining such joy in the coming fame and income he hoped for. He told God that he would tithe twenty percent of his earnings from the interviews about how he discovered the remarkable A Mann or John Stevens; it was getting a little confusing now. He was hoping—assuming— he would be the young hero's agent. Perhaps A Mann was a divine gift. The pastor liked the thought of that.

First Bethel was about to be resurrected.

CHAPTER 30

JACK WAS SHAKEN out of a deep morning sleep by Mary pushing his arm. "When it couldn't get worse, it has," she said, looking down at his slightly confused face.

"Huh?"

"The tree has been burned down." Her voice had a certain fear in it to him.

Jack almost shouted. "In our yard? Which one?"

"Your tree that man tried to hang himself on. I'm looking at the television right now. There are all kinds of fire trucks and police out there. It's quite the news."

Jack was stunned and quiet for a moment as he wondered if Frazier had done this or even Shandra Berry to get more attention. And then he realized that was what the pastor had warned him about. *The pastor tried to save me*, he thought. *The young man must have been going to hang himself again, and Struby burned the tree down. He's right. I'll get blamed. But the email to Meredith will show I had already given up on my demands. So, I had no reason to burn the tree.*

"Oh, this is rich. You announced last night that you were

selling the property. Here it is online." Her face had a look of incredulity, and her eyes started to glisten.

"How could you make a major announcement and not tell me?"

"I made up my mind after you were asleep. I'm getting out. I'm doing what you wanted." Jack felt relieved he had acted quickly and weary of another argument with Mary.

"I don't know if this is good or bad. The damn tree can't be an issue if it's not there, but then they'll be accusing me of burning it next." His voice was filled with resignation.

"Oh, listen, Shandra already is," Mary said. There was a pause as she listened to the television in the next room. "I don't believe this woman. She's asking, 'Has anybody seen Jack Collier? He wanted this tree taken down. Could he have done it with a match and a lot of gasoline?' Just trying to get the story of who destroyed the most famous tree in America."

Jack's first thought was the cryptic words Martin had said about trees not living forever. Surely a major lender wouldn't be up to that kind of power play. It had to be, of all people, Randolph Struby.

"Damn her." Mary could hear the anger in her husband's voice. "So, I'm already being blamed for burning the tree. Martin Savoy could attest to my being at home. He was here late last night, but knowing him, he won't get near it publicly."

Mary was confused, "Isn't he your main lender? He was here?"

"Shocked me too. Right at the back door. His boss admires my work and wants to work out a deal where I put the project up for sale. The pension fund quickly buys it, but I have to leave town for a while."

Mary sat heavily on the side of the bed as though there was no energy left in her.

Her mind was trying to grasp the demand from Martin that her husband run. She stood with a sudden burst of anger that energized her. "You can't leave us; you can't run. That would be the final statement that you were guilty."

Her eyes looked puffy in their days of angst and hopelessness. She was paying the toll, and it was physically and mentally costly.

"It's not just Shandra now. It's the whole social media network. It gives life to lies."

"Now, nothing is certain or absolute. Lies are truth, and truths are lies."

"So, sell the property, and this will be over. You are the toughest man I've ever known. You're not a runner. You can't run away from this. You can't." There was a demand and a plea in her voice.

"Believe me. I don't want to. That's the deal the pension fund demands. They won't ask for a two-million-dollar payment that I owe them. They will keep a similar design and build a civil rights museum in the development. But only if I get completely away from the project.

"Mary, I am now the face of racism in America. This country is being swept by revenge, and it needs so-called enemies to feed it. It has become a crazy place, and you can't fight crazy. I can't have your name hurt anymore. The only way we both can survive is for me to get the hell out of here for a few months."

Mary brushed around him, leaving the room with, "Then do get the hell out of here."

For the first time in his life, Jack felt he had no control over his life. He skipped his usual shower and breakfast and went straight to the office. On the way, he called his attorney and told him he wanted to sell with instructions to call Martin

Savoy. Sell the land. Sell the plans. Deed the area where the tree stood to John Stevens. But tell Savoy that Mary and his three friends had to have some position in the project to save them from losses.

Jack surprised himself in realizing he had no desire to call his three friends and give them an update. A precious bond had been broken. He was a ship loose from its moorings with no ports in sight except for the lender and his Faustian offer.

CHAPTER 31

SEVERAL DAYS OF SECRET LAWYERS' meetings followed, sealing what was a complex transaction. When announced, the city was shocked to hear of the pending sale and that Jack had been offered (which he wasn't) a big design opportunity in Rome. Jack's press release said he was excited to have some of Atlanta's biggest developers and the pension fund take over. He was especially pleased to donate the area where the tree had been to A Mann. It was as though none of the previous recriminations and raging in the media had ever happened. It started a tone of redemption that was especially strong among Black leaders. They remembered well Jack's generosity. They had called him "friend" over many lunches together. But the movement against racism was too central to their culture and identity, and it was a wind they couldn't sail against until now.

Jack talked to his mother every day. Betty's health, with a new medication, seemed better. She said she was proud of her son for stepping away from something so important to who he was. Like her beloved Wade had said, "We are not just defined by our acts of good, but how we make right those acts we are not proud of."

The loss of the tree and Jack's leaving had left Shandra, and the civil rights activists caught off guard and uncertain of where to go with all the energy they had created. She was being courted by CNN for their New York desk, and her mind was starting to escape from Atlanta. She had also heard the rumblings that many Black leaders felt she had hurt Atlanta with her fierceness. But she felt secure in what had transpired and how it had given voice to those Blacks who felt still under the weight of white ignorance and indifference. Knowing the art of communicating, she knew the value of a symbol, and she had created that symbol with the evolved John Stephens.

Jack and Mary had claimed a neutral status in their marriage and personal interaction. She came to accept his leaving as a part of a necessary act of redemption. He had, in the end, given. It also gave needed air between them. Jack spent every evening with his son Paul on the roof, talking of the uncertainties of life and how unknown and unguidable the future could be.

His son said as the night air cooled around them, "Are there any heroes here, Dad? Can we say that A Mann was a hero for Black people in being willing to give his life? For their freedom as he saw it. Maybe. Will the world say that you were heroic in standing alone in your commitment to excellence as you saw it? Maybe." Paul gave a breathy laugh, "What happens when two heroes represent the truth? Can both be right?"

Jack put his left arm around his son's shoulder. "If there was a hero, maybe it was your mother who tried to protect her family against the leader of the family whom she saw destroying it. No, I was just a man standing for what he believed as certain in a world where nothing seems certain."

He kissed his son on the cheek as he stood on the gently sloping roof. "Know that I love my Homeric son who is far wiser than his old man." And he was down the ladder and into the house.

The next day Jack made no attempt to contact Meredith after rounding a corner on Peachtree and almost walking into her. Their eyes had locked in what seemed an eternal moment, both conflicted and confounded by a rush of emotions, then Jack had creased a smile, nodded toward her, and continued his walk. It took every ounce of strength to step away, but they were an illusion, and he had to try to remove all things Atlanta from his mind.

He had been up at six that morning, hours before the flight. Walking into the kitchen, he saw a note from Mary that read, *Text me when you land.* She didn't sign it in her usual manner of drawing a heart with their initials in it, as though they were carved on a tree of lovers. She didn't ask that he call so she could hear his voice. What the note didn't say said everything.

As one gesture of cordiality, a recognition that they were still married, a nod to custom, whatever it was, a pot of coffee had been set on the percolator. She had made coffee every morning of their marriage. The gesture was as revealing in its loyalty to their oaths as was her wedding ring. The singularity, the symbolism, was powerful in a mind like Jack's that sought the ultimate truth in everything. It exacted a heavy weight of guilt on him. The truth here was that his wife, even at a time of profound disappointment in her husband, still had an ember of unalterable love for him.

He had turned his office over to an employee of unusual

talent. There were several projects that needed finishing. Selling the plans and land for Metamorphosis had no impact on the other projects. Hopefully, the other employees would find their way back to work.

At ten o'clock, the massive engines shook the plane's frame with their primordial roar as the Delta started its sprint down the runway at Hartsfield-Jackson International. It would be a long flight to Milan, where he would reestablish contacts with major European developers that admired his work. The flight would give Jack time to think about the fragility of a reputation, a marriage, and of friendships. But the leaving was a failure in the larger sense, he now realized. The pursuit of perfection had forced him to ask himself, *What is the price of perfection?* And it was too high.

He opened the *The Atlanta News* online edition and the *Atlanta Business Chronicle* to see what the media were saying as he left the city he loved. It had been two weeks since he gave his final press statement.

The News, above the fold, storied that the famed architect, the toast of Atlanta, Jack Collier, was rumored to have left the city for a new major project in Italy. It was filled with "sources said" and "rumors are." An adjacent article said that Shandra Berry had been hired by CNN to be senior reporter on their new Justice Desk, where she would ferret out white cops abusing Black men, white supremacists, and all acts perceived as Black discrimination. Her opinions would be seen as a barometer of the state of civil rights.

The corner of Jack's mouth twisted up in a smile. Shandra had escaped the mean streets of Atlanta on the wings of lies. She knew how to work the echo chamber of the media. She knew the power and how sticky an accusation was and how rebuttals didn't stop the hunger of a story of destruction. As he looked at her smiling face in front of the CNN logo, Jack realized that he never stood a chance once she seeded the story. He also had to admire her tenacity. She was so much like him in the strength of her beliefs. And, he felt, there were tragic hurts every day to her race. Her cause was good, he knew.

A second article featured A Mann visiting the White House to be thanked by the President for his passion in holding a light to discrimination. The President felt the attempted hanging was a courageous statement about conviction. In the White House photograph, standing roundly next to A Mann, was the proud figure of Pastor Struby in what looked like a purple bishop's robe. The article also said that A Mann's life story was coming out in a book and that a movie by Steven Spielberg would soon be in production. And it would be filmed in Atlanta, employing many of its citizens. Jack wondered who would play his character.

The article also said that Atlanta's big steeple Black ministers, who had abandoned Jack, joined with several national civil rights organizations in anointing A Mann as a new national civil rights hero. One of them said Jack had left them no choice but to join the movement to save the tree. The story didn't say, and what Jack had heard, was that the ministers were telling their congregations they knew Jack was the furthest thing from being their enemy. But The Movement's current had flowed against Jack. Black leadership's allegiance, the verification that they were true to The Cause, demanded they go against what they knew to be true. Jack Collier was no racist.

Privately, they said they had shot one of their own and worried about who would replace the years of support Jack had freely given their causes. Maybe his wife. Jack felt no recrimination toward them. He knew, in Black Atlanta, they had no choice.

Jack thought, in one sense, they were as much a victim of their past as he was. Besides, The Movement always needed a spotlight to further the cause. Jack was today's spotlight. To be a force in Atlanta politics, the ministers had to keep their backs to the winds. In the past weeks, so many of his friends and the city's leaders had been tested. All had proven to be fallen in the various ways one's actions testify they knew better than their actions.

The News editorializing against Jack was a final strike against integrity for the editor Press. He informed the newspaper's publisher that he would quit at the end of the year after thirty years as editor of *The News*. He would go quietly so his shares of stock and his pension wouldn't suffer, and he hated himself for that cowardice on his part. He had fought his last battle for journalistic integrity, and he knew he had lost.

Jack Collier was going to put Atlanta on the architectural map and bring hundreds of jobs to minorities. But the paper went with the flow.

The *Atlanta Business Chronicle* featured a photo of A Mann with Martin Savoy, several other lenders, and big-name developers who had formed a consortium. They would buy the land and part of the design from Jack, changing the front of the building to accommodate a small, almost invisible, plaque where the tree had stood.

Only Jack cared that the new structure wouldn't be da Vinci-inspired. There was no physical legacy to look at, and honor with the tree cut down and burned up. The new developers were shown in yellow hard hats, grinning as they broke ground with shiny shovels. With them were Atlanta's mayor and several Black ministers known for their activism. Obviously absent was Shandra. The mayor was still angry with her and the notoriety she had pushed of America's Black Mecca being a racist town. She had been banned in the minds of many of Atlanta's leaders. Having a small monument had satisfied them all, as well as the developer's promise to have a large minority included for construction work.

On page two was an article by Meredith on the exploding reality that many Atlanta Public School teachers had altered their students' grades to get higher scores. Jack smiled, sure that she was heading for a Pulitzer. With a sense of loss, he thought their meetings had been like bubbles blown by a child, exhilarating for a moment but impossible to sustain.

In the "Personality" section of the paper, Jack saw a picture of Mary and Cal O'Connor. She was starting a new foundation with Cal as the first board member. It would provide funding on imaginative solutions to single-parent minority children dropping out of school, leading aimless lives. *God, she's a beautiful and wondrous creature,* Jack thought.

The article didn't say that Mary had cried herself to sleep the night before over the loss of the love she had once had for her husband. She had married Jack because of his uniqueness, his commitment to being the best of men, his genius. He was so large in life, and she had succumbed to his brashness and flamboyance. There was an overpowering joy, even jubilance about him. Now, those qualities had proven to be too self-centering for their marriage to survive, at least for now. She was frayed from the hurt of so-called friends who had shown little support when the racist accusations came at her husband.

But Jack knew his wife. He knew she was iron-willed, and

she gained strength in giving her strength to others. She was born to be a servant. He had added a million dollars to her charity foundation. He smiled as he thought of how proud he was of Mary and how much he admired her. And he felt a rising guilt for the hurt he had placed on her.

In Jack's mind, Mary's demand that he abandon his identity as an artist to fit someone else's agenda had made it easier for his wife to slip out of his heart. It was a baptism he couldn't accept. But his mother's revelation that perfection was not a Collier family characteristic had freed Jack from his father's commanding influence. It had allowed him to end the fight to stay true to the project. His coat of armor had been pierced by the past and its terrible culture. Jack could barely deal with the thought of his father being a secret supporter of the Klan. *What secrets and shames we all hide,* Jack thought.

He loved falling in love. Meeting Mary had created a wind that quickened his heart unlike any of his many romances. But the years and the intensity of both of their lives had slackened the urgency they felt for one another. And then, like a mirage, Meredith shimmered on what had become a drying romantic landscape with Mary. Her youth was a tonic that revived his passions. Her beauty was a near perfection Jack sought in life. He was able to put Mary and his marriage in a separate place from his feelings for Meredith. This separation meant guilt kept at a distance. He thought of the way he could put the different parts of his life into their own walled worlds. He didn't like it. He didn't like himself for it, but still, he would push guilt aside.

Jack thought his wife might come to Europe because of the gravity of their past love. But the hurt he had placed on Mary was the past he was sick of. His sights were set on the future. It's who he was out there on the horizon. As the hum of the engines pushed Jack off into a nap, his mind saw the breath-taking hills of Tuscany at sunset, a small village, a postcard restaurant with a sun-goldened woman he knew as "The One" sitting across the table, a local red wine in her hand. A new start was a siren song, and he fell asleep listening, untethered to any past.

ACKNOWLEDGMENTS

To list all of those of both races whose voices ring out here would be to leave someone out. But I must give thanks to four who gave especially important contributions. Alice, my wife, with her endless encouragement and readings and rereadings, I thank you. To Janie, my first editor, who saw value in my story and who slayed the many typo dragons I had created, you're the best. To Kathy, a reader of exceptional insight who read the perfect title, thank you.

A writer without a publisher can be a ship without an engine or a rudder. I am grateful I found both with Publish Authority. The owner Frank Eastland's calm, patient, and supportive leadership was the captain of a dedicated and talented crew. Nancy, my editor, fought the endless typos my seemingly endless rewrites were producing. Raeghan is a national talent with her eye-catching cover and website designs. This is a team committed to excellence in publishing, and I am grateful for their accepting of me and my work.

ABOUT THE AUTHOR

William Anderson writes about lives in transition when being swept by events they can't control. His political biography, *The Wild Man from Sugar Creek*, is such an example. His two novels, *God's Arm* and *Jesus at 65*, are similar studies of people searching for the meaning of their own lives. William lives North of Atlanta with his wife Alice.

For more information about the author, visit his website at
WilliamAndersonWriter.com

 facebook.com/dubanderson

DISCUSSION QUESTIONS

1. Did the novel give a balanced representation of all sides of the current divide in America over race or cultural differences?

2. The character of Jack Collier was written to reflect the complexities of the race issue, especially with southerners who feel they are supportive of Blacks. Did you see this confusion and the shock he was having been accused of being a racist? Was he too unmoving in his refusal to change the building?

3. Was there a hero in this story? If so, who and why?

4. Meredith was an idealistic young woman caught between falling in love and wanting to find the truth as a reporter. Do you think she had moments of being fallen like the other characters in the story?

5. Today's media is very powerful and is both hated and loved. Would you say the media is a contributor to an angry America? If so, how?

6. Jack's wife, Mary, was put through the anguish of having a husband trying to make the perfect artistic creation when it could destroy their love and their family. How do you think she handled her husband's drive for perfection?

7. Did you think John Stevens/A Mann was heroic in trying to give his life for what he saw as an injustice? Can you sympathize with his dishonesty in becoming someone else, or was it a reflection of the pain he felt about his people's past and current oppression? Or was he just over the top in trying to amend the past?

8. Shandra was very aggressive in being critical of today's white race, especially the wealthy like the Colliers. She gave them no credit for their check writing or supporting Blacks in any way. Do you see her tough stance as a strategy for media attention or true belief?

9. How do you think the races and whites of differing beliefs can come together?

THANK YOU FOR READING

Publish Authority

If you enjoyed *The Price of Perfect*, we invite you to share your thoughts and reactions online and with friends and family.